PREHISTORIC JOURNEY:
The First Expeditions

D.L. Narrol

PREHISTORIC JOURNEY:
The First Expeditions

DOUBLE DRAGON

Chapter One

The cool sea showered the crew with falling mist and strong spring winds, which caused the men to clench and shiver. As the music ballads observed the rising of dusk, the twilight set upon the Anglo-Indian empire in the year of our lord 1907. Captain Colin Limmerick sprawled by the bow watching the crew celebrate yet another long night on the Celtic waters. He sat up trying to focus, counting several empty bottles of ale rolling about his feet as he mesmerized himself with a hefty bottle of whiskey. He hoisted himself up and staggered toward the crew, leaning by the stairs that led to the galley. Eddy, the first mate and oldest crewmember, stood beside the towering six-foot four captain.

The Atlantic Mermaid held her own with her sturdy body, two protruding steam pipes, and one mast sail. She cut through the blue-gray waters, too small to be a mechanized steamer, yet too oversized to be a deep-sea trawler

Eddy sighed with exhaustion. "Lad, I'm gettin' too old to keep up with yar strength 'n mischief."

The captain chuckled. "Ye take a rest. I'll haul in the catch."

"Ah, yar a one-man crew. Just look at the size of ya, Captain."

"I do what I can." The captain laughed while flexing his great biceps.

Young Timmy steered the ship to the Dublin Quays while Eddy trailed behind the nine-man crew into the galley. They sat wherever there was an empty stool, placing warm ale upon the wooden table. Colin remained standing, drinking his ale while he gazed at his crew.

Eddy looked at him. "Can't ya find a place to sit, Captain?"

"Standin' I don't mind doin', thanks."

"Despite ya bein' the captain 'n owner of this ship, yar still like a son to me. I can tell somethin's eatin' ya. Is it quid?"

"Quid? It's not."

"Good to hear, Captain," Eddy responded.

"Our *Mermaid*, she brings us some of many good feastin' she does." Colin tried to smile. He finished his last drop of whiskey while noticing the crew comfortably seated around him. "Men, I've got some news for yez." He watched as a few drops of whiskey ran down the side of his empty bottle.

"Tyin' the knot are ya? I bet our Captain is," Eddy tried to guess. "Strange, a man of yar good looks can't find a wife." The crew cackled and drank up.

"Married, ye say? I haven't the luck with wenches, ye know it."

"Come out with it then -- what is it?" Eddy asked. The room grew quiet.

"Men, I'm thirty-nine years old. Ye know as a man ages he starts to ask himself if he's happy?" Colin tried to focus on the crew, who appeared concerned. He brushed his fingers along the sides of his empty whiskey bottle and placed the last drop of spirit upon his tongue. "I don't know how to say this." Colin tied back his brassy-crimson hair, which hung to the middle of his back. "Ye know I've lived in two worlds for the past seven years, tryin' to obtain me university degrees'n run this vessel'n such."

The crew nodded. "We know our captain's a scholar!" Eddy blurted as they all opened another ale. "Yaz the smartest man I've ever known."

"Yer too kind. I just received me acceptance into London University's doctorate course in the Department of Natural History. Sure, you know how much I'm goin' after bein' a naturalist?"

The men broke into hysterics mauling Colin with rugged hugs. "We know yaz could do it, Captain!"

"I'll be meetin' up with me academic advisor next

week in London town. I was teamed with 'em 'cause he's the only professor in the department who specialises in the evolutionary process. Ye fellows know me already, ye know how I'm interested in that kind 'n such, don't you?" Colin asked, blowing the foam from his mug of ale.

"Yeah, we know you're a big smart bastard!" Eddy shouted, then the men broke into chants of excitement.

"What ya goin' to do 'bout us 'n *the Atlantic Mermaid*?" Eddy asked.

"I thought maybe you all could carry on the legacy without me durin' the week. I'll still be yer captain, only I won't be on the ship as often 'cause I'd be spendin' me time at the university'n such. I'll try 'n be here three days a week to fill our largest quota I will." Colin lit a candle, reflecting the light off the freckles of his nose. The sun was starting to set as the crew intoxicated themselves without mercy.

***

The following week Colin planned a meeting with his advisory professor in the afternoon so he could spend the morning travelling to London. His crew dropped him off at Fishguard, where he boarded a train to London.

He finally made it to London, where he tried to make sense of his directions that were scratched on a scrap of newspaper. Pulling off his jacket, he swung it over his shoulder. His tight-fitted undershirt exposed far too much of his brawny flesh for the buzzing Edwardian Londoners. Frayed suspenders were attached to his tattered trousers, which expelled the stench of seawater. He wore three chain necklaces around his broad neck: one gold with a hanging crucifix; a large, heavy silver chain, and a fine silver one. His ear was pierced with a gold earring. He wore heavy boots, which made a hard clinking sound when he walked in his regular, lead-footed stomp.

He scurried out of the train station onto the street level, where he was immediately faced with the thriving hustle and bustle of the crowded streets of London. He

7

continued to walk northbound. Clusters of females passed by staring with blushing giggles. Gangs of young thugs passed by him cursing in their south London cockney slang.

He found the university and made his way up the stairs to the second floor to the Natural History Department. He clenched the newspaper with the directions in his hands, failing to notice his fingers were caked with dirt. He stopped someone in the dim hallway asking if they knew where a Professor Randolph Cushing's office was. The person directed him to the north side of the building. Colin stopped in the hallway, deciding to tie his long hair back so he could look more presentable. His tweed cap's visor pressed his long forelock, which hung past his eyes, against his face. He stopped to catch his reflection in a window where he tried to primp his appearance the best he knew how.

He finally found the correct office and knocked on the door. He found it ajar. "Pardon? Pardon meself?" Colin called out as he pushed his way into a dimly lit well-organised office.

A man in his mid-sixties turned to Colin while he poured himself a cup of tea. The paunchy man had hanging jowls that swung from each side of his face. "Yes?" The man could hear the sound of Colin's jewellery clang as he walked into the middle of the room. He jolted with surprise as the towering, broad-shouldered man approached him.

"Pardon me, sar, but could ye be so kind in directin' me to a Professor Randolph Cushing's office?" Colin asked in his heavy Dublin brogue.

The man's eyes widened. "Yes, I am he. I am Dr. Cushing." The professor squinted his eyes as he tried to focus on Colin, noticing the tattoo of a mermaid and a ship burned onto his arm. "Oh, I see who you are. Yes, you see this cabinet is very large and heavy; it needs to be moved to this side of the room," Dr. Cushing said pointing to a large metal cabinet. "I've been waiting for you all day. What took you so long?"

"All day, sar? I thought I informed ye that I'd be in yer office this afternoon."

"No! No! No! Just move the cabinet!"

Colin squatted to the floor to lift the cabinet. "Ye want it on that side of the room, sar?"

"Yes, I do! Damn it!" He paused. "What are you doing?"

Colin started to lift the cabinet. "Doin,' Sar? Movin' this metal cabinet as ye asked."

"Stupid foreigner, you're supposed to take everything out before you move it!"

"Not necessary, sar." Colin moved the cabinet to the other side of the office with folders and books still in it.

"You look like you could move a house! Now, I suppose you want some kind of a tip?"

"Tip, sar? Can't say I know what yer speakin' of."

Professor Cushing pulled two pence from his wallet. "Here!"

Colin stood still, confused. "Sar, why'd ye just give me money?"

"Look, I don't have time to chat. I'm expecting someone to arrive quite shortly."

"Aye, sar. I've arrived, so I have."

Professor Cushing nodded his head with disgust. "No, no, not you. I'm talking about my new doctorate student

"Oh, ye got yerself another new doctorate student do ye?"

"No, Timothy Duncan is already in his second year of his doctorate, he's my other student. My new student is some chap named Colin Limmerick ... he's got impressive credentials," the professor muttered as he glanced at the clock on his desk. "Not that you'd be interested in that sort of thing."

Colin laughed as he extended his large hand toward Professor Cushing. "It's me pleasure."

9

Professor Cushing pushed Colin's hand away from him. "Be gone! I've got to get prepared for my new student."

Colin placed his hands on his hips. "Sar, I'm yer man. Colin Limmerick so I am!"

Professor Cushing was silent and still. "What?"

"Colin Limmerick so I am. 'Tis grand to meet with ye, so it is," Colin said shaking his professor's hand profusely.

"But, I called the movers to move my office furniture? Aren't you them?"

"Colin Limmerick is me name. The one with the impressive references ye speak of, sar."

Professor Cushing sat down.

Colin smiled. "Sar, for some reason, ye thought I was here to move yer furniture? Sure, I am yer new doctorate student."

"It was you who sent that outstanding reference package? That was you?"

"Sure I am, sar," Colin responded in his deep, calm voice.

"You? How can this be?"

"How can what be, sar?"

"You're, you're a pirate!"

Colin laughed. "Pirate, sar? A pirate I'm not -- a fisherman so I am."

Professor Cushing remained sitting as he tried to slurp his cold tea. "It was you who wrote that lengthy monograph for your research proposal on Charles Darwin's theory of natural selection? That was you?"

"And, so it was, sar."

The Professor rubbed his face. "Go, you need to go now. There is a housewarming ordeal occurring in the university's Great Hall. Just go and mingle with the other students. Get your doctoral student package -- it will be addressed to you with my name marked down as your academic advisor. I can't believe you're Colin Limmerick!

Just go!"

"Professor Cushing, you seem a wee bit piqued, ye do."

"Just go! I have to take this in. I'm going to be working with you for the next four years. I have to come to terms with this some way, somehow."

Colin leaned over Professor Cushing's desk to shake his hand. The professor looked at Colin's sweaty, dirty hands in horror.

Colin smiled as he made his way down the marble stairs of the university searching for the Great Hall. He could see a crowd of people filtering into a middle-sized hall. By the time he got there, they had all had already taken their seats, leaving Colin standing in the aisle. An older man spoke in a loud monotone to the crowd. The students were quiet as they listened to the man welcome the new students to The University of London. Colin fumbled along the aisle. The speaker stopped and glanced at Colin who was still trying to find a seat.

"Who is it you're looking for?" the speaker loudly asked Colin.

"Is this the Great Hall?"

"It is."

"Then I'm in the correct location I am. I apologise I do." Colin bowed his head while he could hear the seated students whisper to one another.

"Come on, come on then, just find a seat anywhere and we will proceed," the speaker said, looking annoyed at Colin.

Colin spotted one seat near the back row as he fumbled through the crowd. "Pardon me, is this seat taken?" he asked one of the few females in the crowd.

The young woman smiled. "It would be yours now."

Colin seated himself and removed his tweed cap. "Hello," he said to the woman, noticing her long, golden brown hair was tied back with a blue felt ribbon.

She smiled as she tried to pay attention to the speaker

but instead grew more intrigued with the stranger sitting beside her. The crowd applauded and the speaker completed his *"welcome, graduate students"* speech.

"Would ye know who the speaker is?" Colin asked the young woman.

She leaned over to him and covered her mouth. "I think he's the chancellor, but I'm not too sure," she whispered.

"Rather long speech it was?" Colin commented, trying to make conversation.

"Yes, rather boring." She gestured a pretend yawn and pulled her student information out of a brown folder with her name on it.

"Where'd ye get that?" Colin asked.

The young woman couldn't help but stare at Colin's brutally handsome smile but tried to focus on his question. "It was handed out as we entered the hall -- yours is probably still by the podium," she said.

"Fetch it I should?" Colin asked nervously.

"You would draw too much attention to yourself."

"I think ye could be right."

The welcome lecture finally concluded, Colin and the woman left the lecture along with the crowd of new graduate students. Colin held his tweed cap in his hand, "Say, would ye like to walk 'round London town with me?"

"Right now?" she asked.

"Now is good." He took notice of her large, dark eyes. She appeared nervous.

"I don't know."

"Sure ye'd like to show a newcomer like me 'round London town?"

"I don't know," she said, turning away from him.

"Ye from 'round here?" he asked as he stepped closer to her.

"I grew up in London, but I'm no Londoner."

"Nor am I."

12

"Really?" she answered sarcastically.

He chuckled and stepped closer to her. "Ye seem like a very proper lady ye do. So proper 'n so beautiful."

She stepped away from him. "You know, I really need to pay attention to the time."

"Ah, ye need to run do ye?"

Her eyes started to wander, for she could not stop focusing on his piercing green eyes. "Yes, I have to be somewhere."

"Where?"

She lowered her eyebrows. "Somewhere -- that is none of your business!"

"Would ye spare some time 'n walk 'round town with me -- just for a minute or two?"

"You're a stranger."

"That I am. Maybe not a stranger for long?"

"You're persistent aren't you?"

"That I am."

"What would your wife say about this?"

He chuckled. "Wife, ye say? There's no wife. I'm still waitin' for the right maiden to come me way." Colin grinned, exposing the dimples in his cheeks.

"All right then."

"Is that a *yes*?"

"I'll stroll about with you."

Colin smiled as he clumsily gathered his notes and orientation information.

They walked to Covent Garden, where several vendors sold food and other merchandise.

"May I ask a lady her name?" Colin tipped his cap toward her, noticing how delicate she was. She was dressed in a floor-length blue dress with several ribbons, which drew Colin's attraction.

"I'm Rosa. Rosa Emanuel." She extended her hand to him.

"Rosa, Rosa, like a flower ye are smellin' so sweet 'n lookin' so lovely," Colin sang as he bowed and kissed her

13

hand.

"I see you're a poet? Not a keen one, but a poet," she commented. "And your name?"

"Colin. Colin Limmerick I am -- Captain at that. Captain Colin Limmerick so I am."

"Limmerick, Colin Limmerick...Captain? I don't think I've ever met anyone with a last name of a city."

"It's common it is, very common wouldn't ye think, lass? Me Celtic ancestors may've had somethin' to do with it or even the Gauls perhaps -- it goes way back ye know."

She paused. "Wait a moment, I heard about you. You're the bloke with the impeccable academic references?"

"Impeccable? I never would have described me references that way as such."

"You're the bloke who's supposed to be impeccably brilliant?" She pointed at him. "You're Professor Cushing's new Ph.D. student? It was you who wrote that monograph for part of the university application on some prehistoric mammal?"

"*Megaloceros giganteus*," he said.

"It's displayed in the showcase in the foyer of the Natural History building. Yes, meglo-whatever! That's you?"

"*Megaloceros*, the Irish elk, the same mammal with two names it is."

"Oh! Did you meet Professor Cushing yet?"

"Briefly, I did."

"I've heard about him. How did it go?"

Colin scratched his head. "I don't know really."

"You don't know?"

"I-- I moved his office furniture around I did."

"Pardon?"

"He had me move a grand lookin' metal cabinet to the other end of his office."

"Why?"

14

"A mover he thought I was. He didn't appear to fancy me much. Two pence he gave me."

"He gave you money? Why?"

"A tip I think it was."

"Dr. Cushing is known as a snobby elitist! Watch out for him. On the other hand, some of his students adore him."

"If he's known as an elitist maybe he won't fancy me bein' Irish."

"Very possible."

"By the way, I'm a Dubliner I am."

"What a surprise."

They continued to walk through the markets of Coventry Street. "Rosa, I wonder if I could ask ye somethin' if I may?" he asked.

"Yes."

"I'd adore yer company, if ye could?" he said, standing very close to her in the streets of the market. Rosa looked up at him as he continued. "Would ye do me the honour of allowin' me to be yer suitor?"

She stepped back. "Are you asking me if you can court me?"

"I understand if ye already have a gentleman. Taken already, I'm sure a pretty lass like ye would have yerself a fine gent, ye would."

"You're asking if I have a gentleman friend?"

"Well, if by any slim chance ye don't, perhaps I could maybe be considered, if this is a wee bit possible?"

"I gave them up a while ago."

"Huh?"

"Men, I gave them up. I don't court anyone."

Colin wasn't sure if she was making a joke. "Gave up men, yer tellin' me?"

"I don't bother with them."

Colin appeared deflated with his lips parted. "I see."

"Don't look so sad, you don't even know me. I'm sure all the ladies are constantly giving you attention."

"I wouldn't say that much, I wouldn't. Somehow, Rosa, I feel as if I've known ye all me life. What ye think?"

"I just met you. I think this is all a bit premature -- not to mention quite abrupt."

His body language indicated some angst as he constantly shifted his weight from one leg to another. "Ye know I pay attention to the ancient Celts I do."

"Ancient Celts?"

"They's me ancestors, they is. Intuition is somethin' not to be ignored. Deep in me gut I feel ye 'n me should be courtin'."

"Really."

"Really, me love, from the spirits of me ancient Celtic ancestors, I need to be your suitor."

She rolled back her eyes. "Look, ignore my last comment. Where would you like to take me?" She asked feeling nervous.

"Where I live I'd like to take ye."

Her eyes focused on the road. "Where do you live?" There was caution in her voice.

"A sea merchant I am, 'n I live on me vessel, I do. Would ye like to see me ship 'n meet me crew?"

"You're a sea merchant? That explains the *Captain* you put in front of your name, and I suppose it explains your clothes?"

"*Me Éadaigh?* Somethin' wrong with me cloths?"

"Well, I guess your clothes are perfect for a sea merchant, but I hardly think they're too fitting for the elitist university community."

Colin glanced down at his chest while he examined what he was wearing. "I've always dressed this way even when I went to university in Dublin."

"That was Dublin, this is London. Professor Cushing probably lost a beat when he saw you walk through his door. Just buy some suits, and all should be well. Oh, and scrub those fingernails," she said. "They do look dreadful."

Colin peered at his fingers. "I don't understand."

"You need to fit in -- that's all I'm saying," she said.

Colin took her hand. "Would ye like to see where I live? This Friday evening a party will be upon me ship. I'd like to invite ye to come as me guest I would."

"A party! Sounds like fun. How do I get to your ship?"

"I'll pick ye up in front of the Natural History buildin'. Ye will come with me on a train to Fishguard, 'n waitin' there will be me vessel already docked."

"Fishguard?"

"Aye."

"This sounds very far and complicated."

"It's the only way."

"I don't think this is possible. I don't even know you," she said pulling away from him.

He placed his arms around her and brought her five foot-five, slender frame toward him, pressing her face against his belly. "Please," he pleaded.

She squirmed in his arms. "If I come, it can only be for a short time."

"Ah, but that's the catch, love."

Rosa's smile dissipated. "There's a catch?"

"You'd have to stay in me cabin for the weekend. I reunite with me crew every Friday through Sunday for our most tryin' catch of the week. I'd have ye back by Sunday."

Rosa stepped away from him. "Then I can't come."

"Please. I really would like ye to visit me ship I would. I want to show ye off to me crew."

"Show me off to your crew? What is this?"

"Not tryin' to offend I'm not."

Her voice lowered. "I never stayed in a man's home before."

"Please, ye must say yes ye do."

"Crew? You want me to stay in your cabin the entire weekend with you and your crew? No, I don't think I

17

can," she said nodding her head while pulling away from him. "I'm Catholic."

"So am I. Isn't that marvelous somethin' in common we's got."

"I hope you go to confession."

"Oh, but I do."

"Of course you do."

"An avid Catholic at that I am."

She stepped closer to him. "Look, I was never with someone like you."

"How do ye mean, Rosa -- love?"

"You have dirty fingernails. You even smell quite disgusting."

Colin hung his head down while staring at the street. "You don't fancy me much do ye?"

"No! No, that's not it! I really like you! You seem very nice. No, please don't misunderstand. It's because you seem different than the blokes I'm used to attending school with."

"Rosa, I would really like to spend some time with ye. I'm invitin' ye to me ship. Think of me as the boy next door."

She laughed. "Boy next door? You?"

"I've been called that before I have."

"No, no you haven't. I would never describe you as the boy next door. Maybe a rough-neck at best."

He scooped her in his arms. "Well? Are ye comin' to me boat?"

Rosa was shaken by surprise. "Put me down, you out-of-control, big lug!"

Regretfully, he placed her onto the road. "I'm hurtin' ye am I?"

"No, no you're not. Colin, why can't you understand? I've only known you a few hours. I can't stay the weekend on your ship with you and your crew. My reputation would be crushed."

Colin's eyes saddened. "I suppose I don't really follow

reputations much."

"That's obvious."

"I want ye to see the world I come from 'is all."

"Why?"

He focused on her as he paused. "'Cause I truly fancy ye, Rosa."

"You don't even know me. What if I was Jack the Ripper's sister or something awful like that?"

He stepped closer to her and ran his hand through her long silky hair. "I don't think that's the case, love."

"If you weren't so nice and so intriguing, I would walk from you this very minute, Colin Limmerick! But I suppose I will have to trust you on this one, God knows why."

"Is that a *yes*, lass?"

"Yes, yes, yes, I'll visit your boat. But you and your crew are not allowed in the cabin where I will be spending the night."

"Me crew will be forbidden, I promise ye."

"They better be forbidden," she enforced.

Colin wrapped his arms around her. "A good-bye kiss I'd love to give ye just now?"

"No!" she said angrily.

"A day kiss right now here on the street?"

She pulled away. "No!"

"I promise I won't hurt ye," he said while he gingerly held and kissed her cheek.

She pushed him away. "You have to stop doing this."

"Why is that?"

"It just isn't proper. I'm a lady, and you're a ..." Her gaze dropped to the road.

He stepped closer to her again. "And I'm a man. Aye, yer a lady, 'n I'm a man -- therefore, we can get romantic with one another, eh?"

She tried desperately not to look at him. "Keep your distance!" she blurted, holding her hands out in front of her.

19

He stood still. "I'd like to at least try the other cheek if I may?"

"No! You may not!"

"Ye have me word I'd never hurt ye. Me ship is a much safer place to be than the streets of London."

"I'm making a big mistake. I don't think I can trust you."

"Ah, but ye can, lass! Please! Ye must!"

"I told you my answer already. I will not board your ship!" she said sternly as her eyes locked with his.

He smiled and remained still.

"You have these dimples in your cheeks which make you look like an honest man," she said.

"An honest man is what I am, love," he stepped closer to her.

Her hands shielded her again. "Stay back! And, don't call me love!"

He walked toward her. "I need to go now. Me crew will be waitin' at port -- I need to take the train, I do."

She started to walk backwards away from him. "You shouldn't keep your crew waiting."

"Sometimes I make 'em wait, but this time I shouldn't."

"I have to go too," she said.

"What time can I pick ye up Friday?"

"Don't know!" She kept her distance.

"I have to work at sea. I'll get clean. I promise 'n pick ye up at half seven?" he continued to walk toward her.

"Half past seven is fine, I suppose," she turned her back on him and began walking north in a near trot.

He grabbed her from behind by the waist. "I have to give ye a kiss good-bye, 'til we meet again!"

She pulled away from him and ran like a bashful teenager. "Until then!" she shouted, getting away from him as fast as possible.

***

The next day Colin was back on *the Atlantic Mermaid*

reeling in the catch with his crew. Timmy, the youngest crewmember, continued to steer the ship. Eddy noticed Colin's cheerful hum. "My -- my, Captain Limmerick, I don't remember the last time I saw yaz this happy. Somethin' happened at the university, didn't it?"

Colin smiled as he pulled the full nets toward the boat. "Met a lass I did. A real lady, I should say."

Eddy slapped him on the back. "I knew it was somethin' this grand, lad! Congratulations! What she like?

"She's beautiful."

"Describe this beauty!"

"She's got big brown eyes, long, golden brown hair that curls at the ends. She's a tiny lass, 'n she's got ribbons in her hair. I invited her here tonight. She's stayin' the weekend."

"Is she the one, lad?"

"Well, we just met, but who knows."

"I'm lookin' forward to meetin' this real lady. I'll tell the boys to be on their best behaviour."

"Thanks!"

***

It was almost 7:30 p.m. Colin took the train from Fishguard Harbour to Waterloo Station. He was clean and smelling good; however, his style of dress had not changed much since the last day he saw Rosa. He hurried northbound to the university's Natural History building where his pace was strong and brisk. He held a rose tightly in his hand. Rosa stood in front of the building a blue dress with a cashmere shawl wrapped around her shoulders. Colin saw her in the distance and picked up the pace even more so.

He stood in front of her in a partial bow. "How now, Rosa?" he said handing her the rose.

She tightened the shawl around her shoulders. "Hello, Colin. Is the flower for me?"

"It is. Yer me flower, ye 'ar," he said kissing her gently on the cheek.

She pulled away from him, realising her nerves made it difficult to breathe. "I packed a small bag. Am I still staying the weekend?"

He slid his arms around her tiny waist. "Ye'ar." He took her bag as they began to walk. "We shall catch the next carriage to Waterloo Station."

"Did you walk here?"

"I did. I always do…don't usually bother with carriages 'n such." Colin hailed a carriage, which took them south to the train station.

As they boarded the train, Rosa tried to keep her nerves in control. They found two seats together, and Rosa immediately took the window seat. As they rode on the crowded train, feeling every bump and sway, Colin noticed how quiet Rosa had become.

"Me dear lady, is somethin' troublin' ye?" Colin asked.

She kept peering out the window, observing the early stages of dusk. "Trouble? I'm not troubled at all, Colin." She continued to stare out the window feeling nervous from the side of his body pressing against her. "Umm Colin, can I ask something of you?"

"Anythin', love."

"Could you not sit so close to me? I'm feeling a little claustrophobic."

Colin's gleaming expression dissipated. "Look at me size, love, I couldn't move away from ye even if I tried, 'n besides, this train is full to capacity, I can't really change seats can I?"

"No… I suppose not."

"Unless ye prefer me standin'?"

"I suppose London to the harbour is too long of a time to be standing?" She gently fluttered her eyelashes while looking away from him.

"Sweet Jesus me dear Lord, I'd much prefer to be sittin' beside ye, if it's dany with ye?" He pressed the side of his body against her even more by moving a little

22

closer. "Just crossin' me leg, 'is all I'm doin', love."

"Look, Colin, I think it's best if you stand the rest of the way!" she said, pointing to the crowded aisle.

"Ye don't mean that, do ye?"

"Get up and let someone else sit down," she insisted.

He stood up in the aisle. A tiny, elderly man moved toward the vacant seat. "Excuse me, lad." The elderly man pulled on Colin's coat sleeve.

"Aye?"

"Is this your seat?" the man asked smelling of mothballs and beer.

"Not anymore, please help yerself."

"Thanks," the man replied as the train jigged enough to throw the man on top of Rosa.

Rosa screamed. Colin yanked the man off her.

"You have obviously won this battle. Colin, go right ahead and sit down," she said.

"I'd much prefer standin'. " His voice oozed with frustration.

Rosa tugged on Colin's jacket. "I don't think I could bear having you stand the entire journey sulking."

He peered down at her while he tried to keep his balance from the bumpy ride. "I can't really say if I ever once met a lass quite like ye. I wish ye'd stop resistin' me 'is all."

She buried her head in her small bag of luggage. "Colin, it is obvious that you know very little about ladies."

He paused with a glare. "I beg yer pardon, love, but I'm afraid I'm not quite readin' ye."

"Never mind."

After some hours passed, the train arrived by Fishguard Harbour. Rosa realised they had reached their destination. She turned her head and found Colin had fallen asleep in the aisle on top of several large pieces of luggage. The train stopped, and the passengers quickly cleared out of the train dragging their bags. Rosa scurried to Colin to shake his arm. "Colin, you need to wake up -- we have arrived!"

His eyes appeared sleepy as he hoisted himself up. He took her bag and awkwardly stomped out of the train. He led her outside to the docks where he pointed out his ship in the distance. He observed her reaction where she appeared anxious and somewhat excited but he wasn't sure.

Colin helped Rosa onto the ship while the nine-man crew stood before her. Their eyes were fixed on her delicate figure. "Men, meet Rosa. We met at the university this week," Colin said with a proud smile.

Eddy took her hands and raised them to his chapped lips. "Ahr, if she aint a beauty, Captain." He kissed her hands, leaving them wet with his alcoholic saliva.

Rosa tried to be cordial. "Hello, hello gentlemen," she said. The men lined up to greet her. Some wrapped their arms around her, some gave her wet kisses on the cheek, and some left her hands dripping in saliva.

Colin pulled Rosa close to his body. "Well Rosa, what do ye think of me crew?" Colin asked in an excited whisper.

"I'm surprised your first mate doesn't wear a parrot on his shoulder," she commented.

Colin's expression changed to confusion. "Parrot?"

Joey pulled out his fiddle while Séamus brought out his accordion, and Murray blew his tin whistle. The music began, and Eddy handed Colin his bodhrán. Three large-busted women climbed onto the ship. They were dressed provocatively, exposing their deep-cut cleavages and curvy buttocks. Their attire was complemented with makeup caked on their faces. Several bottles of ale and whiskey were passed around as the ship departed from Fishguard Harbour for Saint George's Channel. The howling winds blew through Rosa's hair, and she felt the crisp coolness penetrate her bones. Her clothes felt damp to the touch as the mist from the Celtic seas sprinkled upon her. The three women danced in the middle of the ship's deck while the crew stood around howling and clapping. Colin hit the bodhrán with his cipin, keeping the beat of the music. Rosa's eyes widened, almost in disbelief, as the band of fishermen sang "Whiskey in the Jar."

WHISKEY IN THE JAR
As I was goin' over the far Kilkerry mountain
I met with Captain Farrell and his money he was countin'
I first produced me pistol, and then produced me rapier
Said stand and deliver, for I am a bold deceiver

Chorus:
Musha ring dumma do damma da
Whack for the laddie-o
Whack for the laddie-o
There's whiskey in the jar
I counted out his money, and it made a pretty penny
I put it in me pocket and I brought it home to Jenny
She sighed and she swore that she never would deceive me
But the devil take the women, for they never can be easy

Chorus
I went into me chamber, for to take a slumber
I dreamt of gold and jewels and for sure it was no wonder
But Jenny took me charges and she filled them up with water
And send for captain Farrell to be ready for the slaughter

Chorus

25

It was early in the mornin', before I rose to travel
The guards were all around me and likewise captain
Farrell
I first produced me pistol, for she stole away me rapier
But I couldn't shoot the water so a prisoner I was
taken

Chorus
If anyone can aid me, it's me brother in the army
If I can find his station in Cork or in Killarney
And if he'll come and save me, we'll go roving near
Kilkenny
And I swear he'll treat me better than me darlin'
sporting Jenny

Chorus
Now some men take delight in the drinkin' and the
rovin'
But others take delight in the gamblin' and the
smokin'
But I take delight in the juice of the barley
And courtin' pretty Jenny in the mornin' bright and
early
Chorus

As the tune finished a chunky, blond-haired woman made her way to Colin, rubbing her breasts against his body. "When am I invited to yar bed again, Limmerick?" she asked in a vampish whisper.

"Lorelei." He shook his head, not responding to her body language.

"When? Hmm? When is me next invitation to yar bed?" Lorelei shouted as she fondled his suspenders.

He took a step back from her.

Lorelei noticed Rosa. "Who's this, eh?" she asked, pointing at Rosa.

Colin tightened his arm around Rosa and continued to

drink his ale. "Me lass she is."

Rosa looked at Colin. "I am?"

He ran his full lips along Rosa's face. "Ye is."

The two other women stood close to Colin as they watched Lorelei try to pursue him.

The older of the two, Bessy, boldly rubbed herself against him. "Hi, sailorman, missed yaz, I 'av. Yaz lookin' dapper as always," she said. Lorelei appeared angry.

"Ah, Bessy, what ye doin' to me? I'm here with me lass, Rosa. Ye can't pull yer tricks on me tonight ye can't. Not anymore."

Tara, the thinner of the three pushed Bessy away and grabbed Colin's hand. "It's been too long, love. Yaz 'n me had some good times together we's did," she said.

Bessy nudged Tara in the side. "Sailorman 'n me have had better times than yaz 'n Lorelei put together."

Lorelei pushed both women away. "Tara, ya bitch! Go screw one of the other crew -- leave Limmerick to me!" She focused her eyes on him. Rosa pulled away from Colin and tried to focus on the sea.

Another Irish tune began and Eddy took the bodhrán from Colin. Lorelei pulled Colin to the middle of the deck as they both danced to Murray's tin whistle. They both reeled a traditional Irish dance with conviction, kicking their legs back and back -- *one two three* -- *one two three* -- with the hard knocking sound of each treble hitting the floor.

The first mate stood next to Rosa. "Ya better pay attention on how to dance a reel, lass. Yar man, Colin here, can do a mean step he can."

"My man, Colin?" Rosa responded.

The drinking was continuous, causing the men to play rough with each other while they drenched themselves with ale and whiskey. While Colin took a break from Lorelei to help himself to more ale, she approached Rosa. "Ya got Limmerick -- he's yar man, eh? Well, let me tell yaz, I've had'em many a-times before. Ye gotta watch out

27

for'em," she said, clutching a bottle of whiskey. "He's a beast in the bedroom he is. I should know. I've had'em for years in me sack, I have." She blew her hot, alcoholic breath in Rosa's face. "Hangs like a bull he does. He'll surely split a tiny wench like yaz in half."

"Look, if you want him tonight, I won't stop you, whatever your name is."

"Lorelei is me name, missy! Well, it's mighty grand of yaz to step aside 'n let me have'em tonight. Yaz ain't his type, yar not!"

Rosa slowly wandered over to Colin. "Colin, can I ask you something?"

He bent forward to meet her face. "Anythin'."

"These women appear to be prostitutes," Rosa asked, concerned. "Are they?"

Colin continued to watch the festivities. "They've been keepin' me boys happy for a good while now."

"They work on your ship?"

Colin smiled and nodded. "Everyone's gotta make a livin', they's do."

***

The party continued till the early morning with dancing, ale, whiskey, women, and brawling. One of the crew didn't like that another crewmember was getting extra attention from Bessy. Colin sat at the corner of the ship with Rosa, oblivious to any of the goings-on that took place. He placed Rosa on his lap while he ran his large fingers through her silky, long hair. Suddenly, a stool flew across the ship as two crew members battled for Bessy's attention. Lorelei screamed, trying to stop the violence. Colin sprung from his chair, letting Rosa down gently. He broke up the crowd and pried the two men apart. "Ye two gotta stop this feckin' shite! Bessy, make yer decision but leave it off me feckin' ship!" he shouted.

"Ah, children…all men are bleedin' children!" she mumbled, half drunk.

Colin gave Bessy a blank stare. He then glanced at

Tara and then tried to avoid looking at Lorelei.

The two crewmen sulked in the corner inhaling their ale. Lorelei approached Colin as she rubbed her hands up and down his chest. "Hey, don't blame Bessy for yaz stupid men's feckin' brawls! Why don't yaz 'n me hook up 'n go upstairs to yar cabin, where we banged so many times before?" Lorelei spoke loudly, hoping Rosa would hear.

Colin ignored Lorelei. He took Rosa's hand and led her to the ladder up to his captain's quarters.

"Colin, was or is Lorelei your girl?" Rosa asked as he led her through his cabin door.

"She's been a friend for a good while I'd say. I won't lie to ye -- she was me own personal whore for a good while."

"Excuse me?"

He slid his arm around Rosa. "It's not what ye think. After a few tricks, she forbid me payin' her 'cause she wanted to believe we was a couple. I'd give 'er gifts 'n such instead. Sure to keep 'er goin'. "

Rosa pulled away from him. "She's a whore, your whore! Oh my God!"

"But it's not that way, 'cause she refused me quid, she did."

Rosa folded her arms in front of her. "So what?"

"So that means I didn't pay her for sex like as if she was me lady of the evenin', ye know."

"No, I don't know…How about Bessy and Tara?"

"What 'bout them?"

"Were they also your personal whores?"

He paused. "I've slept with them more than five times, maybe more than ten, not sure I am. I won't lie to ye, Rosa. I want the truth to be known to ye," he said, embarrassed.

"What am I doing with you on this ship? Oh my God!" she exclaimed in a panic.

"Well, I mean it was just screwin' 'n nothin' more."

"Nothing more? I think that's something, don't you?"

"Rosa, I never loved any of those wenches."

"Were there other women, perhaps?"

He paused. "Just screwin' it was, not lovemakin' is all. A sailor is what I am. I've been married to the sea since I was fifteen. I used to work on me uncle's boat when I was a wee lad. Despite me love for the sea, I'm also in love with readin' 'n research. I'm an educated sailor, if ye can believe it?" he chuckled, feeling a slight head-rush of embarrassment.

"My, what a checkered past we weave." Rosa forced a smile.

"I'm a rather complex bloke I am." He smiled, looking as if he were waiting for her approval.

"Well, it looks like these three women, or whatever they are, really want you, especially that Lorelei. She looks like she wants to strike me."

Colin started to play with Rosa's hair. "Jealous ye are?"

Rosa laughed. "Colin, I'm not jealous of Lorelei!"

He began to stroke her cheek.

"Stop touching me!" She pushed him away and walked into the middle of his cabin. She took notice of his double bed and smiled nervously. "Nice big cabin."

He recklessly flopped on the bed. "Ye like it?"

"I quite like your ship. Your crew is another story, and so are your three lady friends. Ladies?"

Colin took Rosa's hand and pulled her to sit on his bed. "Tell me 'bout yer-self, Rosa? Did ye ever have a bloke in yer life that ye wanted to marry? Let the truth be known."

"I was engaged when I was twenty-one. He was Spanish from a town just outside Barcelona. I'm originally from there. He was a friend of the family. It was an arranged marriage. It took a year to prepare the wedding. It was going to be colossal. But ..."

"But what?"

"I called it off one month before the wedding. I didn't love him. This was something my parents wanted more than I did. I wanted to go to school and obtain a degree. My family frowned on me for that. My mother thought I should get married and have babies like she did."

"Why didn't ye love him?"

"He was consumed with only himself. Also, he didn't support me wanting to attend university. I too had highly acclaimed references of my last graduating class. I've always had a love for archaeology, specialising in human evolution. He just wanted me to focus on him and only him."

"I hope ye never think I'd ever treat ye that way."

"Colin, you're something different all together. I'm still trying to digest you and your world."

He began to run his hands along the contours of her tiny body. "Are ye sorry you called off yer weddin'?"

"No regrets. That was already six years ago. However, my parents still live in Barcelona. I have nothing to do with them. I haven't even returned for a visit. My father moved here to teach Biology at the East London University, so you could say I grew up in London."

"Yer father is a professor he is?"

"Yes, but I don't bother with my family anymore."

"Don't ever say it or think it! Yer family should be most important in yer life!"

"It's not so bad divorcing one's family."

"How can ye say this? A tragedy it is!"

"I take it you're close to your family?"

"I am.

"You're close to your parents?"

"I am."

"How sweet."

"Me family has been good to me. I can't really complain. There's just one wee thing."

"And, what is that?"

"They's always pressurin' me to marry." Colin started

31

to kiss Rosa's neck as he pushed her hair away.

"I guess this is why I'm here tonight?"

"'Cause ye fancy me?"

She grinned. "Yes, I do like you. You seem very sweet. But there's more underlying reasons to why a modern woman like myself would be spending the weekend on your ship with you and your musical crew."

"What's that?"

"Don't you see, Colin? There are no society girls doing what I'm doing right now. This has made me a renegade."

"Renegade, ye say?"

"If my family knew what I was doing right now, they'd disown me."

"Would ye even care?"

"I made the decision to live an estranged life from my Mediterranean upbringing, and it feels good. I feel emancipated. It feels wonderful to be an independent woman, not really needing parents to run to. And, better yet, not needing a man."

Colin lay on the bed, "I see."

"I'm free!" she blurted.

He began caressing her shoulders. "Colin, no. You promised."

"Yer too lovely for me not to," he said pressing his body against hers.

"No, Colin. You can't do this."

He pressed himself onto her. "Rosa, I want ye tonight, please," he whispered in her ear.

"No, Colin, you need to control yourself."

His heavy breathing frightened her as he started to unbutton her blouse. He pulled his shirt off and began to thrust his body against her. She tried to move off the bed, but his arms were wrapped firmly around her.

"Colin! Stop! Colin, get off me!" she shouted, trying to fight him. He kissed her neck then moved toward her face. She squirmed, but he continued pressing his lips against hers. He moved his tongue into her mouth. She slapped him across the face. He got off her immediately.

She sat crouched on the bed, terrified. "I didn't come here for this!" she whimpered.

Her slap had left a red mark on his cheek. "A woman has never slapped me before. I don't know what got in me," he said, rubbing his sore face.

"If you want to be with me, Colin, you cannot treat me like those three tramps on this ship!"

"Forgive me." His head hung down. "Rosa, I think I'm fallin' in love with ye."

"Colin, this is a little too soon for you to be saying this. I think your over-sexed nature is running away with you!"

He forced a smile. "Over-sexed nature, ye say? I'm sorry I am. Please don't think less of me. I won't do this to ye again."

Rosa took Colin's hand, "Colin, you seem very nice, except for your urges. You see, Colin, your way of life is too different from mine. I don't know if this would ever work."

"I'll change when we go to university -- you'll see. I bought four suits just like ye told me."

"Colin, if you still want to be friends, don't scare me like this."

"Friends? I want to be so much more than friends." Colin kissed her hands. "Don't say friends, love, don't say this," he said with a panicked expression.

"Colin, I just met you. I need time with a man, lots of time. I can't rush into these things. Can't you understand?"

"Do I still have a chance? Please tell me I didn't blow it with ye?"

She patted Colin on the shoulder. "You're used to a world that is unfamiliar to me. I don't know if I can take this, Colin."

"Please dismiss me behaviour, what got into me I

33

don't know."

"Colin, I think it's best if you give me some breathing space. This doesn't look like it's going to work for us."

His eyes grew wet as he turned away from her while still sitting on the bed. "Sure ye 'n me can make this work," he mumbled in a soft whisper.

"Crying? Are you crying?"

He faced away from her. "I'm not!"

"A big strong man like you? A sailor at that is crying over me?"

"Men don't cry! Especially men of the sea."

"Apparently they do."

She placed her delicate hands around his face, "Colin, I think you've had a really long day of fishing, train travel, and then crew festivities. You look terribly tired. Maybe things will look different in the morning. Maybe it's time you leave, and you and I both get some sleep."

His large, muscular body lay on the bed curled beside her.

"What are you doing?" she blurted in a whisper. His eyes closed and he fell asleep beside her. "Colin, what are you doing? You're not supposed to sleep here with me."

Rosa felt it was safe enough to sleep on the same bed. She crawled under the blankets, and he slept on top of the blankets with his trousers on.

Chapter Two

It was October, the time when the university was beginning its new academic year. Colin arrived at Professor Cushing's door wearing a suit. "Sar?" Colin said.

"Colin Limmerick? You look different from the last time I saw you. You actually look civilised."

"Yer talkin' 'bout me grubs, sar?"

"Step in, Colin, take a seat. Sit on that old stool. Sit, Colin. I asked you here today so I can inform you of what is expected of you in the next little while. First, I'd like to know are you doing any course work this term?"

"Course work, sar? Enrolled in two courses at the moment I am."

"Two courses? What are they?" Professor Cushing asked as he dipped his pen-nib in a bottle of ink.

"One course is called *The Philosophies of Evolution* 'n the other is *Theories of Evolution.*"

Professor Cushing wrote the names of the two courses down. "Okay, Colin, which of the two are you willing to get rid of?"

Colin felt uncomfortable in his new suit. "How'd ye mean?"

"Exactly that. Choose the one you can toss."

"Sar, it's me course work. I need those courses, I do."

"Colin, you're only going to do one course for this autumn term."

"Can I ask why, sar?"

"You're going to be teaching my *Introduction To Natural History* foundation course."

"I am?"

"You are."

"Why do I have to withdraw from one of me courses?"

"Time, Colin, time. You won't have any time."

35

"Sar, ye did read me sample of me future proposal that was enclosed with me application, didn't ye?"

"Proposal? It will be a year before we can talk proposal."

"Sar, I've got me ideas ready to go. I really want to submit me dissertation proposal to ye."

"On what? That ridiculous prehistoric mammal you're so interested in? Megla-something."

"*Megaloceros,* or Irish elk, so is its names. I want to prove through me research how it evolved. Its closest livin' relative today is the fallow deer, so I've read in some foreign academic journals. Don't ask me why it's known as an elk. However, sar, in me opinion, *Megaloceros* wasn't an elk at all. It really should be known as the Irish deer."

"Who cares?"

"Sar, I need to prove how Darwin's theory of natural selection is what led to *Megaloceros'* extinction."

"Colin, right now you will have to put Darwin to rest, because you have a course to teach for me."

"I do?"

"You do!"

"What's the actual class size? Maybe I could take both me courses just the same."

"Okay, Colin, suit yourself. You need not worry about the class size of my foundation course, which caters to first and second year students."

"Ah, sar, what is the usual class size?"

"It ranges from about fifty to sixty students."

"For a foundation course that sounds wee small, sar."

Professor Cushing scratched the information on what lecture hall and time the course was being offered on a piece of paper. "There you go, Colin. The course begins next Monday," Professor Cushing handed the information to Colin. Colin forced a smile as he stood up with a good-bye to his professor and left.

***

36

That afternoon Colin walked along Piccadilly Circus trying to dodge the busy metropolitan traffic. The narrow sidewalks spilled over with crowds; several people scattered throughout the roads meandered among the fast-moving carriages and few automobiles. He had just come from the university library, where he had gathered recently published academic work authored by foreign scientists.

As Colin walked through the crowd, he noticed a petite woman with long, golden brown hair trying to cross the busy street. Her dress was long and blue, very simple with ribbons hanging from her sleeves. It was Rosa. He caught up to her before she crossed the street.

"Rosa!"

Rosa turned her head, "Colin! Aren't you handsome in a suit," she said, smiling.

"I don't fancy its feel much, but it's what ye recommended," he said as he focused on her large dark eyes. "Where ye goin'?"

"I need to work in the lab for my first experiment for my archaeology course."

"I'd come along if I had time," Colin said in a low voice.

"I didn't ask you to come with me, Colin. I'm a student just like you. I have little time just like you."

His smile transformed to a frown. "How thoughtless of me."

"What do you have in your hand?" she asked tapping him on the arm.

"I'm interested in academic journals by foreign authors. There's some strange stuff bein' researched all over the world these days that I'm after includin' in me research."

"Oh really? Like what?"

"Time travel, if ye can believe it?"

"Time travel? You mean going back in time to another century or something?"

"Wonderful idea, isn't it?"

"Who is writing this strange information?"

"A Russian physicist for one!"

"Some Russian author is writing about time travel?"

"There's this fascinatin' professor in Russia who writes 'bout the laws of physics behind time travel. Wonderful theories he has."

"You believe this bloke's theory?"

"I have to, Rosa!"

"Why do you have to?"

"I want to prove Darwin's theory of natural selection to me academic advisory professor. I think he's a bit of a non-believer, he is."

"Good luck with Professor Cushing, my dear. You're not going to have an easy go with him."

"Noticed that already I have," he said, feeling a bit nervous.

She grew silent as she smiled at him.

He paused as his eyes began to scan the streetscape. "Would ye like to spend a bit of time with me again?"

"I hope you're not referring to your boat? I think I have too much to do, anyway."

"Can I at least give ye a kiss?"

"Colin, I'm very busy now."

"One wee kiss is all I ask ye." He wrapped both arms around her.

"Get your hands off me!" she shouted, and he released her. "What kind of a man are you?"

"A man who knows a good woman when he sees one."

"Just keep your distance!"

He backed away from her. "Ye don't fancy me much do ye?"

She shrugged her shoulders at him. "Colin, if you would like to court me the way a proper gentleman would do, that could be possible, but your method is for savages. I can't live by your rules."

"So ye *do* fancy me?"

She stopped tensing her body and took a deep breath, "Yes, Colin, I do like you."

Colin clamped his lips onto her, took advantage of her gasp of surprise to thrust his tongue into her mouth. Rosa squirmed and hit him on the back. She tried to scream, but it was difficult with Colin's tongue in her mouth. She tried kneeing him in the crotch, but his crotch was situated much too high for her reach. She finally managed to push him away. He pulled back, noticing they had drawn a crowd of spectators.

"You must be crazy to keep assaulting me like this!" she shouted.

"Assaulting ye? I'm just expressin' me feelin's for ye, 'is all!"

"You're a beast!" She got away from him, leaving Colin standing alone on the street with a crowd of people gawking at him.

***

That weekend Colin managed to find a fair-sized flat across the road from the university Natural History building. He had already begun his two courses and had piles of homework for the following week. He then made his way back to his ship at Fishguard Harbour where he met with his crew.

Eddy appeared glad to see him as they greeted each other with a strong handshake.

"Lad! Yaz here! Yaz look tired," Eddy said.

"Tired, so I am. I didn't realise the scholarly university programme was goin' to be this hectic, I didn't," Colin said making his way to the galley. The crew was glad to see Colin, and they each gave him a friendly slap on the back.

Colin sat at the table. Eddy gave his captain a hard stare. "Captain, where's yar lass at?"

Colin pressed a bottle of ale against his lips, "Lass, ye ask?" Colin gave a pained snicker. "Rosa? She's not me lass no more. We haven't been gettin' on too well. She thinks I'm a beast 'cause I kissed her. I love'er, ye know. But, I guess I need to forget'er I do." Colin started to hand out his crew's pay.

"Ah, Captain, she's just playin' hard to get, she is," Eddy said; the crew seemed to agree.

"She's not. She don't fancy me much."

"Who wouldn't fancy our captain? All the lasses are always in love with yaz. Ye never had a problem gettin' a wench, Captain."

"Only the ones who hate me 'n call me beast," Colin said, inhaling his beer.

"Beast? Not yaz! You're such a gentleman ya' ar."

"Apparently not. Rosa don't fancy me touchin' 'er. She's afraid of me, she is."

"Well, I've seen yaz kiss the ladies, Captain, 'n ya could be a bit too passionate for the dear garl."

"I'm not her type of man 'is all," Colin poignantly said as he finished his second ale while opening a third. His head hung down in sadness at the conversation. His heart ached as he tried to show a tough façade to his first mate and crew.

"Captain, I'm really sad for yaz," Eddy said.

Colin proceeded to get very, very drunk.

Chapter Three

Monday morning Colin trotted through the university hallway to his office. He removed his coat and hat, revealing one of his new vested suits. He dashed down the marble staircase to the lecture hall with his leather bolg in hand. He could hear the crowd of students seating themselves as he bolted through the doorway and onto the lecture platform. He stood at the lecturn with the department's new, high-efficiency microphone attached to it. He pulled out his notes in a panic, failing to glance at his seated students, yet he could hear their conversations going on. Suddenly, he heard more than one person whistle at him. He looked up to the last row to see where the whistling was coming from. It was two females near the last row of the lecture hall. He was mortified to see that the lecture hall appeared to have about two hundred students sitting in front of him. "Cushing lied," he muttered to himself. "That feckin' bastard lied." He stared at the group.

The two young women from the end row kept whistling at Colin with their fingers in their mouths. "Hey! Look up here!" they kept calling to him.

Colin gazed at the gadget known as a microphone as he tried to figure out how to turn it on. "Attention, ladies 'n gentlemen. Just bear with me, while I try to turn on this fancy new, high-efficiency transmittin' microphone." Finally it turned on, creating a noisy feedback echo throughout the lecture hall. "I'll be yer instructor for this foundation course for the duration of the first half. You may address me as Instructor Limmerick. I'd appreciate the ladies at the end row to stop that silly whistling 'n let's get down to business, shall we?" The two young women sank in their chairs. "I know all of ye were expectin' Dr. Cushing to be teachin' this course, but there's been a

41

change in plans 'n I will now be takin' over."

The students talked amongst themselves.

"I would first like to introduce Dr. Charles Darwin to ye all. He was the founder of the theory of natural selection, entailin' survival of the most fit species." Colin paused, glaring at the large group of students, all whom seemed attentive. "What is natural selection?" Colin scanned the lecture hall, looking for a show of hands. His students were still and silent, so he went on. "Random genetic mutations occur within an organism's genetic code. It's the beneficial mutations that are preserved because they are the survivors, they is -- this is the process Dr. Darwin calls natural selection. These beneficial mutations are passed on to the next generation. I hope yer all takin' this down. Over time, beneficial mutations accumulate, and the result is an entirely different organism -- not just a variation of the original, but an entirely different creature. This process can be compared to a prehistoric mammal known as *Megaloceros giganteus*, more commonly known as the Irish elk. This large mammal is the topic of me own research. I'm interested in findin' out how this large mammal grew to its extinction. Its extraordinarily large antlers hindered its feeding in forested lands. It may've had difficulty keeping its head up even. Sexual selection was the reason for such large antlers. Female *Megaloceros* were sexually attracted to the largest, most muscular stag with the largest set of antlers." The students started to chuckle.

"It was unfortunate, environmentally speakin, that this large stag's antlers grew so large it was selected against not to evolve into another species but rather simply died off. This is how natural selection keeps the strongest, most beneficial mutations and throws out those who cannot adapt to the environment in search of food like *Megaloceros*."

***

Colin glanced at his students. "In conclusion, despite

42

the stag *Megaloceros'* size, strength, 'n antlers, it was selected against. Thus, with conflictin' selections, this large mammal grew to its extinction." Colin's Irish dialect echoed through the lecture hall on the microphone. "It has been compared to today's deer. Not an elk rather -- but, that is me own opinion, other naturalists may challenge me on this. This large, prehistoric mammal did not evolve into the deer we know of today -- it stopped evolvin' 'n died off. This is the result of a different organism." Colin took a long look at his class, noticing the two females sitting at the back. He scanned the room again, noticing there were a few female students sitting at the far end. *"Hardly a handful of wenches,"* he whispered away from the microphone. "I will quote from *The Origin of Species* I will, that one species takes advantage of, 'n profits by the structure of another. But, natural selection does profit from another species' downfalls. Natural selection tends only to make each organic bein' as perfect as, or slightly more perfect than, the other inhabitants of the same country with which it has to struggle for existence. And, we see that this is the degree of perfection attained under nature, but natural selection is not total perfection either, keep in mind!"

After two hours Colin's lecture concluded. The students gathered around him expressing their interest with several questions.

When the students left the lecture hall, the two female students from the back row remained. "Sir, we're sorry for our behaviour earlier," one of the young women said with her eyes fixed on Colin.

Colin leaned against the lecturn as he removed his round-framed glasses, "What was the problem, ladies?"

"Sir, we didn't realise you were the instructor of this course. We're terribly sorry."

"Who the hell did ye think I was?" he questioned abruptly.

"You don't really look like an instructor, sir," one of

the females said, with her cheeks blushing.

"If I'm standin' here by the lecturn, then I must be the instructor of this bleedin' course shouldn't I be?

The girls felt intimidated by his size and tone. "Sir, we're terribly sorry!" They both pleaded.

"Why were ye callin' out to me like that when I was tryin' to get the class started?"

The women looked at each other. "Sir, I understand why you're angry with us, but we didn't realise your lecture was going to be so wonderful. It was very enchanting! We especially liked what you said about the Irish elk being sexually selected by the females and how sexual selection worked against the big strong stag, sir."

His stern expression dissipated and transformed into a smile, "Ah, really glad I am that ye absorbed that part of the lecture."

"But, sir, there's something else I'd like to know, if I may? How about human beings?" One woman asked.

"Human bein's?" He continued to lean over the lecturn, but appeared confused.

The young woman smiled at Colin as she recklessly removed the bows from her hair. "Does the same theory of sexual selection happen with human beings, sir? Can females sexually select males for their size?" She flipped her curly fair hair in front of him.

Colin looked at the two young women with widened eyes. He started to gather his notes, stuffing them into his leather bolg. "A male's size ye ask?" He stuffed the last of his notes into his bag. "Until next class, I must run."

"Sir! Are you still angry with us?" the other young woman asked as she boldly pulled at his arm.

"Angry, ye say? Not at all am I angry with yez ladies. Just don't let it happen again 'is all!" he shook his finger at the young women.

"We wont, sir! Thank you! But before you go, and we know you're in such a rush, could you quickly answer the question?"

"Question?"

The two young women looked at each other a burst into girlish giggles. "Can a man be sexually selected through the evolutionary process? Will he become extinct because he will no longer be able to adapt due to his size?"

Colin paused while his eyes scanned the room. "I don't really know what yer referrin' to 'n I really must be off now."

"Just answer *yes* or *no*, sir," the young woman insisted as she looked at her friend with a grin.

Colin took his bag in his hand as he loosened his tie. "A male human bein'?"

"Yes, sir."

"Size?"

"You know, sir."

Colin yanked his tie from his neck, "Ah, this is too much of a puzzle for me, I really must go. It's wee hot in here."

"Sir, you should know the answer to this question. After all, you are a member of the male species." The two young women sprinted to the door of the lecture hall while bursting into laughter. "Until next lecture, sir! We can't wait!" the girls blurted in hysterics and left.

***

After an hour had passed Colin, showed up at Professor Cushing's door. "Sar."

"Colin Limmerick, do come in and pull up a stool!" Professor Cushing said.

Colin sat down. "Sar, did ye have a chance to read through me rough draft of me proposal?"

"I most certainly did, Colin, most certainly did," the professor said as he sipped a cup of tea.

"Well, sar?"

"Well, what?"

"Sar, what is yer take on it?"

"It needs work, Colin. It's all over the place -- it's a

jumble!"

Colin paused almost in a feeze-frame not taking his eyes off his professor. "How, sar?"

"You keep going about this natural selection rubbish! Your Irish elk most likely evolved into that damn fallow deer that you mentioned in your proposal."

"It didn't!"

"Of course it did. You provided photographs of the fallow deer and some artist's sketch of your Irish elk -- they look identical. Of course your *Megaloceros* evolved into that damn deer! You even said it is a deer rather than an elk. You said it yourself in your garbled proposal, Colin."

"Sar, they look nothin' alike, they don't! How can ye even think this?"

"Now, Colin, don't get yourself in a tiff. You seem like the kind of chap who tends to lose control!"

Colin stood up. "Sar, if one studies evolution, one must accept natural selection. I don't see it any other way, I don't! Natural selection is far from perfection, sar, but it makes a hell of a lot more sense!"

"To you, Colin, it makes sense and only you and perhaps Charles Darwin."

"I can understand ye not acceptin' the theory for purposes of yer faith, I can."

"Colin, how about *your* faith? You're the one who wears crucifixes around your neck along with all that gaudy jewellery."

Colin started to sweat; he removed his blazer. "Sar, I practise me faith, but I try not to relate the two, I don't."

"Colin, I probably don't practise my faith as much as you. My distaste for your proposal has nothing to do with faith. It has to do with the mere fact that it just isn't a very good proposal."

"I see."

"Colin, look at your big, rough hands -- these are the hands of a working man, the hands of a sailor, not the hands of a scholar."

"What?"

"Colin, even the way you write is not suitable for academics."

"What's wrong with the way I write?"

"You write like a poet, not an academic!"

"I don't."

"Colin, I'm hoping this academic institution made the correct decision in having you come aboard."

"When do ye want a fresh copy of me proposal?"

Professor Cushing pulled Colin's proposal out of his desk drawer and handed it back to him. "Tomorrow some time."

Colin slid his blazer back on. "Until then," he said as he left Professor Cushing's office.

***

That afternoon Colin attended one of his graduate level courses, **Theories of Evolution.** It was a small class of eight. He found himself a chair, noticing the meek young gentlemen in the room. Colin pulled out his notebook and began taking notes. The professor was an elderly Englishman with bushy white hair.

"Colin Limmerick is your name? You're the prodigy who wrote that great piece on the evolution of *Megaloceros.* That's you isn't it?"

"Prodigy?" Colin paused. "Aye, sar. That piece was mine," he responded, feeling tired and awkward.

"Brilliant piece!" the course professor exclaimed.

"Glad ye fancy it, sar." Colin tried to suppress an exhausted yawn.

"You seem like a fine researcher," the professor said not really caring that he was holding up the class lecture. . "Let's see, would you have that interesting piece with you?"

"Not with me, sar. Sure, our next class I'll bring it along."

"I just read through it once. I liked it. Yes, I liked it

47

very much. Can't wait to see what you're going to do for me in this course," the professor said. Colin gave a friendly smile to his classmates. The class responded to Colin with a blank stare.

After the two-hour class, Colin became acquainted with his fellow students then made his way to the university library to obtain several books on evolution.

***

It was late afternoon. Colin felt he needed to go to the gym to sweat off his stress and exhaustion. He made his way to the men's change room. He threw his canvas gym bag onto the bench and lethargically removed his clothes. Colin recognized some of the young men in the change room from his graduate course, and some were students from the course he was teaching. He slowly slipped on his undershirt, almost falling asleep in the process. He tied his laced rubber shoes and tied his long hair back before making his way to the gymnasium.

There were several free weights as well as a running track. Several of his students said hello as they walked by him energetically. Colin adjusted the barbell to his desired weight of 400 pounds for his dead lift. He started to lift until he worked up a sweat. For the next several hours Colin did several repetitions of every weight in the gym. His deep pant transformed to a wheeze of discomfort, which he ignored. Finally he exited for the showers. It was already 8:00 p.m., and he realised his day was coming to an end.

He walked slowly through the dark streets, carrying his gym belongings and textbooks. Feeling over-worked and lonely, he passed the pub, deciding it was time for a few pints. The place was full of drunken old men and male university students. He planted himself at the bar, piling his things on the floor below the bar stool as he ordered ale in the largest mug possible. He hung his torso over the bar ledge and ignored the goings-on. He drank until closing time.

48

***

Just two weeks into the first half of the academic year, Colin blew off his daily frustrations at the gym working on the bench press. One of his class peers spotted him while he managed to lift a hefty barbell over his head. He was drenched in sweat while gritting his teeth trying to conquer the challenge.

"Come along, Colin, only ten more reps to go," his classmate encouraged him as he continued to spot him. Every vein in Colin's arms bulged.

"Like an eternity it feels!" Colin burst with spit.

"Colin? Where have you been? I thought you vanished off the face of the Earth," a feminine voice gently murmured.

Colin's concentration broke and he almost allowed the barbell to fall onto his chest. His classmate noticed Colin was losing his grip. "Miss, you have to leave. This is a man's gym. You're not supposed to be here. Please stop distracting this man."

"You want me to leave? You think I'm distracting this man? Well, I think I have every right. This man is my beau," Rosa blurted.

Colin almost lost grip of the barbell, accidentally lowering it to his chest. "Shite!" He yelled. "Feck! Help me get this feckin' thing off me!"

"Colin?" Rosa said in a demanding tone.

Colin got a grip of the barbell while his classmate tried to help him place it back on the rack of the bench press. His classmate helped him up. Colin approached Rosa, panting with exhaustion so that he had difficulty talking. "Beau, so yer callin' me?" He immediately sprang up from the bench with his arms out ready to hug her. "I bes' not touch ye. Ye may think of me as a beast or somethin' too awful."

She moved closer to him as he put one knee on the bench. He lowered his sweaty body close to hers. She grabbed his face and kissed him on the lips.

"I missed you," she said.

He was visibly stunned. "Oh dear God, thank-ye," he said, closing his eyes.

"What's the matter, you big lug?" She kissed him again on the lips.

"I'm shocked is what I am."

"No need to be shocked, but remember, my dearest love, you play by my rules," she said, tapping him on the nose.

"I shall clean up then give ye the kiss of a lifetime," Colin said with a gleaming smile. They passionately kissed in the middle of the men's gym.

Chapter Four

It was late spring 1908, and Colin just completed his research proposal. Rosa sat in a chair in Colin's flat while he tried to finish shaving his face in the bathroom. "Shite! I cut me bleedin'face with me bleedin' blade again!"

"Colin, why so flustered?"

"Professor Cushing, that feckin' bastard he is, makes me bleedin' nervous!"

"Colin, wash your mouth! Relax! It will all work out."

"It won't. Hates everythin' I do, the bastard does. Hates everythin' 'bout me, don't ye think?"

"Now don't be ridiculous, Colin, he's just a bit narrow in his thinking."

"Shite!" Colin yelped.

"Did you cut your face again?"

"Ye know on me ship I shave whenever I damn well feel like it. What's some stubble on a man's face? I often wore a full beard when on me ship."

"Respectable, my dear, you must look respectable in the academic world," she said.

He dashed to his bedroom in a struggle to put on his vest over his dress shirt. "Today's the day, Rosa! Cushing gives me the verdict on me proposal he will." Colin grabbed Rosa, holding her tightly to his body. "Won't say anythin' positive he won't, that he never does."

"Take a deep breath, and you'll feel a lot better."

Colin placed his top hat on his head and threw Rosa's shawl over her shoulders. They dashed out to the busy streets.

"I have some work to do in the lab this afternoon. Do you want to meet later for some dinner? I'm a very good cook, and maybe it's time you try a Barcelona dish," she said as she and Colin cut through the regular hustle and bustle of the streets of London.

"Rosa, I would just love it, thank ye, however, I have to spend the entire afternoon with Cushing. I hate 'em! Bastard!"

"Perhaps another time? You will probably spend the latter part of the evening at the pub drinking draught, no doubt."

"I might need to get pissed-up after me time with the old bastard. I wish ye could help me drink me sorrows away, I do."

"Dear, nobody can drink you under the table."

"Now yer goin' 'bout me drinkin' again -- this isn't the time."

When they arrived at the university Rosa went to the lab where she worked while Colin continued toward the Natural History Building. He grudgingly walked through the dark, echoing hallway that led to his advisor's office.

"Colin Limmerick, you're late! In my office with you! C'mon, what are you waiting for?" Professor Cushing pulled out his rusty stool and slid it under Colin's butt.

"I'm not late, Professor Cushing, this is the scheduled time for us to meet."

"Colin, when will you start to lose that Irish drawl of yours? You've been living in London for almost a year now. I still have trouble understanding you."

"Yer in a fury 'bout me Irish brogue?"

"It's like another language."

"About me proposal, sar?"

Professor Cushing purposely tried not to focus his eyes on Colin. "Yes, I have read your proposal." He fumbled for Colin's draft, slamming it on top of his neatly organised desk. "To be brutally honest, it's not a very good proposal!"

"W--What?"

"Colin, this is not some flimsy doctor's programme that you would find in Dublin or some damn place in your far-off land. This is a London university where only scholars belong. This Ph.D. proposal will never get past

52

the Dean's office for approval." Professor Cushing had Colin's proposal rolled into his hand while he kept tapping it on the desk.

"But, why, Professor?"

"Frankly, there is nothing in this proposal that demonstrates an actual research question."

"Is it because I back up Darwin's theory 'n criticise Lamarck?"

"Look, Colin, everyone knows that Lamarck's theory of evolution makes the most sense. Your ideas of what you call natural selection just don't make it. There have been too many criticisms against Darwin. Your ideas of evolution would take a lot longer for such drastic change. And then...and then...and then... you speak of this Irish elk that isn't even an elk as you say. It did not just simply die off because its horns were too large; it evolved into another elk with smaller horns so it could roam through the forests with less trouble finding food. You think you are going to be a prehistoric mammal naturalist? Please..."

"What do you suggest I do to fix it, Professor?"

The Professor pulled a ham sandwich out of a brown paper bag, squishing it in his mouth at once. "I'm just wondering if you're a lost cause," he said with food particles falling from his mouth onto his shirt. "Number one -- you use Lamarck to back up your research. Number two -- drop your research on the Irish elk. Three -- drop out of this doctor's post...Take your pick!" Sandwich particles spewed from the professor's mouth and collected onto the pages of Colin's proposal. "By the way, how's my course doing?"

"The course has almost two hundred students. Gradin' papers 'n preppin' is what I always do. Me own research I have little time for, let alone me course work. Sleepin' is what I rarely get to do anymore. All me time, sar, is spent on yer course."

Professor Cushing laughed. "Priorities, Colin,

priorities. Maybe you need to sell that damn boat of yours. Priorities, Colin, priorities."

"Me vessel is me bread'n butter, sar."

The professor propped himself on his desk. "Look, Colin Limmerick, you fisherman...a true scholar would be willing to starve for his dissertation. You're too damn worried about your bread and butter...I did it...I starved for my dissertation...what makes you so special? One of your biggest liabilities, Colin, is your age. You're too damn old to be a student at this university!"

"Me age? What does that have to do with anythin'?"

"You're too set in your ways. You're too attracted to the smell of money. Well, if it's too important for you to be a successful business man, why the hell are you even bothering with a doctorate degree?"

Colin stared at the floor and took a long pause. "Me first love was always the evolution of prehistoric mammals. The sea was always second, but I had to make a livin',sar. And, I must say, I've grown very attached to me life at sea."

"Someday you should get acquainted with Timothy Duncan."

"Of course, dear Timothy who ye always marvel for."

"He's my other doctorate student."

"Of course he is."

"He doesn't concern himself with the rubbish you do. He's a great deal younger than you, and he could teach you a thing or two about academics."

"I'm sure someday I'll be meetin' Timothy. But, bear in mind, sar, he 'n I are not the same people with the same experiences."

"Experiences, that's the problem here. Timothy doesn't have any -- and you do!"

"Absurd, this is!"

"I don't have to waste so much of my time trying to discipline him as I do with you."

Colin gathered the professor's several pages of

comments on his proposal. "Who's talkin' rubbish now?" He sprang up from the stool and left his professor's office.

He trotted to the lab where Rosa was working and knocked on the door profusely. "Rosa!"

She was examining a small piece of fossilised bone of human skull from her last archaeological dig. She brushed sediments from the fossil, carefully trying not to change its present state. She heard Colin's voice outside. "Colin?" She rushed to the door. Colin was standing in the doorway looking depressed. "Colin, you're upset? It's Professor Cushing?"

He stomped into the lab. "Cushing, I hate'em I do! Feckin' bastard! Piece of shite he is! It's his feckin' job to discipline me?"

"Colin, cool off. Do you want to tell me what happened?" Rosa led Colin to one of the stools in the lab and brushed his hair away from his face.

"He hates me proposal. I should either support Lamarckian theory, don't research the Irish deer, or forget 'bout obtainin' me doctor's degree, he told me," Colin sat rubbing his hands over his face with frustration.

"Oh my God! This is horrible. Do you think this will affect your research bursary?"

"It's sure to, it will."

Rosa paced the lab. "You're going to get the grant and you're going to Ireland to find the elk's remains, it will happen, Colin," Rosa said rubbing his back. "Forget Cushing now."

He took a few deep breaths. "Rosa, there's this phenomenal work done by a Russian physicist I've been readin', have I told ye?"

"You've mentioned him to me."

"He's come up with somethin' brilliant, he has."

"You said something about time travel."

"Time vortexes -- he calls it somethin' else in Russian."

"What are time vortexes?"

55

He stood up and stepped closer to her. "Devices used for time travel, they is," he said in a whisper.

"Excuse me?"

"Dynamic work researched by this Russian physicist, Dr. Sasha Dimitrikov, is what I've been readin'. Time vortexes'n time travel is what he writes 'bout. I--I mean I don't really know how real this all is. It could be rubbish for all I know."

"Colin, what are you trying to prove?"

"Cushing disagrees with me. I need to go back in time 'n find *Megaloceros* in order to prove Darwin's theory of natural selection."

"Colin? Maybe you need to spend more time on your ship. I think Cushing is working you too hard. Go to the Azores, someplace nice."

"Huh? Rosa, I won't disagree with ye there, that scum is workin' me too hard. That shite deserves one of me left hooks, he does."

"Dear, you need to relax about all this. It's obvious he doesn't like doctorate students who challenge him. You know a lot more about this changing world of ours than he does. You're the one who's travelled the seas encountering all kinds of wildlife -- he's pigeon-holed in his stuffy university office still stuck on the horseshoe crab."

"Unfortunately, he's me academic advisor -- what the hell can he really advise me on? Narrow-minded in his research, he is!"

Rosa gave Colin a glass of water. "Please relax. Think about this Dr. Demitrikov and fantasise about your time vortex or something."

"I'm supposed to be meetin' Dr. Dimitrikov right here in London. He's here lookin' for a professorship because his country is in the middle of a revolution."

"This sounds all too surreal, Colin. When do you meet this Dr. Sasha Dimitrikov?"

Colin looked at the clock on the wall. "In an hour to be

exact."

"Oh?"

Colin paced the lab along with Rosa. "The proposal must be accepted in order to get the bursary. This Dimitrikov bloke is a physicist, and I really need his help in order to prove me point."

Rosa pulled Colin's watch out of his pocket, "You are supposed to meet this Sasha in an hour? Where are you supposed to meet him?"

"The Piccadilly Pub I think."

Rosa ran her hands along Colin's jacket lapels. "Have a good meeting with him."

"I wish ye could come along with me, love," he said as he started caressing her petite frame.

"I would if I could." She subtly pushed away his sexual gestures.

Colin dashed to Piccadilly Circus. He ploughed through the busy crowds of Piccadilly in search of the pub. The pub was down the stairs in back of an old building, crowded with men, beer, and tobacco. Colin pulled out a crumpled piece of paper from his pocket -- the instructions Sasha had sent him. It read:

Dear Mr. Limmerick,

I will meet you at Piccadilly Pub at west wall 8:30 p.m. I will look for tall man with hair of red as you instructed. When you look for me look for thin man with hair of yellow. I look Russian.

Dr. Sasha Dimitrikov

"He looks Russian? What the hell is that supposed to mean? That could be anyone in this pub. Sounds absurd, he does!" Colin scanned the crowded pub, noticing men playing darts, drinking, harassing the barmaids, and eating. An older man was playing piano while some of the more intoxicated tried to dance with themselves. "Anyone of these men could be him," Colin repeated to himself.

"You are C--Colin Limmerick?" questioned a somewhat attractive man with a Russian accent. His fair hair was in curls, almost eighteenth-century style; he had a slim build and stood about five foot ten. He wore a grey three-piece suit and tie.

"So I am," Colin answered.

"Come sit there with me," the man said, pointing to the west wall.

Colin followed the man weaving through the crowd.

"You will drink vodka?"

"Wait, Sasha Dimitrikov is yer name?" Colin asked, refusing to sit down.

"Da! Da! I am Sasha."

"How'd ye know I'm Colin Limmerick?"

"You describe yourself in letter as tall man with red hair. And here you are in front of me, tall man with hair not so red but some yellow, some brown. It is you? You no look like doctor student. You look like you should be building railroad, maybe. I buy drinks, vodka?"

"I pictured ye to be a more mature man. Ye don't look a day over twenty-five."

"Correction, Mr. Limmerick, I just have thirtieth birthday."

"Prodigy is what ye is. I'm very impressed with yer work, I am. Ye received me letters requestin' a physicist who's willin' to work with me in Ireland have ye?"

"Da, that is me. I read some your research at my Polytechnic Institute in St. Petersburg, my beautiful city Petersburg. You are clever man also, Mr. Limmerick. So, you are Darwinist? All western people are afraid of Darwinists. Maybe you are devil? Red hair?"

"What?"

"Many western natural scientists fear men like you. You are modern thinker. You are Darwinist, da?"

"What the feck are ye talkin' 'bout, man?"

"World is not ready for scientist like you. You frighten people, especially scholars. You must have no religion if you preach Darwin."

"Ah, but I do. A rightful Catholic, so I am," Colin said.

"Nyet, you think you are. Other Western men must call you -- now what is word? You are blasphemy? Da?"

"Not me, I love 'n respect the Church, I do."

Sasha propped himself up on the table nose to nose with Colin. "You cannot love church if you are Darwinist. Your university must regard you as bad man, da?"

"Look, yer physicist methods need to be applied to me own research, 'is all!"

"Calm down, Mr. Limmerick, I can tell you are crazy man. Let me explain you. I now try to get job as professor at your university in London. My Russia not so good place now."

The barmaid brought a bottle of vodka with two shot glasses. Colin looked at Sasha with a serious expression. "I have read 'bout the revolution in yer country. I'm sorry for ye 'n yer country, I am. There's a lot of turbulence all over the world, even England's imperialism of India. I'm feckin' glad the Boer Wars are done, but what a mess they've left. I was almost called for that one."

"Your England does not compare to my Russia. You western people don't know. You not know true meaning of fighting for real reason. You fight for what? For slop? You British have all freedom. Russian boy like me have none."

Colin gazed at his shot glass. "I'm very sorry to here that."

"You not sorry. You people only know your freedom and aggressive behaviour to conquer, da? To imperialise, da? Look at India."

Colin changed his sitting position, becoming a bit uncomfortable. "I've been followin' Britain's imperialist aggression; however, I'm an Irishman 'n I understand yer feelin's I do."

"You do not!" Sasha shouted, Several of the men at the neighbouring tables turned to him.

Colin's eyes flickered from the dim lights in the pub. "Uh, gettin' back to why we's meetin'?"

"Da, da, of course..."

"I need to go to Ireland to find *Megaloceros*, the Irish deer? I want to prove to me professor that natural selection is not just a theory, but can be applied to this prehistoric mammal."

Sasha did not respond.

"Sure this is over yer head; ye'ar a physicist not an anthropologist."

Sasha slowly lit a cigarette while he glared at Colin. "Mr. Limmerick, you think I am stupid man? Let me explain you. There is problem with natural selection hypothesis. Animal lower on evolutionary scale found many thousand of years ago reproduce in much numbers. Individual survival after birth is mostly result of chance. Most cases natural selection eliminates only sick and deformed. Environmental variations cause evolution -- temperature, population of other animal and other plant life -- all stable for many long years, result is in only limited degree and types of change. You are only naturalist, this is over your head, da?" Sasha laughed as he puffed on his cigarette. "Drink vodka now." He drank down the shot in one gulp. "You want to work with me, you must drink vodka like animal!"

Colin sat back in his chair as he stared at his shot glass. "Ye may be Russian, but I am still an Irishman," he said, then guzzled the shot of vodka in an instant. "Natural selection is only a hypothesis -- but it won't be even ten years from now. It's the evolutionary process that every scientist will be explorin'."

Sasha poured another shot of vodka for Colin and himself. "Drink! You don't need physicist to help you dig bones in Ireland, why you even know of me? Drink!"

Colin drank another shot with Sasha, "I must find the Irish deer 'n I don't mean its fossils. I want to find it. It was nearin' its extinction approximately ten thousand years ago in the peat bogs of County Wicklow. I want to find it alive!"

Sasha drank his shot. "Drink, Mr. Limmerick! Drink! You know my academic journals on *vodovopot* from the Polytechnic Institute of St. Petersburg?" Sasha observed Colin finish his drink and pour himself another. Sasha paused in stillness while he watched the Irish stranger relish in his alcoholic beverage.

His head tipped downward toward the table. "S--s--shite, I can't."

"You can't what, Mr. Limmerick? Drink like animal?" Sasha had already stopped drinking, but Colin continued.

"I'm an ale'n whiskey man me-self." Colin placed the bottle of vodka to his lips.

"Last call!" shouted the barmaid, noticing Colin's intoxicated behaviour. "Eleven o'clock, last call!"

Sasha lit another cigarette. "Aren't you going to tip barmaid, Mr. Limmerick?"

Colin pulled out some change from his pocket, throwing it on the table. Sasha looked at Colin with caution. "Drink up, last call." Sasha shifted his eyes around the room. "You want to use my theory of vodovopot? Listen to me, Mr. Limmerick and don't be so drunk. The fabric of space isn't flat, it curved surface that can be bent. If you bend surface enough, Mr. Limmerick, two parts of surface can be close to each other even though normal space is far apart. If you move from one spot to other that is close to multi-dimensional space but is far apart in three-dimensional space then you, Mr. Limmerick, just have gone through a time vortex -- or vodovopot. Also, is no reason this can't be applied in four-dimensional space allowing someone to move through time as well as space. I am talking about time travel, Mr. Limmerick. Also, Mr. Limmerick, one more important point, I expect percentage of bursary for this job paid in full before we begin experiment, da?"

Colin tried with difficulty to stand up. "Yer theory, Sasha, I know 'n I must see if it takes me ten thousand years into prehistoric geologic time. I need ye to time travel with me. I can't go it alone. Me professor has no interest in me researchin' *Megaloceros giganteus* or provin' Darwin's theory of natural selection. I must observe the fact that this animal could not survive with gigantic antlers 'n such. The end of the Ice Age brought on me *Megaloceros'* demise, it did." Colin shut his eyes against the bouts of dizziness. "Pissed up I am, feck!" He struggled to form his words. "This animal couldn't live in forests like deer we know today. Feck! It was the largest deer that ever lived but died off because of natural selection. Me academic advisor doesn't buy this. Cock-sucker he is! Shite!"

"For brilliant researcher you have mouth like trash can, da?"

"Also, 'n ye'll get paid a percentage of me bursary, don't worry, mate." Colin stood with wobbling feet. "Feck! I'm a mess just now!" He used the table to hold his large physique.

"Mr. Limmerick, you are now very drunk man. You are too big for me to carry -- you must go home on your own and sleep. We will speak tomorrow in library. This vodka is new experience for you. I did not say you to have sex with bottle."

"I--I suppose I've done me-self a fine job with yer brew here, mate. So ye'll help me do this experiment for me research?"

"Da, Mr. Limmerick, I already agree," Sasha struggled to hold Colin up as they tried to leave the pub.

"Mate, why ye say *da*? What's it mean?" Colin

staggered out of the tavern with Sasha.

"It means *yes* in my language."

"You'll have to teach me Russian someday. But, now I need to get to bed, I do."

Colin staggered to his flat.

Chapter Five

Colin walked past Professor Cushing in the main hall of the Natural History building. He tried to avoid his professor's attention by blending with the other students in the hallway.

"Colin Limmerick? In my office, please," ordered Professor Cushing.

"Dr. Cushing, hello, sar." Colin followed behind his professor.

"Well, Colin, have you corrected your proposal?" Professor Cushing asked, shutting the door of his office.

"I have. In me *bolg* it is," Colin said while taking his proposal out of his leather bag. He unbuttoned his coat and removed his top hat.

"I hope you seriously took my advice from the other day," Professor Cushing said, taking the proposal from Colin. "Hmm, the title still mentions your *Megaloceros*. So you still intend on researching this prehistoric mammal do you? It sounds to me that you're getting too deep into something you really don't understand, Colin. For example, when I did my dissertation I tackled something that all of us could comprehend."

"Horseshoe crabs was yer research, Dr. Cushing, in five hundred million years they's barely evolved -- yer right, sar, let's keep it simple," Colin said closing his eyes with disgust.

"Yes, my research problem was about animals that hardly evolved at all in millions of years. Evolution is too new of a theory, and there are too many skeptics. You will fall flat on your face when the time comes to do your final examination! I'm telling you as your academic advisor, don't go near natural selection!" Professor Cushing insisted, waving his finger at Colin.

"Evolution is not too new, sar! Yer havin' problems

with natural selection 'n only that. Ye still livin' in the eighteenth century. We're anthropologists, sar -- it's a changin' science it is."

"Don't forget, Colin Limmerick, who the academic advisor is in this room. I don't like what I'm hearing."

"Good God, sar. Please try not to be offended."

"Offended? You offend everyone! You even look offensive. But, I suppose you can't help it."

Colin was anxious to leave Professor Cushing's office, "Professor Cushing, we's natural scientists here, what ye sayin' to me? We's supposed to study evolution."

"Are you lecturing me, Colin Limmerick?"

Colin took a deep breath, "I'm not, sar. But, what I don't get is why you oppose me structurin' me research around natural selection? Sar, this is Natural History -- we's supposed to find the pieces to the puzzle, are we not?"

"Wrong again, Colin! You are missing the basics of what our academic discipline really is about. You didn't learn anything from teaching my foundation course, Colin. All you really did was compare everything to that damn Irish elk. My students complained to me about your teachings."

"They's was me students, not yers. Ye gave them up to me. Fascinated with me course, they was. They still come to see me in me office. A role model to them, I am. They look up to me, sar."

"Of course everyone looks up to you, Colin, you're quite tall."

Colin closed his eyes with frustration, "Anyway, sar, dash I must now. I do need to mind the time."

"That's you, isn't it, Colin, always running here or there! It's you who has purposely planned your days with limited time -- you're walking on thin ice, Colin, thin ice!"

Colin stood by the door. "I just don't understand what's happenin', sar. Yer the evolution specialist in this department, why is it, sar, ye dismiss everythin' I say?"

"Colin, go back to your ship, go where you belong -- maybe this dissertation is over your head. Perhaps you would be more comfortable doing a research paper rather than a dissertation."

Colin took a step closer to Dr. Cushing, hovering his torso over the desk. "A research paper, ye say, sar? So I can fill empty bullshite pages quotin' Lamarck's theory? I didn't disrupt me fishin' trade for that, I didn't!"

Professor Cushing encased himself in his chair. "You need to leave now. How dare you speak to me in that cocky tone!"

"I was just leavin', I was, 'n I'll prove me theory to ye 'n to all!" Colin placed his hat onto his head and stormed out of the office.

***

It was 3:00 p.m., and Colin was to meet Sasha in the library. He scanned through the stacks and spotted Sasha reading the newspaper. "Sasha!" called Colin. "A bleedin' hang-over is what I have, 'n ye?"

"I did not consume as much vodka as you, Mr. Limmerick. Stop what you are saying now and listen to very bad information. At 7:17 last Wednesday morning, mysterious explosion happened in sky over my Siberia," Sasha said, looking serious.

"What?"

Sasha read from the newspaper. "It was caused by breakup of large meteorite at altitude of almost six kilometres in atmosphere. This is maybe asteroid or meteorite. I was not born in Siberia, but it still my Russia."

"Sasha, I don't know what to say. How awful this is."

Sasha put down the newspaper, "Maybe terrible for me and my Russia but not so terrible for you, Mr. Limmerick. I have theory about energy waves and how we might be able to use them for your research. I can prove my theory of time vortex by using these energy waves. Energy waves either penetrate through Earth's crust or even atmosphere or refocus through constructive interference at various places depending on what waves reflect against and how far they propagate. Meteorite explosion in my Russia could help us find time vortex in your Ireland much easier."

Colin looked at Sasha with amazement. They left the library and walked to the laboratory where Rosa was working.

"Rosa, I would like ye to meet Dr. Sasha Dimitrikov," Colin said, kissing Rosa on the cheek.

Rosa smiled as Sasha took her hand. "Dr. Dimitrikov, the physicist from Russia?"

"Such beautiful lady. It is pleasure." Sasha kissed her hand.

Rosa blushed. "Thank you, Dr. Dimitrikov, and it is my pleasure as well."

"Sasha, I am Sasha."

"Hello, Sasha," Rosa said.

"I have never seen such beautiful lady, not even in all of my Russia."

Colin folded his arms in front of him. "Feck, cut it out!"

"Such beautiful dark eyes," Sasha said in a whisper.

Colin grabbed Sasha's arm. "I said to feckin' cut it out, mate! What's got into ye? I've brought ye here to meet Rosa because she needs to know of yer theory of energy with the recent meteor strike in Siberia that will enable time travel to occur. She's me lass, so hands off!"

"There was a meteor strike in Siberia?" Rosa asked.

"Da, very bad for my Russia but good for Mr. Limmerick. The energy waves will now penetrate through Earth at almost same latitude as Mr. Limmerick's country Ireland, so time vortex theory can take place much easier."

"Incredible," Rosa said with fascination.

"I will do this, Miss Rosa, for Mr. Limmerick but not for anyone else. He seems like so nice man."

Colin felt uncomfortable. "Yer doin' this 'cause I'm a

nice man? Yer doin' this 'cause I'm givin' ye a cut of me bursary money," Colin said as he possessively wrapped his arms around Rosa.

"You want physicist or not?" Sasha asked.

"I want to feckin' time travel. Tell me what I need to do to move this along?"

"Don't worry, Mr. Limmerick, you will find out soon enough," Sasha said, lighting a cigarette.

**

The next morning Colin was back in Professor Cushing's office.

"Well, Colin Limmerick, I have read over your second draft of your proposal," said Professor Cushing, slurping down a cup of tea.

"And?" Colin said expecting the worst.

"It's still a disaster. You are just not a scholar. You don't think like a natural scientist. You think more like a Darwinist, and that's a disaster! Maybe all those years you were out to sea made you think less scholarly, you know being with the uneducated and all." Professor Cushing dropped the proposal on the desk.

"But, changes were made, they was!"

"Well, not enough. I just don't want to read about this Irish elk. Who the hell cares about prehistoric mammals and the natural selection that killed them off?"

"I really tried to connect Darwin with Lamarckian theories, so I did."

"You shouldn't be mentioning Darwin at all! Nobody agrees with him, because he's wrong!" Professor Cushing had a tinge of craze in his eyes as if he had gone mad.

"What I don't understand, Professor Cushing, is Darwin you barely read."

"Yes, I read the first chapter of his *Origin of Species*. I know enough that Darwin is not the way to go when writing your dissertation. To be brutally honest, it's just not accepted in our academic world. You must base your research on Lamarckian theories and my own. You haven't even touched on the horseshoe crab in this proposal. This will not merit bursary money for this mysterious research that you have been plotting. Do it again and do it right this time, or you will be dismissed as my graduate student and you will have to go back to your life on the high seas with the uneducated working class!"

Colin gazed at his professor stunned, not knowing how to respond. He grabbed his proposal and left Professor Cushing's office.

Chapter Six

Late that night, Colin was in Rosa's flat trying to type out another proposal. Rosa stood behind Colin as he sat at the typewriter and tried to help him with suggestions.

"Colin, the only way you can get around pleasing Professor Cushing is to give him what he wants."

"To succumb so I can just gain a feckin' piece of paper?" Colin responded.

Rosa paced around the room appearing electrocuted with disgust. "Colin, you have such a dirty mouth! Do all sailors speak like you?"

"Sorry, love."

"Just say you're going to prove Lamarck's theory and try to match it to your hypothesis by saying the Irish elk's antlers got smaller with each offspring in order to adapt in the forest. Don't say it became extinct because of the size of its antlers. Say it evolved to a reindeer or something. Don't touch on natural selection at all in this proposal. All you need right now is that bursary."

"Ye meanin' for me to have the proposal Cushing's way 'n me dissertation another?" Colin began typing and did not stop until he completed it; he had it on Professor Cushing's desk the next morning.

***

Professor Cushing was eating a messy pastry as Colin presented his completed proposal to him. "My, how fast you crank these proposals, Colin Limmerick. You must not have enough work to do," Professor Cushing said, getting chocolate and cream on his shirt and fingers. "Let me read this third draft of your proposal, I hope this one is the last one."

Colin forced a frozen smile as he made his way to the door. "I'll be back this afternoon for yer critique on it, sar?"

Professor Cushing was already engrossed in reading Colin's proposal while getting pastry all over the pages. "You can come back later today if you wish. You know Colin, I'm not used to having older graduate students like yourself. The younger grads seem to take their time handing in their work."

"Well, I guess us older graduate students are more efficient with deadlines. I suppose this is what the real world has taught us."

"Real world? This is the real world, Colin Limmerick, and don't you forget it! Or perhaps at your riper age, you just cannot be molded." Professor Cushing started laughing, then started choking on his pastry. Colin left Professor Cushing's office feeling angry.

Colin ran through the streets of London, noticing the people on the streets reading the front page of *The London Times*. He could see that the top story was the meteor strike in Siberia. He could hear people discussing the disaster amongst the crowds. He thought about Sasha's idea of using energy from the meteor strike in Siberia and how it penetrated through the Earth's crust in order to find a time vortex for time travel. It all sounded too good to be true. *What if Sasha's crazy?* Colin thought to himself. *But he can't be…*he thought again. *Sasha has written too many academic journals to be crazy. The one who's nuts is Dr.Cushing,* Colin thought. *The man is a complete has-been. Lost in yesteryear's research.* "Cushing is a joke," Colin blurted to himself in a snort of laughter.

"Colin, did you call my name?" Dr. Cushing said licking an icecream cone as he waited at the street corner.

"Professor Cushing! How long have ye been standin' behind me?"

"Long enough, Colin!"

"Sar, did I not just leave ye in yer office some minutes ago?"

"I'm everywhere. Almost like God."

Colin found it difficult to look at his professor without

71

the feeling of repulsion so he stared at the road instead, "Fancy seein' ye outside, is all."

"Outside? Is it so strange to see me outside?"

"I've only ever seen ye in yer office, sar."

"Colin, I always thought there was something wrong with you. I've seen you with that Russian kid, Dimitrikov. Suddenly you're part of the Russian Revolution!" Professor Cushing said with a hacking laugh.

"Umm...Did ye have time to glance at me proposal by any chance?"

An impressive automobile parked close to where the professor was standing. A frumpy-looking woman in her early sixties wearing an extra-wide brim hat sat in the passenger seat while someone else sat behind the wheel. The woman fluttered with her feather scarf trying to flaunt her cheap perfume. Professor Cushing climbed into the backseat. "This is my wife, Colin."

Colin walked toward the vehicle. "Fancy that, sar, ye got yerself a wife, ye do."

"Forty years of marriage, maybe you need to take notes. By the way, my brother-in-law is at the wheel," Professor Cushing said as he shut the door of the car.

Colin over-dramatized the removal of his hat and bowed as low as he could. "Fancy that, sar, ye got yerself a motorized carriage, isn't that brilliant?" Colin said, admiring the vehicle.

"It's a wonderful machine to own. I am part of the small population London has of automobile owners, " Dr. Cushing said through the rolled-down window.

"Well, sar?" Colin stepped toward the window of the car.

"Well, what, Colin?" Dr. Cushing said as he pushed Colin's hands away from the car.

"Me proposal, sar?"

"It's all right this time. Not great, somewhat acceptable I suppose."

Colin stood on the busy street with a smile of relief on

his face as he watched Professor Cushing drive off with his wife.

***

Colin searched for Rosa at her flat but discovered she was not there. He then scurried off to the physics lab to look for Sasha. As he walked through the lab, he saw Sasha speaking with Rosa by the farthest window. He gazed at them from a distance, noticing Sasha was standing too close to her. He tried to remind himself he was now in a university role and what was tolerated at sea was not tolerated in an academic institution. He picked up his pace, and as he tried to focus on them he paused, noticing Sasha was standing even closer to her. "Rosa? Strange seein' ye in the physics lab here with Sasha," Colin called with uneasiness in his voice.

Rosa appeared relaxed when she noticed Colin in the lab. "Colin, Sasha is showing me his plans for his time vortex theory. It's wonderfully fascinating! Sasha's such a prodigy!" she said, gleaming at Sasha.

Sasha blushed as he slowly slid his arm around Rosa's delicate shoulder. "She is too good for my ego, Mr. Limmerick, she is great lady. You are lucky to have such great woman in your life."

"Don't we have work to do, Sasha?" Colin asked, anxiously expanding his chest with air.

"Da."

"Colin, did Professor Cushing review your latest proposal?" asked Rosa.

"That he did, 'n he has accepted it. I will be gettin' me bursary any day now."

Rosa swung her arms around Colin. "How splendid, darling!"

"Would never have made it without ye, love, really I wouldn't 've," Colin said as he kissed her on the cheek.

"You call that kiss, Mr. Limmerick? I can demonstrate Russian style to Miss Rosa if you like?" Sasha said, moving closer to Rosa.

"She don't want me, ye know, doin' things to her. She's delicate, like a rose she is."

"She does not like you touching her? I cannot say I can relate, Mr. Limmerick. I have never had woman not like me touching her."

Colin's eyes rolled back. "Would ye just feck-off already!" Colin pulled Rosa against his body and began kissing her on the mouth.

"Colin!" Rosa screeched with a huge grin on her face. "Colin, you haven't kissed me like that in a long time!"

"Everytime I tried ye pushed me away," Colin said, feeling frustrated.

Sasha leered at Colin. "In Russia Rosa would have many men breaking down door, especially me." He grinned. "Guarantee, she would never push me away. It must be you, Mr. Limmerick."

Rosa appeared confused and awkward. "I should be running along. I have a lot of work."

"Aye, we have loads to do here as well. Bye for now, love." Colin held Rosa's hand for a moment, then she left.

Colin cleared his throat almost in a grunt. "Anyways, let's get to work, Dr. Dimitrikov!"

"Sasha, I am Sasha…you must address me as Sasha. Don't be angry, Mr. Limmerick, you are very lucky man. You people of Irish are' very strange. You are colder than my Russia."

Colin clenched his fists. "Well then, all right. I get ye, man. I'm Colin, call me Colin."

They worked all night in the physics lab writing formulas for the energy transmission from the meteor strike in Siberia. They worked with cold cups of tea and stale sandwiches all night until their vision started to fade with fatigue. They calculated where the energy was reflecting off the earth's core and where the waves had constructive interference.

"Mr. Limmerick, we must go to your Ireland to finish this experiment. We need your bursary. We don't have much time, because constructive interference will only last seventy-two hours. In solid media speed of sound moves up with density of material," Sasha said with angst.

"We have to get to Wales first -- it will take some time to get there from London, it will," Colin said.

"How about your boat, Mr. Limmerick? Miss Rosa tells me you own boat?"

"Nay, me crew is doin' a northern catch just now near Greenland, they is. The train is what we'll do."

"You have crew?"

"I've been a sea merchant all me life. I own me own shippin' vessel'n crew."

"You are sailor?"

"A fisherman, so I am."

"That explains your behaviour. Now I understand."

Colin glared at Sasha. "Understand? What ye understand?"

"You have behaviour like savage -- I was warned about West."

"A savage I'm not. Yer talkin' shite, ye is."

"Enough, Mr. Limmerick, stop your child's play! You say your Professor Cushing has automobile?"

Colin almost gagged. "We can't take Professor Cushing's roadster, Sasha. Have ye gone mad? Besides, I think his motorcar is a 1903 model. It's not in the best of shape."

"Does it run?"

"It does. I saw his wife pick him up with it."

"*Harasho! Harasho!* We must use it somehow."

"What?"

"How much you want to do experiment and meet your fuzzy elk face to face?"

"Sasha, we must wait on this -- we need the bursary in order to obtain all the experimental tools."

"Da, when bursary comes, we use your professor's auto, da?" Sasha lit a cigarette.

"I can't imagine Professor Cushing lendin' us his

motorcar so we can do an experiment he strongly disapproves of."

"Now -- now, Mr. Limmerick, we must sleep and tomorrow you will feel fresh and you will ask your wonderful professor if you could kindly borrow his nice running automobile."

"I think we should just go to Waterloo Station 'n buy ourselves some train fare to Wales."

"Sleep, Mr. Limmerick, go now and sleep," Sasha said, pushing Colin out of the lab.

Chapter Seven

Colin dodged the crowds with his heavy-footed stomp, trying not to get hit by any fast moving carriages. He took his time heading to Professor Cushing's office, hoping he looked presentable enough. He arrived at his professor's door while trying to find a piece of ribbon or string to tie his hair back. He found the professor's door ajar.

Professor Cushing noticed Colin standing behind the door. "Colin Limmerick? Get in here. I have good news for you."

Colin walked in with caution. "Howya?"

"Colin, sit down, yes, sit down. I wanted to give you this," Professor Cushing handed Colin a large brown envelope. "It's your bursary." He sneezed into his sleeve.

"Lovely this is." Colin tore the envelope and found a cheque for £100.00. "Brilliant this is, sar."

"Well, I know you were anticipating its arrival, I looked for you earlier but I couldn't find you."

"I was workin' late at the lab with Dr. Dimitrikov. I'm feelin' a wee bit withdrawn."

"Only God knows why you're with that escapee from the Russian Revolution. He's a physicist, you know. Did you know this? What the hell does a naturalist have in common with a physicist?"

Colin glared at his professor. He sat back and became interested in a hanging thread on his jacket. "I am very well aware he's a physicist." He sighed with frustration. "Professor Cushing, with me experimental research I must do some travellin' 'round the Isles. I must seek out Ireland for me research observations."

"So?"

"Well, me point, sar, is that I need an automobile to get me to Wales. I need to travel to Fishguard Harbour'n connect with the ferry that crosses the Irish Sea. I need to explore the Ballybetagh Bogs, the exact location the Irish deer inhabited almost ten thousand years ago, in County Wicklow. I could easily take the rail to Wales but I also need transportation more efficient than the rail to get me to the Irish deer's prehistoric habitat, sar."

"Wicklow?"

"Aye, sar."

"Never heard of it."

"It's just south of Dublin City, sar."

"I don't really care what proximity it is to Dublin, Colin!"

"Of course ye don't, sar."

"And, you need to use my motorcar don't you?"

"I do. Is it possible, sar?"

"No, it's not."

Colin slowly backed out of his professor's office with a mild wave good-bye. He shuffled his feet through the dark hallways trying to keep his composure. The echo of his boots bellowed via the acoustics of the narrow walls to a morbid beat. He glanced from behind then took a long stare in front. When he noticed there wasn't anyone around, he punched the wall, leaving a large hole in the plaster. He stood still in silence, almost paralysed by his actions. By his feet was a heaping pile of debris left from the wounded wall.

***

Colin and Rosa strolled the dim, wet streets holding hands. The June rains cleansed the streets with freshness while the scent of the rose gardens flourished as each raindrop left a perfumed mist. The roses were in full bloom standing by the busy streets in their English gardens attached to the stone façade rowhouses.

Colin escorted Rosa to his flat. He tore into his apartment and immediately yanked off his tie. "That feels much better," he said puffing his chest as he took a deep breath.

Rosa could smell the whiskey on his breath, which

forced her to turn away. "Did I ever mention how handsome you look in a suit?" she said, staring at the wall. "I hope you keep it on for the remainder of this evening."

Colin fixed himself a drink. "Ye don't want to get bolloxed with me tonight, love?"

Rosa primped her hair, still not looking at him. "No, but I must say I don't mind the occasional grappa."

"Grappa? Now that's a drink!" Colin said slipping off his jacket. "Nice Mediterranean drink for a nice Mediterranean garl, eh?" he said as he unbuttoned his vest.

"What are you doing?"

He sprawled on his small love seat. "Come sit 'er next to me," he said feeling somewhat intoxicated as he gave the cushion a gentle pat. He then tore off his vest.

Rosa stood still, almost frozen. "Why did you just take off your vest?"

"It's too tight? Ye would do the same if ye was me." He smiled.

She encircled the room and whisked herself beside him. He stroked her head, running his fingers through her hair. "We've been together for almost a year. I loved ye from the day I saw ye." He put his arms around her, caressing her delicate body as he started to unbutton the back of her dress.

She pulled away, which he had expected, so he began to unbutton his shirt. He shifted closer to her. He ran his hand against her breasts. "Yer so damn beautiful, Rosa."

"Don't do this!" She pulled away from him. He continued to unbutton his shirt. "Colin, you're drunk again."

He took her hands and placed them on his crotch. "Would ye like to undo me trousers?" he asked.

"I will not!" she adamantly shouted, pulling back her hands. She squirmed and tried to get up.

"I'll help ye." He guided her hands onto each button of his trousers. She tried not to look. "Yer lookin' away, what for?"

"You're wasting your time, Colin. I will not engage in this filth!"

"Filth? Lovemakin' this is."

"We're not married -- we shouldn't be doing any of this."

He forced his body against hers. "Let's get to the church 'n get married then," he said with gasping breath as he struggled to remove his trousers.

"What are you doing?" she screamed in horror, feeling hard matter press against her.

"I haven't even taken off me shorts yet, why ye so afraid?"

"Yet? There will be no *yet*! Stop this immediately!" she cried out while squirming.

He kept his body pressed against hers as he awkwardly managed to pull off his boxer shorts. He locked her body between his crouched knees as he wrapped her tiny hands around his enhanced stiffened mass. They both fell to the floor.

"Are ye likin' what ye seein'? Are ye likin' what ye touchin'?" he blurted in a busting whisper of orgasm.

"Let me go!"

He started to gyrate his pelvis as he held her hands over his penis hovering over her with the support of his sturdy, bulked legs. "I love ye, Rosa. This is lovemakin', it 'is."

"I don't want to touch it! I don't want to see it!" she shouted and kept her eyes closed.

"We've been courtin' for a year. I haven't touched ye. I respected yer wishes, I did, but now I may never see ye 'cause of me time travel expedition. Ye got to let us become one, love, ye just got to."

He was completely undressed. "Yer dress is still on, Rosa. Help me take it off, please," he said feeling flushed with his racing libido.

She could feel his hardness rub against her body, but

her dress was still on. He jabbed his tongue down her throat as he breathed heavily. He kept her hands on his penis, feeling almost faint. His eyes rolled back with lust, trying to hold back his orgasm.

She tried to fight him off. "No! Colin, stop this!"

"Ye don't mean what yer sayin'," he whispered in her ear while kissing her neck.

"I am not one of those sea-tramps you're used to sleeping with whenever the hell you're in the mood! Now get off me!"

He looked down at her hands. His cum dripped down her arms, wetting her torso. "Oh, my God!" she cried.

He gazed at her, panting with some relief. "I'm sorry for soakin' ye so bad, love."

"Colin, cover up, please and get off of me. You are disgusting! I feel disgusting, I must bathe."

"The bath is just there, love," he said, pointing.

"You got your manly fluid all over my dress. Colin, how could you? Are you some kind of savage? I can't marry someone like you!"

He jumped off her and ran to the bathroom where she heard water running from the tub. "You suddenly had to take a bath?" she questioned while trying to gather herself. He gave no response. She heard water running when she walked up to the door. She could hear him moaning, then the water shut off. She knocked on the door, "Colin? What are you doing in there?"

The door swung opened. He stood in front of her naked, drying himself off with a towel. "Ye can't figure out what I was doin'?"

She covered her eyes. "Oh my God! You're still naked! You really don't like wearing clothes, do you?"

He walked around not bothering to get dressed. "I had to finish the job I did."

"Finish? Finish what? Didn't you already do your stuff all over me?"

He puffed his broad chest, taking a deep breath, "I had

to finish is all."

"You men are dreadful," she said pushing him away from the bathroom entrance so she could enter. She shut the door.

"Are ye at least goin' to share me bed with me tonight?" he shouted from outside the door. "I promise I won't get outta hand I won't, if ye don't mind me sleepin'in the raw." He heard the water running from the tub. "Are ye takin' a bath, love?"

"I will have to buy you pajamas!" she shouted to him as she slipped into a frothy tub.

"If it's a gift from ye, I'd like that," he commented.

"Have you no shame, Colin? How did your parents raise you?"

"What's wrong with the way I was raised?" he asked, leaning his face against the bathroom door.

"I'm just asking a question -- I am not being critical of your parents."

He paused as he placed his ear to the door. "I can hear yer in the tub. Why don't ye let me wash yer back?"

"I will do no such thing," she responded.

The bathroom door opened and Rosa charged out wrapped in bulky towels and with dripping hair. "Now put some clothes on or my eyes will remain shut."

He moved closer to her. "I can't believe it, I used to get me full share before I had a damsel, now I'm --," he paused.

"You must have been desperate," she said trying to towel-dry her hair.

Colin laughed. "Desperate? I had the most beautiful wenches in Dublin."

"Then go to them! They're all tramps anyway!"

"Not all of them -- some was good lasses they was."

"Okay, why didn't you marry any of them?"

He was still naked as he pressed himself against her. "None of them was ye that's why. I love ye." He kissed her on the cheek. "Someday soon we'll be married."

82

"I would never marry you," she said looking anywhere but his naked body.

"Ye love me 'n ye'd marry me if I asked," he said.

She turned away from him. "Don't ask me. I have to go. It's getting late. I will not share your bed with you. Absolutely not!"

He took his clothes and handed her her dress as he left the room. She quickly laced her corset and slipped on her dress, looking around his bedroom for a hairbrush. She was dressed but feeling a bit shaken. She exited his bedroom and found him sitting at his desk. He was reading Darwin.

"Aren't you going to take me home?" she asked, relieved to see he was dressed. He lifted his eyes from his book. "I don't want to take ye home. I want ye to stay here with me."

"Yes, my darling, you seem to be having a problem distinguishing love from sex. You see, darling, love is love and sex is sex."

He cocked his head forward. "Yer wrong, love."

"I am right, and you are wrong, darling."

"Married people have sex all the time, love."

"Colin, we're not married people nor will we ever be."

He slid a bookmark on the pages of his book and closed it. He stood in front of her with a poignant expression on his face. "It hurts me to hear ye talk that way, it does."

"Colin, I don't want to hurt you. You're the last person on earth I would ever hurt. Yes, we have been courting for a year. It's been a splendid year. Darling, I do love you."

"Then we should marry, we should!"

"No, we shouldn't."

He poured himself a shot of whiskey and sat. "Ah, you'll change yer mind someday -- I know it."

"Wrong again, my dear -- never will I marry you."

His facial expression saddened. "If ye didn't fancy me

why are ye even with me?"

"I suppose I always wanted to know about fishing," she said.

He kissed her on the cheek and took her home.

***

It was 9:15 a.m. Colin stormed into Professor Cushing's office. "Professor Cushing, I really need to use yer motor car, really I do! A portion of me bursary money I will give to ye!"

Professor Cushing was just in the middle of pouring himself a cup of tea. "Colin Limmerick, you crash into my office first thing in the morning demanding this ridiculous request? Have you gone mad?"

"Sar, I'm bleedin' mad. I really need it, or else me research will be too difficult to conquer. I need it, Professor. I need it."

"Calm down, Colin. Sit down first and talk to me like a civilised human being. When do you need my roadster?"

"The sooner the better."

"Fine then, how about tonight? Can you have it back by 8:00 tomorrow morning?"

Colin's eyes started to shift around the room as he paused. He tried not to react so he continued to pause. "Ridiculous this is. A few months I need it for. I'm sorry."

"A few months? How will I get to the university each morning?"

"Coventry Street is where ye live, couldn't ye walk to the university for a change? It's not a long walk, sar."

"Yes, I suppose I could. Walking is not something I enjoy, as you know. Perhaps I could hale a carriage. Maybe I could get the neighbour to drop me off. Yes, I'm sure I could come up with something. How much of your bursary money do you want to give me?"

"Whatever ye want, Professor."

"I'll talk to the Dean of Natural History and I will get the money from the department's scholar fund. Don't pay me anything from your bursary money, Colin. You need that money for your research; you and I, Colin, need to establish a decent professor-student relationship, hmm? "

"Yer agreein' to this, Professor Cushing?"

"Y--yes, now get the hell out of my office. I have a meeting in an hour with other faculty. Come back around 6:00 tonight, and the car is yours for a few months."

A smile formed on Colin's face, but he kept silent. He fumbled out of Professor Cushing's office in amazement.

***

Colin and Sasha sat together in the university diner for lunch. Sasha smoked a cigarette while eating. Colin looked at him with excitement in his eyes. "Well, Sasha, it looks like we got everythin' we need for our departure tonight."

"I tell you your wonderful Professor Cushing would agree. I think you have love-hate relationship with him. I think more hate than love, da?"

"Just wasn't that hard, it wasn't."

"Of course it wasn't, Mr. Limmerick," Sasha said with his cigarette hanging off his bottom lip.

"Sasha, I forgot to ask ye one thing.'

"Da?"

"Sasha, how can we be certain we'll travel exactly ten thousand years in the past?"

"What you say, Mr. Limmerick? You Irish ask many questions."

"Sasha, what if we end up in the middle of the Crusades or somethin' awful like that? I'm not equipped to deal with human bein's. I'm not that kind of researcher. I don't really fancy people much. They're destroyin' the world with all their filthy industry we got goin' on 'n all the political revolutions 'n such. I'm just not interested in them for me research, is all. It's the animal world I get on with."

"Mr. Limmerick, then you must remove steam in your boat and use only sail. You are polluting world with your filthy technology."

Colin took a deep breath. "I never really thought of me steam trawler as a contributor to the destruction of our planet. Yer right, though, mate, it is. Well, I think what I was really sayin' to ye is I'm against the hatred 'n wars our human world has always been so engaged in."

"You think too much with heart, Mr. Limmerick. I never think about saving planet, who cares."

"I care."

"Only you, Mr. Limmerick."

"Fine then…just tell me, Sasha, how're ye goin' to take us to the time I need to be in? How's it goin' to work?"

"Don't worry. I have controlled how far back in past we go. I will have my transmitter device along with *indicator*."

"*Transmitter 'n indicator* devices, ye say?"

"Da, Mr. Limmerick, purpose of transmitter is teleport us through time. *Indicator* device gauges us to specific time in past we want to be and gauges us back to our time…clever, da?"

Colin appeared reluctant. "Aye, aye. Ye need to tell me more. I'm just not convinced yet," he said with a nervous chuckle.

"My two devices will take us against speed of sound. It will transmit us to our destination time. All I must do is indicate on dial, and we go. Don't worry -- it is programmed to take us back to your Irish elk's time. Don't forget, Mr.Limmerick, I am great physicist! I never make mistake. I am Russian prodigy."

"Okay then," he responded with hesitation.

"Come, let us gather our equipment for our journey," Sasha said swallowing the last bit of his sandwich while putting out his cigarette at the same time.

***

By the end of the afternoon, Colin had completed packing his equipment in the laboratory. He left Sasha in the lab and began to walk toward Professor Cushing's hall. Suddenly Rosa showed up. She stared at him from the end of the hall. Colin gazed back at her as she stepped forward to grab his arm.

"Colin!" Rosa blurted.

"What is it, love?"

"Colin, tell me, will you be using Cushing's motor car?"

"I will. Still dumbfounded I am by him agreein' to let me use it though. I really don't understand the man. Hates me guts, he does, so why is he doin' this?"

"Cushing can be very odd. I think he's afraid of you."

Colin chuckled. "Afraid of me?"

"Colin, you're someone he's never encountered in his entire academic career. You, Colin Limmerick, defy him. Nobody has ever defied Professor Cushing."

"Sure there's been others."

"Perhaps, but none of those others dressed like pirates, ran a fishing trade with their own vessel, and had your intimidating appearance...and..."

"And what?"

She lowered her head. almost touching his stomach. "And, came from working class Ireland," she whispered.

"Ah yes, me workin' class Irish make-up, that is me, isn't it?"

"You're Cushing's worst nightmare. He probably wishes he never responded so positively to your graduate application in the first place."

"Well, I guess I'm in this programme for the long haul."

"By the way, Colin, I'm coming with you tonight to meet *Megaloceros*."

"Huh? Nay, Rosa. Very dangerous it'll be, we have no idea what will happen to us there."

"I love you, and I'm coming," she insisted, hugging him tightly. "I thought about what you said about us getting married."

"Did ye?"

"I think I'd really like to be your wife. I love you, Colin."

"If ye love me so much, how come ye don't quite fancy me touchin' ye?"

"I don't really know, maybe you intimidate me with your size."

"I scare ye?"

"A touch."

"Am I not gentle enough with ye, love?"

"You're gentle but too impatient I think. You try to force things along. Just let things happen, Colin. This is all new to me."

Colin held her tightly in his arms. "Please, ye've no need to be afraid of me, Rosa. Yer protector, so I am. When we's return from this prehistoric journey, I'll buy ye the biggest diamond ever. A huge wedding we'll have."

Rosa held onto him almost in tears of joy. "I'm going to be Mrs. Colin Limmerick."

"That ye will."

"You just have to be patient with me about that sex idea. I hope you don't mind."

"Patient about ye 'n me havin' sex? Are ye sayin' it'll be a long while before we ever…?"

"I have to feel comfortable if we're ever going to."

"Sure, love, I'll be patient, I reckon. But, once we marry that will all surely change, won't it?"

"It could be longer than what you're used to."

Colin loosened his collar. "How long?"

"Long."

"Is there somethin' 'bout me appearance that repulses ye, love?"

"Of course not."

"I suppse I just don't understand."

"Colin, my dear, you're going to have to learn to wait."

"Wait."

"Yes, wait."

"Well, I'm glad we got that out of the way ..."

She smiled as she pulled away from him.

"Sure ye not meanin' to come with Sasha 'n me on this prehistoric journey? I don't really know what the conditions will be."

"My dear, I wouldn't have it any other way."

"I can't imagine doing this time travel voyage without ye. But now I must seek Cushing in his office." They embraced.

She stood still in the hallway smiling as she watched Colin walk to Professor Cushing's door. He hesitated to knock as his eyes were still fixed on her standing at the end of the hallway. He then slowly turned his body toward the door. He took a deep breath of dread and then knocked lightly. "Professor Cushing? I hope I'm not disturbing ye, but I have come for the automobile," Colin said as he noticed the door ajar.

"Hello, Colin, come in. Would you like a chocolate?" Professor Cushing asked, holding a box of chocolates.

"A chocolate, sar? I can't say I do, but thank ye kindly."

"Unfortunately, Colin, I cannot let you borrow my roadster, a sudden change has occurred."

Colin's facial expression suddenly changed. "Oh."

"My wife needs it tomorrow because she promised her sister she would go berry picking with her."

Colin had a blank stare on his face. "Berry picking."

"Yes, Colin, berry picking. It must be done tomorrow morning."

"I--I can't believe this, sar."

"Well, believe it! Now I have more important things to do than deal with your silly expeditions!"

"Sar, countin' on it, I was. Is there still a way?"

"No."

Colin stood in his professor's office almost in denial of what he had just heard. "I better scurry off to Waterloo Station and buy me some train fare," Colin said throwing his arms in the air, not surprised by his professor's behaviour.

"Yes, that will be difficult since you have so much of your alleged equipment to lug around with you for your mysterious experiment. Good day."

Colin left his professor's office in a slow shuffle of bewilderment. He met up with Rosa, taking her by the hand. "C'mon, we're goin' to Waterloo station to buy train fare, we is."

"Aren't we going in your professor's motorcar?"

"Really, why would Cushing want to help me prove him wrong, really? Really, it wouldn't make much sense for Cushing's untouchable reputation, would it now? Feck'em. Really. Feck'em," Colin blurted in a curt tone. "Let's get the bleedin' train tickets. Sasha will be packing up all he needs at the lab, we will meet him there, 'n off we go, we's will."

"Professor Cushing can be a terrible man," Rosa said, feeling deflated.

Chapter Eight

It was early morning with the moonlight still beamed brightly when they boarded the ferry to Dublin. Colin looked at Sasha as they stood on the deck of the ferry. "We are so ill-prepared."

"On contrary, Mr. Limmerick, we very prepared. We will now go back exactly ninety-five hundred years into prehistoric Ireland. The year will be approximately 7592 B.C."

Colin smiled.

"It sounds frightening," Rosa commented.

Soon they docked in the main port of Dun Laoghaire just to the south of Dublin. They carried their belongings off the ship, while feeling the low temperatures of the sea's wind. The heaviest equipment such as cameras, thermometers, gauges, rope, fishing gear, Colin's axe, various other tools, tarps, and boxes of liquor were placed in Colin's arms; Rosa carried delicate merchandise like clothing while Sasha carried part of the camping gear and construction tools.

When their equipment and merchandise was finally moved off the ship, Sasha walked up to Colin, who was standing on the dock, and looked up at his eyes. "Now, Mr. Limmerick, you must buy automobile in your fine country Ireland."

Colin's expression changed. "What? You want me to suddenly buy a motorcar?"

Rosa started to rub Colin's back. "Colin, it wouldn't be such a bad idea."

"Yer agreein' with 'em? Believin' this I can't!"

"You are a foolish man. Do you have better suggestions? How we going to carry all things to bog lands of your Ireland's Wicklow?"

"Colin, you have more money than Sasha and me, you

have the bursary -- just do it!" Rosa raised her voice. Sasha remained at the dock with their belongings while Colin and Rosa took a carriage to the main town to car shop. They found a 1905 English car that was still quite costly for its day. Sasha sat on one of the boxes of their gear smoking a cigarette as he people-watched. He noticed several passengers departing on the ferry carrying several large suitcases. There were families, sea captains, and several ship crews passing by Sasha at a given time. He sat as he watched and smoked. He saw Colin and Rosa parking the new vehicle in the distance. They approached Sasha.

"Mr. Limmerick, it looks like nice automobile, how much you pay?"

"Enough," Colin said. "I was meanin' on usin' that money to repair me vessel."

"Your ship now must wait for repairs."

Colin cranked up the car and drove toward the busy streets of Dublin. He drove to O'Connell Street, where he had to make a stop at the Dublin College University. "Now that we're in Dublin I need to pop into me former university, hope ye both don't mind."

"What for, Colin?" Rosa asked while thrilled with the auto ride.

"Me former academic advisor I need to see. Informed him of me time travel experiment, I did. He wants to see me before me trip, if it's *dany* with yez?"

He parked the car in front of the university, and the three of them walked through the hallways of the university. Colin led Rosa and Sasha to his former academic advisor's office. Colin gave a faint knock on the door. He took the liberty of, opening it and stepping in. There stood a tall, lanky man in his early sixties with thinning hair who appeared to be speaking to two other men.

"Professor Finnegan? Howya?" Colin politely said as he stepped into the room.

92

"Colin Limmerick, hello." Professor Finnegan grabbed Colin's hand with a strong shake.

"Wrote ye about me comin' through, I did, 'n said I'd drop by before me field experiment."

"Oh yes, is that what you're setting yourself out to do now?

"Aye. I'd like ye to meet Rosa 'n me scientific partner from Russia, Dr. Sasha Dimitrikov."

Professor Finnegan shook their hands recklessly. "It's just grand it is." He paused. "I still keep your masters thesis on my shelf right here and show it off to all my students. You wrote about the extinction of prehistoric marine life. I must say you slipped in a lot of Darwin," Professor Finnegan rambled on.

The two guests of Professor Finnegan's nudged him in the arm while they forcefully cleared their throats.

"Forgive my rudeness -- meet two colleagues of mine, Dr. Sharma and Dr. Patel, they're from the University of Delhi -- in India...they're finishing up their time here researching prehistoric botany."

Dr. Sharma was a petite man in his late fifties. "Colin, oh yes if I can call you Colin very well? Can you explain your research experiment further? I would thank you very much in doing so," Dr. Sharma asked.

Colin shook hands with the two men. "I really don't want this idea to get 'round too much 'cause our experiment may very well fail, sar. Dr. Dimitrikov, he is a new professor-scientist, through physics has developed a time vortex theory for the purpose of time travel."

"Really?" Dr. Patel exclaimed, appearing very interested. "Fascinating idea."

"Time travel?" said Dr. Sharma as he looked at Sasha.

Sasha remained expressionless as usual as he stepped closer to the three gentlemen. "I have developed time-travel method. According to my calculations, we should be travelling using force of energy," Sasha added. "This experiment, Mr. Limmerick, will not fail if I am genius

93

behind it."

"If you could so kindly tell me, Colin, what time in history do you intend on travelling to?" Dr. Sharma asked.

"We'll be goin' after the year 7592 B.C.," Colin answered.

"Very unbelievable but all very good. Tell me why that time in history, Colin?" Dr. Sharma asked.

"I'm researchin' *Megaloceros giganteus*, if yer familiar with this prehistoric mammal, sar?"

"Yes, of course, everyone knows *Megaloceros*," Dr. Sharma said to Dr. Patel.

"Nay, sar, ye'd be surprised, how many people have never heard of this animal," Colin said.

"What do you want to prove, Colin?" Dr. Finnegan asked.

"I want to prove that *Megaloceros'* antlers were too large for it to graze in forests, inhibitin' it from findin' food, therefore leadin' to its demise. Darwin said a species could die off completely 'cause of natural selection where a new species can emerge 'n continue to evolve. I'm led to believe *Megaloceros* was sexually selected against for havin' its enormous antlers. His great antlers, sar, was sexually allurin' to its females."

The professors chuckled. "Sexually selected...sakes," Dr. Finnegan said.

"Fascinating. Very well, and you're going to prove this in your doctorate work?" Dr. Sharma asked.

"I am," Colin answered.

"Too much information, Mr. Limmerick, too much discussion," Sasha said shifting his eyes at Colin.

"My Dr. Dimitrokov, if your time travel idea works, you will be famous," Dr. Finnegan said with a chuckle.

"We must go soon -- we say too much already," Sasha said ignoring the professor's last comment.

Dr. Sharma moved closer to Colin. "You are a very good researcher I can tell. I'm very interested in reading your work very much. Dr. Finnegan speaks very highly of you. I will be working here in Dublin for a while longer. Where are you doing your doctorate, Colin?"

"London, sar."

"I make frequent visits there, I like it so very much. Faculty always invite me for the very big academic occasions. Also, my sister lives near the university as well. This is all very well," Dr. Sharma said.

"Please visit me in the Natural History Buildin', sar."

"I am a Natural History botanist myself." Dr. Sharma moved even closer to Colin. "By the way," he with a private whisper, "my daughter will be attending your university this coming autumn. She is debating whether to take a foundation first year Natural History course. Have you ever taught any courses as an assistant to your advisor?"

"Teachin'? I'm teachin' all the time, sar. I'm sure she'd be me student at some point."

"Really? I'd like you to meet her before the autumn term begins. You would really like her very well. She is very funny and very beautiful," Dr. Sharma said in a deep whisper.

"I will be lookin' forward to meetin' yer daughter, sar. What's 'er name?" Colin asked with a smile.

"Amolia. I do not have a photograph of her with me. I will send to you if you wish?"

"Amolia, I'll remember that, sar," Colin smiled.

"I'm sure you will very much," Dr. Sharma said. "Please call her Amoli when you meet her -- it is the most casual way to address her."

"Don't want to be rude, but Mr. Limmerick must continue with experiment. You will have to visit your professor friends another time, Mr. Limmerick," Sasha said, tugging on Colin's arm.

Rosa smiled at the professors as they started to leave the office.

"I'm sure my daughter will contact you before I do. She needs so much help with her courses. She doesn't

95

know if she wants to major in Natural History or not. Colin, you would be the best person to discuss this with her. She is the only girl in our family to attend university," Dr. Sharma said with a grin.

"I'll do me best, sar!" Colin said as Sasha pushed him out of the office. The three scientists stood in the hallway with angst.

"Mr. Limmerick, you waste too much time. Could you not have seen your former professor another time?" Sasha asked, searching his pockets for cigarettes.

"I suppose I could'ev."

"You have so big mouth, Mr. Limmerick," Sasha said. "You tell all! Why is this?"

Rosa took Colin's arm. "Come along, Colin, your chariot awaits us," she said with a gentle snicker.

***

Some hours passed, and the three of them were already exhausted from their journey from London. Using Colin's cartographic research they finally located the exact location the Irish elk last inhabited some ten thousand years ago. They had driven to County Wicklow to the Ballybetagh Bog near Glencullen County, where they tried to search for lowlands, which were difficult to find. The elevation appeared to be nothing but highlands from what they could see from the automobile. The roads were limited and unassumed, which made driving on rugged terrain treacherous. They did not speak while Colin drove. The bumpy roads sometimes made loud cracking sounds, which alarmed Rosa. Glencullen County's dense foliage expelled the sweet aromas of moist shamrock and wild flowers mixed with holly. They finally arrived at what may have been the lowlands, but not necessarily, for the elevation was still higher than Dublin's.

They drove until they could find a spot to set up camp. Sasha could no longer do calculations in search of the time vortex opening, for he needed sleep. They built a campfire and sat around it to stave off the chill from the crisp breeze off of the sea. Colin and Rosa prepared a meal together while Sasha slept against a log until dinner was ready.

***

The daylight slowly faded into a dim mist while they quickly organised their tents and sleeping bags. Colin watched Rosa prepare her own tent and then offered to help her unroll the canvas. Sasha observed Colin fumble while he helped Rosa set up her tent.

"Mr. Limmerick, you want to share tent with Miss Rosa?" Sasha asked as he pulled Colin aside.

Colin appeared serious as he glanced at Sasha. "Ah, what a splendid thought that is."

"I detect something is not right?" Sasha asked. "You engaged to Miss Rosa?"

"Not yet, but soon."

"What taking so long?"

Colin scratched his head. "Not sure, really."

"She must be good Catholic girl, da?" Sasha pried.

"That she is."

Sasha stood closer to Colin. "You ever ask Miss Rosa for sex?" he asked in a whisper.

"Huh?"

"Tell me, Mr. Limmerick, you not ask her for sex?"

"What's it to ye?"

"I cannot believe!"

"What?"

"You not ask Miss Rosa for sex? How can you watch Miss Rosa prepare own tent and you not sleep in it yourself?"

"Feck off."

Sasha looked at Colin straight in the eyes. "You are stupid man."

Colin peered down at Sasha. "What's yer problem, eh?"

"You are sleeping in your own tent tonight?"

They both watched Rosa finish preparing her tent. She

97

knew the two men were leering at her, but she continued to prepare her sleeping bag.

Sasha pulled Colin aside. "Are you feeling manly tonight, Mr. Limmerick?"

"Manly ye ask? What do ye think?"

"I think you want to show Miss Rosa who's boss?"

"If I show 'er who's boss, I'll get slapped."

"Then you are not boss."

"This lass I can't force."

"You are telling me you will not try to get it from her tonight?"

"That's right."

"Are you crazy? Don't you want woman? Pretty woman like Miss Rosa would be nice right now."

Colin continued to organize their campsite. "Look, mate, doesn't want it she says."

"What kind of woman you have in past, Mr. Limmerick?"

Colin paused as he placed the dishes in the picnic basket. "Not like Rosa."

"What is your past with ladies, Mr. Limmerick?" Sasha egged Colin on. "I bet you used to love them and leave them when you were out to sea, da, Mr. Limmerick?"

Colin looked at Sasha and started to get angry. "What are ye tryin' to do? I'm not goin' to reveal me personal life to ye. Ye probably loved them 'n left them hangin' with no explanation whilst in Russia, Dr. Dimitrikov." Colin grit his teeth with an angry smile.

"I see we are two men who have not got anything in long time. I see this, Mr. Limmerick."

"See what? Speak for ye-self, mate!"

"So, you get it all the time, with who do you get it from?"

Colin chuckled. "Since I've been with Rosa I've been devoted to'er."

"Tell me, Mr. Limmerick, you not married. Why?

98

What is wrong with you? Why you never marry?"

Colin tried not to let his temper flare. "A sailor is what I am, mate. The high seas is where I've spent most of me life. Lasses have been in me life, some wanted marriage, but --."

"Tell me more, Mr. Limmerick."

"Nothin' more to tell. Yer probably married to some poor Russian lass who ye left with three kids back in Russia?"

Chapter Nine

The misty morning dew sat heavy on the flora. The three researchers were refreshed and washed from the surrounding water in and around their campsite. Sasha was working vigorously on trying to find the location of the entrance to the time vortex.

"Mr. Limmerick and Miss Rosa, could you both please indicate where you think fossils could be located under ground? You both have archaeology skill, therefore you need to put your knowledge to work right here," Sasha said.

Rosa appeared excited. "I understand, Sasha! The location of the fossils of *Megaloceros* are located here indicating its habitat ninety-five hundred years ago; therefore, the earth's penetration helped by the meteor strike in Siberia is south of the fifty-fifth parallel, and that just happens to be where we are right now in Ireland."

Sasha gave Rosa a hug. "You are correct, pretty lady, you are right!

Rosa continued, "I think this contraption you have in your hands, Sasha, will pick up energy waves from the meteor strike in Siberia and literally open a passage to the past. However, we don't really have a lot of time because the meteor strike already happened over a week ago, and the energy waves are getting less and less with each day that passes."

Sasha took Rosa into his arms, lifting her from the ground, and kissing her on the cheek. "Yes, you smart lady! You beautiful, beautiful lady!"

Colin stood watching them embrace in each other's arms. Sasha walked up to Colin. "You are big, stupid man, and she is little, smart lady!"

"Let's get started," Colin grunted.

"Miss Rosa, I think your big Hercules is getting angry

-- we must stop now," Sasha said with a snide cackle.

"Sasha, can ye shut-up with all yer needlin' 'n be a scientist again? How are we goin' to know where this bloody time vortex openin' is?" Colin asked, trying to refrain himself from showing his anger.

"There will be certain glow or even smell in air that will indicate location of passage to past."

"Can we bring all of our things?" asked Rosa.

Sasha smiled. "As long as Mr. Limmerick carries everything we will be fine."

"I guess the automobile stays here?" asked Colin.

Sasha marched up to Colin with a cross expression on his face. "What you think, Mr. Limmerick?" His voice raised in volume. "Do you think your Ireland had roads ninety-five hundred years ago? The vehicle will be hindrance rather than help. It must stay here!" Sasha answered abruptly.

"What a bleedin' waste of quid that was!" Colin blurted.

Sasha stepped closer to Colin. "Mr. Limmerick, you are scientific researcher, da? Then you must do whatever it takes to get closer to your experiment. Do you understand?"

The three of them packed the equipment they intended to take on their time travel. Colin and Rosa walked through the area trying to see if they could indicate any archaeological evidence. Colin spotted an area where he felt the remains of *Megaloceros* could be located. Rosa and Colin pulled out their archeological tools and began their dig. It was already midday, and the two had found remains of the Irish elk, which meant they were getting close.

Colin knelt on the ground as he gently dug the earth. "Accordin' to what I've been readin' *Megaloceros* may very well've roamed this particular area," said Colin.

"I hope this comes easy. The ground is so boggy. I'm getting really dirty," Rosa commented.

101

"This is part of *Megaloceros'* habitat, but who's to say he didn't reside upon some of the highlands," Colin said as he continued to brush away the earth with his tools.

Sasha sat on the ground sketching formulas for the experiment. Finally, Colin found a piece of an antler, a large piece, which appeared to be well intact. He brushed the sediment off with a large, soft brush and placed it on the ground in awe.

"Sure we know now *Megaloceros* lived 'n died here. So it seems a time vortex openin' is around here somewhere?" Colin questioned Sasha.

"Da, Mr. Limmerick, please start looking for discolour of ground or maybe strange smell," Sasha said as he brushed up against Rosa.

"Discolour of what? What kind of strange smell?" Colin asked, somewhat confused.

"You ask too many questions, Mr. Limmerick," Sasha said as he started to focus his energy on Rosa. "Miss Rosa, you excited about our adventure?" Sasha asked, running his fingers through her hair.

Colin's temper was starting to flare, but he tried to stay focused on the time vortex. Sasha took Rosa's hand as they tried to find clues in the soil. He pulled her toward him and gave her a kiss on the cheek. "You are smart lady, pretty Miss Rosa," Sasha said.

Rosa's nerves began to twitch. "Sasha, Colin is much bigger than you -- do you really want a confrontation with him?" Rosa whispered in Sasha's ear.

Sasha brushed her hair away from her face and kissed her on the lips. "Miss Rosa, I very attracted to you. Are you attracted to me?"

She backed away from him.

"I know you like me. I know this."

She blushed where her eyes met the ground. "I do like you."

Colin stood still as he watched Sasha carry on with Rosa. He grabbed Sasha and punched him hard in the jaw, catapulting him a few feet back. Sasha lay on the ground bleeding while Colin towered over him, breathing heavily with anger. "I should finish ye off ye feckin' bastard!" He debated whether he should strike Sasha again until he heard Rosa's screams.

"Colin, are you crazy? What are you doing?" screamed Rosa as she tried to yank Colin away from Sasha.

Colin looked at Rosa, panting with rage. "Ye'ar me lass. He's got no rights on ye!"

"Just hold your temper, Colin, I'm not impressed with you right now!" she whimpered.

As Colin backed away almost in a hyperventilating stupor, he smelled something he had never smelled before. It was an odd smell, and as he continued to back up, his eyes were affected by colourful light. As he continued to back away from Sasha, the ground's texture was feeling strange under his feet. He was becoming nervous but continued to back up. Then he suddenly vanished. Rosa was dumfounded as she ran to Sasha, who lay bleeding on the ground.

With panic Rosa called out, "Colin? Where did you go?" She helped Sasha up. Blood saturated his shirt.

"Miss Rosa, don't bother calling for him, he is gone."

"GONE?" she screamed.

"Yes, Miss Rosa, your Hercules man just found us our time vortex opening, however, I have paid big price," Sasha said, rubbing his sore jaw.

Rosa tried to wipe Sasha's blood off of his face. "We have to find Colin!" Rosa shouted.

"Wait, wait, Miss Rosa, let's gather our equipment, and we will follow him into time vortex. Unfortunately, he didn't know he was walking into it and now I have to carry all our equipment."

***

Colin walked through an untouched swamp with mist evaporating into the air. The grasses were taller and much

103

more unruly than what he knew of a modern-day swamp. The ground was soft and wet to where he was knee-deep in murky water. He knew at this point that he had backed into the time vortex opening, ending up in some other past time. He was excited yet terrified at the same time. He hadn't any weapons with him, none of his equipment, and no Rosa and Sasha. He walked gingerly through the bog, feeling himself sink deeper and deeper. He heard birdcalls as well as sounds of the grasses rustling in the wind. He cautiously tried to get a glimpse of any wildlife. He tried to move in a direction that would lead him out of the peat bogs and to solid ground. He was soaked in muddy water, feeling the dampness run through his bones, but his adrenaline kept him warm. Suddenly, he felt a small frog swim by his belly; he jumped but was fascinated at the same time. As he slowly moved his feet through the bog he noticed he wasn't sinking as much with each step; he was beginning to walk on a more solid surface. He finally made it to solid ground. It was still muddy, but at least he wasn't up to his waist in cold, muddy water. As the crisp wind howled through his bones, he shivered but continued to walk. Everything looked vastly different to him. The texture of the grass as well as the colour of the soil was different. There were insects but none that he could identify. Then he heard Sasha and Rosa calling his name. He quickly turned to the direction of their calls as he scanned the dense, prehistoric forest.

They were now in the boglands. Sasha carried Rosa on his back due to the water table being much too high for her. Sasha held the equipment as well as Rosa, which made him sink even deeper into the bog.

"Mr. Limmerick! Are you around? Please help us!"

The thick mist made it difficult for Colin to see the others. The constant squawking of birds echoed through the forests, almost drowning out Sasha's calls. Colin was standing on solid ground despite the boggy mud caked over his boots.

"Sasha! Get out of the bog! Walk this direction! I'll try 'n find ye in the midst of the grass!" Colin called out as he spotted them sinking into the bog. Rosa screamed with a panicked quiver in her voice.

Colin sorted himself through the bog and grabbed, who was Sasha holding the equipment and Rosa. He led them out of the bog quickly, feeling the cold breeze howl through the grasses. The three of them shivered with discomfort.

"This solid surface looks fine enough to set up camp, don't ye think?" Colin said.

"Mr. Limmerick, let's continue to walk in this direction where there is less mud. I understand you want to be close to your Irish elk, but we also can't have ill bodies," Sasha said, rubbing his bloody jaw.

Colin walked up to Sasha, who was trying to wipe the blood off of his shirt. Sasha looked up at Colin. "Mr. Limmerick, look what you do to me."

Colin looked at Sasha, feeling misgivings about his actions earlier. "Sorry I am, mate."

Sasha gave Colin a blank stare as he continued to walk.

They hiked to where the ground was more solid and much dryer. The grasses were still and tall. The dense brush became denser, sprouting with tall ferns and clusters of sharp holly.

"Where to set up camp?" Sasha asked, looking at Colin.

"If we can just hike to the mountains we can set up there."

Rosa felt uneasy. She glanced at Colin and Sasha as they continued their trek. Colin used his axe to cut away at the dense layers of holly, clearing the way for Sasha and Rosa to follow.

"Ouch!" Rosa yelped, noticing her arm ooze with blood. "I must have rubbed against something sharp," she said while Colin tended to her.

"Holly bushes they is, avoid'em if ye can," Colin said.

"Such strange trees in your Ireland, Mr. Limmerick. In my Russia we have current growing from trees and many birch. I have not heard of blood from tree. Only in your world, Mr. Limmerick."

Rosa suddenly stopped walking. "I can't go any longer. The elevation is getting to be too much for me, Colin. Can't we set up camp here? I can't imagine climbing up those rolling hills the way I'm feeling right now. I need to rest."

"How selfish of me, forgive me," Colin said, taking bags from Rosa's hands. "We can definitely set up camp here. This is as good a spot as any."

"What we do for fresh water?" Sasha asked.

"There should be some runnin' springs 'round here somewhere," Colin answered.

Rosa flopped onto the soft grasses. "Smell the sweetness of the wild flowers, Sasha. It's so beautiful here!"

"I can only smell sweetness of beautiful lady like you," Sasha responded.

Colin focused on pushing a large log toward their campsite. Sasha made sure Colin wasn't looking as he sat beside Rosa and planted a kiss on her cheek.

"Sasha! No! Colin will kill you for sure!"

"Mr. Limmerick is too busy being strong man. I not afraid of him," Sasha responded, sitting snuggly beside her.

Colin romped back to them, noticing Sasha spring up from the grasses. "It's all settled, we'll set up camp here, we's will," Colin said, out of breath from the heavy lifting and pushing of heavy logs.

"Ah, this will be good, Mr. Limmerick, *spasiba*," Sasha said walking toward Colin.

"We're not on a complete slope, therefore we should be fine with our tents 'n such," Colin said in his low, monotoned mumble.

"Splendid, Colin!" Rosa said as she gestured for Colin to help her up.

Colin held Rosa around the waist as his eyes began to glisten. "Ye still want to pitch yer own separate tent, love?"

Rosa backed away from him, feeling uncomfortable. "Colin, please, not here."

"Da, there could be wild beast in bushes, you may need man to protect you," Sasha said with a snide grin.

Rosa glanced at Sasha. "Wild beasts?"

"Of course wild beasts. You have wild beast standing before you."

"Oh," Rosa responded.

Sasha laughed. "I am speaking to you about Mr. Limmerick -- he is wild beast, da?"

Colin leered at Sasha. "Go feck yerself," Colin said to Sasha in a calm manner.

"Colin! Please, watch your language around me!" Rosa shouted. "I hope you're going to help me put up my tent -- as a gentleman should?"

"Have it yer way, love," Colin said pulling her tent out of a heavy canvas bag. He laid out Rosa's tent, putting it up with care. He lined the inside with several warm blankets, placing her sleeping bag on top. Rosa sat inside the tent as she watched.

"You really know how to take care of me, don't you, Colin?" she said fluttering her lashes.

Colin smiled. "I love ye with all me heart, love -- ye know that."

"I think it's time you join Sasha outside and pitch your own tent," she said.

"Not without me good-night kiss, me love." He leaned toward her to give her a kiss on the cheek then carefully left the tent.

Sasha's tent was already standing as he sat on a fallen log to smoke a cigarette. "Mr. Limmerick, there will be many wild animals in this place?"

Colin stood and stared at Sasha. "Aye, mate."

"Where are we in your Ireland? Glencullen?"

"I think. It's rather mountainous here. Could we seek our beast here?"

"We can die here, nyet?"

Colin paused before he spoke. "Don't know, really."

"I keep thinking large dinosaur will appear, da?"

"Dinosaur?" Colin chuckled. "That I know won't happen. Let's just hope we run into *Megaloceros*. Now we really should get some rest for tomorrow." Colin began to set up his tent.

Sasha flicked his cigarette butt onto the damp ground and knelt by his tent. "I am glad you are so sure of yourself, Mr. Limmerick."

Colin completed setting up his tent. "Until tomorrow, mate," he said.

"Let's hope so, let's hope so."

***

The morning was misty with heavy dew. Colin was the first to rise. He peeled out of his tent, observing the thick fog that hung low to the ground. He pulled a heavy sweater over his bare chest and pulled long johns over his legs. He grabbed his axe as he cut through the tall ferns and climbed some feet of elevation to what he thought was a tree line. As he continued to hike up the highland he noticed his heavy boots were sinking into what appeared to be peat. The soil was light brown and saturated with moisture. There was just a scant cluster of trees, and Colin noticed how they did not continue up the large hill. He stopped in front of a large tree and began to cut away at it.

Rosa awoke from the sound of Colin's chopping; she poked her head out of her tent. "Colin?" she called out.

She wrapped herself in a warm blanket as she started to wander towards Colin.

"Aye, love?" He glanced at her standing below the slope.

"Colin, don't leave to chop wood -- something could

happen to us or you. It could be dangerous here!"

"I just got to finish, love. Maybe ye should wake Sasha. Don't worry, love, we's at peace here, we is!"

"Just hurry up, please!" she called out, walking toward the tents.

Sasha pulled himself out of his tent while lighting a cigarette. "Lovely lady, you speak to Mr. Limmerick? What crazy thing he do now?"

"Oh, good morning, Sasha. Colin climbed up the slope to chop some wood. We need wood to build a fire don't we?"

"How should I know?" Sasha responded as he crawled back into his tent.

"I have a box of biscuits if you care for any. I can see Colin already got to them," she said with a forced smile.

Colin returned carrying large, freshly cut pieces of wood. He placed them in a cluster in front of the tents. "I brought me spear fishin' tools -- we gotta eat, we's do," Colin said.

"Colin, I prefer to eat toast and jam for breakfast," Rosa said.

He chuckled. "Ah, but now, ye'll be eatin' fish, ye will."

Sasha returned holding a rifle. "Now we will hunt and eat like wild animal, da?"

"Wait, wait, what ye got there, mate?"

"This, Mr. Limmerick, is loaded gun. You like?"

Colin backed away from Sasha. "I don't like it, not at all, I don't. We's not supposed to use guns on this expedition."

"You have spear and axe, why is this acceptable to you? Why not gun?"

"Gentlemen," Rosa interjected. "Colin, please allow Sasha to use the gun if it is required."

He looked at her and paused. "Ye takin' his side?"

"Oh, Colin, don't be ridiculous, I think both you men need to compromise."

"This is me own prehistoric journey -- there's no room for compromise here."

"Colin, please, let's begin looking for your prehistoric mammal. We can cook up some fish later," Rosa said.

"I'm supposin' yer right, love. I shan't get meself in a scuffle if I'm plannin' on bein' yer protector."

"Let us go now and find elk," Sasha said.

They began to hike up the slope with Colin gripping his axe over his shoulder. Sasha grasped his rifle as close to his body as possible. Rosa trailed behind them as she gasped for her breath with immediate exhaustion. They began to move laterally along the highland rather than up the slope. They noticed something in the distance that appeared to look like a cave opening. It was almost indistinguishable, for the opening was embedded amongst the crags.

"Perhaps that cave is a dwelling for early homo sapiens," Rosa commented pointing in that direction. They moved closer to the cave. Sasha poked his head into the cave opening. Colin turned away from Sasha to continue the hike. Rosa tried to keep up with Colin's pace. She looked over her shoulder and noticed Sasha still peering through the cave. Something was there. Rosa continued to trot behind Colin. She kept looking back. She could no longer see Sasha.

"Colin, Sasha went in that cave."

Colin stopped.

Sasha stepped in. He heard a vibration, some sort of movement. Something was there. The cave was midnight black. The walls of the cave bled with moisture. It was damp and cold. Sasha took each step with caution. He heard moaning and cooing from something that did not sound human.

Colin entered the cave with Rosa trailing behind. Sasha came across a family of large felines. He stood still. They did not see him, he thought. Colin saw Sasha. Sasha was slowly walking backwards. Colin took Sasha's arm

110

and yanked him out of the cave to where Rosa was waiting outside.

"Mr. Limmerick, what you do? I find wild animals."

"I saw them," Colin kept yanking Sasha away from the cave.

"What they are?"

"Cave lions. Ye found yerself a family of cave lions, Sasha."

Rosa's eyes widened. "Sasha, don't stray from us again. Cave lions were so much bigger and fiercer than the lions of our time."

"They not see me, so we okay."

"They could definitely pick up our scent. They didn't come after us 'cause it seemed like they was in the middle of feed."

Chapter Ten

The morning mist was so thick it was difficult to see. They sat around the campfire cooking whatever small game Sasha could shoot. Colin then went off spear fishing in the stream only a few meters away from the camp. The aroma from the barbeque filled the air and attracted a prehistoric male and female human to enter their camp sight. The male held his spear above his head while Sasha noticed the intruder. Rosa was focused on preparing tea. The male walked to Rosa; he was shorter than her five-foot-five stance. Sasha stood up holding his rifle as he approached the male. The male felt threatened by Sasha's towering height of five foot ten.

"Caveman, you better leave before Mr. Limmerick sees you! Go! Go!" Sasha shouted at the early *homo sapien*. Sasha glanced at the stream, noticing Colin spear fishing unaware of the intruders. The prehistoric male spewed his archaic language at Sasha while trying to take some food from the barbecue. The prehistoric man yelled when he grabbed a piece of meat from the fire. The sound of his yelp caught Colin's attention. Sasha and Rosa could see Colin walking briskly toward the campsite. "We know what Mr. Limmerick will do now. These little people are doomed," Sasha whispered to Rosa.

Colin was carrying a large pale of freshly caught salmon, or a species that could have been an ancestor to modern-day salmon. He stopped. He had heated up with his hard work. He then continued to carry the container of fish as he briskly walked toward the campsite. He noticed two extra beings at the camp.

"What the hell?" Colin called out in a panic, rushing to the male and dropped the container of fish to the ground. Colin stood in front of the male without saying a word. The historic male stood still; Colin was about a meter taller. The male stared at Colin in devastation, not making a sound. He measured slightly above Colin's waist and shook with fear at Colin's extreme size. The prehistoric male moved to the other side, and Colin did the same to block his view of Rosa. The savage human then slowly moved closer to Colin and started to touch Colin's skin. Colin remained still without flinching. The male inched his way as close as he could in order to fully view Colin. He pulled and pinched at his flesh. Colin jolted as a reaction to the sudden discomfort. He noticed that the male looked identical to modern man, except he was smaller and appeared withered and undernourished. His knotted hair was long and dark. His skin appeared Caucasian but with a bronzy-copper pigment. He was wrapped in furry hide that dangled almost to the ground. Colin moved closer to the prehistoric male and poked at him. The male backed off with a scream. Colin glanced at Rosa and Sasha.

Sasha and Rosa remained still and watched from a distance. The female approached Colin. She was also dressed in warm hides almost the same color as her ill-kept long dark hair. When Colin moved close to her, she screamed. She backed off, not taking her eyes off him. He slowly bent his knees trying to lessen the height difference.

She brushed her hands forcefully along Colin's stomach, moving toward his back where she continued to investigate. She plucked a few hairs from his back, causing Colin to flinch. She backed away from Colin with fear as she placed his red strands of hair on her hand, examining them closely. The two prehistoric humans stepped back with fear, still focused on Colin. Colin kept his knees bent almost standing with a slouch and took a few steps toward them. The two backed off even further from him but then the female gingerly returned to him. She slowly walked to him. Colin kept his eyes on her, allowing her to do as she pleased. He turned toward Sasha.

"The concept of fitted clothin'," he said. She poked at Colin so much so he yelped, though he tried to remain silent as he pulled away. The male joined the female in exploring Colin's trousers.

"Female likes Mr. Limmerick's trousers? So strange," Sasha commented to Rosa.

"Shhh! Sasha, this is amazing the way they're exploring one another's bodies," Rosa said. "It's fantastic to see one modern man and two late upper *Paleolithics* explore each other seeing the similarities and differences. It is truly amazing," Rosa said.

"That's their name?"

"Yes, they're definitely late upper *Paleolithic* beings; they lived when the Ice Age just finished," Rosa said.

"I would not know late upper *Paleolithic* from early lower *Paleolithic*," Sasha commented.

"Believe me, Sasha, you would."

"I don't even care."

The male sat on the ground with the female and Colin sat beside them. They both touched Colin's face and began to pull at his hair. The late upper *Paleolithic* couple continued to run their fingers through Colin's hair fondling it and noticing how the texture was different than theirs. They pushed Colin onto his stomach, laying him flat on the ground so they could continue to explore him. Sasha grabbed his gun, concerned about Colin's vulnerable position. Colin lay flat on his belly as they both rubbed their hands along his back, buttocks, and legs. They removed his boots, astonished by them, then noticing his over-sized feet. Sasha glanced at Rosa as he quietly stepped toward the two; however; they were too focused on Colin.

Colin slowly sat up. The prehistoric couple examined his face with their faces rubbing against his. The female opened Colin's mouth and became fascinated by his large teeth. She stuck her filthy hands in his mouth touching all of his teeth with her rough fingers. The prehistoric female sat on Colin's lap, wrapping her legs around him. She licked his face. Sasha chuckled when he noticed Colin's reaction. Colin brushed her knotted hair from her face. She started to react with shrill screams. The male became frantic, wondering what Colin was doing to her. He called to his female in a tribal language. They communicated while she remained with Colin. Sasha and Rosa's eyes widened with amazement.

The male pulled his female off Colin. The male *Paleolithic* sat beside Colin. His female stood a distance away. Sasha moved a bit closer, holding his loaded rifle in his hands. Colin very gently and slowly changed his sitting position to kneeling. When Colin stood up, the male felt angry. The male shook his spear at Colin. Colin grabbed the prehistoric male's spear and tossed it to the ground. The male backed away as Colin stood in front of him watching him scramble to retrieve his spear. The female screamed at Colin.

Colin glanced at Sasha and Rosa.

Colin looked at Sasha. "I just want to find *Megaloceros*, a pact with these *Paleolithics* I'm not interested in really," Colin said as he walked to his container of fish.

"You are crazy man," Sasha said as he lit a cigarette, "and you very interested I can tell."

Colin carried the large, heavy pale of fish closer to the middle of the campsite with the two visitors trailing behind him. He crouched down to scale the fresh catch. He offered some fish to the two visitors; they took it, ogled over it, and immediately darted into the dense brush. Colin watched the prehistoric couple dash into the woods as he still knelt down on the ground to clean the fish. He continued to stare in the direction of their exit.

***

It was early dusk as the three young scientists hiked through the rolling hills of Wicklow. They were interested in exploring the landscape, knowing *Megaloceros* lived in the Irish lowlands. They were dressed in heavier clothing because the temperature had dropped considerably at that time of day.

"I'm interested in findin' whatever I can 'bout *Megaloceros'* habitat -- it's imperative to me research, it is. Just noticin' the highlands here -- the tree line stops three-quarters the way up," Colin, said pointing to the slope, "Look there, if ye look to the very top one can see a brush of fern 'n I even see some dwarf willow, ideal habitat for me *Megaloceros giganteus.*"

"Dwarf willow, how interesting," Rosa commented.

"Why so special tree?" Sasha asked.

Colin looked at Sasha. "There's no more dwarf willow existin' in our own time is all."

They started walking down the mountain slope.

"It's steep," Rosa said, concentrating on not falling.

Colin took Rosa's arm. "Not as steep as ye may think, love. I think they sought shelter in some of these narrow steep-sided valleys, but I'm only guessin'," Colin added. Sasha trailed behind Colin and Rosa as he continued to smoke his cigarette.

Rosa fell forward, but Colin caught her in time. "Don't worry, love, I got ye!" Colin said.

"I guess this is no place for a woman," Rosa said.

"It is if ye want it to be," Colin said as he kissed her on the cheek.

"Colin, I don't think I'm wearing the right shoes for such rough terrain," she said.

Colin scooped her into his arms. "Never ye mind 'bout yer brogues, love, I won't let anythin' happen to ye," Colin said while kissing her.

Sasha rolled his eyes back. "Mr. Limmerick, stop your lubby-dub. Do not forget why we are here. You must do research," Sasha said, stepping on his cigarette butt.

Colin lowered Rosa to the ground and chuckled at Sasha.

As they continued to shuffle down the slope, Rosa saw

something out of the corner of her eye. She looked up the hill in the distance and saw a silhouette of an animal in the far horizon. She stopped trying to make out what the animal was. "Gentlemen! Stop! Just stop walking for a second!" Rosa called out to Colin and Sasha, who were further ahead of her. "Just stop!" she called out.

Sasha looked back at Rosa trailing behind him. "Miss Rosa, don't move -- stay still," he whispered to her.

Colin turned around in awe, almost gasping to take a breath. He remained still. "Magnificent creature, it is me Irish deer. I--I found ye," he said softly to himself. "And we found the stag -- magnificent creature so he is!" The large animal peered down at them, watching every move they made. It stood short of seven feet tall. Its antlers spanned almost six feet in length. It was mighty and strong-looking as it snorted several times while it watched the three time-travellers below.

"I'd say our stag knows enough that man is to be feared. Man is a great predator of this animal, therefore it should always be vigilant 'n ready to attack if need be," Colin said.

Sasha slowly walked in the direction of the *Megaloceros*. "If you want to study beast, Mr. Limmerick, then we get closer."

Colin pulled Sasha's arm. "I wouldn't do that if I was ye," Colin said with a stern look.

"Why we here, Mr. Limmerick? To risk our lives so we can view your elk from distance, da?" Sasha said while pushing away Colin's arm.

"Sasha, don't startle the stag. Ye don't know this animal, don't do it."

"It is big reindeer -- I have seen them in forests in Northern Russia. Mr. Limmerick, I know this animal more than you think."

"Ye don't know this animal -- I don't know this animal, Sasha. It's not from our time," Colin pleaded.

Sasha continued to hike up the slope to where the great

Megaloceros stag stood peering down at them.

"Sasha!" Rosa called out.

Sasha stopped to turn to her. "What is it now, Miss Rosa?"

"Perhaps you should listen to Colin. I think he knows what he's talking about!"

Sasha pulled out a cigarette and began to smoke. "Nonsense." He turned away from them and continued to trek up the slope. He walked slowly toward the animal, carrying his rifle. The stag began to feel violated and moved toward Sasha, who stopped and watched it move closer to him. Colin and Rosa watched from the lower elevation of the brushy highlands. Sasha tried not to appear intimidated by the large beast. He remained still as he puffed on his cigarette. As the animal began to snort and rub its large hoof into the ground, Sasha started to feel intimidated and began walking backwards in the direction he had come. The large animal stood and stared as Sasha made it back to Rosa and Colin.

"Mr. Limmerick, Miss Rosa, it seems to be coming this way. I did not know how big this animal was until I got closer to it. It as big as you, Mr. Limmerick," Sasha said, trying to make light of the situation.

Colin looked at Sasha with seriousness in his face. "Ye came onto its territory, ye did. It's wonderin' what we'ar doin' here. It looks like ye got it all agitated, don't ye think?" Colin said as he continued to help Rosa down the slope, keeping one eye on the great beast.

"If we lay flat on our bellies it may no longer see us at the bottom of the hill," Colin suggested. They lay flat on their bellies without saying a word to each other. They could hear it making its way down the hill, rustling through the dense brush of fern as it moved toward them. Rosa breathed heavily with fear, Sasha was afraid but felt confident that his rifle was loaded with bullets, and Colin was worried about Rosa. It walked very close to their still bodies. It identified Sasha's scent from when he was confronting it closer on the slope of the hill. It grew very interested in Sasha and began sniffing him profusely. The large stag appeared violated by their presence, especially by Sasha. It ran the tip of its antlers along Sasha's back. Then it started to snort and lift its front legs off the ground and back down again. It displayed its anger. The large beast started to jump onto its hind legs and back down on all four over and over again. Sasha tried desperately to crawl away. The beast stomped on Sasha's leg. Sasha yelled in agony. "Mr. Limmerick, let me shoot beast!" Sasha tried to stand up, but his leg throbbed, feeling as if it were broken.

Rosa pulled away. "Colin, do something -- it's going to kill Sasha!" shouted Rosa in tears.

Colin frantically ran toward the gigantic beast, trying to distract it from Sasha. It was difficult to distract; Colin had to get bold, getting close enough to catch its attention. It did finally notice Colin. "Sasha, get out of here!" shouted Colin. Colin was only about a couple of meters in front of it. It slowed its actions, as it felt confronted by Colin. It began snorting at him as it inched its way closer to him. The large animal then stared Colin in the eyes as it backed up, still very focused on him. Colin knew what was about to happen. "Mate! Get Rosa away from here. Charge is what it'll do!"

"Let me shoot it, Mr. Limmerick! It will kill you!" Sasha said, pulling Rosa away.

"No! Colin, listen to Sasha, don't be stupid!" Rosa shouted in tears.

Sasha stood on one leg with his wounded leg dragging behind him. Colin stood directly in front of the beast, holding Sasha's rifle over his head to look like a spear. Colin kept moving, waving his arms to show the animal his dominance. "Back off! Back off!" Colin yelled in a deep, thundering voice, trying to show no fear toward the animal. The animal stood still and began taking a few steps backward. Colin moved a few steps toward the

119

animal still holding the rifle above his head. Rosa and Sasha watched from a distance. Colin kept the rifle above his head continuing to show the beast his dominance. Colin could feel his heart beating vigorously as he kept calling out to the beast. The animal knew enough that man had been a predator, an enemy, and a tremendous threat -- it kept backing away from Colin, snorting with agitation. He stood tall, holding the rifle high above his head. The animal charged at him. Colin ran to the nearby forest area only a few meters away. The beast followed. Colin wedged himself behind two large trees. The animal stopped. Colin continued yelling at the animal. The beast banged the two large tree trunks with its powerful antlers, and Colin could hear the trees almost on the verge of splitting. The thundering sound of the great antlers hitting the tree trunks was almost deafening.

Sasha and Rosa ran up the slope, fearing for Colin, who had to fend for himself in the forest.

The large beast suddenly perked its head, focusing its attention on something else. Colin noticed the animal's distraction but remained vigilant. The gigantic beast slowly trotted away. "It may have heard a call from another *Megaloceros*," Colin said to himself.

Colin and Rosa focused on Sasha's leg. "We brought first aid supplies but they're at the camp," Rosa said. Sasha lay flat on the ground, wallowing in pain. Colin looked at his wound and noticed the swelling and flowing blood. Colin took off his shirt and tore it into strips. He then found a branch, which he used for a splint, wrapping the shirt strips tightly around Sasha's leg along with the splint. "The camp I'll carry ye back to, 'n re-do the dressin' -- I'll use some of yer vodka as antiseptic," Colin said as he carefully placed Sasha onto his back. They made their way to the campsite, noticing smaller prehistoric animals scurry in front of them into the brush. Colin was exhausted carrying Sasha as well as two knapsacks.

When they finally arrived at the campsite Colin pulled out their supply of bandages and dressed Sasha's leg.

"Ye know, mate, do ye know how lucky ye is? An animal that size could've killed ye in one blow, do ye know that?"

Sasha sat feeling his throbbing pain while smoking a cigarette.

"The stag was afraid, Sasha. Ruttin' season's comin' up in the autumn 'n this stag wanted to protect his loved ones, I think. He feared ye approachin' it like ye did. Do ye understand me?"

Rosa stood beside Colin wiping her tears as she looked at Sasha. "Sasha, you did a foolish thing by getting so close to it."

"I feel more foolish to come back to camp on Mr. Limmerick's back," Sasha replied.

"But, mate, yer here 'n ye got a few wounds to yer leg 'is all," Colin said with a smile.

Rosa noticed Colin dripping with sweat trying to catch his breath. "I'm starting to really dislike this place, Colin. It's just too dangerous for three people like us from the twentieth century."

"Animal behaviour lesson number one, we are not to badger or mistreat any of these prehistoric animals at any time. There will be absolutely no shootin', no killin' of these creatures. Understood?" Colin stated firmly.

"Just get me some vodka, Mr. Limmerick, it will ease my pain," Sasha said as Colin helped him get settled in his tent for the night.

***

Some weeks had passed and Sasha's leg was no longer in a splint. It was still bandaged, but he could move it much easier with less pain. He enjoyed Rosa cleaning his wounds and showering him with attention. One afternoon she bent over his leg while disinfecting it. Sasha stared at her as she lifted his leg, which acted like a dead weight oozing with soreness. He continued to stare at her as he watched her act quickly while she gently massaged his leg.

"How does that feel?" she asked with a smile.

"Miss Rosa, you are great nurse," Sasha commented fixed in a gaze of lust.

Rosa laughed as she tugged on his lengthening blond curls. "Sasha, your leg needs some time to heal. I think you will be up and around sooner than you think."

"I thank you, Miss Rosa. This small problem proves I cannot live without you."

She looked at him as she brought him a jug of fresh water. "You're too kind, Sasha."

"Correction, beautiful lady, I only speak truth to you, believe me." Sasha turned his head gazing at Colin in the background chopping wood.

"Sasha," she said, sitting beside him, "who are you?"

"Who I am? I am Dr. Sasha Dimitrikov, great Russian physicist."

"I know that part, but who is inside the man of this great Russian physicist?" she asked, trying to primp her long, knotted hair.

"Maybe you like me to recite Pushkin?"

"No, Sasha, I'm not asking that. Just tell me who is inside you? What is in your heart?"

He lit a cigarette. "My heart, beautiful Miss Rosa, is too complex to explain you."

"Try."

"Fine, let me explain. I am man of great big heart and desire." Sasha paused. "Did you know something?"

"What's that, Sasha?" she asked.

"Did you know it not good for man to ejaculate?"

Rosa's facial expression changed. "Excuse me?"

"Tell your big-strong Hercules, this is not good idea for man to ejaculate."

"What are you talking about?"

"A man who does not ejaculate is much stronger because of build-up. You not know this?"

"Know what?"

Sasha puffed smoke rings in the air very casually. "Have Mr. Hercules ever ejaculate in you?"

Rosa's eyes widened. "Pardon?"

"Tell me, beautiful lady, tell me."

"No!"

"It has been one year you with him?"

"Yes!"

"No ejaculation?"

"God no!"

"What has Mr. Hercules done with desires?"

"I don't really know, I never asked him."

"Very intimate relationship you have with such huge beast of man."

"We're still in the courting stages, Sasha."

"One year! You still in courting stages? What I know of Mr. Limmerick, I don't think he will last long with so long courting stages."

"He has, and he will."

"We discuss about Mr. Limmerick here. He is like bull, he will not last any longer."

"So what are you suggesting?"

"I say you put him out of misery and set him free."

"Sasha, I don't think that is what Colin wants. He loves me, you know."

"And you love him?"

She paused. "Yes, yes I do love him. I love him very much."

"I can tell -- this is reason why you not like him touching you?"

"Look, Sasha, I need to hold on to Colin. There are always women trying to snatch him. He's in high demand, you know."

"You are right! This is very good reason. I understand, Miss Rosa, I understand," Sasha said as he continued to smoke.

Sasha sat on the tree stump at the campsite glaring into

Rosa's eyes. They stared at each other as Sasha moved closer to her. He began to caress her delicate shoulders as she sat closely beside him upon the log. He ran his fingers through her hair.

"You like when I touch you, Miss Rosa?" Sasha asked in a quiet whisper.

"I'm not sure," she said, feeling nervous.

"You don't pull away from me like you do with Mr. Limmerick?"

"Sasha, please."

"You not pull away from me like you do with him."

"Sasha, you shouldn't be doing this."

"You like me more than Mr. Limmerick?"

"No! God, no! I mean, I don't know anymore."

He placed his hands on each side of her face as he brought her closer to him, "You love me?" he asked with a whisper.

She slowly grabbed his wrists. "Sasha," she said, feeling almost lifeless as she tried to push him away.

Sasha's arms embraced Rosa's waist as his fingers kept flinching. He suddenly could feel something crawling over his hands, but he ignored it. Suddenly Sasha jolted with a startling realisation. He flicked his hand away from Rosa only to see an army of prehistoric ants crawling over his hand. He looked at Rosa to discover several armies of prehistoric ants had crawled up her arm and under her clothing. They were red and a comparable size to Madagascar hissing cockroaches. "Rosa! Rosa! What is this?" Sasha shouted.

Rosa felt something crawling on her, but when the large prehistoric ants started to crawl up her neck she realised she was a victim under attack. "Sasha! Oh my God! Help me! What --?"

Sasha tried to brush the mass insect army off her, but there were too many. Sasha grabbed Rosa, trying to carry her, but he was limping so badly he fell to the ground, dropping Rosa in a mud hole where more ants piled on top of her.

Colin was chopping wood in the distance where he heard some faint screams. He stopped chopping and stood still. The faint screams became louder. He kept his axe while he sprinted to the campsite, finding Sasha trying to crawl toward Rosa. She twisted and flinched; her face was covered with ants. Sasha's leg still ached whenever he stood on it. He used his arms while crawling in the mud toward Rosa. She screamed, overwhelmed with the prehistoric attack and almost in a state of shock. "Rosa, try not panic!" Sasha tried to stand up, trying to hop on one foot, but he slid on the mud back into a mud hole. Colin ran toward them holding his axe in his hands. Rosa's screams echoed throughout the forest. Colin panicked as he tried to pick up speed. The impact of each step he took had him skid into a bog of peat and mud. Colin fell forward, flinging his axe into the air. Sasha tried to stand on one leg again, and he finally reached Rosa, who was face down in the mud with carpets of the prehistoric insets crawling on her. Sasha took his shoes off and tried to whack the ants off her body. He tried kicking them off, pushing them off with his hands and arms. Colin finally made it to Rosa.

"Dear God, what's gone on?" Colin questioned while grabbing Rosa quickly, carrying her to the stream, and throwing her in. Colin worked quickly trying to brush the insects off her body. He tore her clothes off. The insects latched onto him. The prehistoric ants filtered onto his arms and behind his neck, so he immersed himself in the water immediately. She was naked, lying lifelessly in Colin's arms with not an insect clinging onto her. Sasha limped to the stream and jumped in as well as he also had clinging ants stuck to him. Rosa cried hysterically; her body was bitten several times leaving large welts. Colin carried her out of the water, and she shivered from the cool winds. He carried her to the camp and into her tent. She was naked and shivering as Colin wrapped her in blankets.

He took her and held her in his lap, as a parent would do for their ailing child. "I'd never let anythin' bad happen to ye, love," he said in a soft whisper.

She looked at him as her body started to warm in the several blankets. "But you just did," she said coldly.

"I'm sorry, love, I'm sorry 'bout eveythin'!"

"Obviously not sorry enough, because if you really were sorry you would never let anything like this happen to me."

Colin rocked her in his arms as she lay lifelessly in his lap. "What can I do?"

"Take me to 1908 A.D."

"Love, I hadn't any intension on bringin' ye to such a place, ye insisted on comin'."

"Isn't that just like you, Colin, slapping the responsibility back onto me?"

"Would ye like me to stay in yer tent tonight to watch over ye?"

"Just until I fall asleep, then you must leave. Don't try anything!"

Colin kissed her on the head. "I love ye. I love ye with all me heart," he said softly to her.

She started to close her eyes, as she felt content enough to fall asleep.

**

Colin completed the tree cutting he didn't finish the day before. He was feeling panicked and saddened about the ant, incident knowing how much Rosa needed to go home.

Sasha limped around the camp trying to get breakfast ready. He noticed Rosa was not leaving her tent. "Miss Rosa, you fine now? I would like to see beautiful face today," Sasha called to her.

Rosa peeked her head out of the tent. "Good morning, Sasha. I really don't know what is good about this morning." She looked around. "We're still here, aren't we?"

Sasha took her hand, leading her out of the tent. "Come, Miss Rosa, and drink tea with me. You look beautiful today."

"No, I don't."

"Miss Rosa, did anyone ever tell you you are beautiful woman no matter what?"

"Sasha, please, Colin could be fishing or chopping wood right now he should be back shortly. Just don't get him mad, please," she said while giving Sasha something to eat.

Colin returned, carrying several chopped logs for the camp. "Rosa, yer lookin' so fair this mornin'," Colin said as he placed the logs next to the fire pit.

Rosa scowled. "Go to hell!"

Colin stood in disbelief as he paused. "Rosa? I'm sorry for yesterday."

"I wish it happened to you instead of me," she said sitting on the stump with her head down.

Sasha put his arm around Rosa. "Miss Rosa, you don't know what you say."

"I know exactly what I'm saying. I hate it here!"

"Well, Sasha, I see your leg is improvin', is that right, mate?" Colin asked trying to change the subject.

Sasha smiled at Colin. "Da, Mr. Limmerick, my leg much better now."

"Glad to hear it, mighty grand this is. I can't tell ye how much healthier I am livin' in this virginal land. I never felt better!" Colin said puffing his chest.

Rosa looked at Colin with bitterness. "Colin, I'm really glad you're loving it here so much. I know this is your dream come true, but you are forgetting that this place has given me horrific allergies; I break out in one skin rash after another. And Colin, I was attacked by these mammoth ants yesterday! They were the size of lizards, and you're in love with this place? You may love it here, Colin Limmerick, but I sure don't. You've become bigger,

127

stronger and your endurance is better than ever. You're the picture of health, Colin. I'm very glad for you. God damn it all, do you want me to applaud you?"

Colin hung his head down. His eyes shifted from side to side like a child who was in trouble from his parents. "I'm thoughtless, aren't I?"

"Colin I'm just letting you know that there are other places I'd rather be right now," she whimpered, burying her head in Sasha's shoulder.

Colin sat on the log and slowly turned to Sasha. "Is there anything I can get ye, mate?" Colin asked.

"Cigarettes all I need, or maybe I need something else." Sasha winked at Rosa, who got up to wash vegetables by one of the tents.

Colin crawled inside Sasha's tent to get his cigarettes. Sasha hobbled to Rosa. He stood closely beside her and gave her a kiss on the cheek before Colin returned with his request.

As Colin rummaged through Sasha's tent, he could feel the cold wind penetrate his body. This was supposed to be early summer, yet it felt more like early winter. Colin pulled himself from Sasha's tent holding the package of cigarettes but decided to search his own tent for heavy sweaters for himself and his two companions. He walked to Sasha and Rosa; they were speaking very closely to one another. "I have sweaters here, please put them on if ye didn't bring yer own. It's cold. This must be the remains of the last ice age it surely is," Colin said.

"I have my own, Mr. Limmerick, *spasiba*," Sasha said as he limped toward his tent to gather some warm clothing.

"Rosa, did you bring warm clothing?" Colin asked.

"Yes, yes, yes, Colin! Can you just leave me be right now?"

Colin nodded his head with sadness.

***

That night they slept in their separate tents tossing and

128

turning, feeling anxious but exhausted. Despite Sasha's ailing leg he managed to crawl inside Rosa's tent. "Rosa?" he whispered to her. "Are you asleep?" he asked gingerly while poking in her tent.

"Sasha, I'm scared. I just want to go back home in my lab and work on experiments. I hate it here." She buried her head in her sleeping bag.

Sasha snuggled with Rosa, holding her in his arms. "Don't you worry, Miss Rosa, I will be your protector. Or should I say Mr. Limmerick is our protector." Sasha laughed. "Wouldn't you prefer to be with man who protects?"

"You're referring to Colin?" she clarified. "Colin is a great man, and I love him very much, but I don't think I can build my life with someone like him. I need someone normal," she began to whimper with a confused expression.

"So you don't wish to marry him someday?"

Her eyes started to fill with tears. "I don't know, Sasha. We were talking about getting married after this prehistoric journey."

"He propose you?" Sasha asked.

"Yes, he did. I accepted because I love him, I think."

"You think?"

"I just don't know anymore, Sasha."

"You don't want marry Hercules?"

Rosa laughed. "Sure, what girl would say no to being Mrs. Hercules, but in reality, he may not be the husband that a woman really needs. I can't seem to imagine myself being married to someone like him."

"Am I husband woman needs?" Sasha asked, feeling nervous.

Rosa laughed while in Sasha's arms. "Don't you want some beautiful Russian girl?"

"Uh --" Sasha kissed Rosa on the mouth, and she reciprocated.

***

It was early morning near the end of dusk Colin poked his head out of his tent feeling refreshed. He walked around the campsite stretching his muscles feeling healthy and strong. He walked around the campsite to limber up as he took in the fresh air breathing in the morning mist. He looked at Sasha's tent. He puffed up his chest, still looking at the tent, continuing to breathe in the moist heavy air. He gazed at Sasha's tent again, noticing how quiet and still it appeared. He moved closer, still noticing the lack of activity inside. He kneeled down, pushing his arm through the tent opening. He poked his head in the tent only to realise Sasha was not there.

Colin walked to Rosa's tent. His heavy footsteps rustled through the grass, which woke Rosa and Sasha still bunked together in her tent. He could hear two people rustling around in the tent. He backed away. He stopped, as he looked around feeling anxious and panicked. He picked up his axe and clenched the handle. He stood still, noticing he had started to shake uncontrollably. He peered at his axe asking himself *what is the right thing to do?* As he continued to think, he realised Rosa had made her choice. A tear slowly trickled down his cheek. He shook in panic, trembling to an almost breakdown. His heart throbbed, aching with excruciating pain. His tears ran off his chin and onto his jacket. He felt alone. He tried not to make a sound as he kept gasping for air. He took his axe and walked toward the nearby trees while allowing the sound of his cries to penetrate the wooded area. For a few seconds he thought he was dead.

Some minutes passed as Rosa and Sasha found themselves waking up to the sound of Colin singing a song. They looked at each other. She threw a shawl around her and pushed Sasha out of the tent. It sounded like Colin sang the song with conviction in his voice. Parts of it were in some old Irish dialect or maybe Gaelic that they both could not decipher. His voice sounded poignant as he violently chopped wood up on the nearby hill. He was chopping huge stumps at a time with his anger and sorrow relentlessly piercing his heart. He sang intensely louder and the vibrato in his deep voice echoed through the terrain. Sasha watched Colin while Rosa felt confused.

Sasha limped toward Colin. "Mr. Limmerick, don't you think you have chopped enough wood for entire year?" Sasha asked, feeling a little intimidated by Collin's axe. Colin withdrew from both of them as he gathered his things by his tent.

"What you doing, Mr. Limmerick?" asked Sasha as he followed Colin.

"I'm goin' to scurry over to *Megaloceros* for me observational research," Colin answered.

"First of all, Mr. Limmerick, we all must be together at all times, otherwise things are too dangerous. You must be half beast yourself, Mr. Limmerick to not fear this place," Sasha said, hoping Colin would smile, but he did not.

Colin stood tall, overlooking Sasha with his arms folded in front of him. "Why were ye in Rosa's tent last night?" He stepped toward Sasha. Sasha backed away.

"You are getting too personal, Mr. Limmerick. Now don't lose temper!" Sasha blurted.

Colin turned away and continued to pack his backpack. "Did ye have sex last night?" Colin asked, fearing Sasha's answer.

Rosa dashed over to Colin. "Colin, we need to chat."

Colin punched Sasha in the face, drawing blood from his mouth. He moved closer to Sasha, punching him again -- this time to the muddy ground. Sasha was stunned with his own blood dribbling down his face. He tried to crawl away from Colin, but Colin went after him, picking Sasha up over his head and throwing him. Sasha struggled to get up but Colin grabbed him again. Sasha tripped Colin, causing him to fall on top of him. They wrestled in the mud. Sasha punched Colin a few times in the face, but Colin was too powerful to control. However, Sasha managed to get away. Colin chased after him. Rosa couldn't stop screaming. Despite Sasha's leg injury, he was still difficult to catch, for his lanky, light frame allowed him to pick up speed.

"Colin, stop!" Rosa cried with the sound of hopelessness in her voice.

Sasha slipped on the mud, and Colin grabbed him, pinning him against a tree trunk. He grabbed Sasha by the hair and smashed his head against the tree several times.

"Colin, my God! Please stop! You must stop, Colin! Stop!" Rosa cried out.

Rosa stood behind Colin, hitting his arm, begging him. He looked at Rosa and allowed Sasha to fall lifelessly to the ground. Rosa screamed, in tears, attending to Sasha's banged up face, two black eyes, bleeding nose, and bleeding, lips. "Colin! Why?" Rosa's cries penetrated Colin's heart. "Why, Colin? Why?"

Colin stood directly in front of Rosa. "Ye want to chat? So feckin' chat then!"

"You're going to kill, Sasha!" She wallowed in her cries until she felt sick.

"Ye don't love me. Ye never did."

Rosa started to rub Colin's arm. "Yes, I do love you."

Colin pulled away. "I have never slept with ye, but Sasha has?"

Sasha lay on the cold, muddy ground struggling to get up. Colin moved toward Sasha and kicked him in the chin, knocking Sasha out cold.

"We was talkin' marriage, now, ye feck around behind me back? Rosa, how could ye do this to me?"

"Colin..." She began to whimper as she focused on Sasha lying on the ground. "Since we've been on this prehistoric journey I have learned things about you that I didn't realise before. You're just not afraid of this place."

"Ye don't love me 'cause I'm brave? A pile of shite this is! I'm sorry I can't please ye, Rosa," Colin said in a low voice as he continued to pant with anger and exhaustion at the same time.

He tied his knapsack around his body. "So now ye decide that you don't want me anymore? We've been through so much together. I would have done anythin' for ye, don't ye know that?"

Rosa tried to embrace, Colin but he kept breaking away from her. "Just don't! Go to yer new man, Sasha! Just don't bother me! I'll just be away for a few hours." He stomped away from the campsite. *"Gráim thú,"* he shouted in Gaelic as he continued to walk from the campsite.

As he left the campsite, a melancholy Irish folk song spewed out of him in his deepest melodic voice:

Will Ye Go Lassie Go

Oh the summertime is comin'
And the trees are sweetly bloomin'
And the wild mountain thyme
Grows around the bloomin' heather
Will ye go, Lassie go?

And we'll all go together
To pluck wild mountain thyme
All around the blooming heather
Will ye go, Lassie go?

I will build me love a tower
Near yon' pure crystal fountain
And on it I will build
All the flowers of the mountain
Will ye go, Lassie go?

And we'll all go together
To pluck wild mountain thyme
All around the blooming heather
Will ye go, Lassie go?

133

If me true love she was gone
I would surely find another
Where wild mountain thyme
Grows around the blooming heather
Will ye go, Lassie go?

As Sasha remained on the ground, Rosa put her ear to his chest to make sure he was still breathing. She tried to wash the blood from his face and cover him with blankets. Colin's song faded into the distance. They were alone.

After an hour had past Colin stopped walking in the spongy bog to take a drink of water from a tiny spring, which delicately trickled in and about the rocks. He heard noises from the grasses; as he tried to focus through the dense mist he realised he wasn't alone. Poking through the fog were two large antlers showing a magnificent span. *Megaloceros* stood approximately twenty meters from him appearing to feel fairly at ease with Colin's presence - - it too took a drink. Colin's actions were gentle as he wondered if this was the stag they had encountered the other day. He slowly moved closer while pulling his notepad from his bag; he began to record what he saw only to notice the stag had a female with him. "Ruttin' season to be in autumn, it's wee early for that yet." Colin said to himself. The two large animals saw Colin moving closer. He had his camera with him, which he positioned himself to take photographs. He didn't dare approach the female *Megaloceros* because her mate would most likely react in a violent rage to protect her. The female moved closer to Colin; the bog acted as a liability if he needed to make a sudden dash. Both large beasts were intrigued with Colin as if they could sense he wasn't a threat. Colin followed the beasts to the lowlands, continuing to jot down his observations. The beasts stopped almost with an abrupt jerk. The tall grasses rustled in the wind more vigorously as several flocks of birds flew overhead. The two *Megaloceros* stood still, then suddenly sprinted toward the treeless terrain. Colin knew something was wrong. A pack of mangy, loping canines suddenly appeared with eyes poking through the thick grassy blades. Their breath was heavy and their fangs apparent. The prehistoric wolves bounded closer and closer to him. He gingerly looked to each side of himself, making sure they weren't surrounding him. They looked like modern-day timber wolves, except larger. He had his axe with him and held it tightly in his sweaty hands. He knew that if they swarmed him he would have a slim chance of surviving. They scampered through the grasses looking hungry as they salivated over the sight of Colin. He could pick out the alpha male and female in the pack and watched every move they made as they paced their way closer to him. When they got closer, he started to swing his axe, making aggressive sounds: "Yeh! Get Back! Yeh!" They backed off as he moved toward them. He made abrupt movements with his arms as he kept swinging his axe. Some of them leaped at him while trying to nip at his thigh. He kicked but withdrew quickly, not wanting his legs used as easy access. He appeared aggressive and dominant, not feeling the cold air that howled through the trees. The alpha male and female backed off, realising Colin was too dominant for them. Colin's heart pumped with adrenaline. His clothes almost looked painted onto his body. He slowly backed away, fearing they would pounce in front of him at any second. As soon as he saw no signs of them he began to run through the forested area, holding his axe tightly.

In the early evening Rosa paced their campsite. "Sasha, I'm worried about Colin -- he never travels with any weapons."

"Don't worry about Mr. Limmerick, Miss Rosa. He fears nothing except his Professor Cushing," Sasha said while smoking a cigarette. "He has axe, don't worry."

"I suppose you're right. Colin is quite happy here,"

Rosa agreed. Sasha pulled Rosa close to him. Rosa smiled, feeling a comfort in Sasha's arms. "By the way, Sasha you never told me about where you're from?" she asked.

"I am from St. Petersburg, Russia, you know that. My city is beautiful, but now is revolution and I don't want. I wanted to come to west. Political upheaval in Petersburg three years ago -- workers went on strike complaining to Russian Czar asking for reform.

"A czar is like a king, isn't he?"

"You not know what czar is?"

"I'm just asking you to clarify."

"You people from West know so little, da? Anyway, we have *Bloody Sunday* because government troops killed many people. After this there was strike and all was stopped in my country. Now there is Soviet council called Soviet of Workers' Deputies formed by revolutionaries. We not have great czar, but I'm afraid of revolutionaries. I fear Bolsheviks. My country is not nice place now. It used to be great place. My city, Petersburg, was compared to Paris. Now all has changed. This is very sad for me."

"I'm so sorry, Sasha," Rosa said. They embraced each other. "Can you take me to Russia someday?" she asked.

"Not now. It is bad place. But when government is stable I will take you. I promise," he said, kissing her on the lips.

Suddenly Colin appeared, out of breath. He stood and watched Sasha and Rosa kiss.

Rosa noticed Colin. "Colin, I was so worried!" she gasped, running to him. "Colin, it's not that warm out here. Why are you sweating?"

He could barely speak. "Wolves, there is." Colin struggled with his words.

"Wolves?" she questioned.

"Sasha, I'm after ye helpin' me build a log fence 'round our tents. I've already chopped loads of wood. In the mornin' we'll get started," Colin said.

"Then lets go home, Colin!" Rosa pleaded.

"I can't. I just started me observational research of *Megaloceros*. Can't go now, not yet. I just spotted a male 'n female by the small water body at the foothills. The female had shrubs 'n such in 'er mouth -- he did not. The males were starvin' I think."

"According to Mr. Limmerick it is much better to be eaten by his research," Sasha remarked.

"At all times, we've got to keep the fire burnin', we's do," Colin said, pulling his wet clothes off his body.

Chapter Eleven

Twelve weeks had passed since the three time travellers arrived ninety-five hundred years into the past in the Wicklow Mountains. One evening while eating dinner, Colin was lying down resting against a log. He appeared ill kept with his very long hair and bushy copper beard that he had neglected to shave over the past few weeks. Sasha's blond curls had lengthened and there was stubble on his face. He had become quite gaunt and weak. His leg had regained most of its strength, but he still hobbled with a definite limp. Rosa's hair was longer, tangled, and ill kept. She had become weak and sickly on this journey where she found herself constantly battling colds and viruses.

It was the end of August, and Colin had been documenting scientific observations on the stag *Megaloceros* and its mate. The two *Megaloceros* had been making a few appearances at the campsite. Rutting season was near; therefore, Colin didn't want to aggravate them or stand in their way. Sasha and Rosa were terrified each time the large animals got too close, but Colin welcomed their presence. He would lag in the distance behind them as he watched the female venture into the dense brush while the stag remained by the pond.

Colin continued to watch Sasha and Rosa in each other's arms as he drank down his last drop of ale. He sprung up from the ground feeling quite drunk as he staggered a few meters away from the campsite. He could no longer sit and watch the new couple fondle each other with their eyes. He kept his distance as he began to sing.

Bridgit O'Malley

Oh Bridgit O'Malley, you left me heart shaken

With a hopeless desolation, I'd have ye to know
It's the wonders of admiration your quiet face has
taken
And yer beauty will haunt me wherever I go.

The white moon above the pale sands, the pale stars
above the thorn tree
Are cold beside me darlin', but no purer than she
I gaze upon the cold moon 'till the stars drown in the
warm sea
And the bright eyes of me darlin' are never on me.

Me Sunday it is weary, me Sunday it is grey now
Me heart is a cold thing, me heart is a stone
All joy is dead within me, me life has gone away now
For another has taken me love for his own.

The day it is approachin' when we were to be married
And it's rather I would die than live only to grieve
Oh meet me, me Darlin', e'er the sun sets o'er the
barley
And I'll meet ye there on the road to Drumslieve.

Oh Bridgit O'Malley, you've left me heart shaken
With a hopeless desolation, I'd have ye to know
It's the wonders of admiration your quiet face has
taken
And yer beauty will haunt me wherever I go.

Rosa pushed herself away from Sasha and approached
Colin. "Colin, I didn't know you had such a beautiful
voice," Rosa interrupted, as Colin sat on the soft wet
ground not really caring how damp and uncomfortable it
felt. He stared at the black sky, startled by the sudden
howl of the wolves in the distance.

Rosa stood next to where Colin sat. "Colin, we need to
talk."

139

He tried to get up but failed. Then his intoxicated body tried enough where he stood up feeling rather unbalanced. He peered down at Rosa. *"Conaím thú*, Rosa," he whispered to her in Gaelic.

"Colin, I don't understand what you're saying."

"Tá tú go h-álainn," he said in sad whisper. "Yer beautiful."

Rosa held Colin's hand. "Colin, I'm twenty-eight years old, I've been thinking about marriage lately, and since we have time travelled, I realised I can never marry you. You're such a good man. There is so much I love about you."

He found it difficult to look at her.

"Colin, our worlds are so different."

"Settin' me free are ye, love?"

She cleared her throat. "What do you mean?"

"I'm free now? I can be with whomever I wish, isn't that right?"

She pulled away from him. "Free? Yes, I suppose you are free, if that's the way you wish to put it."

He gave a blank stare. "I suppose I don't really know ye. Never did."

"I'm just being realistic."

"I see."

"Colin, you want to be set free? Go a head and find your new lady. Maybe you'll find her at the local brothel or something."

He stood with a slight waver, looking away from her. *"Póg?"* he said in Gaelic posed as a question as he pulled her close to his body and kissed her lips. "Fine then, I'm no longer yers 'n ye mine."

"Colin are you going to be alright?"

"Grá mo chroí," he said softly to her. He pulled her against him and kissed her again on the lips.

She looked up at him with her big brown eyes. "What are you saying to me?"

He stood tall, peering down at her with a smile of

140

sorrow. "*Gráim thú Rosa.*" He told her he loved her as he brushed her hair away from her face.

"Speak to me in English."

He didn't respond.

"It seems to me that you're used to always getting what you want in life."

He chuckled with anger. "Nothin' in me life has ever come easy for me, I'm just not one to give up so easily 'is all."

"I'm sorry, I didn't mean to offend."

"Well, that's that isn't it?" He continued to struggle to hold himself up. "I hope ye know we're not returnin' to our time just yet. We best remain here so I can continue me research on *Megaloceros*."

"We've been here almost all of June, all of July, and mostly all of August. Colin, we want to go home. Are you ready to go back?" Rosa asked in a soft voice. "Colin, I look dreadful. This trip has not agreed with me at all. You're the one that looks like the picture of health not me," she pleaded.

Colin stepped away from her. "I--I suppose when we do return to 1908 A.D. ye 'n Sasha will marry won't yez?" Colin asked while slurring his words.

"I really hope you and I can remain good friends. We will be working in the same laboratory together. It's very possible Sasha will someday soon propose to me. You have to learn to deal with this and not with booze, my dear."

"Aye, it's me drinkin'. It can't solve me problems now can it?" Colin looked away from her. "A fishin' merchant is what I am. I've worked damn hard to get where I am today. I'll just continue 'is all 'n just be who I am, without ye."

"All right then, when do ye want to leave?"

Colin glanced at her shaking his head with disgust. "Ye don't fancy this place much do ye?"

"Sasha and I want to leave tomorrow -- he's been

searching for indicators of the time vortex."

"Tomorrow, ye say?"

"Colin, we're already packed and ready to go. We can no longer live in this environment. Maybe you can survive here, but Sasha and I cannot."

Sasha watched them from the camp. He lit a cigarette while feeling nervous. He felt even more nervous when he saw them both approach the campsite.

Colin walked directly in front of Sasha. He looked down at Sasha's face with a gaze of rage. Sasha took a few steps back.

"Okay, Sasha, leavin' tomorrow we will. Everythin's packed 'n ready?" Colin said.

"We ready to leave. It's you who still must pack, but we can help you, Mr. Limmerick."

"Help? No need for yer help," Colin paused as he stared at the ground. "Ye love Rosa?"

"Mr. Limmerick, can we talk about something else?" Sasha asked.

"We arrived here with me 'n Rosa a couple, 'n now we's leavin' with ye 'n Rosa a couple. You want to chat 'bout somethin' else, do ye?"

"Mr. Limmerick, I cannot tell a strong-willed woman like Rosa what to do or who to choose -- if she wanted to refuse me she would already do so."

Colin looked at Sasha, realising he was right. Sasha put his arm around Colin. "I was not planning this. I am very sorry."

Colin got very close to Sasha. "Ye know I want to smash yer bleedin' head just now, but I won't. I couldn't do that to ye. I considered ye a friend, mate. But, I'd like to beat ye in the ground anyway."

Sasha wiped his sweaty palms along the sides of his pants. "Da, Mr. Limmerick, *spasiba.*"

Colin staggered to his tent to pack his belongings. "It may take me a good while to get packed 'cause of me research gear 'n all."

***

The next morning the three time travellers packed their tents and sleeping bags, leaving the log fences that surrounded their tents intact. Colin was quiet and distant from the others. Sasha heard a noise rumbling in the grasses. The three time travellers looked at the direction of the noise. It was the stag *Megaloceros* and his female. They were running through the grasses as if they were being chased. Colin and Sasha moved closer while Sasha made sure his rifle was loaded. Rosa raised her eyebrows in fear. The male and female *Paleolithics* were spotted with raised spears chasing the two *Megaloceros*. Colin panicked and ran rapidly toward the *Megaloceros*. When he caught up with the large beasts he found the female lying on the ground with a spear in her throat. The stag was badly wounded in the leg. Sasha and Rosa ran after Colin. Colin was feeling was so devastated that he ran after the prehistoric human beings. He caught up to the male and pulled him into the bog. Colin punched the male *Paleolithic* relentlessly in the face as they wrestled in the peat. Just as Colin grabbed the prehistoric man's throat and almost strangled him, Sasha came up from behind Colin and whacked him behind the knees with his rifle. Colin's knees buckled, causing him to fall face first into the bog. This gave the *Paleolithic* man enough time to get away.

"Mr. Limmerick!" Sasha yelled. "You are foolish! These people have to eat! Stop interfering with their lives!" Sasha helped Colin out of the muddy bog as they walked toward the slaughter. The bull was on the ground moaning in agony. Sasha handed Colin his rifle. "Do you want to do this or do you want me to do it?"

Colin pulled Sasha's rifle from him. He pointed the rifle at the animal's head and fired. The sound of the gunshot startled several birds in the trees above.

"Death." Colin paused. "We can wish all we want, but that don't really change what is," Colin said poignantly.

"Human beings came to this planet with an agenda."

Sasha walked toward Colin. "This is prehistoric world, Mr. Limmerick," Sasha said with sternness. "Mr. Limmerick, we must go now, let's go!"

Colin's body language showed that he agreed.

***

They followed Sasha as he led the way to the passage into the present. They followed the signals to where they found the time vortex opening before. There was a distinct discolouration along the soil and even amongst the misty air. That same pungent scent filled the air, and they followed it as their guiding marker. Their voyage was a rough ride through the passage of time -- much rougher than their ride to the past. Their belongings also travelled through their passage, at times smacking them hard within the vortex of turbulence.

The time travellers crash-landed on the ground. They remained still. Sasha opened one eye and noticed Rosa lying next to him with one of their heavy bags pressing on her. He quickly rolled over to push the weight off of her belly. "Miss Rosa! Wake up, Miss Rosa, please wake up!" he said as he started to abruptly shake her body.

She opened her eyes. "Sasha, is it over?" She felt blood trickling off her forehead.

"You are hurt, my Miss Rosa. Please let me help you up," he offered, brushing debris off her knotted hair.

"Colin, where's Colin?" she asked in a panic.

Colin was a few feet away from them trying to hoist himself up. "Sasha, this wasn't an easy ride back, it wasn't," Colin commented trying to catch his breath.

Rosa looked at Colin as she stood up. "Colin, you should look at yourself." She started to laugh. "Your hair is so long and messy. You haven't shaved your face in ages. You're going to scare everybody in London."

He brushed debris off his jacket with a slight chuckle.

"Colin, I really liked your *Megaloceros*. I'm glad we met them. They were dynamic animals. You're right: they

144

did struggle in the forested areas -- the stags couldn't adapt. I can see them eventually dying off from starvation because their antlers didn't permit them to roam the forested lands. You were right, Colin. Dr. Cushing is wrong. However, it is possible they could have evolved into deer in our time."

Colin rubbed his belly, feeling nauseous from the rough ride home. "The fallow deer is the only alleged living relative in our time, but its relationship to *Megaloceros* is too slight to even say. In my opinion, I don't believe it is a living relative. All the research I've done indicates there are really no livin' relatives. I still stick to me theory 'n to Dr. Darwin's. Species do cease to exist. Not everything evolves."

"Mr. Limmerick, we live in turn of twentieth century where Dr. Darwin is considered devil. People, not all, but many, are ignorant. You are true Darwinist, and your name will someday be written in history and biology books. I hold great reverence for you, Mr. Limmerick." Sasha shook Colin's hand.

Colin stood partially in the peat. "Thank ye. By the way, mate, what year is it?"

"According to indicator it is year 1908 A.D. Can you not tell?"

"Well, I'm still ankle deep in bog, 'n I just wanted to be sure 'is all."

"How does this Wicklow land look to you, Mr. Limmerick?" Sasha asked.

"It looks like the Wicklow I've always known 'n loved."

"We're finally home," Rosa said.

"By the way, Sasha, good show on yer time vortex invention," Colin commented as he extended his hand to Sasha.

Chapter Twelve

It was early September, 1908, A.D. Colin drove his automobile to Dublin from Wicklow. Rosa sat in the passenger seat while Sasha sat in the rumble seat. "Me parents live in downtown Dublin. We need to bathe 'n eat. Ah, parents, may God bless 'em all," Colin said as he forced himself to laugh. "Ye know, Rosa, I always got on well with me parents."

Rosa stared at nothing. "That's good, Colin."

"Bein' their eldest son 'n all…ye know what I'm sayin'?"

"No, Colin, what are you saying?" she asked.

"Well, bein' the eldest I always felt a sort of responsibility over me younger brother, Ethan. I always wanted to please me parents," he talked out of the side of his mouth while he kept his eyes on the muddy road.

Rosa paused. "Well, Colin, I'm glad you're family is so perfect."

"I'm wishin' I could say the same for yer family."

She sighed. "Colin, not every family is like yours. You just have to accept that. Consider yourself lucky to have come from such a well-adjusted home."

"Aye, that ye are so right. I'm very blessed that I am," he said. "And, how's 'bout yerself, mate?" he asked glancing at Sasha while trying to dodge the flocks of sheep sitting on the winding road. "Ye get on with yer parents all right didn't ye?"

"My parents are dead," Sasha answered back.

Colin's smile dissipated. "I'm sorry to hear that," Colin responded. "What happened?"

"Killed in revolution," he answered with little interest in the topic.

"Sasha, I didn't know!" Rosa blurted.

"What is to know? They die in revolution. Many die in

revolution."

"I would have liked to have met your parents, Sasha," Rosa said.

"Why?" Sasha asked.

Rosa turned to Sasha sitting in the rumble seat. "Why?"

"Da, why you ask such silly things? They never know you and…you never know them."

"Oh, Sasha, you sound as if you're emotionally disturbed by this. I am so very sorry," she said.

"Emotional disturbed? Nyet."

Colin glanced at Sasha. "What Rosa's sayin', Sasha, is she's afraid ye could be hurtin' 'n such. Are ye?" Colin asked.

"Nyet."

"You mean *no*, Sasha?" Rosa asked.

"Look, they sometimes good -- sometimes not so good. Father sold black market chickens -- he make many rubles," Sasha said.

"Black market chickens, eh?" Colin expressed as he continued to drive.

"In time of revolution, not so much food. Government overthrow and policies change to commune life. One must be able to survive, so father would sell black market chickens in back alleys of Nevsky Prospect."

"I'm sorry yer family had to undergo such turmoil, mate," Colin commented.

"Good rubles for chickens in Russia. It is delicacy," Sasha said. "One day, father fight against Bolsheviks and he lose."

Rosa straightened her posture. "Sasha, what a sad story," she said. "This must have all happened quite recently."

Sasha lit a cigarette and began to smoke.

***

They arrived in Dublin at a quaint row house that sat on a narrow road just off O'Connell Street a few blocks

147

north of the Liffey. Colin parked his car in front of the house. He and his two colleagues didn't move as they watched the cool wind blow through the stillness just as it did in their journey through time. Tiny Atlantic droplets sprinkled over their heads as the sun made a quick appearance and left. They looked at each other as they vacated the automobile, carrying their personal belongings to the front doorstep. They stood at the front door as Colin gave an aggressive knock. A tall, burly man in his early seventies with bushy white hair opened the door. The man's face lit up with joy when he saw his son standing in the doorway with two other people.

"What the hell has God brought to us this fine day?" the man blurted with excitement.

"Dad, I hope ye don't mind me comin' for a short visit with two friends?" Colin said.

"Get in with yaz, get in!" the man expressed. "Me dear God! Grace, get here!" the man called out to his wife.

"Brian? This hollerin' I'm hearin' from ya is too much!" a medium-sized woman in her late sixties said as she hurried to the door. "Colin, is this 'bout?" the woman asked with concern. She spotted Colin. "Dear God! Our son has come to us!"

Rosa glanced at Sasha.

Colin's parents Brian and Grace embraced Colin as they pulled him into the house.

Brian Limmerick stood directly in front of his son; Colin was about four inches taller. They looked nothing alike except for the ample hair. "No offense, but ya all look like ya just stepped out of a bleedin' war," the man said, noticing their ill-kept appearance.

Rosa was feeling embarrassed as she tried to quickly primp her tangled hair. "I do apologise for our dreadful appearances."

"Skin 'n bones yaz two look," Brian Limmerick said to Sasha and Rosa. "But, not our Colin, strong as an ox he looks as always. Where in the world did ya go?" Brian

Limmerick asked.

"We have been through many things," Sasha commented.

Brian looked at Sasha. "Do I detect a foreign accent? I'm not thinkin' yar from England are ya?"

"I am Russian."

Brian looked at Grace. "Russia?"

"My country has revolution now."

"That's right, I read about that in the papers, your country is goin' through some enormous change," Brian commented.

"Dad, Mum, Sasha is an accomplished physicist-researcher who's been takin' part in me academic research," Colin interjected.

"How very interestin'," Grace said as she paused and glanced at Rosa. "Look at your hair, lass. What ya do to it?"

"We didn't get a chance to groom ourselves during Colin's scientific experiment," Rosa said."

"Scientific experiment? Cavemen is what yaz have to look like in order to do a scientific experiment?" Brian asked.

Colin put his arm around his father. "Dad, bore ye we won't with all the wee details of why we look this way," Colin commented.

"Why? What did yaz do? I want to know. That's our Colin always doin' somethin' life-threatenin' to prove a cause. Deep-sea fisherman he is, ya know. He's had his own merchant ship for twelve years now. He's encountered many deadly situations on the high seas, he has. However, made a lot of quid, he has with the trade. Never had to worry 'bout our Colin makin' enough money. Imagine, our Colin a doctor of Natural History. Our eldest son is the most successful in the family. He's the one with the brains, he is," Brian rambled on.

Grace Limmerick led Colin to the parlour, placing a plate of biscuits before him as she tended to the pot of tea

149

on the stove.

"Make yourselves at home. Sure yar all stayin' a while. It's been too long since we last saw Colin, " Brian suggested. The men sat in the parlour drinking beer while the women prepared the table.

"Colin, ya remember that Connelly garl who used to live on our street?"

"Vaguely," Colin responded as Sasha sat beside him smoking.

"She married a banker, 'n off she went to join some of her relatives in Canada. Immigrated there, she did."

"Good for her."

"She used to fancy ya. Yaz was just teenagers then. Her grandparents lost their potato farm in the great famine -- you must remember her."

"Vaguely," Colin replied, more interested in his beer.

Suddenly the front door swung opened, and a tall, lanky man with straight black hair took off his hat and jacket while entering the home. A tall, slender, blond woman followed from behind with two infant boys trailing behind her.

Colin looked at the four extra guests and started to grin.

"Colin?" said the tall, lanky man.

"Ethan!" Colin shouted as he stood up to greet the man.

Rosa and Grace entered the parlour as they watched Colin and Ethan embrace each other. The two men both stepped back to stare at one another.

"Look at ya, ya big lug. Ya grew yarself a beard."

"I did."

"Ya look quite scary," Ethan said. "No one will dare pick a scuffle with ya."

Colin placed his arm around Ethan. "Sasha, Rosa, this is me baby brother, Ethan."

Rosa stepped closer to Ethan. "It's so nice to meet you," Rosa said while Sasha stood up and smiled.

"This is Mary, me sister-in-law 'n their two sons, Jamie 'n Paddy," Colin added as he scooped up his two nephews into his arms.

Mary smiled at Colin. "Ya don't look scary at all."

Grace stood next to Mary as she pulled her toward the kitchen. "Dinner's ready, Brian help me place the roast on the table," Grace asked.

***

Colin glanced at his parents as he showed Sasha and Rosa to their seats. Dinner was served.

"Tell me, Rosa, do ye have yourself a fine gent waitin' for ya somewhere else?" Grace asked.

"Well --" Rosa said, sipping on a glass of red wine.

"What's a nice girl like you doin' travellin' with two handsome fellows on some science experiment?"

Colin shifted his eyes toward his mother. "Mum, ye make a grand roast 'n spuds, I must say."

"Thank ya, Colin," Grace said while playing with her food.

Colin took a deep breath and swallowed his last forkful of potatoes. Grace and Brian Limmerick looked at each other in silence. Colin re-filled his glass as he piled a second helping onto his plate.

Ethan glanced at the table. "Looks like me big brother let another wench go by, eh?" Ethan laughed.

"Ethan!" Grace shouted.

"It appears Rosa isn't Colin's wench at all," Ethan said.

"Ethan, yer right on that one," Colin responded engulfed in his meal.

"Colin, yar gettin' a wee bit long in tooth, wouldn't ya say? It's time ya settle yourself with a pretty lass like Rosa," Ethan said.

Colin guzzled his whiskey as he turned to Ethan in silence.

Rosa stopped eating. "This is getting rather embarrassing."

"Doesn't your womanising life get a bit stale at times, Colin?" Ethan pressed.

Brian glanced at Grace as they both remained silent.

Colin looked at Mary as he reached for the potatoes. "Mary 'n the kids are lookin' well, they is," Colin said with a forced smile.

Mary winked at Colin; she couldn't stop smiling.

"What ya doin', woman? Are ya winkin' at 'im?" Ethan scowled.

"Just eat yar meal," Mary grumbled.

Colin ignored Ethan's concern and continued to eat.

"Colin, remember what ya used to do to me before I married Ethan?" Mary asked with a girlish snicker. Rosa and Sasha cleared their throats as they continued to eat. Brian and Grace were too consumed with their grandchildren to take notice of anything else.

Ethan sprang from his chair and dashed into the parlour. "Ah yes, scientific Colin! Dr. Colin, ya will soon be, won't ya?" Ethan's shouting was so amplified that it penetrated throughout the house. "No good for nothin', university is, if ya ask me!"

"Who asked ya?" Mary snapped back at him while she tried to finish her meal.

Brian stood up. "Now, Ethan, yar jealous!"

"We don't see the bleedin' bastard for ages, he drops in whenever he damn well pleases, 'n then he flaunts with me wife. I want to kill the bastard!" Ethan hollered hysterically from the parlour and paced around the room.

Colin re-filled his glass and continued to eat.

Grace sat beside Rosa. "You should've seen them when they's was tots. Did ya know Colin is six years older than Ethan? Hard to tell isn't it?"

"I suppose ..." Rosa smiled.

"Whenever Ethan got in trouble, there was Colin to the rescue always fightin' his battles," Grace added.

"Colin's back in town all right!" Ethan shouted from the other room.

152

Brian sat next to Sasha and tried to smile.

Grace looked at Colin. "Ya know, Rosa, did ya know Colin paid for this house for Brian 'n me?"

"How thoughtful," Rosa said.

"Tell me, what son does such brilliant things for his parents?" Grace asked.

Ethan re-joined the table. "A son who needs to make that kind of quid so he can afford his string of whores!" Ethan scowled.

Colin sprang from his chair and approached Ethan.

"No!" Grace shouted while Mary held her sons in her arms.

Colin grabbed Ethan by the neck and drove a forceful punch to his face.

"No!" Grace shouted. Brian ran to Colin. Ethan lay on the floor with his mouth dripping with blood.

Rosa looked at Sasha while they sipped their tea. Sasha cleared his throat again.

Sasha turned to Rosa. "Rosa."

"Yes."

"I know same feeling as Ethan," Sasha said quietly while rubbing his jaw.

Chapter Thirteen

That evening the three time travellers returned to London, each going to his or her own residence. Colin sat in his flat. He clutched a photograph of Rosa in his hands while glancing at the pile of notes he had made while time travelling. He sat at his desk as he skimmed through his notes, trying to organise them into a file system he could understand. He reached for his specs while sipping a glass of whiskey. Eventually he finished the bottle and he lowered his head onto his folded arms, onto his desk. He prayed to God and slowly fell asleep.

**

It was late afternoon when Colin showed up at Professor Cushing's door.

"Colin Limmerick? What the hell happened to you?" Professor Cushing asked while munching on pieces of chocolate all well laid out in a decorative bon bon box.

Colin sat on his professor's cold, rusty stool holding his *bolg*. "I'm back from doin' me research."

Professor Cushing propped himself up on the desk to get a closer look at Colin. "I can see that you're back, Colin."

"I've made some ground-breakin' discoveries I have, sar."

"Tell me, Colin Limmerick, what research did you do? I feel like you're keeping things from me. Just look at you, you look like hell!" Professor Cushing said, placing his tiny spectacles upon his nose.

Colin pulled out a one-page draft of his hypothesis with a description of his apparatus of how his experiment was accomplished. Professor Cushing read through the information in front of him.

"Me researched evidence will be submitted to the head administrator of higher degrees in doctoral studies 'n the

154

dean. They're goin' to marvel over me work, they's will."

"You just came back from a journey in time ninety-five hundred years in the past? Ridiculous, ridiculous," he said, skimming over Colin's work.

"I'm plannin' on showin' me proof to the head administrator of the Department of Natural History as well, sar. I met two professors from India just before me journey in time. They's currently workin' with Dublin College University. I've informed them of me time travel."

"Colin Limmerick has made a discovery? Impossible!"

"Believe it, Professor Cushing. I did the journey with Dr. Sasha Dimitrikov, the physicist from the Polytechnic Institute of St. Petersburg, Russia. It was his discovery of time vortexes by usin' penetratin' energy, which was transmitted from the meteor strike in Siberia back in June. Also, Rosa Emanuel came along as well. She is a human evolutionist."

"Yes, I know of your Rosa Emanuel. She is also a Darwinist like you. And that Dimitrikov kid should have stayed in his country to help fight off those revolutionaries."

"Russia ye don't know much about, do ye, Professor?

"Should I?"

"Yer supposed to be a social scientist aren't ye? An expert, am I correct, sar?"

"You're questioning me?"

"I am."

Professor Cushing propped himself on his desk looking at Colin. "You're the student. I'm the academic advisor. This is who I am, the professional with the impeccable reputation within this academic institution -- not you!"

Colin took a deep breath. "What is it that I've done, sar? Support me ye haven't regardin' me research ideas. Why?"

"You continue to disobey me, Colin. You have no

interest in Lamarckian theory or even my own discoveries of the horseshoe crab. What is all this rubbish about going back in time to see your Irish elk face to face? You have no business in this university institution! You're no genius! Besides, look at you, you never did look like a graduate student," he said, waving his finger at Colin.

Colin looked at him with piercing eyes. "No doctoral student, Professor Cushing, has ever done anythin' this life-threatenin' for the mere purpose of research! I will be teachin' the courses ye wish not to teach this autumn because yer too consumed with some crustacean that barely evolved over millions of years. Well, me journey through time happened, 'n I've got proof." Colin stood up and noticed a porcelain figure of the horseshoe crab sitting on Professor Cushing's desk. Colin took the ornament in his hand and smashed it against the wall. He looked at Professor Cushing's facial expression of devastation. "Yer stupid research on the horseshoe crab is dull! Waste of bleedin' time readin' this old junk! Tell me what scholar would?" Colin stormed out of Professor Cushing's office, leaving pieces of broken porcelain littered on the floor.

Colin rushed into his own office and he sat at his desk with his hands over his eyes. Sasha suddenly appeared at the door.

"Mr. Limmerick, why you sit alone here in office? In some hours from now there will be doctoral lunch in courtyard. Why you look so upset?" Sasha asked.

Colin smiled. "Oh, it's me advisor again….he's a feckin' bore he is."

"Forget him, come to lunch. You work too hard, Mr. Limmerick, come."

"Don't fancy gatherin's when I'm not feelin' up to it 'n all. Besides, I bes' get to the laboratory 'n examine some of the samples I brought back from our journey."

"Mr. Limmerick, go to your home now, put on nicer clothes, shave your face, and attend graduate lunch. You must."

It was a sunny September day as several doctoral students from different disciplines gathered at the university courtyard for a catered lunch. The dean's representative for Colin's defense committee attended as well as several other faculty members. Sasha spoke to other physicists with Rosa at his side while other natural history students gathered together to discuss their research.

Rosa noticed a group of females gather together while sipping on glasses of wine. She suspected these students were in nursing and pedagogy as well as others female-based disciplines. The group of females chatted amongst themselves, giggling and carrying on. Rosa focused on the women as she finally realised what they were ogling over. Colin had entered the courtyard dressed in a three-piece suit and top hat. His tie and suspenders were cherry red as well as the pin stripe pattern on his trousers and blazer. He was wearing his gold earring, his heavy silver bracelets and his three chain-linked necklaces. He wandered into the courtyard, noticing the female attention he was receiving. He tipped his hat to the ladies and smiled as they blushed and giggled with excitement. He then stopped to remove his hat as he tied back his long hair with a black ribbon. The young women were all smiles as they slowly moved closer to him. Noticing there was an opened bar, he helped himself to a glass of whiskey. He decided to make his way to a group of gentlemen that he knew from his programme.

One of the young women marched to the group of men who were chatting with Colin. "Colin, would you mind joining us?" the young woman asked interrupting their conversation.

Colin excused himself to the men he was speaking with and made his way to the young women. He removed his hat with a smile. "How'd ye know me name?" he asked politely.

"Everyone knows who you are. There's a rumour going about that you're very charming, is this true?" the woman asked with blushing cheeks.

Colin took a sip of whiskey. "Charmin', ye say? Ye'd have to come to that conclusion yerselves I think."

"You're dressed so…so magnificent," the young woman commented.

Colin bowed. He took one of the young ladies' hands and kissed it.

"Finally, someone appreciates the way I dress, fair lady," Colin said softly.

The dean's representative for Colin's defense committee approached him. "Colin Limmerick, you're the doctoral student who's proving Darwin's theory of natural selection using a prehistoric mammal as the focus of your research?" one of the elderly, distinguished looking gentlemen said to Colin. The females were silent.

"Aye, sar."

"I was speaking to Dr. Dimitrikov over there by the fountain. So you and he travelled through time?"

The females suddenly wore serious expressions on their faces.

"We did, sar. Rosa Emanuel, the lass standin' beside Dr. Dimitrikov just there, also came with us on our prehistoric expedition."

"He developed a time vortex theory, he tells me."

"He has, sar."

"This is remarkable! Absolutely astonishing!"

"Ye didn't speak to Dr. Cushing 'bout this?"

"He tells me nothing. However, he is a very private gent."

Colin guzzled his glass of whiskey, and then licked the droplets off his fingers.

"Colin, you do know that I will be participating as a member of your defense committee?" the scholar said, trying not to stand too close.

"I think Dr. Cushing has pointed ye out to me once

158

before, sar."

"You… travelled through time?" One of the women asked in awe.

"Aye. I just returned from a prehistoric journey I did."

The women whispered to themselves. "You're so brave," commented the young woman.

Colin blushed. " Brave? I'd rather say that I'm a curious bloke." He smiled as he continued to enjoy his dry spirit. "Besides, the man ye all should be marvelin' over is right over there by the fountain. He's the genius behind the time travel," Colin said. "Dr. Sasha Dimitrikov is the man who made time travel possible."

"Ladies, can I take Colin from you for a short moment? I would like to introduce him to other faculty. He just came back from a journey through time. If all his evidence proves his expedition, then he will have changed modern science forever," the dean's representative interjected as he tugged on Colin's arm.

Colin placed his hat on his head and smiled at the women while walking away with the dean's representative.

Rosa approached the group of women. "Not so fast, ladies, stop your salivating, it doesn't look very proper on you."

The women glanced at each other as they tried to hold in their laughter. They didn't seem very bothered from Rosa's behaviour.

Rosa stepped closer to the women. "If any of you think you have a chance with him -- you better get that idea out of your heads."

"Really?" one of the women responded.

"He still wants me." Rosa laughed fiendishly.

"Oh," the woman said.

"Look at the way he dresses -- would you be caught dead with a man who dresses that way?"

Colin stood beside Sasha as other faculty members gathered around them in awe of their prehistoric journey.

"We have photographs, plus, samples from time in history we travel. We will prove to faculty that we really do this journey," Sasha said.

Another faculty member patted Colin and Sasha's backs. "This is something that needs to be told to the world."

"I documented when I was there, sar. I could definitely turn this into a book -- in fact, sar, I intend to. But, first, a great deal of me chapters in me dissertation will be based on me findin's whilst on this prehistoric journey."

The group of women called over Colin. He excused himself from the faculty members and helped himself to another whiskey. The women continued to call to him, almost making spectacles of themselves. They stood by a four-foot-high stone wall. Colin walked to them while trying to sip from his drink at the same time. "Ladies," Colin said removing his hat and feeling tipsy.

"So, you're becoming quite the famous scientist, Colin," one of the women said.

"Famous? Nay." Colin guzzled his drink then sat on the ledge of the stone wall. The women clustered around him. He loosened his tie.

"Will you remember us when you're famous?" one of the women asked with a girlish giggle.

Colin chuckled as he felt his drink penetrate him a little more strongly. "Don't be silly, ladies, If anyone won't be famous he sure as hell is me." Colin inhaled the last bit of spirit.

One of the women tried to prop herself on a campus stone wall but had difficulty. Colin lifted her upon his lap. She stared into his eyes. His intoxicated state brought his eyes to hers. Their lips touched and transformed into a passionate kiss. The other females tried to look at something else. The dean's representative noticed Colin and the young woman in their act of passion. He glanced at Sasha. Sasha shrugged his shoulders.

"My, my, my, we have a Casanova in our doctoral

programme do we?" the older faculty member commented.

"Forgive him, sir, he sometimes forgets reality," Sasha responded.

"Well, I also noticed he knows how to put it away, doesn't he?" the dean's representative said.

"He still recuperating from time travel."

Chapter Fourteen

Colin walked down the hall of the university. There was a gentle tap on his shoulder. "Are you Colin Limmerick, the man I have heard so much about?"

Colin turned his head.

"Was it almost ten thousand years into the past?" the man asked.

"Me time travellin' was ninety-five hundred years into prehistoric Ireland to be exact, sar."

"Can I call you Colin?"

"Please, sar."

"Oh, I beg your pardon, forgive me, my name is Sir Binghamton. I am a Natural Historian as well as MP of doctoral studies at this university institution."

Colin gave a slight bow as he removed his hat. "What a pleasure it is, sar."

"Colin, I want to learn all about you. You're a fascinating chap. This institution is so pleased to have such an asset as you. Even *The London Times* is printing your story. Tell me all about yourself."

"Ye want to know about me? Sar, there's really nothin' to tell."

"Poppycock! I'm sure there is loads to tell!"

"What ye want to know, sar?"

"Everything, Colin, everything!"

"Well, sar, I'm sure ye can tell that I'm an Irishman."

The man began to chuckle. "You are a rarity, aren't you?"

"A rarity, sar? I can't say I know what yer referrin' to."

"You're so genuine, so real."

Colin smiled, not really knowing how to respond.

"Colin, you are aware you need a second reader for your dissertation?"

162

"Fully aware, sar."

"Has Dr. Cushing appointed that person yet?"

"He hasn't."

The elderly gentleman laughed. "Randolph, he can be a..."

"An arse, sar? He can be an arse."

"Do I detect some --."

"Some crap, sar. Aye, sar, crap's been flyin', it has."

"There was a graduate lunch a few days ago, and I heard from some of the faculty who attended that they were greatly impressed with you and your extraordinary time travel."

"I'm hopin' they was."

"Can you prove this expedition really occurred?"

"I can, sar. I have photographs 'n samples of rocks, grass, jars of water, pieces of other matter that I can show ye, sar."

"Good. Then we're all set."

"Set, sar?"

"I'll most likely be your second reader for your oral examination board, and next Friday evening is the Graduate Studies Research Conference and Awards Gala in the main conference hall. The gala was pre-arranged by two well known professors of prehistoric Botany from the University of Delhi who claim to know you."

"I know these gents, I do."

"Please, we want you to be our honoured guests. You and your two cohorts, that Russian physicist whiz kid Dimitrikov and Miss Rosa Emanuel. The theme will be a tribute to Dr. Charles Darwin. The two professors of prehistoric botany from the University of Delhi have notified me they are currently doing their research in Dublin -- a Dr. Sharma and a Dr. Patel, if this rings a bell?"

"It does."

"Well, they will be in London next Friday and will be attending the gala. Could you perhaps bring some evidence of your time travel and do a little lecture about your research? Colin, you're a fascinating man. We all want to learn about you and your research."

Colin was almost in a trance of bliss. "A tribute to Darwin ye say, sar? Surprised I am. It has always seemed to me that most loathe Dr. Darwin. Many think he's a heretic or somethin' like that. Darwin's theory conflicts with the church, it does, sar. I'm a Catholic me-self."

"My God, you must feel like you're battling your own faith against the science of Darwin. I admire your courage, son." The elderly professor gave Colin a slap on the shoulder. "You are very right about this, Colin, but remember Darwin is not completely rejected from the academic world. I most certainly don't reject his theories, and I'm with the Church of England myself."

"Me academic advisor hates the whole idea, sar. It's been quite turbulent for me, I must say."

"Colin, this is a battle you have engaged yourself in. Many young academic researchers like you have, in fact, given up trying to prove Darwin's theory through their research. There's been far too much resistance."

"Kiddin' yer not, sar. I'm treated like an outlaw 'cause I want to prove Darwin's theory of natural selection as scientific fact. I'm in jail already, I feel," Colin said.

"Colin, don't worry about any of the ignorance that flies around concerning Darwin. You keep doing what you've been doing. However, you and your two colleagues will be our honoured guests. How does that fit you?"

"It does fit me brilliantly, sar. It will be me pleasure, a great honour. By the way, will me academic advisor need to be present?"

"Randolph Cushing will have to be present to reap the benefits of having such a prodigy for a graduate student as you." The man slapped Colin on the back and walked away smiling as he kept repeating the word, *'Fascinating.'*

***

164

That evening Colin worked relentlessly in his flat on his presentation for the gala. Rosa and Sasha knocked on his door, finding the door ajar and stepping in. Colin was at his typewriter.

"Colin? We heard about the gala next Friday night," Rosa said, smiling while she and Sasha held hands.

Colin smiled as he took a bite from a sandwich and continued to type. "Did ye hear Dr. Sharma 'n Dr. Patel will be present?"

"Great, Mr. Limmerick, great. How about your Professor Cushing?" Sasha asked.

"Uh, Cushing has to be there. He's me academic advisor. Why should that feckin' piece of shite reap the benefits of me time travel experiment? I smashed his bleedin' porcelain horseshoe crab against his feckin' wall earlier today, I should have smashed his feckin' head rather!"

Sasha laughed and poured Colin some whiskey in a large beer mug. "You broke his toy horseshoe crab?" Sasha handed the large glass to Colin.

"Next time I'll break his feckin' head with me bare hands if he gets me feckin' mad again."

"No you won't, Colin. Your fighting days are over, my dear. You should be acting like a scholar not a thug," Rosa said.

"And Mr. Limmerick, your professor Cushing will get you mad again. We all know this, da?" Sasha lit a cigarette with ease in his actions.

"Anyway, the gala is this Friday and we all need to prepare for it. It's a tribute to Dr. Charles Darwin." Colin's tone lowered when he got a glimpse of Sasha holding Rosa's hand.

Sasha strolled into Colin's bathroom to look at himself in the mirror. "I don't know if I can be seen like this, Mr. Limmerick, I've lost thirty pounds. I look bad, da?"

"So, ya'r a wee bit thin. It doesn't seem to bother Rosa, does it?"

Rosa nervously primped herself and forced a smile while she puttered around the room.

Colin continued to type, trying to ignore the throbbing pain of his still broken heart. Rosa watched him type in silence, feeling awkward.

Sasha laughed.

Chapter Fifteen

That evening Colin showed up at his vessel. He was glad to see his crew since he hadn't seen them in over thirteen weeks.

"Our captain's returned to us, lads! Captain Colin's back!" shouted Eddy. The crew jumped at Colin, giving him masculine hugs as they stood on the deck. They bombarded him with questions of wonder, not really knowing where he had been for so long.

"Captain, the picture of health ya look. Where was ya at?" Eddy asked.

"Would ye believe me if I said I was on vacation?"

"Nay, captain, we know ya. I don't think yaz ever took a vacation in yar life," Eddy replied as the crew and he passed Colin a pint of ale.

"I've got yer pay to pass over to yez." Colin smiled while drinking his pint. The men roared. Colin removed his hat. He noticed Lorelei, Bessy, and Tara, approach him. He smiled while he removed his jacket.

Lorelei gave him a long, sensual stare. "Limmerick? Yar finally back are yaz? Where the hell 'av ya been?" She stood bluntly in front of him rubbing her body against his.

Colin stood looking down at her as she fondled with his vest. "Lorelei, what are ye doin'?"

"I'm not used to seein' ya lookin' so civilised." She smelled of gin, her make-up was thick, and her dress was much too small for her busty frame. "I've missed ya. Where's that bitch of yars?"

"Bitch?"

"That university bitch." She rubbed his chest. His eyes shifted with awkwardness. He paused, then reciprocated by running his hands along her bust. Lorelei tried to primp her ill-kept hair while fluttering her eyelashes at him. "I think it's time a garl gets herself lookin' gorgeous don't ya think?" she said, while grabbing her purse making her way to the lavatory. Colin watched her, knowing in his mind how the evening was going to end.

Young Timmy in the wheelhouse waved his arm to Eddy and the ship was in motion. Colin paced around the deck and gave his crew their orders. Tara and Bessy made themselves comfortable.

"Captain, we've got to get a catch of mackerel to the harbour by morinin'," Eddy said.

"I'll change these clothes, 'n we'll get the catch to the harbour long before then."

Tara made sure Lorelei was out of sight as she made her way to Colin. "She's such a slut isn't she, love?" Tara asked as she maneuvered herself to get close to him.

"Define slut," Colin asked as he prepared the nets to be cast into the water.

"Ya know what I mean. I mean whore. As if ya didn't know," Tara said, slapping him on the belly.

He stood straight with his arms at his sides. "What ye want, Tara? Can't ye see I've got work to do?"

"I was rememberin' our last night together. Remember, love?"

"It could have been maybe two years n'some months ago, maybe," he said, not looking at her while he worked.

"Why don't we have a reunion then?" she suggested.

"What ye want, Tara? Ye want me to mount ye tonight?" he asked with an aloof tone.

"Hurry up before Lorelei gets back!" she gasped with angst.

Colin glanced at Eddy. "I may be with Lorelei tonight."

Eddy nodded his head as he continued to work, trying to ignore their conversation.

"How'bout when yaz done bangin' er, ya can come 'round, eh?"

"How much?"

"Whatever yar willin' to offer, love."

"Don't know, Tara. We was together maybe a few times, ye 'n me, I really don't know, but surely ye can get some of me boys tonight."

"I had'em all too many a times before. It's yar turn."

He chuckled at her as he began casting the nets in the water. "How much ye want?"

"Lorelei won't take yar quid, is that it?"

"I'm more than happy to pay Lorelei 'n ye. How much?"

"I won't take yar quid either. Eight times it was. I counted. Let's go for nine, c'mon, love!"

"Eight times?"

"Ya fecked me eight times, I know, I counted."

"Was it that many?"

"It was."

"Tara, are ye offerin' me a feck or are ye doin' a fine trick? Make up yer bleedin' mind."

"I'll take whatever ya think I'm worth. I'd definitely let ya have me for free, but a garl's gotta eat."

"No doubt."

"Ya once whispered in me ear that ya think I'm beautiful."

"Did I?"

"Ya did."

He took a deep breath. "I think I may be with Lorelei tonight, yer friend Lorelei," he reminded her.

"Friend, yaz say? She's no friend."

"Tara, please let me do me job just now."

She stepped back. "Please, nothin'. Ya know exactly what she is."

"What are ye?" he asked.

"A lady is I."

Colin glanced at Eddy. "Tara, look I really can't say."

"Lorelei was never yar garl! She was yar whore she was!"

Colin looked at Tara. "Tara, what the feck do ye want

169

from me?"

"I want ye tonight, love," she said. "I know ya want me too."

"I can't tonight."

"Tomorrow night?"

"Maybe. I can't really say." He finished casting the nets. "We's supposed to be dockin' at Dublin city."

"Can't believe yaz takin' that slut over me tonight!" Tara shouted.

"It's not that I prefer her to ye -- we'll have to make it another night, 'is all."

Lorelei returned with fresh make-up on her face. Her facial expression changed when she noticed Tara standing close to Colin.

Tara tugged on Colin's suspenders, trying to push her away.

"Let go of him, bitch!" Lorelei shouted, giving Tara a shove.

Eddy stood between the two women. "Look, this shoutin' must stop! Yaz ladies are aboard me captain's ship. Yaz should act appropriately, not like smut!"

"Be off, Tara!" Lorelei ordered as she watched her walk to the stairs that led to the cavity of the hull.

***

As the evening ripened, half the crew, Lorelei, and Colin sat around the deck chatting and getting drunk. The fiddler and piper in the crew started to play jigs and reels. Other prostitutes were also on board, and some of the crew danced with them, growing more intoxicated and exchanging sexual gestures with each other. Colin sat next to his first mate with Lorelei on his lap. Eddy noticed Colin didn't push Lorelei's gestures away.

"Captain," Eddy whispered to Colin, "where's Rosa?" he asked while they sat on the side bench located on the deck.

The music continued to play as everyone celli danced, ate and drank ale and whiskey. Lorelei pulled Colin to where everyone was dancing. The men would change partners as they danced around the women, showing off their three steps. Colin would take a few swigs of ale from time to time as he continued to dance a few steps with Lorelei and then re-joining Eddy on the side bench.

Colin sat next to Eddy, watching Lorelei dance with some of the crew.

"Captain, where's Rosa?" the first mate asked again.

Colin shook his head. "Didn't make it, Eddy," Colin said with saddened eyes.

"What the hell happened?"

"She left me, she left me for someone else, she did." Colin drank down his ale.

Lorelei returned, grabbing Colin by the hand pulling him toward the dancing. "C'mon, Limmerick!"

Colin danced with her while Eddy sat and watched. Lorelei unbuttoned his shirt, smooching with his belly while they continued to dance. "Lorelei, could ye let me speak to Eddy a wee bit?" Colin asked in a cordial manner.

"Why is that?" she asked.

"I've been away. Can ye free me up a wee bit?"

She slapped him on his belly. "Go!" She continued to dance her version of a sloppy hornpipe.

Colin sat beside Eddy. "I think I need to get pissed-up, 'n I can't do it if I'm dancin'," Colin said opening another ale.

"I'm sorry it didn't work out for ya, lad," Eddy said with poignancy in his voice.

Colin was silent. Lorelei brought Colin a large, unopened bottle of a fine spirit resembling the colour of strong tea. She opened it in front of him. "Drink up, Limmerick!"

Colin smiled and took the bottle from her. His first mate looked at him strangely. "Captain, ya drinkin' 'n mixin' more than usual tonight I can see. Yar gonna put yarself out real bad."

"I'm never goin' to stop." Colin chugged from the bottle while gagging at the sweet syrup passing through his throat.

Lorelei heard an Irish ballad play and lured Colin for another dance. He saw the deck in streaks; nobody seemed to look whole to him. He stumbled a few times as he tried to dance with her. His large body mass kept slamming into the other crewmembers. His eyes started to close on him. He could no longer make coherent conversation. Lorelei unbuttoned his trousers, yanking him to the ladder leading him to the captain's quarters.

His first mate appeared startled. "Captian, can yaz speak? Ya overdid it tonight, Captain! Lorelei, yaz not bein' fair to 'em!"

"Nay, it's good for me, good ye know," Colin drunkenly slurred as he tried to climb to his cabin with Lorelei. "Don't worry 'bout me." He clumsily climbed up the ladder. He grabbed Lorelei, throwing her over his shoulder and making his sloppy climb to his captain's quarters.

Colin's first mate stood at the bottom of the ladder looking up to him. The drunken crew looked at each in silence.

Joey staggered over to Eddy. "Hey, Ed!" he shouted, stinking of scotch.

"What ya want? Can't ya see I'm worried 'bout our captain? He's gonna do sometin' he'll regreat. Can't ya see?"

"Ahr, ee's alright. Ee's a big lad 'n he can take care of 'emself alright," Joey said.

Eddy gave Joey a shove. "Go play yar fiddle 'n stop botherin' me. The captain shouldn't be with Lorelei just now. I think I saw 'er fillin' 'is veins with rum, I did."

Joey looked at the crew while some of them crawled on the deck. Tara and Bessy sat in the galley waiting for their next clients to come along; some of the crew lay in their bunks at the bottom of the hull with the other girls.

172

Colin threw Lorelei on his bed. Her loud, screeching laughter echoed throughout the ship. He pulled off his shirt and trousers. She continued laughing and flicked off her shoes. He pounced on top of her, roughly tearing off her dress. She screamed in ecstasy feeling him ravish her. He used his strong legs to maneuver his mass as he recklessly injected her with a pounding thrust. Her jarring screams startled the crew in a freeze-frame of silence on the deck. Colin gave a few more thrusts and her eyes rolled back almost in panic from his power. He leaned over her, pinning her arms to the bed above her head.

"Take it out, ya feckin' bastard! Take it out! Yar killin' me!" she shouted to him in agony.

He let out a big sigh, then flopped on the bed beside her. "Since when ya'r all tight 'n virginal?" he asked with a mumbling slur. "At least I finished me job."

She sat up on the bed and stared at him as he lay on his back staring at the ceiling. "Yaz got all yar sauce all over me, 'n everywhere else for that matter. I must say, yaz a messy fecker. Was ya tryin' to saw me in half? I got good mind to slap ya 'cross the face, ya filthy savage!"

"So why don't ya?"

"I got good mind to," she said, fondling his penis.

"Leave it be, if ye don't want anymore."

"I want more alright,"

"Ye just told me to take it out!"

"When a man's yar size, one must do it in stages, ya feckin' bastard!"

"Fine."

"I could go all night with ya. I think I now know what bestiality is," she cackled.

"Shite, let me feck ya again then," he said rolling upon her and thrusting his penis inside with gyrating jolts. It took longer than the first time, and Lorelei started to scream with pleasure-pain. Colin ignored her pleas. He continued to thrust. She was feeling so soar that she screamed urging him to pull out. He did. He lay back onto the bed, and his head fell back onto the pillow. "Feck, let me sleep off the liquor, eh? Ah dear Lord, let me die," he said, closing his eyes.

It was early morning dusk when Eddy awoke to a sound he could not really decipher. His pocket watch sat on the night table beside his lower bunk as he propped himself up to see if any of the other crew members were awake. He gazed at his watch; it read 5:30, but he still continued to hear a raspy coughing sound coming from the upper hull of the ship. He threw on his night coat and climbed up the ladder to the deck. The twilight was dissipating as the sun began to rise. He tightened his night coat around himself to block the damp winds that came off the sea. He walked toward the wheelhouse, spotting Timmy almost half asleep. The cracking, coughing sound was coming from the lavatory platform, which was halfway to the captain's quarters. Eddy climbed the ladder to the lavatory, where he saw Colin naked with his head in the toilet bowl in the middle of a violent vomit.

"Captain! Yaz so sick! What can I do for yaz?" The first mate yelled out as he stood in the doorway of the lavatory.

Colin upchucked while shivering profusely. "I'm feckin' poisoned I am..." He paused with his body hunched over the toilet. "...help me." His head hung lifelessly in the toilet bowl.

"Captain, ya may need a doctor! We might have to take ya to a hospital!"

Other crew gathered around, wanting to help their captain.

"One person I need in 'ere! Men, please go!" Colin garbled as he continued to vomit.

Eddy remained in the bathroom watching his captain continuously be sick. Colin sat on his butt on the cold bathroom floor in an uncontrollable shiver. Eddy wrapped a towel around him. "Captain, I warned yaz last night. I knew it was over when Lorelei handed ya a bottle of rum.

What was ya thinkin'?"

"Rum?" Colin questioned with his head hanging in the toilet bowl.

"Captain, I tried to take it from ya, but ya were out to kill yarself last night. There wasn't anytin' I could've done."

"I drank a feckin' bottle of rum, ye say?"

"Ya did."

"I feckin' hate rum."

"I know that, Captain."

Colin looked at his first mate. "Ed, last night, what else I did?"

"Well, I think ya may've screwed Lorelei."

"Did I?"

"Captain, I know yar hurtin' 'bout Rosa, but ya can't kill yarself over'er!"

"Shite, I fecked Lorelei, I did?"

"I'm pretty sure that's what ya did, Captain. She got nasty 'n made sure ya got bloody pissed so she could get her ways with yaz!"

"I was seduced by a wench, so I was?"

"I'm afraid so, Captain."

"Shite--."

"Captain, Lorelei has seduced ya before. She knows ya all too well."

Colin sat on the cold bathroom floor with a towel wrapped around the bottom half of his body. Everytime he tried to stand, he would relapse to vomit again.

"Captain, yar like a son to me. I hate seein' ya mess up like this. Don't get stupid over a lass. Worth it she's not."

"She didn't want me anymore. We was discussin' marriage 'n such. I loved her so much. I never felt this way for a lass." Colin held his belly, as he felt queasy again.

"Captain, did ya want to screw Lorelei last night?"

"How should I know? I guess I did," Colin continued to hold on to the toilet bowl as he vomited. "This has got to stop," he said with discomfort and pain.

"The boozin' or the screwin?" asked Eddy.

"Both."

"Lorelei has always had her hooks in ya, Captain."

"I can't do this anymore. Me feckin' life's a mess."

Eddy tried to help him from the floor but every time he would, Colin would collapse to vomit again. "Colin, ya got everythin' goin' for yaz. Yar as sharp as a whip, yar fishin' trade is a success, yar knock'em dead handsome, what more do ya want?"

"Love."

"Captain, love is right 'round the corner waitin' for ya. So, it isn't Rosa. The next one will be the right one."

"I've got to change me lifestyle. I think Rosa left me 'cause of who I am."

"Who would turn down a wonderful lad like yourself? Only the man upstairs knows why a good woman leaves a good man."

Lorelei entered the lavatory noticing Colin sitting on the floor naked with a towel hanging over his shoulders. "Limmerick, so this is where yaz hidin'? Get up! What yaz doin' on the feckin' floor?

Eddy grew angry. "Ya purposely got me captain stinkin' drunk last night so yaz could get knocked up by 'em!"

Eddy tried to help Colin up. Colin stood on the cold floor, naked and holding the towel around his shoulders as he continued to shiver.

Lorelei laughed at Colin. "There yaz standin' in front of me stark naked with the stench of bile in the room. Well, Limmerick, I must say it was the best yet lastnight. Yaz certainly know how to perform for a garl," she said, moving closer to him.

Colin ran his hands through his long, disheveled hair. "I don't remember last night." He tried to walk, still feeling nauseaus as he leaned against the wall for support.

"What? How can ya tell me that yaz don't even

remember our finest night together?"

Colin looked at Eddy. "Feck," Colin said, trying to take a breath. "Finest night together, yer sayin'?" He lowered his head, making it to the toilet as he violently burst into a graphic upchuck while bellowing in excruciating pain.

"Lorelei, please, you need to leave this ship. We'll drop ya off in Dublin. Just leave the captain just now. He needs a doctor," Eddy said feeling protective.

"Limmerick, ya 'n I have built quite a life together. I think its time ya stop usin' me for sex 'n start committin'. Ya're not gettin' any younger, yar playboy days are numbered." She scowled.

"Build a life together, yer sayin'?" Colin questioned with his hands over his stomach, wallowing in pain. He slid against the wall onto the floor. "Ye 'n me are just friends, we is," he said with his head between his knees.

"Friends, don't feck, Limmerick! I'm not that kinda garl. I expect some sort of commitment outta yaz. It's time, Limmerick!"

"What do ye want, garl -- a ring?" Colin asked forcing out his words in a sickly manner.

"It's time, don't ya think?"

"Ye want me to give ye a bloody ring?" He breathed deeply with his head between his knees, with Eddy by his side.

"Lorelei, yaz need to go now. Leave Captain Limmerick be. He's quite ill, can't ya see?" Eddy said.

Colin looked at her with his glassy, bloodshot eyes. She began to cackle with laughter. She blew Colin a kiss and left.

He lay on his side on the cold floor, passed out. Eddy called some of the crew to help move him up to his bed.

***

It was late afternoon as the *Atlantic Mermaid* docked at the River Liffey. Lorelei and her female colleagues exited from the ship. The crew sat in the galley drinking

177

strong tea. Colin stumbled down the ladder from his cabin and made his way into the galley. His crew pretended nothing was wrong as they continued to eat their lunch while Colin made his appearance. He glared at the crew and stumbled over to the table still looking ill. He poured himself a cup of tea. The crew had fried up some fish, which turned Colin's stomach. He leaned against the wall holding his tea and tried to focus on something else.

"Nice to see ya join us, Captain," Eddy commented.

Colin nodded as he leaned against the counter noticing the men had taken all the chairs. "Are we doin' off or on shore today or feckin' what?" Colin asked in a sour tone.

"On shore today, Captain," Eddy replied.

"When ye blokes wanna get started?" Colin asked as he searched for a chair.

"Anytime you want, lad," Eddy said.

Colin rubbed his unshaved face. "I need to get to me parents. I'll be off for just some hours. When I return we'll do the daily catch." Colin slipped his jacket over his bare chest and placed his cap on his head. "So, then, men - - take yourselves a break."

They reacted happily to Colin's request.

"Captain, yaz realise yar not wearin' a shirt?" Eddy pointed out.

"Ask me if I feckin' care?" Colin stormed off the ship and onto the dock.

Eddy followed Colin onto the deck and threw him a sweater. "It's gettin' rather chilly, Captain!"

***

Grace Limmerick heard a thundering knock at her door. "Who could that be with such a disturbin' knock?" she asked while unlocking the door. She was surprised to see Colin standing in her doorway looking so ill. "Colin? Pleasant surprise it is to see me lovely son standin' in our doorway. Did you come to join us for tea, love?"

"Sure to feckin' puke me innards out, I will," Colin blurted and staggered into the house.

178

Brian heard voices as he tore down the stairs to see who it was. "Colin? Fancy seein' ya here on this fine Saturday mornin'."

Colin sat at the kitchen table with his head buried in his arms. Grace and Brian stood closely beside him. "Colin, love, how are ya feelin'?" Grace asked with a concerned look on her face. She looked at her husband. "Brian, fetch Ethan 'n Mary. Somethin's wrong with Colin."

Brian took a few seconds to understand the urgency of the situation. He grabbed his sweater and headed for the door.

"Isn't it convenient that Ethan and Mary only live a few rows down? They're always close enough if ya need them, love," Grace said to Colin.

When Ethan, Mary, and their two small sons arrived, Colin's head was still buried in his arms at the table. "Is something wrong with Colin?" Ethan asked, looking at his parents.

"We don't really know," Grace said, fidgeting about.

Ethan tugged on Colin's hair. "Colin, are ya asleep or what? Say somethin', man."

Colin sat up. "Take a good feckin' long look at me. Look at me, 'n what do ye see?"

"Colin, what's goin' on with ya?" Brian asked.

"Colin! You're lookin' a wee bit rough, dear," Grace squealed. "Dear, have ya caught yourself a cold?"

"Tell me what ye see, mum?" Colin asked again.

Ethan walked closer to Colin. "I see a miserable, hung-over, still pissed-up sailor," Ethan responded.

"Ethan, how can ya talk this way to your older brother?" Grace asked.

Colin stood up and began to sloppily pace the room. "Mum, Ethan is correct!" Colin pointed out bitterly.

"Colin, please tell mum what's botherin' ya!" Grace shouted in a panicked state.

"Mother, ya always looked at Colin with rose-coloured

179

glasses," Ethan said. "Can't ya see he's stoned outta his mind?"

"Stoned? Nay, little brother, that was last night. Today, I'm just a waste of feckin' time!" Colin abruptly said.

Grace lunged for Colin's arm. "Please, dear, come sit down. Ya need to calm yourself."

"Mother, he's hung over, can't ya see that?" Ethan said getting frustrated.

Colin continued to stagger around the room. "Well, Mum, feckin' take yer rose-coloured glasses off 'n realise yer eldest son is a feckin' drunk that can only bag whores 'n nothin' more!" Colin leaned against the wall, still feeling woozy.

Colin sat down, slamming his head on the table, burying his head in his arms, and feeling so sorry for himself that he began to cry.

Ethan approached Colin, patting him on the back. "Colin, the booze is makin' ye this way. I hate to see a grown man cry."

"I have such a feckin' headache, I do! I feel like shite, 'n ye know what? I'm shite-faced almost every feckin' night!"

"Colin, ye don't need to be tellin' us all this just now!" Brian said in his usual helpless tone.

"All I do is feck whores! I'll never marry, I'll never have children -- only bastards, 'n I'll never be with anyone unless they've slept with the hurling team." Colin stood up with unsteadiness.

"Ethan, your children are here, tell them their uncle has lost his mind or somethin'!" Brian shouted in a panic. "Mary, get the little ones outta here!"

"I've gotta run, I have a job to feckin' do. I've got to make some quid so I can pay me crew 'n the bills. Me ship, she needs repairs, lots of 'em!" Colin muttered on his way to the door.

Grace followed him. "Dear, is it a lass you wish ya

180

had?"

Colin looked at his mother and kissed her good-bye. "Wish? I don't wish for anythin' anymore!" He grabbed his cap, placed it on his head, and left in a fluster.

"My God, Ethan, have ya ever seen yer brother this way?" Brian asked.

"I have. Yaz two know nothin' of yar son. Ya never did. Yaz like braggin' 'bout his successes to everyone, but ya really don't know 'em," Ethan lectured his parents.

"We know our sons well," Brian insisted.

"Ya never did. He's your favourite 'cause he paid off your bleedin' mortgage where I never could. He's your favourite 'cause he makes better quid than me. He's your favourite 'cause he always got the high grades in school. He makes this workin' class family carry some prestige. But, as soon as he finished secondary school and he was workin' on Uncle Kevin's ship, he was learnin' the fishin' trade. Uncle Kevin was your older brother, Father, who drank, had fast women, and made loads of quid with his trade. He was a businessman. He was built big and strong, he was excitin', and ya was jealous as hell of him, Father!"

"I was never jealous of me brother, bless his soul!" Brian replied feeling cornered.

"Yar terrified yar prodigy son will end up like Uncle Kevin! Ya just don't want to see it!" Ethan insisted.

Grace ignored the conversation. Brian sat down at the table, placing his hands over his face. "Colin is nothin' like me -- he is the spittin' image of your uncle Kevin, 'n you're right, Ethan, it scares me to death."

"Uncle Kevin was a dynamic man with charisma, good looks, skill, 'n brains," Grace commented.

"Sometimes when I look at Colin, I can't believe how much they're alike -- it's frightenin'." Brian wiped a tear from his eye.

Mary moved closer to Brian. "Brian, how did Uncle Kevin die?" she asked.

181

"I don't really know exactly. I heard from his crew it was a boat accident, but I know better. Died of syphilis or else he died a drunk, the good Lord only knows," Brian said.

"I asked Colin if he still goes to confession. He said he does whenever he can. I think he has a lot to confess," Brian said to his wife, trying to hold back his sorrow.

Ethan held Mary's hand. "What are ya both so afraid of? Colin is a grown man and has been for a while. Ya never spent so much energy on me, not ever," Ethan confessed.

"Ya? Never had to worry 'bout our youngest, not ya, Ethan. We always knew what ya were up to. Ya married Mary, got a job with me at the hotel. Ya bought a house down the street from us. Always a good lad, Ethan," Brian commented.

"Don't get us wrong, dear. Colin is also a good lad. He tends to his drinkin' a bit much at times. He will soon marry 'n settle down, you'll see. I know some spinster daughters from the ladies I attend church with. They would love to meet a nice, charmin' man like Colin," Grace said.

"Nice 'n charmin' man? Mother, Colin is not nice or charmin'!"

Grace looked at her husband, "Brian, can ye believe how jealous Ethan is of his big brother?"

"Mother, Colin is a sailor!"

"So?"

"Mother, he's rough!"

"Well, this rough sailor ya speak of is also a darn good scholar. What woman wouldn't that impress? He's brilliant, he writes academic papers 'n has been since he got his masters degree. Now he has this secret experiment he's workin' on. Proud of 'em, I am, very proud!" Grace preached to Ethan.

"Mother, he's a bleedin' Darwinist! Don't ya know what that means?"

"What's a Darwinist?" Grace asked, looking at Brian.

"Mother, he's like a heretic! If he's a Darwinist, he doesn't accept our holy book!" Ethan shouted to his mother with frustration.

"Hold your tongue, Ethan. Are ya sayin' Colin rejects the Bible?"

"That's precisely what I'm sayin', Mother."

"Colin does not reject our holy book. He is a good Catholic!"

"Mother, please, see him for the man he is. Don't forget when he was sixteen, he gave the Flannery's youngest daughter a bundle of joy. He destroyed the poor garl's life. Didn't her parents take her far away to some convent to have the baby? She was forbidden to ever see Colin again. I don't think she was the only one he did this to either. He's a bleedin' sailor!" Ethan preached.

"I question a garl who allows a young healthy man to take advantage of her." Grace puttered around the dining room, finding odds and ends out of place.

Chapter Sixteen

That following Friday evening, the Conference Gala Tribute to Dr. Charles Darwin was held in the Great Hall at The University of London. It was a formal affair with cocktails and hors d'oeuvres. A small orchestra playing Handel in the background added to the occasion. Older retired professors entered the gala in black and white tuxedos with matching top hats. The women were dressed in long gowns and had feathers in their hair.

Animated artwork of *Megaloceros giganticus* dominated the entrance of the reception area. The guests mingled and discussed *Megaloceros* and time travel while they helped themselves to cocktails and food. Colin entered the premises wearing a black, white, and grey tuxedo and top hat, and the crowd began to gravitate toward him. He greeted the crowd while trying to remove his white gloves with great difficulty.

He felt someone tap his arm. Rosa was standing behind him. He smiled at her beauty with relief.

"Nice evening attire, big boy. You look good enough to be put on top of a wedding cake," she snickered.

He scanned her black dress and hair tied high with white ribbons. His eyes softened to her beauty. They gave each other a mesmerizing stare.

"So, where's Sasha? I need ye both here tonight, so I do," he said.

"He's over there chatting to a group of old stuffy professors. You can see him if you look for the halos of tobacco smoke," she said. "He's working hard trying to dazzle the faculty so they can hire him for a professorship -- after all he is the time vortex inventor. It's really his invention that made you the star tonight, Colin."

Colin gave her a blank stare. "Ah yes, Rosa, I'm here tonight livin' off Sasha's brains 'n hard work. Try to understand, Rosa, a Darwinist yerself at that, it is still considered unorthodox to accept Dr. Darwin's theory of natural selection. I'm provin' me theory that me chosen prehistoric mammal died off due to natural selection. Rosa, ye know this shite already! Why the hell am I justifyin' meself to ye? Ye just want to hurt me, 'n I don't know why." He turned his head to look over the arrving guests.

"Temper, temper, Colin. I guess you flare up more often when you don't have a drink in your hand. You should probably get one as quick as possible so you can handle this evening with more poise," she said callously.

Sasha made his way through the crowd. "Mr. Limmerick, finally we meet again, were you out of town recently? I did not see you in lab…"

"I've been workin' hard on me vessel. I've had several quotas I needed to fill."

"Of course, our sailor man needed to work on high seas. When do you start teaching your foundation course?"

"Next week. It's Cushing's foundation course again. He hates that one, he does," Colin added.

"You will have many students in lecture hall?" Sasha asked.

"Don't know, really. More than likely I will have a large group once again. It's either the foundation course for first year students or the second year course on the lack of evolution of crustaceans. Cushing gave me a feckin' choice this time. Can ye feckin' believe how stupid that is? Who the hell cares 'bout this shite? Cushing's courses are as useless as a chocolate teapot, they is," Colin vented.

Sasha glanced at Rosa. "Mr. Limmerick, leave your temper in your Wicklow. Just relax and enjoy evening. This is our night tonight, da?" Sasha said while placing his arm around Rosa and planting a large wet kiss on her lips. They continued to kiss romantically for a few seconds.

Colin uncomfortably fiddled with his bow tie.

"Sasha, we're in a public place," Rosa said with a giggle.

"Does not Rosa look pretty in new dress, Mr. Limmerick?" Sasha said, running his hand over her breasts.

Colin stared at the guests while scanning the room for the bar.

Sasha laughed while engaged in his kiss with Rosa. "Mr. Limmerick? You look like you are in other world. Something wrong?" Sasha asked while he puffed on his cigarette

"I need a drink, I do," Colin whispered in a low tone. "Sasha, Rosa, excuse me if ye would. Just realised that I need to get some hard stuff in me gut."

"Over there, Mr. Limmerick." Sasha pointed. "They do not have vodka so I will have to try something else. You people have no creativity when it comes to spirits," Sasha complained.

"Aye, I know ye are a vodka man at heart. Sorry ye can't find what yer body requires, mate." Colin patted Sasha on the back before making his way through the crowd. He could barely make it to the bar because many faculty tugged on his coat sleeve and calledd his name.

"Colin Limmerick!" Dr. Sharma called out. Colin was finally holding a glass of whiskey. Dr. Sharma stood next to Dr. Patel.

"Hello, gentlemen. It's so nice to see ye both again," Colin said while shaking their hands.

"Colin Limmerick, so we all meet again. It is so very good to see your smiling face. I would like very much to introduce my beautiful daughter, Amoli. I told you about her. She is my youngest daughter of only nineteen. She will probably be a student in your class for this upcoming term, Colin. She is very excited about attending such a very nice place as the University of London," said Dr. Sharma as he gave his daughter a gentle shove toward

Colin.

She stood directly in front of Colin wearing a fine, see-through sari, which barely covered her ample breasts and exposed her belly. Colin's eyes widened. He quickly buttoned his jacket.

"I have heard so much about you, Instructor Limmerick," she said in a tiny voice.

"Ah, ye have? What have ye heard?" Colin asked, trying to bow as low as he could to meet her four-foot-ten height. He focused on her voluptuous, curved shape, almost bewildered by her risqué attire.

Rosa wasn't too far away as she inched her way close to Dr. Sharma, watching how his daughter could not take her eyes off Colin.

Amoli stepped closer to Colin, and a few people who rummaged through the dense crowd accidentally pushed Amoli into Colin. "Oh, my!" Amoli blurted with a nervous shrill.

When Colin stopped her from falling, her breasts pressed against his crotch. "It is getting' rather crowded in here, isn't it?" Colin commented as he tried to hold her steady.

"Thank you, sir, for not letting me fall. I wouldn't want to rip my dress," she said with a tiny giggle.

Colin smiled awkwardly at her while guzzling his whiskey.

"No, no, I wouldn't want to do that, sir."

Colin towered over her. He struggled not to fix his eyes on her prominent cleavage.

"You are so big and strong for a naturalist," she said with a juvenile giggle.

"Why can't a naturalist be big 'n strong?" Colin asked, smiling so hard that the dimples in his cheeks extenuated.

Dr. Sharma laughed. "Do you not find my daughter to be the most beautiful girl you have ever seen, Colin?"

"The most beautiful, ye ask? Aye, that she is."

Amoli forwardly took Colin's arm and buried herself

in his bicep.

"She has had many suitors where none were anything she desired, but maybe she was waiting for you to come along, my friend," Dr. Sharma said in a whisper to Colin.

"Me?" Colin half understood what Dr. Sharma was intending.

"There are some professors I must speak with now. You can introduce my daughter to some of the other graduate students and faculty or show her around the university since she will be a student here -- do excuse us," Dr. Sharma said as he walked away with Dr. Patel.

Rosa pushed herself beside Colin. "Well, well, what do we have here?"

"Rosa, meet Amoli, Dr. Sharma's daughter. She should be enrolled in me up-comin' foundation course."

Amoli looked at Rosa while still buried in Colin's arm. "Who's she?" Amoli pointed.

"This is Rosa, Amoli -- she time travelled with me."

"Oh."

Rosa noticed how Amoli would not physically unattach herself from Colin. "So, tell me Amoli, are you old enough to be attending a university institution?" Rosa asked.

"Yes, I am old enough -- but perhaps you are too old?"

Rosa peered at Amoli then looked at Colin. "Such a sweet little thing. My, my, Amoli, did you forget to dress for this event?" Rosa stepped closer to Colin. "Colin, this gala is attended by your former and future students -- what's so special about Amoli?"

"Amoli is Dr. Sharma's daughter, is all," he said in a whisper.

Rosa looked at Amoli head-on. "What courses are you signed up to take this term, Amoli?"

"I am enrolled in Instructor Limmerick's foundation Natural History course. I want him to teach me everything he knows," Amoli replied in a high-pitched giggle.

"I'm so glad ye have an interest in Natural History,

188

Amoli. I will be lookin' forward to seein' ye in the course," Colin said with a smile.

"Tell me, Amoli, do you even know what Natural History is?" Rosa asked.

Amoli looked at Rosa and Colin with a startled laugh and paused. "I can't really say that I know. It fit my schedule, and Instructor Limmerick will be teaching it. Aren't those two reasons good enough?"

Rosa pressed her lips tightly together, glancing at Colin. "No, Amoli, that's not good enough. Instructor Limmerick is very rigid with his classes. He demands a lot from his students. I hope you're ready to work, because you really won't have time for anything else, do you understand, Amoli Sharma?"

"A dictator is what ye make me as, Rosa? Amoli, I think Rosa is just tryin' to prepare ye for a hardy workload. Rigid is not the way I would describe meself," Colin said, trying to ease Amoli's nerves by patting her gently on her bare shoulders.

"Well, I intend to work my very hardest. I won't disappoint you, sir," Amoli said.

The master of ceremony was Colin's dean's representative. He made his way to speak at the microphone, asking everyone to take his or her seat. The room was quiet. The spotlight focused on the frail, elderly gentleman. "Good evening, faculty members, graduate and undergraduate students, ladies and gentlemen. We are here tonight as natural scientists to remember Dr. Charles Darwin. He was our own British naturalist born in 1809 and passing in 1882. One could say he was the grandfather of evolution in showing us the way with his theory of natural selection. I will quote him from *The Origin of Species*: ' *I have called this principle, by which each slight variation, if useful, is preserved, by the term Natural Selection.'* Natural Selection has been proved as the most correct theory over and over again due to the several archaeological artifacts discovered over the years.

However, it has recently been proven with a drastic experiment done by venturing back through time. A Ph.D. student of ours has recently come back from a journey into time. He has proved to the world that his chosen prehistoric mammal of research became extinct due to natural selection." The guests spoke amongst themselves in high volume. "For all you non-believers, this conference gala is for you. But, first I would like to introduce our time-travelling Ph.D. student's academic advisory professor, who has backed them with all the support they needed so they could make this time travel possible. This man is a great scholar at this institution who has devoted his life as a natural scientist to the Lamarckian evolutionary theory behind the evolution of the horseshoe crab. I would like to call Professor Randolph B. Cushing to the lecturn." The audience gave a round of applause as Professor Cushing waddled onto the stage to the lecturn. Colin sat with Rosa and Sasha with Amoli at his side.

Dr. Cushing pulled the microphone toward himself. "Ladies and gentleman," he said as he cleared his throat. "I have been Colin Limmerick's academic advisor for two years now. When Colin first came to me he was reluctant to accept Darwin's theory of natural selection as part of his research. He introduced his idea of researching the Irish elk, scientifically known as *Megaloceros giganteus*. He came to know a young scholar from some far-away place who knows something about time travel. I encouraged Mr. Limmerick to change Natural History forever by using time travel."

Colin caught the waiter's attention. "Four bottles of whiskey ye need to bring me," Colin asked in a whisper. Sasha and Rosa glanced at Colin with concern.

Professor Cushing called Colin to the platform. "Let me introduce to you my Ph.D. student, Mr. Colin Limmerick." The professor wore a fake smile as Colin walked to the stage trying to calm his own anger. The crowd stood up and applauded. Professor Cushing handed an academic award to Colin.

"Thank ye, academics 'n friends, I can't tell ye how surprised I am that all this is happenin' tonight. "I just completed a prehistoric journey, thirteen weeks of livin' in a completely different century. It has been speculated that our journey took us approximately to the year 7592 B.C. I travelled ninety-five hundred years in the past. The premise of me voyage included me strong belief in Darwin's theory of natural selection. Ye see, I am so headstrong that *Megaloceros giganteus* grew to its extinction 'cause of its over-sized antlers inhibitin' it from feedin' on foliage from forests, leavin' it to die of starvation. Lamarckian theory, on the other hand, says that Megaloceros kept evolvin' to our modern reindeer. Ladies 'n gentlemen, that's a pile of rubbish! Lamarck says a species will evolve to adapt to the environment, while Darwin says those most capable will survive -- this is survival of the fittest, natural selection. Thus, new species will later emerge in order to adapt to the changin' environmental conditions." The audience began to chatter amongst themselves.

"Ladies 'n gentlemen, yer probably all wonderin' how me two colleagues 'n I survived in the prehistoric untouched wild. Darwin's concept of survival of the fittest definitely came into play! We was in constant confrontation with prehistoric *Homo sapiens*, wild, prehistoric mammals 'n such, but we survived. We survived, ladies 'n gentlemen, 'cause of survival of the fittest. We was the fittest!" The audience broke into an uproar. Colin stood on the stage behind the lecturn, feeling his adrenalin run through his veins. "I would like to introduce me two colleagues, Miss Rosa Emanuel and Dr. Sasha Dimitrikov." The audience applauded. "I'm sure yez all have some questions. Please feel free to ask. He is the man who should be speakin' to yez now -- he's the inventor of the time vortex. He is the man who took me

191

and Miss. Emanuel through time."

Sasha stood at the lecturn. "I am Dr. Sasha Dimitrikov." The audience stood up with applause. He gazed at the crowd with his usual, expressionless face.

A man stood up in audience. "Explain how you went back in time?"

"I am physicist. I study in my country Russia about energy penetration given by meteor strike. I don't know if British know about meteor strike, which happened in my country last June -- in Siberia. We left for prehistoric journey in June just when meteor waves penetrate through earth -- same latitude as Ireland. So, we go back ninety-five hundred year to see Mr. Limmerick's *Megaloceros*." The room was quiet. Sasha gave a slight bow, pulling away from the podium.

Rosa then stepped behind the podium. "Hello," she said, stretching herself toward the microphone. The crowd applauded. "My name is Rosa Emanuel." She smiled while glancing at Sasha and Colin standing behind her.

Another person stood up in the audience. "Excuse me, Miss Emanuel, how could a young woman like youself live in such an unruly environment like that and with two men?"

Rosa smiled. "I felt very protected by these two gentlemen. As far as the unruly environment is concerned, I personally wouldn't time travel again." The audience stood up with an uproar of applause.

Colin's dean's representative re-entered the stage and encouraged a round of applause for the three time travellers. "Our university's institution has three genius time travellers who have accomplished something no man or woman has ever done before." The audience roared. "These three time travellers look great without a scratch. They accomplished the impossible. This will change Natural History as well as the laws of physics forever. Colin Limmerick, it is an honour to have you as our own student in the Ph.D. programme in Natural History here at the London University. You are a fascinating man." The audience continued to stand with applause. "And also, I think it is in order to present Dr. Dimitrikov with an Honourary award for his genius in discovering the route to time travel," the elderly scholar announced to the roaring crowd as he handed Sasha the award.

Colin stared at the audience, who continued to applaud him. He was almost in disbelief that all those people were gathered in the large conference hall to see him. The three time travellers walked off the stage while the applause continued.

The festivities commenced as the orchastra began Handel's *Hornpipe*. The crowd thickened. Reporters and faculty tried to get a word with the three time travellers. Amoli kept her eyes fixed on Colin, not letting him out of her sight.

At one point Colin got lost in the crowd while he helped himself to some food and whiskey. Professor Cushing approached from behind him. "Nice performance, Colin Limmerick. You are quite the showman. Academia is not a sideshow, you know -- it is serious and requires great thinkers! Great scholars!"

Colin was feeling tipsy from his whiskey consumption so he ignored his professor.

"I think you aren't starving enough to be a graduate student of mine. You really don't feel it in your blood, do you? You're too damn busy with that damn boat of yours trying to make as much sterling as possible! Your priority should be your research and only your research!" Dr. Cushing lectured.

Colin leaned against the wall, appearing more interested in his spirit.

"If you were a serious researcher you would quit that fishing trade of yours and live in poverty like the rest of us!"

Colin chuckled and almost gagged on his drink.

"My God, you're as dumb as you look...yes, poverty.

I started in a middle-class home before I reached this tenured professorship!"

"May the cat eat ye, 'n may the cat bes be eaten by the devil," Colin grunted with a snarl.

"I beg your pardon?"

"Go feck yerself," Colin responded in a deep whisper.

"What did you say?"

"Nothin'. I said nothin' that would interest ye."

"Colin, I've been telling you for a long time now that you are not graduate school material -- especially doctorate material!"

"Go n-ithe an cat thú is go n-ithe an diabhal an cat."

"Excuse me?"

"Ah, there I go slippin' into me brogue, sar. Sorry, I am."

"I'm doing you a favour by giving you the opportunity to be my teaching assistant! You should be thanking me for this!"

"Teachin' assistant is a bullshit term, that is! I should be called teachin' slave, rather!"

"Where do you get off waltzing in this academic institution looking like a thug-pirate demanding special privileges?"

Colin struggled to stand straight without tripping. He stepped closer to his professor and guzzled his drink. He let out a loud, cracking chuckle.

"This is what I mean Colin -- you tend to be very savage about how you go about things. I think you should return to the high seas where you belong! You look much better with a harpoon in your hand than a book, anyway. You're, you're unprofessional!" Dr. Cushing said, pointing at Colin as if he were a naughty child.

"Yer after callin' me unprofessional? Look who's callin' the kettle black! I'm unfortunately stuck with ye. It's a sad situation, Professor Cushing, so it is."

"I think you and I are stuck with each other, Colin."

"I think ye just want to torture me, so ye do?"

194

"Colin, you're paranoid. The whole world is not out to get you."

Colin looked as if he was going to punch Professor Cushing. Sasha saw this and grabbed Colin's arm. "That is enough, Mr. Limmerick! Time to say goodnight to all nice people," Sasha said, pulling Colin away from his professor.

Amoli stood in the crowd watching Colin exchange dueling words with Professor Cushing. She approached Colin while Sasha tried to calm him. Professor Cushing was no longer in sight.

"Excuse me, why do you look so upset?" Amoli asked Colin.

Colin didn't hear Amoli; he leaned against the wall in the corner of the room still trying to collect himself. Sasha walked away a few feet and lit a cigarette.

"Um, do I call you professor, or mister, or Colin?" Amoli asked.

Colin heard Amoli's tiny voice as he looked around and saw her four-foot-ten structure standing in front of him. He peered down at her. "If I'm yer teacher in autumn, lass, ye can call me Instructor Limmerick. I'm not a professor just yet."

"Why are you so very upset, sir?" she asked.

His eyes scanned her voluptuous shape.

"Are you fine, sir?" she asked.

"I suppose now that yer here. I'm just fine now."

She rubbed her fingers over his black satin vest; he was a bit surprised she took the liberty.

"Do I really have to call you instructor?"

"If I'm yer teacher so ye do," he said as he gently placed her hands at her sides. "Ye are a tiny, wee thing aren't ye?" he said noticing the top of her head barely reached his waist.

She fluttered her long black eye lashes at him along with her enchanting smile. "Instructor Limmerick, can I ask you a question?" she said as she bashfully buried her tiny face in his jacket.

He felt a bit awkward about her gestures "Do ye always do this when ye first meet a bloke?" he asked.

"No, no, I don't, sir," she answered in a tiny whisper.

He smiled as he tried to back away from her. "What's yer question, lass?"

"Sir, when is your birthday?"

He chuckled. "Birthday? Why ye ask?"

"I may want to surprise you on that day."

"Ye just met me -- me birthday shouldn't be special to ye."

"Please, sir, it would be very nice if you informed me to when it is. I hope it already hasn't past."

"February one -- it is," he said.

"Oh, how very nice it is that you have a birthday approaching!"

"Not really."

"Birthdays are days of very much celebration! Hmm, let's see, what else can I ask you tonight?"

"What's to know, lass?"

"I am so very intrigued by you, sir. I would like to know everything."

He grabbed her hand, leading her outside onto the campus grounds. He brought her behind a brick wall as he held her close to him. "All right then, what ye want to know?"

"Where do you live?"

"Just down the road in the House Place flats, number 19."

"Can I visit you there sometime?"

"Lass, what are ye tryin' to do to me?"

"You are a very clever man who will some day prove his own theories through his own discoveries," she said as she fiddled with the buttons on his vest.

Colin straightened his posture. "Oh, really?"

She held tightly onto him, immersing herself in his long jacket. "Yes, really, sir."

"How -- how, profound of ye to say, lass."

"Thank you, sir," she said with a girlish giggle.

"Provin' me own theories through me own discoveries, ye say?"

"Yes, sir," she answered.

"Ye know it's funny ye should even mention that, lass. I've got pages 'n pages of notes based on me own ideas."

"Really, sir?"

"Do ye know what else?"

"What else, sir?"

"Extinction is a part of who we is. Did ye know that, lass?"

"Oh."

"Someday the human race could be no more -- 'cause ye know why, lass?"

"Why, sir?"

"'Cause we is a bunch of bothersome bastards, we is. We's after destroyin' ourselves, so we is," he continued in his intoxicated slur.

"Oh, sir, that's not a very romantic thought."

"Romantic thought, ye sayin'?" Colin tried to hold himself up while taking a deep breath.

"Yes, I thought you brought me out here so you could be romantic with me."

"What are ye doin', lass?"

She fondled his clothes. He gently took her hands, pulling them off of him. "What are ye doin', lass?" he said, feeling nervous as he realised he had consumed too much alcohol.

"Don't you like me, sir?"

"Oh mother of God, help me with the female species. I keep feckin' up!" he said looking at the sky.

"What are you talking about, Instructor?"

"Nothin', nothin', I've had a bad year, is all. Look, Amoli, it looks like the guests are startin' to leave. I really should find yer father 'n take ye to 'em."

Amoli took Colin's hand. "We don't need to find my

father right now. He's chatting with some old professors. It would be very boring for me. I'd much rather spend some time out here in the moonlight with you."

"Ye would, eh?" He smiled at her. "Look, lass, I really need to get home, I do, 'n ye need to be with yer father."

"Do you not like me touching you, sir?"

"Huh?"

He bent over toward her as he scanned her curved body. He noticed her full hips and fleshy buttocks. He tried to pull his hand away from her. "Amoli, the truth of the matter is, I drank too much tonight 'n I really need to get home."

"I am so very sorry you aren't well."

"I feel like I'm goin' to turn into a monster or somethin'. I haven't been holdin' me booze well lately," he said, making his way to the wall to lean against it.

"I'm sorry."

"Amoli, stupid is what I get when I'm pissed-up, plain stupid I get. I do things I end up regrettin', I do. I don't want to do anythin' I may regret tonight, understand me, lass?"

"Do you want to do something tonight? Maybe you could take me to your flat?"

As he gently tried to push her away, he awkwardly tripped on a rock. He fell on the well groomed lawn. The guests were leaving in their carriages and automobiles. Large crowds of people walked by not noticing Colin lying on the ground due to the darkness of the night.

Amoli rushed to Colin and crouched on the lawn against him. "Instructor Limmerick, are you alright?"

His hair hung over his face. "Amoli, ye can't be with me tonight -- ye have to leave me be. Can't ye see I've had too much to drink?"

"Then let me help you, Instructor!" Her tiny hands started to massage his back.

He abruptly sat up. "Leave me be, Amoli! Please, go find yer father. There are people everywhere. I can't be seen lying with ye in the dark." He tried to stand up but failed.

Rosa and Sasha strolled out of the building, and Rosa stopped suddenly in disbelief of what she saw. "Colin? What are you doing outside in public on campus grounds with her?" Rosa pointed. Colin jolted. He looked at Rosa in silence. Amoli held onto Colin's jacket.

"Colin? Answer me, please," Rosa demanded.

Sasha smiled. "Good for you, Mr. Limmerick -- enjoy yourself."

"Sasha, what are you saying?" Rosa shouted.

"We better leave Mr. Limmerick alone. It has been long night. Let us go, Rosa," Sasha pulled her away.

Colin tried to stand up, rejecting Amoli's help. "Feck! I've got to get ye to yer father or I'm goin' to get in some kind of shite tonight somehow someway." Colin finally fumbled his way to a standing position.

Amoli looked into his eyes. "For a man as nice as you, you use a lot of bad language."

"Amoli, can't ye see I'm not at me best just now!" He grabbed her hand, pulling her back into the university to find her father. He yanked her through the large foyer as the crowd strolled out of the building.

Finally, Dr. Sharma spotted Colin. "Ah, Colin, there you are! It is easy to spot you in a crowd. Did you and Amoli enjoy the fine sights of the campus?" he asked, standing next to Dr. Patel.

"Father, I had the best evening of my life!" she blurted with excitement.

Colin battled with his alcohol consumption as he tried to stand straight. "Sar, ;tis late now. Must be goin', I will." He gave a semi-bow as he shook Dr. Sharma and Dr. Patel's hands. Amoli extended her delicate hand to Colin, and he awkwardly bowed to her and sloppily tried to kiss her hand.

He left, slamming into other guests as he made his way outside and taking the back alleys to his residence apartment building.

Amoli and her father watched Colin depart from the gala. "Father, why is he walking with so much difficulty? Is he ill?" she asked.

"Ill? No, I do not think so. He is Western, you know. It is written we of the east will never ever understand men of the west. Please keep this in mind, my dear daughter."

On Monday morning Colin rushed to his students in the lecture hall. He was hoping, as he dashed with his *bolg*, that the class size wouldn't be over two hundred students. He walked into the lecture hall and noticed the room was completely full with first- and second-year students. He guessed there were about three hundred people sitting in front of him. Amoli sat in the front row with a female classmate. He loosened his tie, adjusting the lectern microphone to his height.

"Greetin's 'n welcome to the Natural History Foundation course. I can see we once again have a full house. For those of ye who don't know me, me name is Limmerick." He sighed with frustration. He noticed Amoli waving at him while he was trying to deliver his lecture to the class.

"In this course, we will be examinin' the theories of Dr. Charles Darwin, the grandfather, I feel, of evolutionary theory. In me mind, it's all fact not theory. However, ye don't have to believe what I'm sayin' to yez. God is not who I am. Keep in mind, all professors 'n instructors are biased in their own way." He paused to catch his breath. "Ye'ar a large group; therefore ye will be broken into smaller tutorials. I'm the lead instructor of this course, I am, so ye will also have other tutorial instructors. I will also be teachin' one tutorial. If Professor Cushing had his way, I'd be teachin' all six tutorial,s I would." The students broke into laughter. "By tomorrow ye will know who yer tutorial instructor is."

***

Colin lectured for two hours until his throat felt raw.

200

When the class ended, several students gathered around to inform him that they had attended the gala the previous Friday. Amoli stood behind the crowd wedging herself in.

When everyone else had left, Amoli stood beside Colin's lectern. "Good morning, Instructor Limmerick. You taught a very interesting class today." she clutched her books against her ample breasts.

Colin tried not to stare at her figure, bouncing his gaze around the room. "I'm glad ye enjoyed it." He began packing his things into his *bolg*. "Now, I should be in me advisor's office in thirty minutes, so I don't really have a lot of time, I don't."

"Is your advisor that old, ugly, pudgy man who gave you the award at the gala?"

"Aye."

"I'd like to meet him. When I think of it, you and him were at odds at the gala, weren't you?"

"I'm sorry ye had to see that, lass."

"I suppose it's none of my business to know why, sir?"

"I'm afraid it isn't the most interestin' information for ye."

"I want to know all about you, Instructor Limmerick," she said, standing closer to him.

Colin took a step back, feeling uncomfortable. "Look, lass, I'm after bein' upstairs to prepare for the blood-bath with me professor."

"Blood-bath?"

"I can't really explain now." He gestured that he really had to go, so she followed him.

Colin made it to his graduate office, which he shared with another graduate student whom he had never met. He sat at his desk shifting through the notes he made on his time travel expedition while Amoli watched.

"Instructor, when will you be finished seeing your advisor?"

Colin's expression was long and miserable. "I don't

know really. It could be hours, unfortunately."

"Would you like to come to my dorm for tea afterwards?"

"I have to study for me comprehensive examinations, prepare me lessons for our class, then I'll be goin' to the gym, 'n then maybe to the pub."

"You don't have any time?"

"I don't. I'm sorry."

"Instead of going to the pub would you like to see me instead?" She wrote her address on a piece of paper.

He sat still in his chair as he took a deep breath. "Lass, I must sound like a cad to ye. What man would choose a pub over havin' tea with a lovely, kind lass like ye?"

"Will you come for tea?"

"Aye, I will but don't forget I'm yer instructor."

***

Later, Colin showed up at Professor Cushing's office.

"Take a seat, Colin, take a seat," Professor Cushing said, drinking tea.

Colin insisted on standing. "Sar, I've got three hundred students this semester. Could ye get another graduate teachin' assistant to take half me load?"

"No. Colin, I want to know if you have any of your dissertation chapters to submit to me," he said, spilling tea on his shirt.

"I have chapters three 'n four, sar."

"You went a head of your requirements? I told you to work on chapter three only! How long are they?"

"Chapter three is approximately fifty pages, 'n chapter four is 'bout the same or a tad more." Colin pulled them out of his *bolg* and handed them to Professor Cushing.

"Obey, Colin! Obey, Colin! You must obey in order to pass this programme! You need discipline!"

Colin shook his head as he leaned against the doorframe. "Ye'ar a wee bit perturbed 'cause I did more work than what was asked? Blyme!" Colin chuckled with disgust.

"If I tell you to do ten chapters in one week, you better damn well do them! If I tell you to do one chapter in a year, you better damn well do it too! Do you understand, Colin Limmerick?"

Colin nodded. "Now that ye have chapter four in yer hands, are ye goin' to read it? Or do I need to take it back 'n wait for yer cue?"

"So cocky, Colin, you are so damn cocky sometimes. No, no, I'll just read it. But, don't let this happen again. You know this is the kind of thing Cambridge complains about! Students need obedience!"

"Me comprehensive examinations are comin' up, by the way."

"Yes, I know they are. You better start studying. I think I read that you will be writing in November. Are you nervous about it, Colin?"

"I never get nervous over exams," Colin said, staring at the floor with his arms folded in front of him. "I only give meself the jitters if me vessel hits an iceberg or some damn thin' like that..."

"Too much confidence, Colin Limmerick? You need to start studying now if you want to remain in this programme."

Colin smiled. "I know I'll pass them -- there's no need to worry, sar." Colin walked out of Professor Cushing's office.

That evening Colin completed his weight training ritual at the gym. He entered the change room and showered, making sure he smelled clean. He combed his long, wet hair and dressed in the suit he wore that day. He stood in front of the mirror looking tired but dapper. He said goodnight to the other men in the change room and then made his way to Amoli's university undergraduate residence.

As he entered the women's residence there were several first- and second-year women students ranging from ages eighteen to twenty-two gathered together and chatting as one student played the piano. Colin noticed there was a front desk where he asked if he could see Amoli Sharma.

Colin made his way up two flights of stairs to first-year residence. He came to a long hallway with several dorms. He looked for Amoli's dorm number and found her door at the end of the hallway. There were several female students passing him in the hallway as he made his way to Amoli's door. He knocked on the door. Amoli swung opened the door. "Instructor Limmerick! I'm so happy to see you!"

Colin leaned against the doorframe as he took off his hat to greet her. "Is it too late for me to come?"

"No, of course not, did you just finish up at the gym?"

"I did."

She grabbed his hand, pulling him into her confined dormitory room, which consisted of a single bed, desk, closet, and sink. "Come in, Instructor Limmerick. I hope you don't mind that my place is so tiny?"

"I must say, I feel like a very old man walkin' through this undergraduate residence," he said, loosening his tie.

He stood inside her room as she gestured for him to sit on the bed while she sat on her desk chair. "Is the only reason you are here is for tea?"

He chuckled. "I'm not here only for tea. Ye so kindly invited me. Quite rude, I've been. I wanted to make it up to ye."

He sat on her tiny single bed as he watched her dash out of the room to get the tea that she had already prepared. "Here it is -- tell me if it's not hot enough for you." Her palms were sweaty as her nerves took control of her. She was dressed in a traditional Indian sari. "Would you really have gone to the pub tonight?" she asked, pouring him a cup of tea.

"I go almost every night, lass," he said, taking a sip of tea.

"Why? What do you do there?"

"Get pissed outta me mind."

"I heard when western men get drunk, they do it because they have troubles. You don't have troubles, do you, Instructor Limmerick?"

"Aye, all men have troubles, lass."

"What's wrong? You do seem like something is bothering you?"

"Aye, lass, somethin' is botherin' me."

"What?"

"I don't want to bore ye with me messed-up life," he said finishing his tea.

She filled his cup again, still feeling nervous. Some of her housemates peeked in her room from time to time to catch a glimpse of him.

"I know our foundation course is very large. Is that what's bothering you?"

"Aye, that's part of it."

"I didn't like that woman you introduced me to at the gala. Is she important to you?"

"Rosa? She's a friend,"

"A girlfriend?"

"Former girlfriend."

"How former?"

He looked deeper at Amoli and laughed. "She's not important to me if ye must know."

"Good."

He removed his coat.

"I can pour you another cup. Can you wait right here, Instructor Limmerick?"

"Where'm I goin' to go?"

She rushed off. She approached the dorm stove located in the common area and sighed with frustration. She gathered a few pieces of wood and threw them in the bottom cavity as she slammed the trap door shut. Her two female housemates crowded her demanding details about her male guest. The water took some time to boil, which had Amoli feeling nervous about keeping Colin waiting.

"He's your teacher?" one housemate asked in disbelief.

"Yes! Yes! Yes! He's my teacher! Did you get a good look at him?"

"I want to see him up close. It's hard to tell what he looks like if you only have a second to look. For what I did see, he's quite tall."

The housemate looked at Amoli. "I don't even think men are allowed in this dorm. You could get in trouble."

Amoli poured the hot water into the teapot and rushed back to her room with her two dorm mates following behind her. "Instructor Limmerick, I have boiled more water," she said, dashing back into her room with her two dorm mates.

Colin had fallen asleep on Amoli's bed. He lay in his binding suit curled in a fetus position.

"Instructor Limmerick? You've fallen asleep!" Amoli gasped, trying to put the pot of tea down on the desk.

"Your teacher fell asleep on your bed, Amoli!" her dormmate said, standing in the doorway to Amoli's room.

"What do I do?" Amoli asked in a panicked state.

"He's your instructor?" the other roommate asked, peeking into the room.

"Yes, he teaches natural history," Amoli blurted frantically.

"I'm signing up to take natural history the first chance I get," the other roommate commented.

Amoli sat on her chair, staring at Colin while he slept. "Do you two think he looks troubled?"

"He's sleeping what else could you gather from this?" the other housemate commented.

"Shhhh! You're speaking too loud. Maybe we should let him sleep," Amoli suggested.

"Where are you going to sleep tonight, Amoli?" the roommate pried.

"I don't know. I promised him no fooling around. I guess I'll have to sleep on the floor."

"You're a fool, Amoli," the other housemate said. "I say either sleep with him or wake him up."

"I just don't know what to do," Amoli stared at him, noticing how uncomfortable he looked in his suit. She carefully tried to loosen his collar so he could breathe easier.

The roommate examined Colin. He was in a deep sleep letting out the occasional loud snore. "Is this the instructor who time travelled?" the housemate asked, pointing at him.

"Yes, now keep your voice down!"

"My, that's unheard of. How does one time travel? Did he ever talk to you about it?

"No, he doesn't tell me very much."

"Not a good sign, Amoli," the housemate said.

"Is he married?"

"No!"

"Does he have a special lady friend?" the other roommate asked.

Amoli nodded. "No, thank God. I met his former lady, though. I don't like her."

"You're not supposed to like the former woman, Amoli," the housemate said.

"I suppose not. I don't really know much about him. He's a good teacher. My classmates seem to really like him. And, he sounds Irish, I think. Maybe he's from Scotland…he could even be Welsh."

"So, we know his name, he travelled through time, he's a good teacher, he had a lady friend, he sounds Irish or something, and he's handsome. You're not doing well, Amoli. You have this man sleeping in your bed and you really don't know him. And, to make matters worse, he's your teacher," the other housemate said.

Colin's eyes flickered and slowly opened. He glanced at Amoli and her two friends. His eyes kept closing on him from exhaustion. He turned his head as his eyes slowly opened.

"Instructor Limmerick, I'm sorry we woke you," Amoli blurted.

"Is it that I'm dreamin'?" he asked.

"Instructor Limmerick, you're in my room at my university residence," Amoli answered.

Colin sprung from her bed. "Shite!"

"Professor Limmerick, you must be very tired -- you fell asleep on my bed," Amoli said awkwardly.

"Got to go I must!" he said looking for his jacket.

"Sir, you don't have to go now do you?" Amoli pleaded.

"I do."

"Would you like another cup of tea, Instructor Limmerick?" Amoli asked.

"Another cup of tea, ye ask? I'm afraid I can't," he said as he made his way to the door.

Amoli followed him down the stairs of her residence building.

She took his arm before he left. "No kiss goodnight?"

He smiled and kissed her hand.

Chapter Seventeen

It was a rainy morning. Rosa sat in the Natural History Department's teashop reading while sipping tea. Amoli entered and pulled up a chair beside her.

"Amoli? Hello," Rosa said.

"Hello. Instructor Limmerick mentioned to me that you used to be his lady, is this true?

Rosa's facial expression changed immediately. "Is this so important?"

"There's nothing else I have to say except I'm getting to know Instructor Limmerick quite well these days."

Rosa slammed her teacup on its saucer. "What are you getting at, little girl?"

"Nothing."

"Nothing? You come sit here and spew some rubbish about you knowing your instructor really well? I don't even know you, go play with your dolls!"

"I was with him last night," Amoli said in an instigating tone.

Rosa's eyes widened. "Excuse me? Where?"

"He was in my bed!"

"Instructor Limmerick was in your bed?"

"Yes, he was, you can even ask him!"

"I will do just that!"

"He's not your gentleman anymore. I think you need to understand this. Besides, I even saw it!"

"Saw what?"

"I saw it! You know what I saw!"

"Oh my God! No! You didn't!" Rosa said shrilly.

"I saw it, and it's colossal!"

"What do you know about the male anatomy?"

"What do I know? I know that I saw the instructor where it counts!"

"You little bitch! You should listen to yourself. Some

good little Hindu girl you are! Wait till your father finds out." Rosa paused. "I don't believe Colin would have shown you anything."

"Instructor Limmerick showed me a lot last night!"

"You have no right to talk about him this way -- besides this man is your teacher, don't forget!" Rosa shouted.

"You have no right to even think of him anymore." Amoli stood up from the table. "Well, I have to get to Instructor Limmerick's class. I don't want to be late." Amoli exited the teashop.

**

It was late in the evening when Rosa poked her head into Colin's flat. "Colin?" She said. "Are you decent?" she asked with reluctance.

Colin was at the typewriter working on chapter five of his dissertation. "Rosa, come in. Sasha isn't with ye, nay?"

"I don't really know where Sasha is. He's probably playing with his physics formulas -- what else does he do? Him and that stupid time vortex!"

Colin continued to work away at the typewriter, ignoring Rosa's comment. She moved closer to him. "Colin, I have to ask you a question."

"Aye?"

"Are you interested in Dr. Sharma's daughter?"

"Huh?" Colin stopped typing. "What prompted that question?" he asked.

"Colin, listen to what I'm saying to you! Do you find her attractive?"

"Amoli?" Colin remained sitting in front of the typewriter. "I see where this is leadin'. Of course I find her attractive."

"Colin, she's too young for you. She's just a child!"

"And suddenly yer me mother? Rosa, is this what ye came here to tell me tonight?"

"Colin, she's not even white, and she's not even

Catholic, doesn't that bother you?"

"She's female, and that's good enough for me."

Rosa's voice spewed with desperation. "Colin, I need to know what's going on in your head these days."

"Why?"

"You and I have a history together. I've always been there for you, and I need to know if you're exposing your *you-know-what* to young girls."

"What?"

Rosa rubbed Colin's shoulders while he sat in front of his typewriter. "Colin, Amoli approached me today like a crazed little girl giving all this information about you exposing your, um, your manliness to her."

Colin stood up abruptly and began to pace the room. "Rosa, what ye tellin' me? Number one, it sounds to me that ye 'n Amoli had a scuffle. Number two, Sasha is yer man -- ye should be tellin' him this rubbish. I will not answer yer silly questions. I will not."

Rosa felt embarrassed. She held her head down trying to hide her tears. "You're so distant from me now Colin -- you never used to be."

Colin walked to his stash of ale. He opened a bottle with his teeth and drank it in one breath. "Distant? Ye should be hearin' yerself, Rosa. I think I'm goin' to get stinkin' drunk tonight."

"Can you just stay sober for a minute?"

He stepped closer to her. "Ye don't want me anymore, remember?"

"Colin, remember how we used to be?"

"Go to Sasha! Why are ye even here?"

"I need to know what you did with Amoli last night."

"Why?"

"Colin, no woman knows you like I do. Amoli doesn't know you at all! Look at you -- you can't handle anything without me to guide you!"

"I will do as I wish without yer consent!"

"Colin, this is the first time you ever raised your voice

211

at me!"

"Ye need to leave now."

"Colin, there was a time you would have never asked me to leave. What has happened to you?"

Colin slumped on the loveseat in the middle of the room. "What the feck are ye sayin, garl? Yer man is Sasha! Ye made that decision loud 'n clear!" he said as he swished ale from one side of his mouth to the other.

Rosa nestled beside him on the loveseat. "I know I did, and I do love Sasha."

He stood up, pulling away from her. "Then go! Stop tryin' to feck with me head! Leave little Amoli out of this!"

"Colin, it's the booze talking, not you! Tell me what you did with her last night?"

"Yer not serious?"

"I have to know!"

"Ye need to leave."

"Please don't drink anymore tonight. Just tell me so you can put my mind at ease," she pleaded.

"I just started drinkin'. I'll tell ye when it's the booze!" he shouted as he made his way to the door, gesturing for her to leave.

"Colin, I'm sorry. I'll go because you want me to," Rosa said, storming out of his apartment.

"Feckin' right I wan't ye to..."

***

The following morning, Colin was in a meeting with Dr. Sharma. He went over his samples of the foliage he'd brought back from his prehistoric time travel.

"Well, Colin, I think we have gone over quite enough for today. I thank you for this very interesting research," Dr. Sharma, said packing up his notes. "By the way, Colin, changing the subject, are you aware of my daughter's feelings for you?"

"Feelin's, sar?"

"Well, she has had many suitors in India, but none of

212

them have been successful candidates."

"Candidates, sar?"

"Her very nice dowry is looking the way it should when a young woman is ready to marry."

Colin's eyes widened. "Dowry? Dear God! What are you sayin', Dr. Sharma?"

"Well, this isn't easy to explain to a western man like yourself, but my daughter has come to me so I can ask you if you would have her hand in marriage?"

"What?"

"I know this is rather sudden, but she is nineteen, which is rather old to marry. Our family would welcome an Irishman into our home, because England's imperials have created an Anglicized India that we cannot change."

"You want me to marry yer daughter 'cause England's imperializin' India? Absurd this is!"

"Colin, my son, don't you see, I would like western grandchildren very much, especially grandsons. Oh yes, indeed, please try for grandsons."

"Sar, this isn't right at all! If it's the English ye fear with their Imperialist attacks on yer country, can't do anythin' 'bout that. I'm sorry. I'm not an Englishman, sar."

"Colin, but you are white and my daughter is brown. It is so much easier to live as a white man in this day and age. Besides, my daughter tells me that she wants to be your wife very much."

"Sar, please!"

"She loves you, you know."

"I barely know yer daughter, Dr. Sharma."

"Don't you think she is beautiful?"

"She is."

"Then it is settled."

"Nothin' is settled!"

"You will take her dowry very much."

"Dowry?" Colin pulled his watch out of his pocket. "Look, I have a defense committee meetin' in a few

213

minutes. Sar, please don't mention this dowry to me again. I really must be goin'."

"You are a busy man, Colin, we will speak of Amoli again."

***

Colin showed up at the dean's representative's office out of breath. Two elderly professors sat next to Professor Cushing dressed in dark suits, sipping on tea while munching on biscuits.

The dean's representative stood up and shook Colin's hand. The professor of natural history who was Colin's second reader also stood as he nodded hello. "Welcome Colin, Colin the Darwinist! Please sit down and help yourself to tea and biscuits if you like," the dean's representative offered as Colin tried not to focus on Professor Cushing, who made no attempt to greet him.

Colin's second reader for his dissertation smiled. "Colin, I've read your proposal several times, and it is absolutely fascinating. You are a brilliant man," he said.

Suddenly the door swung opened; the two elderly gentlemen grinned as they welcomed their guest to the meeting.

Colin's second reader smiled as he looked at Colin. "I hope you don't mind that I invited Dr. Dimitrikov to our meeting."

"Mr. Limmerick, so we meet again," Sasha said while finding himself a chair.

Colin stood up to shake Sasha's hand, "Sasha! Pleasant surprise it is. Gentlemen, it's interestin' Dr. Dimitrikov has been invited to me defense committee meetin'."

The dean's representative sat back on his chair at his desk as he began to twiddle his thumbs. "It's time vortexes, Colin, time vortexes, and all sorts. What's gone on here is a groundbreaking scientific discovery."

"Da, discovery of time vortex changes science forever," Sasha said as he leaned forward toward Colin.

214

"Even for you, Mr. Limmerick, this changes dissertation. Your fuzzy elk is not only celebrity, but now we can visit him whenever we like."

Colin sighed with a chuckle. "*Megaloceros*, I find, is far from a celebrity, Dr. Dimitrikov. Gentlemen, please I just wanted to prove me point that Dr. Darwin's research stands as pure fact, is all," Colin said.

"Colin, you must include a few chapters on Dr. Dimitrikov's time travel discovery -- how can you not?"

Colin rose from his chair. "Sar, I find no difficulty in that, but I will also do me best not to sensationalize the method in which I made me prehistoric journey."

The two elderly scholars looked at each other as they began to laugh.

"Colin, you are the real thing aren't you? You remind me of the type of character that I used to read about in adventure novels when I was a child," the second reader said as he snorted with laughing tears.

"Pardon me, sar, I don't quite understand," Colin said as he watched the two scholars laugh in hysterics.

Sasha stood next to Colin. "Mr. Limmerick, they think you look and act like pirate, da?"

Colin folded his arms in front of him. "Well, feck that if that's the bleedin' case. Gentleman, am I bein' laughed at?"

"No, no, no, Colin, we think you're the best Ph.D. student this university has yet to have. You're a brilliant. Please, sit down and lets discuss this a bit. Please don't go displaying that hot-blooded Irish temper," the dean's representative said with a grin.

The second reader interjected. "Colin, what we were discussing before you came in is that you need to include a few chapters on Dr. Dimitrikov's time vortex method. Colin, it would make your dissertation incredible -- it would make this department of natural history almost legendary. Colin, you have proven two very vital scientific discoveries: one, Dr. Darwin was correct in his theory of

215

natural selection, and two, time vortexes exist, which will be part of your methodology."

Sasha looked at Colin as he pulled a pack of cigarettes from his jacket. "Mr. Limmerick, does this information suit you?"

Colin cordially smiled. "It does."

Dr. Cushing leered at Colin. "This is rubbish," he said spilling tea on the desk.

The natural history professor looked at Dr. Cushing with a smile. "Randolph, what seems to be the problem?"

Professor Cushing kept staring at the floor. "I'd like to know what Colin will do when he finishes his Ph.D."

"Oh, yes, Colin, that is a prime question. What are your plans?" The dean's representative asked.

"Plans? Well, I'm hardly the age of many of the Ph.D students in this faculty. I've been runnin' me own fishin' vessel for some years now -- 'n I don't expect to be leavin' it any time soon. However, me dream has always been to explore me own theories 'n such."

"So, do you plan on continuing your life as a fisherman? Perhaps you would be more in your element," Professor Cushing asked rudely. "I think anything that deals with academic research would probably be out of the question -- don't you quite agree?"

"I'd like to see if University College in Dublin may need me, or I may apply at one of the other universities here in London," Colin commented.

"Colin, why bother? If you do obtain your Ph.D., what are you really going to do with it? I mean, you are *working class Irish* -- don't you have financial responsibilities to your clan or some damn thing like that?" Professor Cushing asked with a sneer.

Colin leered at Professor Cushing. "Aye, sar, me clan's expectin' me to provide for them -- this has been goin' on since the end of the twelfth century," Colin responded.

The room grew silent. "Ah, gentlemen, um -- tell me,

Colin, will you time travel again?" asked Colin's second reader.

"I will."

Sasha looked at Colin in shock. "You will?"

Colin sat back in his chair. "Aye, we -- meanin' ye 'n me -- will surely time travel again, Dr. Dimitrikov," Colin said sternly.

"Will you return to your *Megaloceros'* time?" the dean's representative asked.

"Aye, I may," answered Colin.

The two professors were in awe with Colin while Professor Cushing shook his head with disgust. "Gentlemen, please, this is not a circus side show. Most of us are scholars in this room. I think Colin is a bit of a thrill-seeker, don't you think?"

"On the contrary, Randolph, I find Colin to be the bravest man that I've ever met," the natural history scholar commented.

"Oh, yes, Colin has no problem risking his life in a time-travelling time vortex in search of scientific answers. This is all so fascinating," the dean's representative added.

Sasha rose from his chair. "Wait, gentlemen, please. Mr. Limmerick cannot go on such expeditions without me accompanying him, da?"

"Dr. Dimitrikov, me good friend, Sasha, we's goin' to time travel again, we will, don't ye think?" Colin asked as he forced a few biscuits in his mouth at the same time.

"Dr. Dimitrikov, how can you not venture through that magnificent time vortex again? You and Colin need to do this again -- I think it's your calling," the dean's representative said.

"So, Colin, if you ever decide to time-travel again, will that be your new profession?" Dr. Cushing asked.

Colin appeared engrossed in the several biscuits he was eating. "I will be researchin' me own theories, sar, 'n I will perhaps have a professorship somewhere," Colin answered.

"Colin, maybe you should be a ship-builder. If you weren't so robust a chimney sweep might be just perfect, if by any chance you tire of the fishing trade. Colin, I'm not sure if you should obtain a professorship in another university -- your workload would double, and all your thrill-seeking would have to come to a dead halt," Professor Cushing said.

Colin abruptly stood up. "Professor Cushing!" Colin called out as he clenched his fists, stopping himself from saying another word. He looked at the floor as he continued to stand.

"Yes, Colin, do you have something to say?" Professor Cushing asked.

Colin slowly sat down as he loosened his tie and tore it off from around his neck.

The dean's representative was shocked at Professor Cushing. "Randoph, please! To me, Colin has in a sense married his research. No other young researcher that we have encountered has ever reached his level of competence. He performs experiments that are life threatening. Neither you nor I could ever accomplish what he has. I know you dislike his Darwinist beliefs, so what? Lamarck is old research," the Dean's representative said.

Professor Cushing waved his finger as he stood up in front of the men in the room. "Darwinists are not welcome in the academic world! Darwinists do not belong in the Social Sciences, especially *working class* Darwinists who know nothing except how to draw in their catch! I will not pass Colin Limmerick's defense! He will fall flat on his face! He will fail! I've already read some of his dissertation chapters, and frankly they're unacceptable! I will not pass him, nor will I put my reputation as an academic on the line! No! Never!" Professor Cushing stood up and stormed out of the room.

Colin sat in his chair looking at the other two professors.

"Oh my, what's got into Randolph? He used to be

such a pleasant fellow," Colin's second reader said.

"What's going on with him?" asked the dean's representative.

Colin stood up with the intention of making his exit. " Well, I can tell ye for sure, gentlemen, he hates me bleedin' guts."

"But why? We've read some of your work -- it's absolutely impeccable," the Dean's representative said.

"He can't get past who I am," Colin said as he made his way to the door.

"Who you are?" the dean's representative wondered.

"Ye figure it out, sar. I really don't understand the man," Colin said.

Sasha stood up alongside of Colin. "Also, gentlemen, I no think Dr. Cushing likes Russian scientists either."

"Sasha, he doesn't bother with ye, is all. But, it's me he can't deal with," Colin said.

The two elderly gentlemen looked at each other in shock.

"What do I do 'bout Dr. Cushing? Is there a way I could change me academic advisor?" Colin asked as he clenched his top hat in his hands.

"Oh, Colin, I'm afraid that's impossible at this stage. I know you have requested this before, but Randolph has a reputation in this department. I'm very sorry. You're a nice enough chap, so I know you can work this out, hmm?" the dean's representative said.

Colin put on his hat and tried to be cordial as he and Sasha left the office.

***

It was late afternoon, and Colin was in his office grading papers for his foundation course. He was so tired he slowly dropped his head onto his desk and fell asleep. Amoli noticed his door ajar and stepped in.

"Instructor Limmerick?" she said in her delicate voice as she stood holding a crystal platter with a cake on it.

Colin lifted his head. "Amoli?"

219

"Instructor Limmerick, everytime I see you, you're asleep. Is something wrong with you? Do you have troubles?

He sat back in his chair. "Would ye like to sit down?"

"First, I'd like to give you this. I baked you a cake."

"Dead feckin' brill ye did," he whispered to himself.

"Pardon?"

"I'm just sayin' to meself that this cake is lovely." He pushed his long, hanging forelock from his face. "Ye baked this for me, ye did?"

"Yes, just for you. I hope you like chocolate," she said, feeling butterflies in her stomach.

"I do."

"Would you like a piece now? I brought a knife, plate and fork as well," she said with her nerves over-reacting.

"I would like a piece now, but yer goin' to have to share it with me. There's only one plate, lass."

She cut a piece almost a third of the cake's size. "I hope you like it," she said, handing it to him.

"I will, I'm sure." He put a forkful in his mouth as she watched him eat it with bated breath.

"Do you like it?" she asked.

"I do," he said with his mouth full of cake. "Ye need to help me eat this very large piece." He held a forkful of cake to her. She came around the desk getting very close to him as he placed the forkful into her mouth. He then took another forkful for himself. He held another forkful for her, but she then sat on his lap in order to get close enough. She took the fork from him and fed the cake to him while she sat on his lap.

Suddenly the door opened. It was Professor Cushing holding Colin's two chapters. "Colin Limmerick? Is this what you do in your spare time here in this academic institution?"

Colin tried to swallow down his last bit of cake. "Now the fun begins, lass," Colin whispered, shifting his eyebrows up and down.

220

Amoli jumped from Colin's lap. Colin sat back in his chair waiting for Professor Cushing to begin. "Just place me chapters here on me desk, sar."

"Who is this foreign girl? And what was she doing sitting on your lap?"

"Eatin' cake, sar. We was both eatin' cake."

"Eating cake?"

"Aye, eatin' cake. I know ye just marvel for dessert, sar. Ye really should try some -- it's quite lovely."

"You better be damn lucky she's not one of your students!"

Colin stood up, intimidating his professor with his size. "Don't ye worry, sar. I wouldn't be so stupid."

"By the way, Colin, the chapters..."

"They stink?" Colin replied sarcastically.

"Right-o!" answered Professor Cushing.

"Don't rush off, sar. I'm after givin' chapters six 'n seven to ye." Colin placed them in his professor's hands.

"I don't know why I waste my time reading this rubbish. Rubbish is all you seem to give me, Colin. All this animated jumble on Darwin. I'm telling you this is not even publishable."

Colin stood leaning against the wall with his arms folded in front of himself while Amoli sat on a chair trying to understand the dynamics of the professor-grad student relationship.

"All I can say, sar, is happy readin'!" Colin said.

Professor Cushing started to walk away. "By the way, Colin, I should have these chapters ready Friday morning, and I will expect you in my office to go over them."

"I can't, sar."

"What did I hear?"

"I'm busy Friday, all day, sar."

"Busy? With what?"

"Me crew needs me on me vessel. I've got to do me regular three-day weekend with them. We have to meet our quota of mackerel for the weekend. It's gettin' to be a

221

regular thing it is. Ye won't really find me 'round campus on a Friday much, sar."

"Priorities, Colin, priorities. You put your working class life ahead of your academic world. This is what seems to suit you best." Professor Cushing left Colin's office.

Amoli looked at Colin as he continued to lean against the wall. He remained silent while she stared at him.

"As ignorant as a bag of arses he is," Colin blurted.

"This man is your professor? He gave you the award at the gala?"

"An act, it was." Colin sat back at his desk staring at the half-eaten piece of cake.

"You said this Friday, Saturday, and Sunday you're working on your boat? Do you own your own boat, Instructor Limmerick?"

"I do."

"You must be rich!"

"I'm not."

"You're a Ph.D. student? And, an instructor?" she asked, feeling surprised.

"And a time traveller 'n fisherman," he added.

"That explains why you're falling asleep everywhere."

Colin smiled. "It does."

"Instructor Limmerick, could you take me on your boat this Friday? I'd really like to see it. I think it would be fun."

"Not this time, lass."

"I would really like to come this time."

He looked at the piles of papers he had to still grade. "Amoli, I'm just too busy to even think 'bout it. I have to make me fishin' quota by the weekend's end. I don't have time to attend to yer needs when yer on me ship. I'm sorry. Me ship is a trawler. It has a purpose to fish 'n sell to the markets. I have deadlines, lass. Try to understand," he said while rubbing his tired eyes.

"So, is it impossible for me to come some other time?"

"It is, lass."

"It's impossible?"

"Ye'd have to stay a few nights, 'n that's impossible, don't ye think?"

"Why is it impossible?"

"It just is, lass."

Her head hung low, showing disappointment in her face. "Sir?"

"Yes, lass."

"I want so badly to learn about you, and I feel your life on your boat is a big part of who you are which I know nothing about."

"Ye need not know 'bout me. It's not that important for ye."

"Oh, but it is important for me, sir."

He patted her on the head like a child. "I don't understand why," he said.

"Someday you will."

"Someday?"

"Sometimes boats are given names. Does your boat have a name?"

"It does."

"What's its name?"

"The *Atlantic Mermaid* she is."

"*Atlantic Mermaid*? That's a pretty name for a boat."

She stood up, feeling rejected by him. "Don't forget to finish your cake, Instructor Limmerick," she poignantly reminded him.

"Don't give me that face, lass."

She appeared as if she were going to cry. "I will leave you now. You are a very busy man. I just wanted to learn very much about you." Tears started to roll down her round cheeks.

He sat straight in his chair. "Amoli, why ye so sad?"

She turned away from him. "Nothing, sir, it's nothing."

"It's somethin'. Child, do ye want to tell me what's

223

botherin' ye?"

"Nothing is wrong, sir. I should be going anyway." She made her way to the door.

"Amoli, I thank ye for the cake, really I do."

"As much as I like you being my teacher, sometimes I wish you weren't," she said with a sniffle. "Sir, I very much wish you would not call me child."

"Forgive me, lass."

"Sir," she said, facing him. "Sir, don't you see me as a woman?"

"I do."

She slowly left his office. Colin slid his glasses onto his face and continued to grade papers.

***

The weekend was hectic on Colin's ship. He and his first mate worked day and night to draw in their fresh catch of mackerel. Late that Sunday night Colin and his crew brought their catch to Dublin, where the distributor waited for their arrival so he could get the fresh catch to the markets. It was after 10:00 p.m. when they made it to Dublin. Colin was paid handsomely for the completion of his assignment. He and the crew were tired. It was already November but the cool sea still felt warm to their over-worked bodies. They kept the boat docked at the Dublin Quays, as they headed to their favourite pub downtown. Lorelei and Bessy met them at the pub where Colin and his crew stood by the bar drinking as much ale as they could. Colin sat at the bar trying desperately to intoxicate himself. He kept his eye on the time knowing he had to be back in London to teach his class the next morning. He kept his distance from Lorelei.

***

The next morning Colin was feeling exhausted and slightly hung-over but he managed to get through his class lecture with success. He had his graded papers with him, which he distributed to the front of the lecture hall. His head throbbed as well as his eyes burned from sleep deprivation. His muscles felt sore every time he moved. He lectured for two hours, feeling a deep hoarseness in his throat from the ample tobacco that filled the pub the night before.

"When all of yez are into yer tutorial groups, yer instructors will be informin' ye of an upcomin' class excursion. In the next hour, ye all should be in yer tutorial groups, check yer schedules of what room yer suppose to meet in."

The students filtered out of the large lecture hall.

Amoli lagged behind as the students left. "Instructor Limmerick, I'm in your tutorial, so I'll wait here with you until it's time to go," she said.

He wanted so badly to undress her in his mind but was too exhausted to even try. "Amoli, I have a meetin' with the other tutorial instructors now, so ye can sit 'n wait here, no good it'll do ye,"

"Oh, I see, you are having a meeting. You're very busy all the time. But, then I I'll see you in room 234, it's upstairs at the far end of the building I think," she said feeling nervous.

"Amoli, not in me tutorial group yer not. Read me class list I did, yer name wasn't there as it wasn't," he said as he folded his arms standing in front of her.

"But, I am, sir. Have you looked at a recent role list of your tutorial class lately?"

"Can't say I have, lass."

"My name is on your tutorial group list, sir," she said moving closer to him.

"Lass, what ye doin'? Ye switchin' yer tutorials? What for?"

She looked away from him. "You can't figure it out, sir?"

He awkwardly nodded his head. "Gotta run I do. Can't really stay to chat. I'll see ye in room 234 in less than an hour," he briskly left the lecture hall leaving her with a smile on her face.

Colin made his way to his office, the tutorial instructors were waiting in the hall for him. "Where we meetin'? Colin asked them as he tore into his office to gather the course of study and course information.

"We are meeting in room 234, Colin," one of the male tutorial instructors answered.

"Convenient that is. Me tutorial is in that same room," Colin announced.

Five men in their late twenties and early thirties sat at the largest table in the room. Colin made his way sitting at the head of the table. "Gentlemen, just wanted to know if yer experiencin' any problems teachin' Darwin?" asked Colin.

They unanimously replied 'no'.

"Brilliant then, a field trip is in need at this point it is. Students must choose a mammal 'n research its evolutionary patterns. I think I'm goin' to take me tutorial group to County Wicklow in Ireland," Colin said. "I have typed out the on-site assignment for all of yez. You can choose wherever ye want. It doesn't have to be as far as Ireland," Colin said.

"Colin, Wicklow, Ireland, isn't that where you did your time travel?" one of the student instructors asked.

"It is."

"Won't it cost too much money to get forty students to Ireland?" another student instructor asked.

"Not if I take them in me sea vessel it won't," he said.

"You have your own boat?" the first student instructor asked.

"I do. I've run me own sea merchant trade with me own ship 'n crew for a good while now.

"Impressive," another student commented.

"Ye can take yer students wherever ye please as long as ye know the area 'n ye know they will have some success in studying a mammals' evolutionary patterns. Ye need to run it by me first if ye can," Colin suggested.

The four men discussed the course until the hour was

226

up. They wished Colin well as they left the room to meet with their own tutorial groups.

Colin sat at his desk as a group of fourty students entered the classroom seating themselves. Amoli shyly entered the room with another female student as they found seating near Colin's desk. They were the only two females in the tutorial.

"How was your meeting, Instructor Limmerick?" Amoli called out to Colin as he tried to get prepared for the tutorial.

He walked to her. "Lass, the meetin' went well," he said finding her appearance and girlish behavior quite refreshing.

"Class, I think it's time we do some field work by examinin' the chosen mammal of yer choice 'n track it's evolutionary patterns. Please try 'n choose a mammal whose habitat is in the British Isles, it makes life easier it does. Also, make sure it's a species, which does show significant evolutionary patterns, it may have had several predecessor links. In other words, don't do the horseshoe crab, I'm afraid ye won't get anywhere with it," Colin suggested. Some of the students who knew of Professor Cushing's research interests started to laugh. "I have an initial task for yez all to try. It's tracking evolutionary patterns of the species of yer choice by lookin' at already published data, if ye will." Colin handed out the task to his students. He pulled a trolley of books into the middle of the room expecting his class to find the data they needed. The students worked diligently on the assignment. Amoli felt somewhat overwhelmed with the scientific jargon but worked with her girlfriend the best way they knew how. Colin purposely strayed from helping Amoli hoping she could solve her own tasks.

***

When the large lecture class met again two days later Amoli approached Colin after the lecture. She felt reluctant approaching him where she felt he had been

227

behaving aloof.

"Instructor Limmerick, you gave me a C grade on my paper," she said, "Why?"

He rubbed his tired eyes as he stood at the lectern watching the large group of students exit the lecture hall. "Why, ye ask? That's what it deserved, lass."

"I thought I'd get better than this. I worked so very hard on it. I really wanted to please you."

"Please me? Please yerself, lass. Read through me corrections so ye can understand why ye got the grade ye did."

"I thought you liked me, sir," she said.

He stood straight flipping his long forelock back. "I do fancy ye, lass."

"A lot?"

"Yer a good student, lass."

"Just a good student?"

He sighed with frustration. "Yer grade is yer grade 'n ye can't really change that."

"Well, I'll try to improve next time, sir."

"Good."

"Sir, would you like to have tea with me?" she asked holding her graded paper in her sweaty hands.

"I can't. I've got a meetin' with yer father now."

Amoli hung her head down feeling sad. "I understand."

Colin sighed with exhaustion. "Lass, we can have tea later. I just can't right now.

He gathered his papers stuffing them into his *bolg*. "I've gotta run, lass." He tucked his leather bag under his arm and left, leaving Amoli standing by the lectern in the lecture hall.

Colin found Dr. Sharma standing outside his locked office door. "Colin, you are ten minutes late," Dr. Sharma said watching Colin fumble with his key to open his graduate office door.

"I was speakin' to yer daughter, sar," Colin said

228

swinging his door opened and pulling out a chair for Dr. Sharma.

Colin slumped on his desk chair out of breath. "Sar, ye mentioned last that ye wanted to see me photographs'n samples of me prehistoric journey?"

"Colin, my assumption is that some plant life from 7592 B.C. has not evolved too extensively. It can be related to your academic advisor's horseshoe crab. This species hasn't really evolved at all in five hundred million years. Isn't that something?"

"It is."

"My question, Colin is why? Why does some plant life rabidly evolve and other plant species do not?"

"Sar, ninety-five hundred years ago is not all that long ago when one looks at geologic time for drastic evolutionary changes to take place," Colin replied.

"Yes, you are very right."

Colin displayed his samples of prehistoric plant life from his time travel journey to Dr. Sharma.

Dr. Sharma examined the specimens. "You have changed science forever, do you realise this?"

Colin smiled. "Perhaps, sar."

Dr. Sharma touched what looked like a few blades of grass. "What is this, Colin?"

"Grass, I think, sar."

"Grass? It looks so -- so, unusual. It is so much more coarse than the grass we know today."

"All livin' things on our planet are constantly evolvin', sar -- even grass. Grass couldn've been destroyed easily, sar, by another plant species -- it was naturally selected, sar, to withstand all interferences from other plant life as well as other life, -- therefore, it prevailed to survive."

Dr. Sharma looked at Colin with a smile. "But, grass has changed in just ten thousand years, which contradicts what you just said."

"Not all livin' organisms evolve at the same rate, sar. A lot depends on whether it is naturally selected -- where

229

some stop evolvin' 'n die off just like *Megaloceros*, who could no longer cope with the environment due to be sexually selected by the females 'n therefore ceased to exist."

"What I do not understand, Colin, is why are you in so much constant struggle to prove Dr. Darwin's theory of natural selection? This makes so much sense for my own research as a botanist. What is the problem?"

Colin took a deep breath. "Sar, if I knew the answer to that question, our academic world would be a different place I'm sure it would."

"If only you would give my beautiful daughter the time of day. Colin, I like you so very much. I would like to have you be part of my family. Please stop pushing my Amolia away," Dr. Sharma said.

"I'm her teacher, sar. I have to be professional 'bout this. Besides, I don't think she and I would be right for each other."

"Why do you say this?"

"Sar, please, try to understand, she's a wonderful lass, but there is an age gap."

"I am fifteen years older than my wife. Is age the problem?"

"Sar, not just age, I'm not who ye think I am."

"What do you mean by this? Is it because we are from India?"

"Sar, I'm not part of the English elite. I don't come from some of the finer stock the other English men come from at this university."

"Nonsense."

Colin stood up. "Sar, look at me, do I look like I'm from the right stock to ye?"

"Colin, you always look so very presentable to me."

"Sar, don't let me tailor-made suits deceive ye!"

"Colin, I can look very much past anyone's façade. I think with you, the only façade you wear is your suit."

Colin sat down. "Sar, yer too kind, but I'm not what

230

ye think."

"I see you as a very much brilliant scholar with very nice manners."

Colin looked away from Dr. Sharma. "Thank-ye, sar."

"Tell me, Colin, you aren't in the process of wooing another lady are you?"

"I'm not."

"Then why do you speak like this to me?"

Colin sat back in his chair. "Maybe I've been a single man too long. It's too late for me to marry, sar."

"Too late? No, no, please think about her dowry."

Colin focused on a filing cabinet instead.

"Please Colin, when the course ends, which is the end of December, please consider courting my lovely daughter," Dr. Sharma said. "You're comprehensive examinations are near are they not?"

"They are."

"You're a busy man, aren't you, Colin?"

"I am, sar. Sleep doesn't happen enough far me."

"Well, I wish you the best of luck with your examinations. Please keep in mind Amoli loves you very much."

"I can't understand this, she knows nothin' of me, sar."

"Have you ever heard of love at first sight?" Dr. Sharma asked.

"Aye."

***

That evening, Colin sat alone in the pub drinking until he could no longer see straight. Sasha joined him. "Mr. Limmerick, what you doing here getting so drunk?"

"I have another problem I do."

"So many problems, Mr. Limmerick, what now?"

"Dr. Sharma is trying to get me married off to his daughter, Amoli."

"Well, I must be honest with you, if you did get married to Miss Amoli, it would be better for me and

Rosa."

"Come again?"

"I think Rosa is confused about both of us. She likes having me around but she still loves you."

Colin started to laugh. "A bitch she is."

"I think Rosa is confused girl. Us men are used to having many women all the time. Rosa thinks she can do same. She is not man."

Colin finished his whiskey and ordered another. "She broke me heart she did. Ye feckin' bastard I should'ev busted yer legs when the time was right."

Sasha took a deep breath. "Mr. Limmerick, tell me how is relationship with Miss Amoli?"

"A student-teacher relationship we have. She's me student 'n I her teacher, nothin' more."

"You must try to make it more, Mr. Limmerick."

"I can't."

"You must!"

"She's beggin' to come aboard me ship."

"So do it!"

"I can't."

"Why not?"

"I may have to feck'er if she's aboard me ship that's why not," Colin answered with a drunken slur.

"So, do it and enjoy!"

"I first must finish teachin' the course for this term. I can't feck'er if she's me student."

"This is true, Mr. Limmerick, but course ends before Christmas holidays, da?"

"It does."

"This is soon, you can do it then."

"I'll take her on me vessel after the students receive their grades."

"Will you marry her?"

"I barely know the lass."

"You must have sex with her first then you will know?"

232

"Maybe."

"She has nice body, Mr.Limmerick."

"She does."

"You will like her when you give it to her."

"I like her now."

"Give her ring."

"When do ye plan on givin' Rosa a ring?" Colin asked.

"In time."

"I should've busted yer legs when the feckin' time was right."

Sasha tried to laugh it off. "Mr. Limmerick, think of Miss Amoli. She is so young and pretty."

"I think of her all the time."

"Give her ring!"

"Feck off, mate!" Colin drank up and left money on the bar counter. Sasha was left in the tavern.

Chapter Eighteen

It was the first week of November Colin had been preparing for his comprehensive examinations where he finally felt ready to write. He entered a medium sized lecture hall with a few other Ph.D. students who were also writing. The room was dead quiet as Colin walked up the aisle stairs to find a seat. He scanned the room noticing how nervous the other students appeared. He wondered why he wasn't that nervous as he climbed the stairs.

Each exam was presented as a package that was personally addressed to each Ph.D. student. The examining committee paced around the lecture hall for the duration of the four hours.

When time was up, the students were dismissed until the next day. Colin made his way out of the lecture hall noticing how serious the students looked as they left for the day. Amoli stood outside the door.

Colin approached her. "Howya, waitin' for me are ye?"

"Hello Instructor Limmerick," she said with a bashful smile. "How do you know that I am waiting for you? Maybe I am waiting for someone else."

He laughed. "And, so ye may."

"Did you just write your exams?"

"Got another in the morin' I do."

"Was it difficult?"

"Some parts was."

"I have really missed you, sir."

"Ye have?"

"Would you like to come to my dorm for a very nice dinner tonight?"

Colin looked at Amoli with a surprised expression. "A forward wee thing ye is aren't ye?"

"Please."

"How kind of ye, but I must get to me residence 'n study for tomorrow."

"You're not supposed to eat when you write exams?"

He paused for a few seconds. "I am," he said talking into his chest.

"Please, I would like very much to cook for you tonight."

"That's just not possible."

"Why?"

"I'm sorry," he said as he started to back away. "'Till next time…"

She stood in the hallway outside the lecture hall as she watched him walk away.

***

It was a Monday morning Colin lectured the large group with the other tutorial leaders sitting behind him. "The last week of November we will be doin' our excursions with our tutorial groups, just to keep yez updated," the students were in an uproar of discussion amongst each other.

When the class was dismissed after its regular two-hour duration the students cluttered around Colin where he stood by the lectern. Amoli stood behind the crowd clutching her books where he noticed her. The students slowly left the lecture hall leaving him alone with Amoli.

"Hello, sir," she said in her tiny voice.

He smiled, "Hello, Amoli."

"I can't wait for the excursion. Even though it's getting cooler outside will we be camping?"

"We will," he responded with a smile.

"It's going to be fun won't it?"

"It will," he patted her on top of her head and they left the lecture hall.

Chapter Nineteen

That evening Colin sat in the Piccadilly Pub with Sasha ready to indulge in his regular intake of whiskey.

"So, Mr. Limmerick soon you will be on class excursion back to terrible place we find time vortex some months ago, you will enjoy, da?" Sasha asked.

"Hope to," Colin said as he drank his first shot of whiskey for the evening.

Sasha pulled out a cigarette and lit it. "Rosa asks about you all time. What I do?"

"Don't steal other bloke's women, ye bleedin' shite--head!" Colin said partially with a sneer.

Sasha smoked his cigarette. "You have Miss Amoli now don't you, Mr. Limmerick?"

"She's me student 'is all!"

"When course ends -- she will be for you, da?"

"Maybe."

"I may have professorship at London University..." Sasha said trying to change the subject.

Colin sat straight in his chair. "Wonderful that is, Sasha!"

"You happy for me?"

"Ye deserve it, mate! Tell me 'bout it!"

"They say me I only be considered for physics professorship if I involved with London University. They say me they want me have interest in London school maybe because I am foreigner? What they want?"

"Get involved? How do ye mean? Guidelines perhaps have been given to ye?"

"Read letter they give me," Sasha said handing the letter to Colin.

Attention Dr. S. Dimitrikov,

The Department of Physics has gone over your credentials and would like to thank-you for expressing your interest in applying for the professorship post in our department. We are pleased to say we are impressed with your portfolio but encourage you to involve yourself with any internal or external events that go on at our university involving any of the following sciences: Natural Science, Chemistry, Physics, Biology, Geography, Natural History, and Behavioral Science.

We look forward to hearing from you,

Yours truly,
Dr. A. R. Thompson,
B.S.C./M.S.C./PhD. Physics

"Promisin' letter this is, mate," Colin said handing it back to him.

"What does involvement in university mean?"

Colin poured himself another shot. "Well, would ye like to come with me on me class excursion to Wicklow?" Colin asked with a smile. "That would be university involvement it would."

"Back to your Wicklow?" Sasha replied.

"I could use yer help, mate," Colin said while gesturing the barmaid to bring more drinks.

The barmaid brought Colin another bottle where Colin paid her with a generous tip.

"I am not built like you, Mr. Limmerick. I don't want," Sasha repeated.

"Come along, mate. The fresh air will do ye some good so it will," Colin encouraged him. "I'm not after time travellin', a class excursion 'is all."

"Does Rosa come too?"

"Why?"

"Miss Amoli comes?"

"She will. She's me student don't forget, she has to come along, " Colin said watching Sasha's body language.

Sasha continued to puff smoke rings into the air. "Maybe I will come then."

"Ye touch Amoli, I kill ye," Colin said looking menacing.

"I will go on trip for you and just for you," Sasha said putting his cigarette out on a glass ashtray.

"And for ye, mate."

***

It was the last Monday in October 1908 Colin stood at the Fishguard docks in Wales dressed in a lumberjack jacket, a tartan scarf wrapped around his neck, heavy boots, and a tweed cap on his head with his bushy reddish sideburns sprouting out. The Atlantic Mermaid had docked in front of him, where his seventeen-year old crewmember, Timmy steered the ship with the first mate, Eddy. Eddy and Timmy lowered the plank as they walked to Colin standing on the edge of the dock.

Eddy handed Colin an orange. "I brought ye this, Captain, yaz like citrus I know."

"Very kind of ye it is," Colin said starting to peel the orange rind with his teeth.

"Where's ya class at, lad?" Eddy asked while passing an orange to Timmy.

Colin put his arm around Timmy. "A wee bit late they is," Colin answered. "Are ye ready to steer me garl to Wicklow?" Colin asked his young crewmember.

"Aye-aye, sar," Timmy answered.

Colin had brought four large knapsacks of necessary items for their camping excursion in the damp peat bogs of Ireland's east coast. "Men, glad 'n greatful I am yez both are helpin' me today. Hope yer not feelin' bad that the rest of the crew got a day off?" Colin asked.

"Thank-yaz, Captain for the bonus pay. We would've done it for yaz no matter what," Eddy said.

"That I know," Colin said as he finished his orange. "Got any more of these?" "A crate of 'em is lyin' in the hull," Eddy answered.

Colin noticed his class walking toward him, thirty-six young males between the ages of 19 and 21 with Amoli and her female classmate, Patsy. Amoli was dressed in boy's overalls and a flannel shirt with a heavy coat and her girlfriend was dressed in a similar way.

The group of young men greeted Colin. "Good morning, Instructor Limmerick! You look just like a fisherman!" one of his tutorial students commented as he shook Colin's hand as a friendly gesture.

"I think I will be a fisherman on this trip I will -- we gotta eat," Colin commented with a smile as he greeted his class. "People," Colin called out to his class members, "Just walk up the plank to me ship 'n leave yer bags on the deck, we will set sail soon we's will. Usin' the sail today, it's a less costly way," Colin commented as he checked all his student's names on his clipboard as each one entered the Atlantic Mermaid. Soon the plank was drawn into the ship and the vessel set sail for Saint George's Channel.

"Captain!" Eddy shouted to Colin. "We're settin' sail now!"

Colin waved to Eddy. "Grand!"

The students sat on the deck organising their notes for the trip and their belongings.

Amoli stood in front of Colin. "You look very nice today, Instructor Limmerick."

"I do? I look like a scruffy fisherman don't I?"

"I think you look nice."

"Thank-ye, little lass. Ye wearin' boy's clothes ye are. Ye can't help but look lovely all the time, eh?"

Eddy looked for Colin. "Captain! Can ye come'er for a minute?" Eddy was with the young crewmember steering the ship in the wheelhouse.

Colin trotted over to Eddy and the young

crewmember. "Ye called me?"

"Captain, we're goin' to Wicklow are we?" Eddy asked.

"That we are."

"We'll let yaz 'n yer group off 'n off we'll be?" Eddy said.

"Aye, we have to do a bit of a wee carriage ride to the peat bogged lands."

"Do I track the rest of the crew at Dublin city?"

"Aye, tomorrow pick them up at the quays. I won't need ye again 'til Thursday I won't. We's gonna do a wee bit of campin' we will. But, it's been a mild November I can honestly say," Colin said.

"Lucked out yaz'av, lad, lucked out," Eddy commented.

Colin smiled. "I've got two females with me who wouldn't appreciate cold campin' nights, glad it's balmy I am."

Six hours passed as the Atlantic Mermaid docked at Wicklow. "Captain, I'll see yaz all Thursday!."

As the class carried their belongings off the boat Amoli tried to keep up with Colin's pace. "Instructor Limmerick, I really like your boat. It's very nice."

"Now ye can say ye've been on me ship," Colin said.

"Yes, I can but this is not the way Miss Emanuel was on your ship was it?"

Colin walked his strong brisk pace as he carried his two knapsacks and two backpacks. "Ye always askin' me questions, little lass, why?"

Colin had pre-arranged seven carriages to be waiting at the Wicklow port to take him and his class to the Ballybetagh Bog near Glencullen County located along the river valleys exactly where he, Sasha, and Rosa had travelled in the late spring in search of the time vortex opening. Amoli insisted on sitting beside Colin in the carriage where she buried herself in his chest. Colin felt uncomfortable with some of his male classmates in the

240

carriage with him but let her be.

The carriages dropped them off as close as possible to the peat-bogged lands of Wicklow. They hiked for several hours to the destination Colin had indicated near the time vortex. "Okay, ye all should have yer tents therefore ye can start pitchin'. If ye need me assistance I'm here for yez," Colin said.

Ten thick canvassed tents went up in a circle around the burning fire pit that Colin had started. They matted several blankets at the bottom of their tents for insulation. Colin spent most of this time helping Amoli and Patsy.

Colin later placed a fishing rod in Sasha's hands as he held his fishing spear. "Come mate, we bes' do some fishin' for the class," Colin said. They walked half a kilometer from the campsite to a small stream. During their walk through the tall grasses to the stream Colin noticed several small animals scampering through the grasses. He first didn't pay attention to them. When he did notice the animals he froze in silence. Sasha continued his hike realising Colin had stopped.

"Mr. Limmerick where you are?"

"Mate, did ye get a look at some of the small wildlife 'round here?" Colin asked.

Sasha was too busy lighting a cigarette. "We are in jungle, what you want to see?"

"Take a look at some of the small mammals. Some of them look like a species that I know is already extinct," Colin commented.

"I like you better drunk, Mr. Limmerick," Sasha said taking a puff from his cigarette.

As they made their way to the stream Sasha noticed in the distance a large brown bear trying to catch a fish on the opposite side. "Look at that, Mr. Limmerick, we are not only ones fishing," Sasha pointed to the bear.

Colin dropped his spear in awe of the bear. "Holy feck!"

"You are afraid of brown bear? I bring rifle, it is fully

loaded, don't worry I have all under control."

"Sasha, that's a brown bear is it not?" Colin pointed at the animal.

"Da, Mr. Limmerick, da! I think you need drink, fast. In my city, Petersburg, there are many brown bear all over city."

Colin squinted his eyes to focuss on Sasha. "What?"

"Mr. Limmerick, you are crazy man. In front of *Winter Palace* we have black bear and brown bear and they dance for us -- so very nice."

"Huh? What the feck are ye sayin'?"

"I say you, I have rifle I will shoot it -- do you want?"

"The brown bear has been long extinct in Ireland it has," Colin said running his hands violently through his hair.

"Well, you must be wrong because it standing right there trying to catch fish. It cannot be extinct! Maybe it came from Scotland or some place or even my Petersburg."

"Correction, mate, the brown bear has been extinct in the Isles for a long time now!" Colin said in an irritated panic.

"You not God, Mr. Limmerick! Remember that! You not always correct. You have made error. We stay here, we catch fish and we go, da?"

"I want to be with me class just now," Colin said as he rubbed his face.

"We must catch fish. You really need drink! Next you will say you saw wolf...awhooooooh!" Sasha said nudging Colin.

The two men remained at the stream and caught a great deal of fish.

***

That night Colin and Sasha slept in the same tent as did Amoli and Patsy also shared a tent. The rest of the young male students shared two or three in a tent as the campfire continued to burn providing warmth.

Sasha and Colin discussed the day. Colin crawled into his sleeping bag while Sasha put out his cigarette as well as the kerosene lamp. Colin could hear Amoli and Patsy chatting in the next tent where he could detect that the conversation was about him.

"You are like celebrity, Mr. Limmerick," Sasha whispered to him in the dark tent. "Miss Amoli can't take her eyes off you. You are lucky man."

Colin was half asleep too tired to even listen. In a few minutes the campsite was dark without a sound. The class of campers was exhausted from their first day on site.

It was early dawn approximately 5:00 a.m. Colin had rolled toward one side of the tent. He slept on his side where his face was only about an inch from the canvas. Suddenly the hot breath and loud snorts of a creature penetrated through the canvas. Colin's face flinched but he continued in his deep sleep. The hot breath saturated his face where he opened one eye. The snorting of a wild creature became apparent. 'Somethin's out there' -- he said to himself. Colin opened both eyes as he laid purposely still, 'Somethin's out there' -- he said again. He could hear rummaging through the grass of footsteps of some kind as well as snorting and growling. He slowly sat up pushing his body close to the tent -- opening that was buttoned shut for the night. He undid some of the buttons of the tent flap to see what had entered their campsite. He gazed through the flap noticing a silhouette against the flame of the campfire of what seemed to look like a pack of wolves. He jolted, as he looked at Sasha sound asleep in his sleeping bag, "Sasha!" he whispered. "Sasha! Wake up!" he blurted in a whisper.

"What now, Mr. Limmerick? I was sleeping too good to be awake. What you want now?"

"Shhhhhh! Ye gotta be quiet. A pack of wolves is visitin' our campsite. What shall we do?"

"Take rifle and blow off their heads," Sasha said burying his head in his pillow.

243

"Don't want to alarm me class I don't. A gunshot is not what I want."

"Go! Go away Mr. Limmerick. Let me sleep. Go make coats out of them," Sasha gasped half asleep.

Colin reached over Sasha picking up his loaded rifle. He lit the lamp and slowly made his way outside the tent. The wolves stopped and stared when they spotted Colin. He tried to act as aggressive as possible despite his fear. He stood tall outside the tent aiming the rifle. Some of the wolves tried to approach him from the side by weaving around the tents. Colin started to run toward what looked like the leaders of the pack. He began to shoot bullets in the air as he ran toward them. The lower ranked wolves tried to attack by approaching him from the back and sides. Colin purposely used jerky movements as one aggressive wolf started to nip at his thigh. Colin tried to kick the wolf with his heavy fishing boots where the wolf yelped with a squeal. The higher ranked wolves tried to attack Colin from head-on where he had to shoot one of them dead. The pack ran chaotically throughout the campsite. More than half the male students jumped out of their tents trying to help their teacher as they heard the commotion. They threw rocks and acted aggressively by showing their numbers. Amoli and Patsy crawled out of their tent not understanding what was happening.

Sasha stood outside the tent. "Girls go back in tent, wait for this to come to end. It is dangerous for girls," Sasha cautioned them.

"What's going on, Dr. Dimitrikov?" Patsy asked.

"Your Instructor Limmerick is getting morning exercise this is all," Sasha replied.

The disabled pack bolted into the trees.

"Instructor Limmerick? What happened?" One of the male students asked.

Colin stood by the campfire holding Sasha's rifle while standing in his underwear and boots in a cold sweat. "Wolves entered our camp I guess," Colin said trying to catch his breath.

"Wolves sir, you told us that wolves have been extinct from Ireland for a long while now," the same male student said.

"I did didn't I?" Colin responded as he began to shiver.

"Instructor, I don't get it do you?"

"Well, did I mention to yez that the only place in Ireland that still has families of wolves is right here in Wicklow?"

"That sounds absurd, sir," the student said.

"I'm gettin' rather chilly standin' here in me drawers I am," Colin said with a shiver.

***

It was mid morning the class cooked by the campfire and made tea for breakfast. Colin lay out his sleeping bag by the campfire so he could doze off due to the exhaustion from what happened at dawn. As he lay flat on his back with his cap over his eyes he began to speak out to his class. "Ye goin' to begin yer research assignment after breakfast yez are," Colin said feeling sickly from the event of the early morning and alcohol withdrawal symptoms. "Yer to identify yer animal ye are -- be happy with yer choice 'cause ye have to live with it," he called out as his cap remained over his eyes to block out the daylight.

"Sir, we can't change our choice of animal?" Patsy asked Colin.

"Ye can't," Colin replied.

Amoli crawled beside Colin to where he lay and began to caress his stomach. The male students began to chuckle while they watched Amoli's actions.

"Lass? What are ye doin'?" he asked feeling interrupted. "After ye choose yer mammal for this study, ye need to examine its habitat, so where does it live? Describe it, what does it need in order to live?" Colin continued.

Amoli started to run her tiny fingers along his legs as

245

he continued to lye down. The male students talked and whispered to one another. "Lass!" Colin raised his voice. "Then ye need to document its appearance. Describe its appearance."

Amoli continued to lightly fondle him. Colin sat up, "Lass! Ye can't be doin' this! Please!" Colin shouted. Amoli felt hurt from his raised voice while the students laughed. "What group does this animal belong to?" Colin continued. "The fun part then, try 'n find its fossilized relatives if ye can," Colin announced as he sat in a kneeling position so he could keep an eye on Amoli's actions. He was in a foul mood where his body craved alcohol and sleep. "Yez all need to get this down as documented notes ye do 'n I want them on Thursday when we leave, does everyone understand?" Colin stood up noticing Amoli sitting on the ground sulking.

"Lass, ye need not despair over such silliness. We're here as researchers 'n nothin' more," Colin said as he towered over her. "I'll be choppin' wood while ye all get started," Colin walked off with his axe.

The students worked hard the entire day trying to find an animal in its natural habitat that they could research. Colin cautioned them to work in groups so no one is left alone in the peat bog lands.

**

The next morning the group prepared a hardy breakfast while Sasha sat in his tent writing out formulas regarding his time vortex theory. Colin was still feeling the affects of withdrawal where his head hurt. He felt miserable. He sat with the group not demonstrating his usual raging appetite. He was quiet just observing what he saw.

Amoli sat beside him and planted a kiss on his cheek in front of the class. "Good morning, Instructor Limmerick," she said smiling.

He didn't react. The males in the class tried not to take notice as they continued to eat breakfast. "Instructor

Limmerick, what did I do? Don't you like me anymore?" She asked.

Colin tried not to swear as his body clenched from alcohol withdrawal. He ignored her romantic gesture.

"Why are you acting this way toward me?" she shouted as she stomped off into the distance where the top of her head was easily camouflaged by the tall grasses. Colin was surprised by Amoli's reaction. He pulled his round spectacles out of his jacket pocket and placed them on his face. "I bes' go after her," Colin said to the class.

Colin kept looking in the direction she ran to. "I need to find her she has me worried she does. None of us should be alone 'round here, none of us," Colin started to walk almost in a trot to the direction she ran. It was approximately a half-kilometer from the campsite. He kept his glasses on where he saw a large cave. "Amoli!" he called. "Amoli! Where are ye, lass?" he kept calling. "Amoli, I'm sorry! Forgive me, please!" He walked through a maze of large boulders that almost resembled ruins. He heard a delicate voice crying behind the boulders. He spotted Amoli sitting on a rock crying. "Amoli!" Colin ran to her. "Amoli, yer so sad ye are, no need to be," he said kneeling to her where she wrapped her arms around his neck and held on tight with a harder cry.

"You're acting like you don't like me!" she shouted.

He pulled her off the rock and started to direct her toward the camp. "Lass, ye know that isn't true I'm just not me-self lately. Nothin' to do with ye, it isn't. Come, lets return to camp."

As they started to walk a cave lion appeared about ten meters from them. It stared at them in wonder.

"A lion!" Amoli screamed.

Colin gingerly bent over. "Lass, get on me piggy back style. Do it now, do it slowly," he said in a soft whisper.

She wrapped her arms tightly around his neck as her stomach rested tightly on his back and her legs wrapped around his stomach. Colin looked at the closest tree as he slowly moved toward it trying not to stare the animal in the eyes. The cave lion remained still but then started to leap forward as Colin tried to make his way to the tree. The tree was a deciduous species where it appeared to have sturdy branches. Colin climbed up the tree busting several branches with his large body mass. The tree waved with the extra weight but appeared sturdy enough. He tried to climb as high as he could without causing the tree to buckle. He placed Amoli on a higher branch. The cave lion was huge in body structure but too burly to climb. It made its way to the tree trying to claw at Colin. Colin kept kicking it with his heavy steel boots. Amoli screamed and cried. The lion kept trying to grab hold of Colin's foot but Colin kept kicking it away. Its claws were huge and razor sharp where it did grab hold of Colin's boot. Colin tried to put all his strength into retracting his leg away from the large feline. The animal wouldn't let go as Colin struggled. The strength of the animal was unbeatable. It had wedged its claws so deep into Colin's boot it managed to pull it off. Amoli belted a continuous scream.

"Colin climb higher!" Amoli shouted.

"I can't! If I do, I'll bust the tree with me weight! I have to stay here!"

The cave lion encircled the tree trying to figure out how to get at the couple. An hour had passed where the lion finally gave up deciding to find easier prey. Colin could see his chewed boot sitting at the bottom of the tree. He broke off a sturdy branch. His sailor knife was kept in his back pocket where he carved a sharp point at the end of the branch.

"What are you doing?" Amoli asked.

"Makin' a weapon I am."

They remained high in the tree for some time after the lion's departure. Colin slid down the tree with Amoli on his back. He tried to fit his mangled boot back on his foot but it no longer felt the same. Colin walked away from the tree with Amoli on his back breathing heavily with the fear the large feline would re-appear.

"Amoli, we shouldn't speak, let's just get out of here 'n not draw attention to ourselves," Colin said.

They arrived at the camp where Amoli tried to keep up with Colin's quick pace as she held his hand feeling almost dragged. He carried his large pointed branch in his other hand.

Patsy ran to them. "We've been worried sick! What happened?"

Colin fell on his knees beside the campfire. Sasha moved closer to find out what had happened. Colin tried to speak. "Attacked we was". The class gathered around him.

"Almost didn't make this one," Colin said trying to catch his breath. Colin's eyes were glassy with almost a crazed stir. "Attacked we was," Colin took a deep breath puffing out his chest and not feeling oxygen reach his body. His eyes rolled back and he passed out falling on his back with his legs still contorted in the kneeling position.

"Dr. Dimitrikov, help us! What's wrong with Instructor Limmerick?" Patsy called out.

Sasha looked at Amoli. "Tell us, Miss Amoli what you two encounter for so many hours?"

"A very big lion came out of nowhere," she said still shaking.

"Lion? There is problem with this place," Sasha said trying to get Colin to come to. Sasha noticed Colin's boot mangled. "Your boot looks like problem happen, Mr. Limmerick."

Colin opened his eyes. The class stood around with Amoli and Patsy on each side of him. Colin glanced at his pupils then scanned to Sasha and then to Amoli. Amoli held his hand.

"Sasha?"

"Da, Mr. Limmerick, I am here ask anything of me," Sasha responded.

"Ye 'n me must discuss matters."

Sasha and the male students helped him up. "There is definitely problem here, Mr. Limmerick," Sasha said. "Please let Mr. Limmerick alone -- we must discuss matters."

Colin grabbed Sasha by the shoulders. "Sasha, was the time vortex left opened when we did our prehistoric journey some months ago? Tell me the truth! What the feck is goin' on here?" Colin shook Sasha not letting go of him.

"Get your hands off me," Sasha took a few steps back," After wolf incident I began checking notes and tried to figure out what went wrong."

Colin took a step closer to him. "Okay, what went wrong?"

"Time vortex gap was never closed that is all," Sasha said calmly.

"I thought so! Do ye know what species me class has chosen to research?" Colin asked in a rising rage.

"This assignment is to be handed to you Thursday, da?"

"Guess what some of their chosen animals are, mate?"

"Mr. Limmerick, you are raising voice!"

"Guess, mate!"

"I do not know. What they researching?"

"One of me students is doin' the auk. He found a family of auks here in Wicklow that he has decided to study, mate," Colin stood tall with his arms folded in front of him.

"What is auk?"

"A long extinct penguin-like foul that hadn't the use of its wings. The auk had been known for its large beak unlike penguin's small beak," Colin couldn't control his frustration. "Mate, what the hell is me student doin' his research on the auk for? He's spotted a family of auks right here in 1908 A.D.?"

"We must try to close time vortex, but first we must

shoot cave lion."

"What?"

"Look at your boot, Mr. Limmerick, do you want to
see your pupils look like that? Take your pick, be animal
protector or protect your students!"

Colin looked at Sasha feeling helpless as he paused for
a few minutes. "The lion's cave is in that direction," Colin
pointed.

"Come with me and gun and we will destroy it. Look
at you, since we have come on trip you have not slept and
barely eaten. You are mess, Mr. Limmerick."

"This class excursion has been hell for me it has."

"You have darkness under eyes, you look bad. Come
with me now and we will destroy it. You need good-night
sleep."

"Sasha, we had no business playin' God we didn't.
What did I want to prove? I've proven nothin' to Dr.
Cushing, it's a fiasco," Colin said feeling defeated.

"You are not playing God, Mr. Limmerick, you are
playing researcher."

"We opened a time vortex to do the impossible we did.
We went back in time ninety-five hundred years so I can
prove I'm a true researcher to Dr. Cushing? No matter
what I do, mate, Cushing will always hate me for who I
am. So now, we're goin' to take the life away from an
innocent animal? What have we done to evolution?"

"Mr.Limmerick, we must destroy it right now!
Pazhalusta!" Sasha pleaded. "It is prehistoric animal, Mr.
Limmerick! Prehistoric animals do not count -- it is okay
to kill them!"

Colin stared at Sasha with disgust.

They returned to the camp as Sasha checked his
supply of bullets.

"Don't want anyone to leave this campsite. Men,
please whatever sharp objects ye may have make them
readily available. Dr. Dimitrikov 'n I need to do somethin'
right now," Colin announced to the group as they sat

251

around the fire.

"Instructor Limmerick, you and Dr. Dimitrikov are going to shoot the lion, right?" one student asked.

Colin looked at the young man and the rest of his pupils. "Aye," Colin looked at Amoli, "Don't leave this campsite! Understand me, lass!" Colin said as he violently shook Amoli.

Amoli hugged him. "What's going on, Instructor Limmerick? I didn't know Ireland had lions," she said.

He looked at her. "It doesn't, lass."

Colin grabbed his axe and left the campsite with Sasha. He directed Sasha to the cave. They tried their best not to make a sound being only too aware of the feline's keen sense of smell. They stood behind the maze of boulders just before the opening of the cave. They waited roughly for forty-five minutes until Sasha heard the grasses make a rustling sound. He tapped Colin on the shoulder to make him aware, Sasha raised his rifle where he started to aim it in the direction of the sounding grasses. Colin's heart started to pound as he saw the same male cave lion look like it was trying to find a place to bask in the sun. Sasha needed to move closer to the beast where Colin followed holding his axe. The aim still wasn't accurate enough, for Sasha had to move even closer for perfection. The lion was lying down but perked its ears to the sound of Sasha and Colin. It immediately stood up trying to see where the noise was coming. It then saw the two men. Sasha's aim was perfect at this point. The lion started to charge as it accelerated with each step. It was only a few meters where it started to leap toward the men. While it was in mid air, Sasha shot it in the belly. It roared in agony.

"Sasha! Shoot it again! It's suffering!" Colin shouted. Sasha fired another bullet in its head. It was still.

Colin glared at Sasha and paused.

***

Colin and Sasha tried to walk to the area of the time

vortex. "It was in this area we found time vortex, Mr.Limmerick," Sasha said.

"How can we close it?" Colin asked with a worried pant.

"Easy!"

"Easy?"

They walked in small circles around the grassy landscape.

"I know what to do in this case."

"What then?"

"We must go back to past and close it upon our return to 1908."

"What?"

"We find time vortex and go through time again, we did it before we do it again."

"Any alternatives?"

"Maybe, but I do not know yet."

Colin grabbed Sasha by the shirt collar and smacked his head against a tree. "Yer full of shite!"

"Get your hands off me now! Stop this! I like you better as a drunken scientist! Leave me alone!" Sasha raised his rifle aiming it at Colin, "You touch me again. I blow your head off!"

Colin slammed him against the tree letting go of him. "Alright! How the feck are ye goin' get us outta this mess?" Colin shouted.

"Why should I? You wanted to be famous researcher not me! You wanted to prove Darwin to your Professor Cushing! You are the one who put us in this mess, Mr. Limmerick! Now your sweet little Miss Amoli is in this mess with you and she is so in love with you to even see what kind of beast you really are!"

"Ah, the feck with ye!" Colin stood still looking at Sasha as he paused. "Sasha, we can't go back in time we can't. I've got a class of thirty-eight students here with me includin' Amoli. I--I don't know what to feckin' do!" Colin looked up at the sky placing his hands over his face.

"Dear God, tell me what to do?" he asked with a wimper.

Later in the afternoon Colin watched his students sitting by the fire jotting their observational notes. Colin stood behind them watching them write. "I see that many of ye have chosen interestin' animals to research," Colin said to his class as he walked around reading over their shoulders. "I see some of ye are researchin' bats, shrews, hedgehogs, badgers, stoats 'n..." he continued to rummage around quickly skimming their notes as they continued to write, "Ah yes, the auk, the wolf, the brown bear, aye 'n *Megaloceros*?" he continued to walk around with panic. "...'n, *Paleolithic* man, which, a) does not follow the assignment 'n, b) who the hell saw a *Paleolithic* man...?" he sat on a rock rubbing his tired eyes. He stood up looking at his class. "Who here saw a bleedin' *Megaloceros*?" Colin asked with agnst.

Amoli walked to him. "I did, sir," she said in her tiny voice.

"Ye did?"

"Are you angry with me?" she peered up at him with her large dark eyes.

"I'm not angry with ye. Ye saw a *Megaloceros giganteus*? Where, lass?"

"Not too far from that opened field of grass over there, you know where there aren't many trees," she said. "I saw more than one. Maybe five or six, I don't really remember."

"Five or six?...I would like to see these animals I would," he said while he kept blinking his eyes in surreal disbelief.

"I'll take you to *Megaloceros* and his family," she said. As she was speaking, a few young auk's waddled behind the closest tree.

Colin caught a glimpse of them. "Me dear God! This is fantastic!" Colin tried to slowly move close to the birds. "Beautiful birds they is or was," Colin said in a soft voice of confusion.

254

"You really love animals don't you, sir?" Amoli said.

"Notice how they're wings is of no use to them," Colin said wanting to get closer to them, "Sasha, fetch me the camera in the tent if ye can?"

"They look a lot like penguins," Amoli commented.

"All but their large hooked beaks 'n tiny atrophic wings they do," Colin replied. He took a carrot lying beside the fire and walked close enough to the animals to lure their attention. The animal was timid but slowly got closer to him where it took the carrot from his hand. Sasha managed to take a few photographs.

"Aren't they spectacular birds?" one of the students commented.

Suddenly the ground felt a bit unsteady where it started to shake. The rumbling of the ground lasted for only a few seconds. Colin stood and stared at Sasha and his students.

"What is that?" Patsy asked in a panic.

"Something has gone bad," Sasha said as he calmly lit a cigarette.

"Gone wrong? What's gone wrong, Dr. Dimitrikov?" a male student asked looking worried.

The rumble of the ground lasted almost a minute. "I don't recall a fault line bein' this close to Ireland," Colin said.

"Are you referring to earthquakes, Instructor?" Patsy asked.

"The closet fault line is still too far to create such a noticeable tremor, but I'm no expert I'm not," Colin said.

"What are you talking about, Instructor Limmerick? What is a fault line?" one of the male student's asked feeling bewildered.

"I was a readin' an academic journal on earthquakes statin' the planet sits on a series of fault lines. I always read new state of the art science, which always seems to make sense to me," Colin said.

"You're a brilliant, instructor," Patsy said. "I would

255

have never thought of that.

The rumble of the earth began again where the trees swayed and a distinct sound of a chaotic thunder continued at a constant. The auks ran away quickly. Colin felt this was no earthquake. He stood away from the camp looking in a distant direction. A group of *Megaloceros* charged at him. He stood in disbelief of what he was seeing. "Shite! feck!" Colin shouted. A series of other prehistoric animals followed the group of *Megaloceros*; wooly rhinos, wolves, bison, cave lions, and several more ran in a stampede heading for the campsite.

Colin grabbed Patsy and Amoli throwing both over each of his shoulders racing to a tall sturdy tree where he placed them on a strong branch for safety. "Men! Find a tree 'n climb it! Do it now!" Colin shouted. The rest of the students scattered. Sasha stood still aiming his rifle. Colin pushed Sasha's rifle away. "What the feck are ye doin'? Find a bleedin' tree! Ye can't shoot these animals!" Colin shouted.

The rumble of the ground worsened as the stampede approached the camp. Amoli and Patsy were terrified screaming with terror in their eyes. Colin made sure everyone was safe. The stampede was almost before him but he managed to leap onto a sturdy tree swinging on a branch and breaking it. He crashed hard onto the ground almost in front of a raging *Megaloceros*. Amoli and Patsy saw this from their view where they screamed thinking their instructor wasn't going to make it safely. He rolled away from the *Megaloceros* and seeked another tree that could carry his weight as he weaved between the stampede. At this point, the stampede ran through the camp and Colin was caught amongst them. He scanned the area trying to find a strong enough tree. He noticed about ten meters away there was a mature tree. He needed to get to it without being stomped by the stampede. He wasn't the fastest sprinter especially with one mangled boot and a large wood and metal bladed axe in his hand. He tried to dodge the prehistoric animal hysteria by running behind one tree at a time. The trees were fairly spaced from one another, which made him take longer strides for safety. There was dust, grass and mud flying through the air causing poor visibility. Colin tried to reach the tree where he took a dash with every bit of strength. A charging bison was coming toward him where he failed to estimate his speed with the animal. He almost ran past the bison but it managed to clip the back of his leg, which sent him flying through the air landing on his belly. He was in a haze of dust feeling stunned where he slowly raised his head noticing a pack of wolves coming his way. Most of the wolves leaped over Colin but some actually stomped on him in the process. Amoli watched with baited breath. He tried to stand trying to make his way to the tree where he pounced onto a branch and swung himself up the tree with all his strength. He watched from above noticing that these animals were being chased. *"What could be chasin' these animals?"* he asked himself. He tried to see far beyond the stampede to see what was chasing them. Then he saw yet another stampede behind the hysterical animals. It was a large tribe of *Paleolithic* people running with spears in their hands. Colin's class watched the event in awe. Sasha was in a tree feeling not too impressed by the episode so he fondled his pockets for a cigarette. The mass stampede lasted for about fifteen minutes and then there was silence. Colin made his way down the tree first. He was muddy with dust caked on his hair, face, and body. He looked around to make sure the stampede was over. He looked at the camp feeling surprised nothing was destroyed. Many of the animals strayed from the fire and weaved between the students' tents. Colin helped Patsy and Amoli down from the tree. Sasha and the rest of the students made their way down the trees.

Amoli and Patsy wrapped their arms around Colin holding him as tight as they could.

"I thought I was going to loose you, Instructor

Limmerick," Amoli said in tears. She cried with her face buried in his belly.

"I'm alright I think," Colin said.

Sasha walked to Colin. "Mr. Limmerick," Sasha said watching Colin trying to console the two girls in his arms.

"Mr. Limmerick, we got problem, da?"

"We do," Colin answered.

"I told you what we must do, did I not?" Sasha said finding it difficult to light a cigarette.

"Ye did."

"Come, I must speak to you in private."

Colin tried to pry the girls off him. "I need to speak to Dr. Dimitrikov now. I'll be back in a second I will," Colin said.

Sasha walked toward the area of opened field where the stampede had just taken place. He flicked his cigarette butt onto a muddy puddle. "Mr. Limmerick, there is problem here in your Ireland."

"No feckin' kiddin'," Colin replied.

"Did you look in mirror lately, you look like either mud monster or sandman."

"I have a good feckin' idea what I look like. All I know is we made a hell of a mess," Colin said.

"Mess is putting it lightly, Mr. Limmerick. Now, I told you what we must do to fix problem did I not?"

"You said we need to go back in time again."

"Da, we must go back to approximate time 7592 B.C. and return to 1908 A.D. and close time vortex while in process. *Vy panimayitye?*"

"Huh?"

"Do you understand?"

"Oh, I do."

"When you want to do this time travel?"

"Not today, tomorrow me first mate, Ed, comes to pick us up with me vessel. Have to go ourselves ye 'n me, not with the class."

"Longer you wait worse it gets, your Ireland will be in

big trouble. Cannot have cave lions running around countryside."

"Realise that I do. Have to come back Friday, though. Me crew is gonna think I'm really screwed up."

"They already know, Mr. Limmerick."

"Thanks, Sasha."

***

Later that afternoon the class cooked by the campfire where Colin sat on a log with Amoli beside him. She collected a large plate of food and passed it to him with a bashful smile.

A male student stood up and approached Colin. "You brought us here to this prehistoric nightmare. I think there's loads you're not telling us, Instructor Limmerick!"

"What is it ye need to know?"

"Our lives have been on the line ever since we arrived. What's with all these prehistoric animals roaming about? Who's this Dr. Dimitrikov? He doesn't even teach at our university! He's some bleeding foreigner who smokes a lot of tobacco!"

Sasha looked at the student and continued to smoke. "It is obvious that you know nothing. Shame on you! Speaking to your instructor with so disrespect way. In my Russia, there would be no tolerance for students like you!" Sasha said with a cigarette hanging from his lips.

"Who cares about Russia!" the student blurted. "I think our instructor is just a façade. All you do is push Darwin down our throats and time travel! What are you trying to do, live out some childhood fantasy?"

"Instructor Limmerick, please ignore him. We're all a bit shaken by some of these experiences whilst on this exursion, sir," another student intervened.

"I understand, " responded Colin.

***

The following morning the class cleaned up the campsite leaving nothing behind. They waited by the shore for the Atlantic Mermaid to dock. The students were anxious to board the ship.

Eddy greeted Colin with opened arms. "Captain, glad to see yaz! How was it?"

"I wouldn't repeat this I wouldn't," Colin said fumbling in the galley for ale.

"Poor lad, yaz been dry for four days. How did ya manage that?"

Colin found a bottle of ale and tore it opened with his teeth. "I didn't."

"Captain, yaz can't get shite faced yet, yaz still got students here and it's 10:30 in the bleedin' mornin' it is," Eddy said. They watched the students slump on the deck with ailing fatigue.

"Just one feckin' beer is all," Colin said as he inhaled it.

It was a calm day for the *Atlantic Mermaid* where it eventually docked at Fishguard Harbour.

***

It was a windy Friday morning in December, Colin and Sasha were on the *Atlantic Mermaid*. Eddy walked to Colin slapping him on the back. "Ya got somethin' up yar sleeve ya do, Captain. Why ya goin' back to Wicklow today? Ya just got back yesterday."

"Some loose ends need to be tied 'is all."

"Where's that cute little foreign lass who fancies ya so much?"

"Home I suppose," Colin answered.

Sasha smoked a cigarette while he stared at the sea. He observed the crew work with Colin to drag the nets.

***

They docked at Wicklow, Colin and Sasha were dressed in warmer clothing this time.

Eddy watched the two men carry their equipment off the boat including Colin's axe and Sasha's rifle. "When do yaz want me to pick yaz up again?" Eddy shouted at Colin as he stepped onto the dock.

"Can ye give us ninety-six hours? If I'm not here by

then I'll probably be dead!" Colin shouted.

"Captain, what the hell are yaz up to?"

"Ye wouldn't believe me if I told ye!" Colin swung his arm waving at Eddy as if it were the last time.

Eddy had a serious expression on his face. "What's that lad up to I wonder." Sasha had his *time indicating device* with him as well as several slide rules for his calculations. Colin carried the food and water as well as camping gear and weapons.

They continued to walk away from the shoreline as Sasha noticed a small prehistoric animal scamper in front of them. They both paused to look at the animal. "Problem is still here, Mr. Limmerick."

"Do we need to find the exact area where we found the time vortex?" Colin asked.

"Da, we must," Sasha answered. "We know how long we will be in time warp did you tell your Professor Cushing?"

"I told'em he had to complete the course himself. He wasn't pleased -- he hates undergraduates he does. Besides, do we really feckin' know how long all this shite's gonna take?"

"Only some weeks before course is over, da?"

"Aye."

"By the way, did you say Miss Amoli we are doing this today?" Sasha asked.

"I told her nothin'."

"Why you not say her?"

"'Cause she's not me lass 'is all."

"Not yet, Mr. Limmerick."

"Probably -- not ever."

"Mr. Limmerick, you must have drink or something -- you not yourself. Do you not like Miss Amoli?"

Colin searched his knapsack for an unopened bottle of whiskey. He recklessly opened it as he placed his lips upon it. "Stop the bleedin' questions already, man! It's just I don't know much 'bout time vortexes 'is all!"

"You know more than average man."

"Feck all is all I know," Colin blurted as he began to inhale the whiskey. "What did Rosa say when ye told her 'bout our new escapade?"

"She laughed at me and told me I am crazy man."

"Did she want to come?"

"What you think?"

"Not at all I suppose."

"You are right, not at all. She say never again."

They walked for about an hour until they reached the approximate area of the location of the time vortex. They placed their belongings down and Sasha pulled out his *time travel indicator*. As he did that Colin heard a sound in the tall grasses he looked up and saw a large stag *Megaloceros* standing roughly ten meters from them. Colin and Sasha ignored it as they continued to work. It moved a few steps closer to them feeling curious about their presence.

"Okay, time vortex is just in this area, we must look for signs indicating exact location and get ourselves through it. Remember, Mr. Limmerick, no guarantees of the time in history it will take us because meteorite has already happened six months ago."

"The important thing here is we close the gap on our departure back to 1908. We will arrive back in 1908 won't we?"

"What you afraid of, Mr. Limmerick?"

"Don't want to end up in 1808 or 2008 -- somethin' awful like that."

"I told you we always return the exact year we depart."

The *Megaloceros* started to move closer to them where it started to charge. Sasha pushed Colin and his belongings into the time vortex where Sasha followed.

Chapter Twenty

Colin and Sasha lay on the ground. Sasha slowly opened his eyes noticing unfamiliar surroundings. He sat up and brushed debris off his shoulders and arms. "It so hot!" Sasha blurted loudly as he removed his jacket. He removed his hat as he slowly stood up. "Why so hot if we in Ireland?" he asked himself, hoping Colin would wake up. Colin lay flat on his back perfectly still. "Mr. Limmerick, please you must wake up!" Sasha said pacing around noticing their belongings and equipment had come safely through the time vortex. Sasha unbuttoned his shirt. "So hot! Why so hot? I must check my *time travel device* to see what time we are gauged at." Sasha found the device lying on the grass and picked it up. "My God! We are forty thousand years in past? Incorrect! Am I reading this correct?" Sasha removed his coat, then his shirt, and wiped the sweat off his face with it. "Why so hot? Mr. Limmerick! Please wake up!" Sasha kneeled to Colin. "Why you not wake, Mr. Limmerick? I'm sorry for all bad things I did to you in past. Now, you must wake up! Please! *Pazhalusta*, Mr. Limmerick!" Sasha tapped Colin's face.

Colin slowly opened his eyes.

"Thank God, I thought you dead man!"

Colin rolled over and started to vomit on the grass.

Sasha watched Colin. "I am glad, Mr. Limmerick, so glad."

Colin lifted his head and glanced at Sasha. "Yer glad I'm barfin' me feckin' guts out?"

"Mr. Limmerick, I am glad you alive and well."

"Alive, I am, mate. However, I'm not sure 'bout the well part. It's so feckin' hot!" Colin grunted in the midst of feeling ill.

"Mr. Limmerick, you don't take time vortex travels

well do you?"

"I guess it's like bein' sea-sick, mate, only sea-sick is not me problem, it's these damn time vortexes! I feckin' hate'em I do!"

"You and I both know time travel is something you cannot stop."

Colin sat up. "Cut the shite on yer analysis of me, mate. Why the feck is it so bleedin' hot?"

"I thought you could answer this question."

"What does it say on yer *time travel device*? Are we in the future, the past, the present? What? Ah, the feck!" Colin asked as he removed his jacket and hat. "Are we still in Ireland or are we in the Caribbean?"

"We are forty thousand years in past and yes we are in your Ireland."

"Forty thousand years in the past ye say?" Colin stood up as he yanked off his tie. "That's not possible, mate, yer device isn't workin' very well."

"Why you say this?"

Colin felt irritated by the extreme heat as he started to unbutton his shirt. "Sixty thousand years, mate is the second half of the Ice Age."

"This is disaster! My *time-travel device* has never been wrong."

Colin took his shirt off as he wiped the sweat from his body with it. "Me hair's too long for heat like this!" Colin started to walk through the long grass until he heard a rustling sound.

"Is something there?" Sasha asked.

"Shhhhh! Somethin' is definitely not far from us," Colin was drawn to the noise until he was visible to a prehistoric spotted hyena. "Ssshite!"

"I must get rifle, Mr. Limmerick!"

"Ye won't! It's already in the middle of a feed. Leave it be," Colin backed up to the time vortex location. "We're in the Ice Age alright."

"How is this possible with such heat?"

"Interglacial it is."

"What is interglacial?"

"Interglacial periods is what we's in now. The Ice Age consisted of a series of extreme cold phases known as glacials. Wedged between each phase were interglacial periods, which could be tropical-like temperatures. I fancy the heat, but this is a strange stagnant heat that I've never experienced before. The South of France isn't like this, really."

"I'm glad you know what you are talking about, Mr. Limmerick."

"Someone has to."

Sasha glanced at him while trying to compose himself.

"Anyway, do ye want to investigate the area' er what?"

"I do not know. Does your Irish elk live in this time?"

"It does."

"Good, you can do more research on your elk. I can figure out way to leave this place."

"Leave? We just got'er, mate?"

"Do only wild beasts live in this time?"

"Uh, if Rosa was here, she'd say *Paleolithic* people would be rulin' these lands she would, or would they be *Mesolithic*? I'm no expert on human evolution, that's Rosa's expertise."

"I should have asked her to come. She will do anything for me."

"Colin chuckled. "Anythin' ye say?"

"No big deal. I see primitive people on last time travel? Do they have brains?"

"*Paleolithic* or *Mesolithic*?"

"Both."

"They's do."

"I will use rifle if one is near."

"Ye won't! We may not even come across any. We may be attacked by somethin' else all togather."

"You speak as if you welcome this idea."

265

"Just put yer gun away. We's here to investigate."

"I have not problem with investigation."

"Brilliant of ye. Lets grab our things 'n set up camp somewhere. Maybe we need to walk toward the sea, if the sea was even existin' at this time."

"No Irish Sea?"

"It may've just been formin'. It wouldn've been as wide as we know it, I think. I was readin' a German academic journal which speculated that Ireland may have been attached to England at one time ye know."

Sasha looked at Colin with a serious expression on his face. "I will stick to laws of physics."

The two men gathered their equipment as well as their personal belongings and head in the direction of the sea. They noticed several different animal species that looked unfamiliar to them. Sasha noticed a large animal in the distance. "Mr. Limmerick, I see rhinoceros, this is Ireland why is such animal here?"

Colin fell to his knees suffering from heat exhaustion then tied back his hair. "Rhinoceros used to live here, mate. Woolly rhino was its name, so it was."

"It is too hot here for you, Mr. Limmerick?"

"Strugglin' I am with this heat. I need to take me trousers off as well." He lay on his backside on the grass while pulling off his pants. "I feel so lethargic I do," Colin said lying in his underwear.

"Do not fall asleep, Mr. Limmerick. I am not naturalist I do not understand these beasts!"

Colin rolled on his stomach. "I promise I won't fall asleep. I just feel so damn awful."

Sasha gazed at the silhouette of the rhinoceros. "This African animal is approaching us, Mr. Limmerick."

Colin forced himself up. "Forgive me, mate. I'm just not adaptin' well to this climate."

Sasha held his rifle close to himself. "Is this woolly rhino dangerous?"

"Modern day rhinos in Africa aren't really, only if ye

266

catch'em by surprise they's likely to charge. South East Asian rhinos of our time may even be more tame."

"Why it approach us?"

"It smells our sent, grand sense of smell they have. They can't see for shite though."

"It knows we are here?"

"It does."

"Is this good thing or bad?"

"Good."

The two men set up camp near the sea. "We's need to build sturdy shelter'er otherwise, things could get nasty," he pulled out his axe.

"Nasty?"

"Sasha, this is the first time I've ever seen ye so worried. Usually nothin' fazes ye."

"I am not fan of wilderness, especially if wilderness is forty thousand years old."

"Need to chop some lumber for us I do.

"We should dove-tale wood to make shelter strong enough to withstand wild beast attack."

"We don't have ourselves any nails so yer idea is a good one."

Colin chopped and he chopped collecting enough lumber for a decent sized sturdy shelter with enough left over for firewood. They completed their project in the middle of the night noticing several nocturnal animals scamper throughout the grasses with their glowing eyes.

In the morning Colin rose early investigating the environment outside the wood shelter. He wasn't wearing any clothing for it felt more comfortable in such stagnant heat. He walked to the sea jumping in for a swim. The waves were unruly containing various life forms Colin had never seen. The harder the swim the more Colin was attracted to this activity. As Colin started to swim to shore he noticed Sasha smoking a cigarette. Colin made his way to the shoreline. "I think we can catch ourselves some grub," Colin called to Sasha.

267

"Mr. Limmerick, there could be sea life in this water that is not very good."

"Feck that shite, these waters are great they's is!"

"We will have to survive on only fish?"

"We can eat mammal meat if ye want. We can hunt like the natives."

"What natives? We have not seen any."

"Not yet, mate, not yet!"

Colin climbed a tree cutting a long almost straight branch with his axe. "I'll turn this into me fishin' spear."

"Mr. Limmerick, you should cover up. Sun is very hot."

"If it weren't for yer drawers ye'd be naked too, mate!"

"Mr. Limmerick, how will we survive here? I should work on time vortex and get us back."

"We'll survive! Better yet, we'll love it so much we'll forget 'bout the time vortex so we will! I'll learn to make me own beer even, shall we look for barely 'n hops?"

Sasha rolled his eyes back. "Can we try to hunt now? I will get rifle."

"Yer not gonna fetch yer rifle are ye?

"How will we feed ourselves?"

"No guns!"

Colin sat on the grass as he carved a spear out of a branch. He held it as he jumped back into the water. He swam under water fascinated by the sea life. He saw several reptilian creatures with noticeable sharp teeth, which he stayed away from. He swam to the top trying to spear some sea life but every attempt failed. "Losin' me touch I am?"

Sasha watched by the shoreline noticing upon Colin's return that he was empty handed. "Where is breakfast, Mr. Limmerick?"

"Ye don't want fish for breakfast do ye? Come, we'll hunt a large mammal, like mammoth or somethin'."

"Mammoth? They are Siberia's ancient children."

"Ah, but they lived in me Ireland long ago too."

"Mammoth are here?"

"They should be accordin' to the time we's now in."

"It is surprise to me."

Colin wiped the sweat from his forehead. "Feel the sun growin' in its intensity, mate?"

"Da, it is very hot, too hot."

The two men walked through the forest leaving their campsite. Sasha wore only his boxer shorts and shoes as he carried his rifle. Colin was naked, except for his tall boots and held his axe tightly in his hand. The sun penetrated through the trees causing Colin and Sasha to sweat profusely. Colin used his axe as a machete to cut away at the dense foliage in search of food. Suddenly Colin stopped in his tracks as he pushed away some of the brush. "Sasha, shhhh! I think I see a meal."

"That is your fuzzy elk, nyet?" Sasha pointed at a large antlered animal.

"It's no *Megaloceros*, that's some kind of reindeer. *Megaloceros* looks nothin' like that."

"Who cares! Get out of my way so I can shoot it," Sasha aimed and fired.

Colin pushed Sasha to the ground. "Are ye feckin' crazy, man? I said no guns 'n I mean no guns!"

"What is difference if you chop off its head or I shoot it?"

"Don't get smart with me!"

"I say what I think."

Colin peered down at Sasha. "That's yer feckin' problem, yer always tellin' me what ye think!"

"Reindeer is no longer here. We must have strategy for our hunt, Mr. Limmerick."

"Strategy, yer right. Maybe it's time we look for somethin' we can feed on for a good while, like mammoth."

"Good while...how long is good while, Mr. Limmerick?"

269

"As long as it takes."

They hiked through the brush for hours but no luck with their hunt.

"Mr. Limmerick, we must find small lake or pond to drink, I am very thirsty."

"I'm with ye on that one, mate," Colin said hacking away at the thick foliage with his axe as they continued to hike. "I'm wonderin' if we could set a trap. We could push boulders off a cliff or somethin'. We bes be ambush hunters, what ye think?"

"We must scout this area more and see where we can practice this strategy."

"Okay, mate. But, now I think we's really need to hydrate our bodies from this heat." They came across a running stream where the water was fresh and palatable. Colin stood in the stream squatting down as low as he could, splashing the crystal-clean water to his face as he started to drink from his cupped hands. Sasha stood and watched with his rifle tucked under his arm.

Colin looked at Sasha with water dripping from his face. "Ah, what I'd do right now for a swig of good Irish whiskey!" Colin shut his eyes with droplets of water dripping from his thick auburn lashes. "I can taste it I can, it tastes so feckin' brilliant it does as it trickles down me throat," his tongue lapped up any droplets that fell from his face.

"Mr. Limmerick, you need to be in reality -- you not taste whiskey -- you taste only water."

Colin opened his eyes, he looked at Sasha and slowly rose from the stream. They went to bed that night on empty stomachs.

Chapter Twenty-One

The following afternoon, Colin moved several rocks and boulders, one by one, near a cliff by the sea. He worked relentlessly without any food or rest.

"Mr. Limmerick, I don't understand your endurance. I am so hungry and weak, aren't you?"

"I try not to think 'bout it."

"Mr. Limmerick, this cliff overhangs on thin strip of land beside sea. Would mammoth be so close to sea?"

"They's swimmers they is. Big migrators they is too, that's how they ended up in yer Siberia."

"Very good, then I guess we wait by boulders until prey comes?"

"We sit 'n wait, we do. We's best get to it then."

They sat against the boulders waiting for the large animals to pass below, soon it was dark and they fell asleep. Below the cliff a family of mammoth started to pass by. Sasha opened one eye hearing the rumbling sound of the beasts below him. He gingerly crept along the boulders to view what he had heard. "It is mammoth! Fantastic beasts! Mr. Limmerick, you must wake up, our prey is below us!"

Colin opened his eyes. "Prey?" Colin smiled as he crept behind the boulders. He tried his hardest to see in the dark. "Magnificent creatures they is." Colin started to push the largest boulder with Sasha's help. Every vein in Colin's biceps bulged as he pushed the boulder with all his strength. "C'mon, Sasha, push harder!" Colin demanded gritting his teeth as beads of sweat poured off his face.

Sasha pushed as hard as he could. "We must hurry or beasts will get away!"

The boulder toppled over the cliff falling on the matriarch's head killing her instantly. The other mammoth family members stopped in horror as they looked up focusing on Colin and Sasha. They suddenly started to stampede away.

The two men made their way below the cliff with their rifle, axe, and spear in hand.

"We did it, Mr. Limmerick, we kill big fuzzy elephant! Now we have food for very long while."

"We need to build a fire right 'er 'n cook the meat. In fact, I'm so hungry I could tear the flesh from its bones right now!"

Colin chopped portions of the animal to cook on the fire that Sasha built. The aroma of the fresh kill filled the air. They ate without saying a word to one another. Sasha noticed how Colin tore away at the cooked flesh eating without even taking a moment to breathe. Sasha ate not paying attention to their new visitors. A family of spotted hyenas encircled them. Sasha felt uncomfortable but Colin kept eating without bothering to acknowledge the intruders. Sasha slowly placed the meat down. The hyena circle only shrunk a little where the animals made a point of keeping their distance. Sasha sat still keeping his eyes on the prehistoric animals. Colin continued to eat.

"Mr. Limmerick, I cannot eat another bite."

Colin was silent as he continued to tear away at the flesh.

"Mr. Limmerick? Are you alright?"

Colin did not answer.

"Mr. Limmerick!"

"Can't ye let me eat?"

"What do you think of taste?"

"Don't feckin' care, as long as it's meat."

"Hyenas are moving closer to us."

"Let'em join us for dinner, it's alright by me."

"They're hyenas, Mr. Limmerick." The hyenas kept their distance where the fire pit kept them alert.

Colin stopped eating as he gave Sasha a cold stare. "Don't feckin' give a shite if they's hyenas! They don't bother me -- not at all!"

273

Chapter Twenty-Two

A few days had passed Colin and Sasha were getting used to hunting prehistoric mammals. They kept themselves well fed as well as rested in their new environment. One hot afternoon they hiked through the grasses and forested areas in search of food when Sasha noticed wild horses roaming in the background. "Horses are here?"

"Ah, fantastic, wild horses they is!" Colin said holding his axe.

"Wild horses. These are great animals, Mr. Limmerick."

"Should we hunt them, mate?"

"I cannot imagine eating horse but we may not get opportunity in long time."

"I'll use me axe 'n spear, don't use yer gun."

"Let me have your spear and we will catch one."

"Do we need a plan of ambush?"

"I do not know. We need to eat I know. They run very quickly, how we catch such animal?"

"I'll throw me axe or ye can throw the spear -- we can only hope for the best."

Colin held his axe tightly in his hand as he crept low in the grasses. Sasha did the same. Colin targeted a large male when he began to run. Forgetting to take a breath, he chased after it. The horse tore through the grasses to get as far from Colin as possible. As Colin continued to run with every bit of power in his body, another human-like figure started to run along side of him. Colin flung his axe at the horse killing it instantly with a deep wound to the neck. He ran to the dead animal realising the person standing next to him was not Sasha. He noticeding a stocky male measuring around five feet tall. The male was holding a spear of its own as it started to rip the flesh from the dead horse. Colin stood there watching with anger. Sasha held his gun close to him as he made his way to where Colin was standing. Colin punched the male on the back trying to pry him off the carcass.

"Get the hell away from me prey, ye thief!" Colin shouted as he grabbed the male pulling him away. The male looked at Colin and started to yell in some kind of tribal language.

"Sasha, look at the bastard, he's tryin' to take away our meal!"

"Mr. Limmerick, this is some kind of caveman. This is not like you to be so disrespectable. Let him have horse. We have become expert hunters, we can get something else."

"This one is ours 'n we's gonna eat it!" Colin grabbed the male thrashing him to the ground.

The male remained on the ground as he gripped onto Colin's ankles pulling him toward him. Colin hit the ground hard. Colin crawled toward the male and grabbed him by the neck. The male elbowed Colin in the neck where he gasped.

"Mr. Limmerick, let him go! Stop this!" Sasha shouted with concern.

Colin stood and leered at the male. "Fine, take the bleedin' carcass ye bloody bastard!"

Sasha pulled Colin away from the male. "What species is this, Mr. Limmerick?"

"Hmm, what would Rosa say? I think I just had meself an encounter with a *Neanderthal*. I'm surprised to find them in Ireland."

"He did not seem afraid of you."

Colin tried to wipe the dirt off his body. "Did ye see the size of the bloke? He was wee small he was! I could take'em in a flash I could!"

"Mr. Limmerick, he looked like he could be strong."

"No more than I."

"We cannot survive in this place. I cannot and you

cannot!"

"Look at me, nothin' would dare cross me path."

"You are man, Mr. Limmerick! You are not made of super human substance! You are just man!"

"Yer speakin' to me like I'm some kind of nut!"

"You are some kind nut! You must ground yourself, Mr. Limmerick! Think of Miss Amoli. Think of what she is doing right now. Don't forget Miss Amoli. Don't forget how much she cares for you."

"I know she fancies me. I suppose I get on with her as well."

"We must return to our time so you can tell her this."

Colin paused looking at Sasha. "I just donno if I can, mate."

"What are you saying, Mr. Limmerick?"

"I never really fit in to our world ye know. I always felt like an outcast."

"What? You must be crazy!" Sasha stood up facing Colin.

"I'm tellin' ye how I feel."

"Are you telling me you want to stay here?"

"I am."

"You so stupid sometimes, Mr. Limmerick. You cannot be serious! What has happened to you?" Sasha whimpered with frustration.

"Me 'n Amoli haven't really established anythin'. She isn't me wench. She's half me age 'n from a totally different culture. She'd never understand me, I'd just frustrate'er."

"Mr. Limmerick, you are experiencing alcohol withdrawl! You do not mean what you say. You talk silliness!

"How'bout ye, Sasha? Ye got shite like this ye left behind in Russia?"

"It no so easy to leave Russia, but revolution push me out," he paused. "I say you this -- we must invent method of closing time vortex or else your Ireland is at great risk!"

276

"Well, feck, ye'r the expert are ye not? Ye find a bleedin' way to close up this feckin' distaster!"

"Nyet, Mr. Limmerick, we find method -- together, da?"

Colin stepped closer to Sasha. "Alright then, how we goin' to close the time vortex?"

"I have developed method you may or may not agree with--."

"Carry-on."

"Dodecagon, da?"

"Huh? What's that?"

Sasha sighed with frustration. "We must build plug, da?"

"Yeah, alright."

"Dodecagon is plane figure with twelve sides and angles."

"Really."

"Now we need material to build."

"Alright."

"You, Mr. Limmerick so enjoy being caveman you can construct tool -- you have axe, da?"

"I do."

"We must begin to gather material. Use your strength, Mr. Limmerick, use your axe, use your brains."

"This sounds absurd it does."

"I will tell you one thing, Mr. Limmerick, you better listen good. When I figure out how to get back through time vortex I will go with or without you! Do you understand?"

"Leave me here? I don't care really if ye do."

"You will never taste your whiskey again if you remain here! Who will you screw?"

"Me-self."

"I have strong feeling now, that I would like to punch you in face," Sasha clenched his fists and stormed off in a rage. "You are such ass sometimes, Mr.Limmerick!"

"Yer doin' loads of name callin' ye is!"

277

***

Late that afternoon Colin and Sasha gathered materials. Colin chopped down several trees while Sasha gathered branches. Colin chiseled away at large chunks of granite. They combined soil with tree sap to create an adhesive for their invention. They worked in the heat for several hours. Colin's muscles throbbed with soreness as he collapsed on the ground.

Sasha slouched onto a rock with exhaustion. "Mr. Limmerick, we must build such great stone to role down ramp to collide with stone wall we will soon build."

"What the feck ye sayin'?" Colin questioned as he panted with exhaustion.

"We must build dodecagon at 6 meters and mass of fourteen tonnes. Ramp must be exactly at 56 meters to release energy enough to close time vortex."

"Absurd this sounds!"

"No so fast, Mr. Limmerick -- we also must build stone wall with your great muscles and power."

"What?"

"Mr. Limmerick, you are romantic -- you not understand physics! We must release energy in correct place at correct time or else this journey is waste of time."

"Couldn't we have just brought dynamite?"

"Hah! We need kinetic energy no chemical energy!" Sasha shouted as he waved his finger at Colin.

"Oh."

"I already tell you we must release correct amount energy, not too much -- just at correct time -- not too early, not too late. What you not understand?

"This sounds impossible it does."

"Nothing is impossible, until we decide it is."

"Can I ask ye somethin'?"

"What is it, Mr. Limmerick, what?"

"Would ye like to explain the meanin' of this bleedin' ramp we's supposed to build with no resources 'n this feckin' stone wall ye speak of?"

"I say you already, we must create explosion -- we must have energy to plug time vortex opening and for us to venture out of time vortex. Why you not understand?"

"Is this similar to the meteor strike in Siberia's explosion which initially got us through the time vortex?"

"Da, you now undersand."

"Alright then -- lets get huntin'," Colin said waving his axe in the air. "I don't know if we should try another mammoth. We left so much food behind we's did with the last one. At least the hyenas had a brilliant time with our kill," Colin said trying to catch his breath.

"Lets try smaller animal. We do not have families to feed. It is just you and I."

Chapter Twenty-Three

It was early morning Colin woke before Sasha taking his axe with him to the nearby pond. He bathed and returned to their camp. Sasha was already up smoking a cigarette. Colin grabbed Sasha's rifle tossing it to him. "Go fetch us somethin' to eat!"

Sasha took the rifle and wandered into the brush. Colin grabbed his axe and began to chop down trees for firewood. The two men worked relentlessly to build the dodecagon. They found a sloped hill where Colin began to build the ramp from several logs and mud. Sasha sat on the grass and stared at his physics equation:

$$PE = mgh = \tfrac{1}{2}\, mV^2 = X \, BTU \; of \; Energy$$

Colin glanced at Sasha. "What ye writin' there?"

"Very important to have scientific plan of action."

Colin walked to Sasha peering over his shoulder. "What's yer formula mean?"

"Potential energy equals mass multiplied by force of gravity multiplied by height equals half mass multiplied by velocity to power of two -- equals British thermal units of energy."

"I see."

"You understand, Mr. Limmerick?"

Colin backed away to continue his work. "Physics is not me focus, man."

"I have thought through several equations of formula and all will be successful -- believe me."

"I'm supposin' we don't have much of a choice now do we?" Colin gathered several thick tree branches.

"Nyet."

"By the way, mate, how come I'm doin' most of the physical labour here?" Colin asked while he rolled a log down the slope.

"You want help? I will give help."

"I'm tryin' to hammer these stakes into the ground so they can keep the logs tightly knit together. I hope the dodecagon will flow down this slop of logs at the speed yer lookin' for.

"As long as log no have jagged surface so dodecagon can slide down hill."

"I'll make sure of that."

"You are good labourer, Mr. Limmerick," Sasha chuckled then began to gather tree branches. "It has to be strong so it will collide with stone wall to create energy."

They worked on the ramp and the dodecagon until the middle of the night. They would stop for the occasional rest and even hunt for a small meal just to give them the fuel they needed to continue. Colin was beyond exhaustion dripping in his own over-worked sweat glands. He compiled pieces of bark to use so he could sand down the cut logs that he had fascine to the slope with the wooden stakes. Sasha continued to create stakes from the wood of the branches. It was so dark they could barely see. Sasha touched his nose from time to time to test his bearings. They then realised it was easier to build a fire and bare the heat while they worked. When they felt they could no longer work they each took a flaming branch to find their way back to their hut. They lifelessly bumped their way to their wooden hut and immediately fell onto their sleeping bags into a deep trance of sleep.

***

The new morning broke with extreme heat causing both men to wake at the same time. They washed up, caught their meal and made their way to the ramp. They stood on the top of the slope beside the dodecagon looking down at the logs where Sasha noticed something just wasn't quite right.

"Logs and dodecagon look good, Mr. Limmerick, da?"

"They's look fine to me," Colin said as he noticed the

heat was starting to intensify. "Somethin' wrong, mate?"

"All tree branches we gather yesterday are now gone. *Pachimu?*" Sasha asked feeling frustrated.

"Huh?"

"Why our branches not here?"

"A cave lion ran off with 'em?" Colin answered.

"Think, Mr. Limmerick -- you are animal expert -- why would lion want branches? They make no nest?"

"Well, of course not. I don't feckin' know why the feckin' branches are missin'!"

"You and me, Mr. Limmerick, spend long hours yesterday gathering branches -- now they gone...why?"

Colin walked around the area. "There's no feckin' sign of 'em. It's like something took 'em, eh?"

"Da, but logs still look in-tact, no?"

"The logs look just fine they's do. But, how the branches left this site I can't really say."

They started to search through the brush smelling the aroma of meat. "Looka there, mate!" Colin pointed to a cave settlement. "I bet *Neanderthal*s live in that cave dwellin'. Someone must be cookin' some grub on the barbeque," Colin said moving closer to the opened fire by the cave.

"They look like people or are they apes -- I cannot tell difference," Sasha said loading his rifle.

Colin stopped and slowly turned his head toward Sasha. "They's look nothin' like apes. I don't get how ye see that?"

"I don't understand many things about you, Mr Limmerick."

"Looks like they's cookin' up a large mammal of some kind."

"They must be expert hunters."

"That they is but not as keen as me they's not."

Sasha tugged on Colin's arm. "Mr. Limmerick, they hunt large game everyday. You are fisherman with modern technology -- you have trawler. This cannot be compared. This species knows these lands -- you do not!"

"'Tis me home it is."

"Mr. Limmerick, this is forty-thousand years in past. This is alien to you!"

"Ye know what I'll do, just to prove to ye that I can survive here -- I'm gonna snatch that slain animal from *Neanderthal* 'n his family."

"You want to steal their food?"

"Hyenas do it all the time. Besides, these wankers stole our wood!"

"What has happened to you, Mr. Limmerick? This is not like you at all. Do not steal their food!"

"Darwin said survival of the fittest did he not?"

"But, you are not fittest in this situation, Mr. Limmerick!"

"Look at me!" Colin pounded his chest, "Look at me size'n strength! I've got the brain capacity, the strategy, 'n the physique! I'm gonna take their food 'n they'll be kissin' me arse in the process 'cause I'll be their new master!"

"Mr. Limmerick, we need to go back to our time. This is not working. You were so nice boy before, why is this happening to you?"

Colin walked in the midst of a gathering of *Neanderthals* cooking what looked like a wooly rhinoceros. Colin stood by the roasting animal. The family of *Neanderthals* stopped what they were doing to move toward Colin. Colin took his axe and began chopping at the dead animal to release it from the fire. Sasha watched from the brush. Three male *Neanderthals* stood in front of Colin feeling somewhat intimidated by his size. One of the males was the one Colin had encountered earlier -- he appeared to be the strongest. He stood directly in front of Colin. They stared each other down but not a word was said. Colin stepped a little closer to him then remained still. The primitive male stepped forward as well and continued to stare at Colin. He then punched Colin in the stomach.

The blow surprised Colin. He doubled over where he felt winded. "So, ye want a fight for yer food do yez?" Colin could barely blurt out a word. The *Neanderthal* remained still and watched Colin straighen up.

Sasha sat in the brush un-noticed as he covered his eyes. "Why has Mr. Limmerick turned into such ass?"

Colin ignored the three *Neanderthals* and continued to cut away at the roasting carcass from the fire. The three prehistoric males leaped onto Colin's back bringing him to the ground. The family of *Neanderthals* gathered around the commotion. Colin was on his belly trying to buck the three beings off. They hit him hard on the back of the head, blood dripped in front of Colin's eyes. The male who had the previous encounter with Colin pierced Colin's shoulder flesh with his teeth. Colin shouted in agony but managed to roll over and get the three males away from his backside. Colin vigilantly focused on the three males while he tried to stand up. One of the males charged at Colin and thrashed him to the ground. Sasha watched from the brush holding his rifle securely in his hands. "Should I shoot, or is this against Mr. Limmerick's wishes? He would rather die this way than have me save his life with gun. He is more crazy than I thought."

Colin was confronted by one of the other males and was violently punched to the ground. The male *Neanderthal'* s stare viciously pierced through Colin. Colin lay flat on his belly with his face buried in the soil. Sasha watched hoping Colin would come to his senses. The *Neanderthal* wrapped his long sturdy arms around Colin's body almost crushing his bones. The prehistoric male picked up a rock and smashed it over Colin's face. Colin lost consciousness. The *Neanderthal* stood on Colin's chest thumping his feet on him. Sasha watched Colin lay on the ground drenched in his own blood.

The stocky male *Neanderthal* roughly placed Colin beside the roasting animal carcass. Sasha's concern heightened where he realized what the *Neanderthal*'s intensions were. "This is nightmare," Sasha whispered to himself, "They want Mr. Limmerick for next feed? *Nyet! Nyet! Mnye plokha!*"

Suddenly there was stirred commotion within the family of *Neanderthals*. There seemed to be panic on their faces. Another tribe of beings entered their settlement. It was beings that appeared to be more human in appearance. "What would Rosa call these people?" Sasha asked himself. *"Homo sapiens? Paleolithic, Mesolithic?"* I do not know -- I am physicist."

The human-looking tribe tried to pull Colin away from the family of *Neanderthals*. The head male *Neanderthal* grabbed Colin's legs trying to pull him away from the human-looking tribe. The human-looking tribe let go of Colin and shook their spears and hand axes ready to fight. The *Neanderthals* pulled out their flint hand-axes also ready to fight. Colin gained consciousness feeling stirred by the strife of the two groups. He slowly tried to crawl away. The human-looking tribe shot a thin spear into Colin's arm. The head male *Neanderthal* grabbed Colin lifting him above his head. Sasha was mortified. "How is this possible?" Sasha whispered to himself. What seemed to be the male dominant leader of the human-like species gouged the Neanderthal, who was lifting Colin in mid-air; allowing Colin to crash to the ground. The two male dominant figures began to duel with each other as Colin slowly tried to crawl away. Sasha watched. The groups were heavily involved with their own tribal disputes. Colin made his way to the dense brush leaving a trail of blood. Sasha remained still.

When it was dusk and the Neanderthal settlement appeared quiet Sasha searched for Colin in the dense scrub. He noticed the foliage had red drippings, which led him to Colin. Sasha found Colin lying beside a tree trying to clean his wounds with whatever resources he could find.

Sasha kneeled beside him. "Neanderthals were very strong species, Mr. Limmerick."

Colin slowly turned himself toward Sasha. He felt pain with every movement. "That they was or is. Feck, I donno how to phrase me tenses anymore. I hurt that's all I know."

"You have some terrible experiences here, Mr. Limmerick, but I so happy to see you."

Chapter Twenty-Four

It was already late morning, the intense sun penetrated through the cracks of the hut causing Sasha to wake from his restless sleep. He lethargically scanned his surrounding area noticing Colin was not with him. He reached for his cigarettes beside his sleeping bag, lit up and began to smoke. He jolted with adrenaline and sprung from his sleeping bag. He went outside with his rifle clutched to his body in a stir of panic. Colin sat by their unlit fire pit while sipping on a container of spring water. Sasha stumbled to Colin dropping his rifle to the ground with relief.

"It's gone, mate," Colin said staring at nothing.

Sasha stepped toward Colin. "What? What is gone, Mr. Limmerick?"

"The dodecagon. It's no longer at the top of the ramp. It's feckin' gone I tell ye. I think those beasts swiped it. We's fecked we is."

Sasha felt almost paralyzed by Colin's words. "Neanderthals took dodecagon? I cannot believe!" He threw his hands in the air.

"I'm no match for'em. They can easily take me down. Do we got enough bullets?"

"Maybe not for entire Neanderthal community."

"We'll have to make another then."

"What? Make another what?" Sasha backed off where the intonation in his voice sounded like a whimper.

"Another dodecagon."

"No, I cannot, Mr. Limmerick -- I have no strength left. I will surely die in process."

"But, if we don't do this we'll feckin' die anyways -- don't ye think?"

Sasha looked at Colin and paused. "We still not yet have built wall below ramp. We must not stand around we must get to work.

Colin tried to be cordial. He stood up toward Sasha. "Ah, ye got it in ye to never give up, mate."

They immediately got to work on the wall at the bottom of the ramp working for hours in the penetrating sun. Colin tried to chisel chunks of rock while Sasha used mud for brick mortar. The sun's intensity heightened during that afternoon, but Colin continued to chisle chunks of rock almost dulling the edge of his blade. He then decided to take a break where he eased his body onto the dense cushy grass. He closed his eyed as he lay in the tall grasses almost in a trance. "Sasha, I think I'll imagine somethin' tranquil just now."

Sasha started to smoke. "Da, something good you can dream."

"I'm visualizin' me-self with a beautiful lass."

"What she look like?" Sasha asked as he enjoyed every puff from his cigarette.

"Beautiful dark skin 'n eyes she's got. Hair is long 'n black like the night.

Sasha held his cigarette between his fingers as he blew a well-formed smoke ring. "You describe Miss Amoli?"

Colin paused. "I suppose so."

"We must hurry and close time vortex so we return to our time, Mr. Limmerick," Sasha said relishing his cigarette.

Colin sat up. "I know what I'm goin' to do!" he shouted while standing up with a sudden burst of energy.

"What?" Sasha asked.

"I'm goin' to fetch our dodecagon I will. I'll get it back from those prehistoric pirates!"

Sasha followed him. "No! Mr. Limmerick, your axe now has dull blade, you are no match for them! You cannot!"

Colin suddenly stopped. "Yer right, mate. They'll bust me skull they's will. But, what we can do is ambush them."

"Ambush? How we do?"

"Either a land slide er a pit trap should do it."

"Land slide is what we do to wooly mammoth?"

"Aye."

"What is pit slide?"

"We dig a large pit where they all can fall through."

"Where we get shovels?"

"We might have to make'em."

Sasha smoked his cigarette down to no butt to discard. "I like first idea better."

"Fine then, we need to follow their path 'n see if there's a way to push a large boulder off a cliff just as we did with the mammoth."

"It is good thing your biceps grow bigger everyday because I not have strength to be pushing boulders off cliff."

"Perhaps we can push a large boulder off a cliff whilst bein' pushed by a log er we can make a type of springboard for launchin'."

"Oh, so much labour, Mr. Limmerick. I know you like this work. Use more your brains, Mr. Limmerick, not so much your brawn."

***

Late that afternoon Colin and Sasha made their way toward the Neanderthal cave while they moved vigilantly through the brush. They peered through the bushes noticing several Neanderthals outside the cave. Suddenly several male Neanderthals rolled the dodecagon in front of the cave.

"How they move it with so much ease?" Sasha asked in a whisper.

"Strong little bastards they is," Colin whispered back.

The Neanderthals formed a circle around the dodecagon as they began to chant.

"They's treatin' it like it's some kind of God?" Colin discovered. The two men slowly made their way back to their campsite.

Colin sat by the fire-pit. "Okay, so the dodecagon is their new found God?"

"This could be big problem."

"Well, yeah."

"I'm referring to not having cigarettes to smoke, Mr. Limmerick," Sasha said.

"Oh."

"So, what we do now? Do we steal their God?"

"Aye, we do -- but first we ambush their master alpha -- he's the strongest one who almost killed me."

"You think we will be able to take dodecagon from them once we kill master?"

"I need yer strength to help me move that thing outta there as fast as possible -- cause they's goin' to come lookin' for us."

"Strength? What strength?"

"This is our only chance, Sasha."

***

The next few days Sasha and Colin concentrated on tracking the main Neanderthal's hunting pattern. The two men stood on top of the same cliff they had been for the mammoth ambush. Below them, they would watch the male Neanderthals from above noticing how they would walk in single file to hunt and gather.

"They hunt along this path," Colin said to Sasha.

"We must try to get this done as quick as possible."

Colin and Sasha located a boulder large enough to kill the lead male Neanderthal. They both faced the challenge of rolling it to the cliff's ledge. They slowly directed the boulder to the ledge of the cliff where Colin rolled his body down the slight slope of the ledge as he almost blacked out with fatigue.

"My God, Mr. Limmerick, I think you really are Hercules," Sasha said placing his head between his knees. "I apologize for having so less strength."

Colin tried to catch his breath. "We need to fatten ye up, mate. I need ye to be healthy for this er we's fecked.

290

Remember, It's all very nice ye call me Hercules but I can't compete with those bastards. We make one wrong move we'll be done I tell ye."

Colin said while Sasha didn't see any more Neanderthals as they peered down from the cliff.

"When we see Nenderthal walk this path that is located below us?" Sasha asked while easing himself to the ground with exhaustion.

"Perhaps we did the other day," Colin answered, as he lay sprawled on the grass.

"We must sit and wait da?"

Colin gazed at the sky. "Sure."

Sasha lay on the grass finding himself almost falling asleep.

Some hours had elapsed as the two men continued to wait where there were no signs of any Neanderthals. Colin lay back and took a rest.

"Mr. Limmerick! Mr. Limmerick! Wake up! I think Neanderthals are below us walking along path. We must hurry!" Sasha shouted. He shook Colin's shoulder.

Colin opened his eyes. "Huh?"

"Come help me push boulder off cliff -- help me spot master male Neanderthal!" Sasha said.

"I must've been havin' a dream," Colin said as he sprung up from his relaxed state. He crouched into the grasses. He and Sasha peered down from the cliff watching several Neanderthal males walk in single file holding hunting equipment in their hands.

Colin noticed the last Neanderthal was the largest and seemed to be walking with a different posture than the other males. "Sasha! I think it's 'em!" Colin pointed out.

"You sure?"

"Feck -- I hope so."

The two men pressed their bodies against the boulder, hoisted it up the slight slope to the very edge. They watched the alpha male walk below the bluff where they perched watching the group. As soon as he walked

291

directly below them, the boulder fell from the sky dropping faster than they thought and hit the ground completely decimating the alpha male.

The Neanderthals halted their activity immediately looking up spotting the two men above on the cliff. The Neanderthal males scattered in all directions holding their sharp hand-axes firmly in their hands.

"Run!" Sasha shouted.

The two time travelers ran to the dense brush without looking back. They could hear cries from the Neanderthals as they cut through the dense forest. Sasha noticed a few Neanderthals in the background.

"Duck down, Mr. Limmerick!" Sasha yelled as he tripped Colin to fall into the deep grasses. "Don't move," Sasha whispered clutching his rifle.

About five or six Neanderthals cased the area holding their weapons with great vigilance. They looked up at the trees as they tried to pick up a different scent of the two men. Colin and Sasha lay flat on their bellies trying not to move. They could hear the rustle of the grass as the prehistoric beings encircled the area drawing closer to the two men. The Neanderthals then sniffed their way to where the two men lay. One Neanderthal noticed Sasha's blond circles and stomped on the back of Sasha's leg slashing it.

Sasha yelped, jumped up trying not to look at the blood spilling out of his leg.

Colin grabbed Sasha throwing him over his shoulder and ran holding his axe in his other hand while he darted into the dense forest. The Neanderthals ran after them. He managed to dodge their flinging rocks while he meandered through the brush.

"My leg! My leg! Why prehistoric mammals always get my leg?" Sasha cried in wailing pain.

Colin tried to dodge the dense trees; leaping over fallen logs, while trying to avoid unstable surfaces as he left the Neanderthals further behind. Colin noticed a small opening that looked like a cave -- he pushed Sasha toward the opening where he had to crawl on his stomach along the muddy ground into a dark cavity. Colin was directly behind Sasha but at the same time watched the Neanderthals approach. As Sasha's entire body fit into the cavity, Colin then lay on his stomach to also enter. He got his head into the cave but his shoulders were much too broad. Sasha was on the other side trying to pull Colin's head. Colin tried to bust some of the ruble with his shoulders but he still would not fit. Colin tried to force his shoulders through the cavity so much so his skin was deeply scraped with blood.

"It's no use, Sasha. I just won't fit 'is all!" Colin kept forcing himself but the Neanderthals were only a few meters away running toward him with vengeance and fury.

The Neanderthals grabbed hold of Colin pulling him away from the small cave opening. They pulled his hair and kicked him to the ground. Colin tried to crab-crawl backwards on the ground as he kept his eyes on the raging prehistoric creatures. The Neanderthal that stood the closest to Colin tried to intimidate him with extreme rage. Colin managed to trip him to the ground. Colin took the *Neanderthal's* hand axe and mangaged to fling it at one of the other charging *Neanderthals* who received the blade between the eyes.

Sasha poked his head out of the cavity and quickly crawled out clutching his rifle. "Good throw, Mr. Limmerick!"

Another *Neanderthal* leaped onto Colin's back forcing him to the ground. They began to wrestle. Colin managed to throw a few punches at the *Neanderthal's* face but he was resilient enough to pin Colin's arms to the ground. The Neanderthal sat on Colin's chest to demonstrate his defeat.

Three *Neanderthals* encircled Sasha as they threw their hand-axes at his head but Sasha was fast enough to dodge the flinging blades. Colin buckled his legs trying to pry the Neanderthal off his chest as they both hung on to each other falling to their side as Colin managed to scuff himself away enough to stand up, realising his axe was left in the cave cavity. He vigilantly walked backward toward the cavity but two Neanderthals walked toward him holding hand axes in their hands.

"Sasha!" Colin shouted as the Neanderthal thrashed Colin to the ground. "Sasha!" Colin shouted in desperation.

"Mr. Limmerick?" Sasha answered as he dodged punches and throws.

The *Neanderthal* kicked Colin profusely as Colin dragged himself away from the Neanderthal. "Where's yer gun?"

"I have!"

"Get this fecker off me -- shoot'em! He won't stop till he kills me!" He hoarsely gasped out of breath.

Sasha leaped on top of a large rock, aimed his rifle and fired. "I may have only three bullets left!" he shouted. One of the Neanderthal fell dead beside Colin.

The remaining *Neanderthals* stopped with fear of how the Neanderthal fell to his death. They backed away and started to speak to each other acting out fear and rage. The remaining two Neanderthals backed away from the two men and retreated to the forest.

Sasha looked at Colin. "You think they will confront us again, Mr. Limmerick?" Sasha asked. He swung his rifle over his shoulder.

"It isn't over just yet. We still need to get our dodecagon back so we can get the hell out of here."

"Well, we killed off a few Neanderthal and frightened away others. We may have chance?"

"Shite, I donno," Colin said to Sasha. "Feck, it really bothers me that we could be changin' evolution. This wasn't supposed to happen it wasn't."

***

Later that day, the wounded male Neanderthals went back to their residing community to complain to the females about the two men. They were distraught in a panicked state with the dodecagon still sitting beside their fire pit. Colin and Sasha poked their heads through the dense brush as they viewed the Neanderthals congregating together appearing almost terrified.

"Sasha, how many bullets ye got?" Colin asked in a whisper.

Sasha sat back. "Three. I say you already."

"That's it?"

"Da."

"Shite."

"Mr. Limmerick, this dodecagon of ours is large and heavy -- if we do get hold of it -- how we return it to top of slope so we create energy?"

Colin suddenly noticed a young wooly rhinoceros standing a few meters away from the dense brush. "We could become animal trainers we could?" Colin suggested.

Sasha noticed the animal grazing in the field. "Mr. Limmerick, sometimes your ideas do not fit you."

"We could train that rhino to be our oxen for the big pull. What ye think?"

"I don't. That is young animal -- where his mother?"

"Who cares? We could collect some tubers or somethin' 'n feed it to the youngster, don't ye think?"

"This is getting bad, Mr. Limmerick. I was correct about you."

"Correct 'bout what?"

"You are some kind of nut."

They gathered several roots, grasses, reeds, and vine branches. Colin saw the young rhinoceros and made sure he was completely in front of the young animal, for he did not want to take it by surprise. He approached it where the animal trotted a few meters away from him but Colin kept approaching it.

"Mr. Limmerick, maybe I should return to that cave

cavity and retrieve your axe?" Sasha shouted standing as far from the rhino as possible.

"Yeah, go a head 'n fetch it. That would be a brilliant help it would."

Colin got closer to the animal where he extended his hands to it trying to lure it to his collection of vegetation. The animal was at first reluctant but slowly came around to move closer to him. As it got very near it started to pull away at the roots in Colin's hand as the greens fell to the ground and Colin observed while it feasted.

Sasha made his way back to the cave cavity. He noticed two young *Neanderthals* had Colin's axe. Sasha ran toward them trying to scare them off. When they saw Sasha they ran from him in terror dropping the axe to the ground. Sasha returned to the spot where Colin was feeding the young rhinoceros.

"Mr. Limmerick, we may not have so big problem getting dodecagon back now!" Sasha shouted as he startled the rhino to run away.

"Feck ye, Sasha! What the feck is wrong with ye? Ye scared'em silly ye did!" Colin shouted back.

"Well, I am so sorry. Try and get him back."

"I don't know if that can happen now. Shite!"

"Mr. Limmerick, I think Neanderthal clan is afraid of us. They fear us. Two Neanderthal children were playing with your axe -- when they see me they run away very fast."

"Is that so?"

"Mr. Limmerick, beasts not understand us -- they fear us, da?"

Colin stood up. "Well, that's good news I suppose. Lets get back to our rhinoceros 'n get 'em to haul the dodecagon back to the top of our slope. I don't know 'bout ye -- but I'm really feelin' the wounds from our prehistoric blokes. I think I need to see a doctor -- how 'bout ye?"

"Of course, Mr. Limmerick, me too."

The two men found some food and went to sleep in their hut.

**

It was a new morining, Colin and Sasha gathered several roots and grasses to feed to the young rhinoceros. Colin trekked through the tall grasses as he waved the roots in the air so the rhinoceros could pick up the sent. Sasha continued to gather as many roots and dry grasses as possible.

"Mr. Limmerick, where is your rhino friend?" Sasha asked forcing himself to continue gathering.

Colin continued to sway the vegetation around. "I don't know. Ye should've realised I was with 'em 'n ye should've never scared 'em off."

"I am sorry, Mr. Limmerick," Sasha said noticing a roundish animal standing in the near distance. "Mr. Limmerick! What is that?"

Colin squinted to get a closer look. "I think our young friend has returned," Colin said.

Colin held the vegetation in his hand as he gingerly approached the young rhinoceros. "C'mon, I met ye yesterday. I know ye really fancy roots 'n such," Colin said in a calming whisper to the animal.

The rhino backed away from Colin but did not run. It stayed focused on Colin's gestures. Colin crouched down to his knees extending the gathered roots to it. The rhino slowly moved toward Colin and began to eat from his hands. Sasha stood in the distance as he observed Colin establish a trust between him and the animal. Colin slowly stood up. He lured the young rhino in the direction of the *Neanderthal* cave settlement. Sasha continued to gather roots and kept Colin's supply well nurtured.

The young rhino followed Colin as he continued to feed it with the help of Sasha's constant supply. Sasha made sure he had a good supply of rope that they had brought with them through the time vortex. The two men arrived to the cave settlement noticing the dodecagon was

297

still apparent. There were several female and juvenile *Neanderthals* who watched and stared at them. Sasha threw one end of the rope to Colin as they tied the wooly rhinoceros to the bulbous object. The rhino was so intrigued with the roots it did not seem to mind that a rope was tied from its waist to the large structure. Colin continued to feed the young rhino roots but two female Neanderthals abruptly interrupted him. One of the females fussed over Colin almost hindering his connection with the young rhino.

"Sasha! Can ye keep this wench off me?"

Sasha tried to wedge himself between the female *Neanderthal* and Colin. She began to touch Sasha. She stepped toward Sasha thrashing him to the ground. Sasha slowly stood up. He felt dazed. She then kicked Sasha in the stomach, which had him lay flat on his front side. He slowly raised his head as he got glimpse of her strong foot approaching him again for a second kick. He quickly rolled out of the way and sprang up noticing Colin in the distance entering the thick brush with the animal and the dodecagon. Another female *Neanderthal* approached Sasha from behind where she swiped his gun. He turned to her and managed to trip her to the ground where she lost grip of the rifle. He dove for the rifle as he immediately sprinted into the dense brush leaving the two Neanderthal females.

Colin managed to lure the young rhino near the top of the cliff where he released it from the dodecagon. The young rhino stood and stared at Colin, where it still managed to get the remaining supply of roots and tubors. Colin didn't want to hurry the rhino along so he sat and waited for Sasha.

Some hours had passed Colin and Sasha pushed the dodecagon to its exact placement on the cliff. Colin couldn't help noticing how beat-up Sasha looked but he decided not to comment realising he looked the same.

They returned to their campsite feeling the throbbing

pain mixed with exhaustion. "I have *time travel device*, it should help me indicate where time vortex is located, remember, the reason we came on this prehistoric journey is to close time vortex so we do not destroy 1908, especially your Ireland," Sasha said.

"I realise that, I just need to rest a wee bit I do. I'm not at me best," Colin said turning toward the hut.

"Stay here and rest, I will look for time vortex. I too am not at my best."

Colin tugged on Sasha's arm. "Don't go far, we's got to leave soon."

"I understand this already," Sasha took his rifle by his side as he ventured away from the camp. "If I fire gun again it better be for good reason -- we cannot afford to waste bullets."

Colin fell instantly asleep feeling somewhat safe in the hut they had built.

Sasha exited their hut making his way through the thick foliage trying to re-trace his steps of where they entered this prehistoric time. His device was directing him in a westward direction.

Colin slept until he felt a banging against the wall of the hut. He immediately alerted himself. "Sasha! Sasha!"

BANG! BANG! BANG! BANG! BANG! The sound was thundering almost piercing Colin's ears. The hut rumbled as if something outside the hut tried to tear it down. Colin stumbled trying to stand up still feeling the throbbing pain of his multiple wounds. He grabbed his axe and placed his ear to the walls of the hut.

"What the hell's out there?" He said. Colin gestured the sign of the Catholic cross across his chest and began to pray. He ran his ear to one side of the wall where he felt a being of some kind pressed against it. In a sudden instant a large horn jetted through the wooden wall of the hut skinning a thin layer of Colin's belly. Colin jumped back as a sudden reaction noticing a wooly rhinoceros was charging at the wall. "What the feck?" Colin took the risk of running out the door of the hut. He managed to dodge the animal running amongst the trees. The rhino was relentless as it began tearing at the trees. Colin ran deeper into the forest gripping his axe firmly. He noticed the rhino in the distance waiting for his return as it snorted and buffed its foot against the muddy ground. "What rhinoceros in its right mind would do this?" He watched the large beast try to rip its way through the forest. "Is this the mother of our baby root'n tuber eater?" He asked himself as he continued to hike through the forest. He cut through the brush with his axe and noticed a lone wolf scavenging for food from a previous kill. Colin didn't let the wolf's presence bother him where he by-passed it as it ate away at the meatless carcass. At first the wolf took a step back when it saw Colin but then it decided to follow him. Colin continued to cut away at the dense brush trying to keep his pace despite his pained exhaustion. The wolf started to follow closely behind him where he could feel the wolf's hot breath against the back of his legs. He turned around where the wolf backed off a bit showing its canines with a low growl. "I can't believe this, this behaviour is so unlikely for me own time. No lone wolf would ever act this aggressive," Colin said to himself. He held his axe above his head as he started to swing at the animal. The animal only slightly backed off showing its aggression.

Sasha made his way back to the camp noticing the hut destroyed and no Colin. "Mr. Limmerick?" Sasha walked through the site noticing that there was a drastic change in the campsite. Even the bear pit where they had their cookouts appeared to be stomped on. "Oh my God, what has happened here?" Sasha put his hand against his forehead in disbelief. "Mr. Limmerick! Please answer me!"

Colin appeared carrying a dead wolf on his back. "Mate! I fetched us some grub!"

Sasha expressed a sigh of relief, "Mr. Limmerick, so

glad to see you! What happened?"

Colin placed the dead wolf over the dislocated fire pit. "A wooly rhino decided to show me *who's boss*. Look at me belly, I have yet another scar from this feckin'exedition."

"Mr. Limmerick, I'm sorry you had to experience this. I thought rhinoceros are not aggressive unless provoked."

"Obviously, mate, this is a different time. We don't have wooly rhinos in our time, we have rhinoceros, 'n beautiful animals they is."

"I did find time vortex, it is not far from camp it is not exactly same location as when we arrived, but very close. We must gather our things and go. I hope we will return to 1908 A.D. There is possibility of not returning to our time but yet another time."

"Well, if we do, mate, I hope it's the Renaissance or somethin' grand."

"Why you hope for Renaissance?"

"The women, the women were supposed to be beautiful."

"You are wrong again, Mr. Limmerick. They had big foreheads and no eye-lashes!"

They cooked Colin's animal kill and ate hardily. They gathered their belongings where Colin followed Sasha as they trekked through the forest.

"Mate, we's not in the forest anymore, I thought ye said it was close to where we arrived?"

"We were not really in forested area when we arrived. It is more wide opened here," Sasha said. "Maybe time vortex needs more space to operate, I do not know. I have my indicator, it is telling me it is around here we must find time vortex."

As they searched for the location of the time vortex, Colin heard a heavy rumble where the ground vibrated.

"Mr. Limmerick, would you know why earth is moving?"

"A possible earthquake maybe. I really don't know."

Suddenly a team of angry wooly mammoths appeared from behind the eroded bluffs. Colin and Sasha stopped and stared at the animals not understanding why this stampede was occurring.

"Are they charging at us, Mr. Limmerick?"

Colin gazed at the oncoming stampede. "Feck, ye know they is. We gotta run or die!"

Colin and Sasha ran to a narrow strip of forest that divided them from the dodecagon, their ramp, and their stone wall. Colin made it to the trees before Sasha. Colin turned around noticing Sasha was cornered by two of the mammoths. Colin's eyes widened, "These animals want to destroy us, why?" Colin asked as he tried to make his way closer to Sasha and the two mammoths. "Is this revenge?" Colin asked himself. "Sasha! Use yer gun! Use yer gun!"

One of the mammoths knocked Sasha down causing his rifle and *time indicator* to land in the shrubs. Colin saw this and approached the mammoths. He waved his arms still holding his axe tightly in his hand. One of the mammoths turned its attention to Colin moving its large mass almost stepping on the *time travel indicator*. Sasha lay flat on his belly noticing one mammoth was moving closer to him. Colin yelled waving his arms trying to draw the beasts away from Sasha and the *time indicator*.

As Sasha lay on the grass he tried to crawl out of sight of the two prehistoric elephants. "What is that smell?" Sasha asked himself. "Mr. Limmerick! Now is time to release dodecagon down ramp to hit stone wall! We must now create energy!"

Colin ran in front of the two wooly mammoths drawing them toward him.

"Mr. Limmerick, the time vortex, I have located exact location of time vortex! You must listen carefully and watch carefully!" Sasha shouted with hoarseness in voice. He crawled to his *time travel indicator*.

"How can I do that when I'm dodgin' these two

prehistoric hell-raisers?" "Follow scent of time vortex, Mr. Limmerick! Remember it has strange smell! We must go to dodecagon and push it down ramp. Then we will vanish into time and you must follow! Do you understand?"

Colin managed to move closer to Sasha as he scooped up the *time indicator* and helped Sasha up as they tore through the deep brush making their way to the dodecagon. They quickly tied their rope, which was lying beside the dodecagon, around the large object as they held on to the rope tightly leaping back through the brush to the time vortex location. The two mammoths were still standing where the two men had left them. When the mammoths noticed Colin and Sasha they started to screech in a chaotic state. Colin and Sasha yanked as tightly as they could on the rope but nothing happened.

"Shite! Why's it not workin'?" Colin shouted with panic.

"Rope could be stuck on tree!"

The two men quickly vanished into the forested strip finding that the rope was snagged on a tree branch. Colin and Sasha worked quickly to untangle it as they burst back to the time vortex area where the mammoths were swaying from side to side with frustration. Colin and Sasha tried to stay out of the two large beasts way as they made their way to the time vortex.

"Okay! Hurry, 'cause I'm 'bout to be stomped!" Colin shouted as he and Sasha yanked as hard as they could on the rope.

"We were thinking when we brought so much rope!" Sasha shouted. They heard a crashing noise realising the dodecagon rolled down the ramp crashing into the wall as Sasha held his *time indicator* and leaped through an undefined opening. Colin could no longer see Sasha, he tried to make his way to the time vortex. Colin followed Sasha and leaped into the time vortex.

Chapter Twenty-Five

The journey through the time vortex was traumatic. Colin and Sasha found themselves in a chaotic vortex pulling them through a spiral of pressure and pain. They found the journey took longer before where this time the nuclear force acted relentlessly. As they were centripetally pulled through the vortex, prehistoric animals started to appear where they too were caught in this spiral of hell. Colin was half unconscious feeling he could no longer deal with this near death experience. He slowly faded and stopped resisting the vortex's pull. Sasha stayed alert choosing not to panic. He held his time *travel indicator* close to him as he noticed a family of *Megaloceros* struggling through the spiral force along with other prehistoric species.

The two men lay flat on their backs submerged in deep crisp snow. Sasha looked around and realised he was still holding his *time-travel indicator*. He raised it to his face as he continued to lie on the snow -- the dial read 1908 A.D. He sighed with relief. His body ached realising he could barely raise his head. He continued to lie flat on his back noticing he wasn't wearing a lot of clothing. He worked his eyes as he scanned the scenery from side to side. He noticed Colin lying flat on his back about six feet away.

"Mr. Limmerick!" Sasha called out but heard no response from Colin. He tried with all his strength to move his arms that it took so much effort out of him he started to sweat. "Mr. Limmerick! Wake up, Mr. Limmerick!" Sasha started to move his arms, which were almost numb from pain. "Mr. Limmerick! Please answer me! Big strong beast like you better not be dead!"

Sasha slowly rolled onto his belly and began to crawl towards Colin. Every cell of his body penetrated with immense pain he had never felt before. Sasha crawled on the snow until he reached Colin's face. Sasha placed his ear to Colin's mouth, "You are breathing -- so, why won't you wake up? Mr. Limmerick! Wake up! Please wake up, Mr. Limmerick?"

Sasha nudged Colin's shoulder but he did not move. Sasha crawled on top of Colin's chest and started to apply pressure. "Mr. Limmerick, please wake up!" He grabbed some snow and rubbed it on Colin's face. Colin's eyelids flickered.

"Mr. Limmerick, you hear me I know you do!"

Colin slowly opened his eyes. He looked at Sasha and smiled. "Snow? I'm lyin' in snow?"

Sasha tried to stand up winching with pain in the process."Da, it is snow. I feel like I died and came back to life, Mr. Limmerick. I feel so awful."

Colin tired to stand up. "Where's we at?"

"We are in 1908, we are home, but time vortex experience was bumpy ride."

"I feel noxious. I'm goin' to puke so I will," Colin rolled over to his side and vomited on the snow.

Sasha started to walk around as each step intensely hurt. "By the way, Mr. Limmerick, time vortex opening is closed and animals are back in their place."

"How'd ye know this?" Colin asked wiping the bile from his mouth with his hand.

"We went through long vortex."

"Pretty bad was it?" Colin expressed trying to stand up but felt dizzy instead.

"Not so good for you, Mr. Limmerick."

Colin's knees started to buckle as he bent over and started to vomit again.

"You passed out, Mr. Limmerick, you missed the scenery. Prehistoric animals were pulled into vortex. It seems inter-dimensional forces pulled animals in and pushed us out to our desired year -- as indicated on my *time-travel indicator*."

"Yer *time-travel indicator* is fecked so I think," Colin stood up but felt another bout of nausea come before him.

Chapter Twenty-Six

It was 9:00 p.m. Friday, most of the undergraduate students from Colin's foundation course showed up at the end of term party. Several students from other courses were also present. It was located in the graduate student common room. Amoli showed up with her friend, Patsy, carrying large platters of food. Amoli made Indian cuisine as she was dressed in traditional Indian dress. Her bright pink and blue sari was in two-pieces showing her ample bust and middle. The females present gawked at Amoli's attire. "Look at the way that Indian girl dresses. She looks ridiculous!" some of the females whispered to one another.

Patsy brought a homemade stew in a large pot as she laid it on a long table with several other dishes brought by other students.

"Amoli, do you think Colin will be present tonight? Is he back in London?" Patsy asked.

"I have asked so many people. Not a one has seen or heard from him. I am very sad."

"You are aware how busy of a man he is, Amoli?"

Amoli let out a sigh of frustration. "I only know too well." Amoli stared at the floor and tried to keep her composure. "By the way, I was planning on showing the students here a traditional Indian dance. A friend of the family, Deep, will be coming shortly and will bring his drum, the dhol, and I will dance to his beat."

"That should be interesting," Patsy commented.

Amoli sighed with disappointment. "But, I wish I could show Colin this dance so very much."

"You can show Colin privately some time. I'm sure he would really like it if you danced for him," Patsy added.

"I don't think he knows very much about my culture, Patsy," Amoli said feeling anxious.

Several platters of food were placed on the long table as the guests began to filter in closer to 10:00 p.m. There was another table where only alcohol was placed and guests could help themselves. Two English musicians showed up, one entered the room holding a lute and the other with a violin. Deep followed as he entered the room making his way to Amoli. He was holding his dhal drum.

Amoli was already on her second helping of food while she laughed and joked with Patsy and Deep until she heard the door open. She quickly turned and saw Sasha enter the room where Colin followed. Amoli froze in shock. She turned away. In the corner of her eye she could see the shadowed silhouette of Colin wearing a long coat and top hat.

"Amoli? Did you see who just walked in?"

"Shhhhhh… quiet! I don't think they saw me. Look at me stuffing my face like a pig!"

"Amoli, I think Colin wouldn't mind if he saw you eating. Don't be silly."

"I don't know where he went for such a long time. I don't know whether to be angry or glad."

"Amoli, he's not your beau, at least not yet."

"Amoli?" Colin said.

Amoli slowly turned her head as she heard Colin's deep calming voice. "Yes, hello, Instructor."

"Address me as Colin, please. No need to call me Instructor anymore, the course is long done."

She turned away from him. "It's been so very long since I last saw you," she said.

He took off his hat and coat. "I suppose it has, lass."

"It has been an eternity, Instructor Limmerick," she said.

"Please, address me by me first name. I've got to find a closet for me coat'n hat I do, be right back," he said as he wandered off.

Patsy glanced at Amoli and began to laugh. "Happy?"

"Do I look appropriate? Do I look pretty? Oh my, he

grew a beard. He looks so very handsome -- except for his black eye."

"Is he the type that fights with chains and knives in street allies?" Patsy asked.

"I don't think so," Amoli answered as she began to bight her nails.

"Amoli, just relax," Patsy assured her.

He walked back to Amoli and lusted over her provocative clothing. He rubbed her naked shoulders and gently glided his fingers along her cleavage. "Brilliant dress, lass. Yer spillin' out everywhere aren't ye?"

Amoli's facial expression appeared shocked. "Sir, I never heard you speak to me like this."

"Like what?"

"Like a man rather than a teacher, sir."

"Well, I'm not yer teacher anymore, so I think it's suitable don't ye think?"

"You don't like my dress?"

He bent down as low as he could for his face to meet hers. "Ye look so bleedin' luscious I'd like to eat ye."

She didn't know whether to laugh or take him serious where she could smell alcohol on his breath. "Would you like me to fix you a drink?"

"Do ye know what I like to drink?"

"No, sir, I don't."

"Well, on the booze table there, I put down three large bottles of whiskey I did. Me contribution it was. I'd like to take one of those bottles back I would," he said still crouching down to speak to her.

"Do you want me to get one of those bottles for you, sir? Can I get you a glass?"

"No need. I would like a bottle just for me-self I would. Better yet, lass, I'll waltz over there 'n fetch it me-self," he said while playing with her hair.

She tried to get a grip of her nerves as she watched him take the bottle off the table and start to drink from it. Patsy looked at Amoli and smiled. They watched Colin shuffle back to them as he stood in front of Amoli peering down at her while he chugged from the bottle.

Amoli watched him intoxicate himself as she finally got enough nerve. "Sir, it's been so very long since I last saw you. Would it be very rude to ask you where you have been? I have very much missed you."

His drunken smile dissipated. "Where've I been ye ask?"

"I thought you left London forever and I'd never see you again. You did not say anything about your departure. I looked everywhere for you, I asked people if they knew where you were -- nobody seemed to know anything. I was so very sad."

He paused. "Lass, I had no idea. Sorry I am. So deeply sorry," his voice lowered with guilt.

"Oh well, I am so very glad you are here and I am actually seeing you in front of me."

"I felt like havin' a few pints 'n good craic with people 'is all."

Her eyes widened. "You didn't come because of me?"

He grew tired of crouching in his drunken state and started to kneel on the floor placing his hands on her cheeks. "Especially for ye I came, lass," he lowered his face and kissed her on the nose. Patsy caught a glimpse and backed off into the background.

"Did you try the dish I brought? Colin, you're not eating anything! Would you like to try my curry chicken?"

"What is it?"

She scurried to the long table of food to pile a heaping of food on a plate. She passed it to him. "I made it myself," she said smiling.

He immediately felt repulsed by the smell. She placed a fork in his hand and encouraged him to eat it. He hesitated, but started to pile a fork full into his mouth.

"Well?" she said.

His face turned red as he started to cough food particles out of his mouth. "Spiced it is!" he gasped and felt his throat swell.

She ran to find a glass of water, which she quickly gave to him. "Drink this, sir. Whiskey won't fix your inflamed throat!"

He was doubled over and continued to cough and choke. Other students were drawn to his distress as well. They also brought him glasses of water.

Patsy got close to Colin. "Instructor, you need to be careful with Indian food, you're stomach isn't used to it."

"Foolish I feel," Colin said. He straightened up and started to feel better.

"You don't like my dish?" Amoli asked.

Colin kneeled down to wrap his arms around Amoli's waist. "I do, perhaps I'll have to work me-self up to it. " Colin noticed Sasha signaling him to join him. "Lass, will ye excuse me, Dr. Dimitrikov needs me for a wee second he does," he stood. She watched him vanish into the crowd.

She turned around realising Rosa was standing behind her. "Miss Emanuel?"

"So you're trying to poison Colin with your Indian cooking?" Rosa asked with her hands on her hips.

"Curry chicken is a very popular dish in the East."

"Then maybe you should be preparing it for a nice young Indian chap who would appreciate it!"

"When did you arrive, Miss Emanuel? I did not see you enter."

"I just arrived. I was working in the lab."

"Colin is speaking to Dr. Dimitrikov over there. Did you see Dr. Dimitrikov yet?"

"Yes, I did. Stop trying to divert this conversation, Amoli. Stop trying to hook Colin because it won't work!"

"I do not understand you, Miss Emanuel, your suitor is Dr. Dimitrikov why would you care if I'm interested in the Instructor?"

"Colin is my friend and has been for a good while now. I know everything about him and I want to spare him from someone like you!"

Amoli panicked. "What are you talking about?"

"You only want him for superficial reasons!"

"Like what?"

"Not only is he handsome, he's also brilliant, he has a few quid to his name from his fishing trade."

"You obviously do not know about an Indian girl's dowry? I also have a few quid to my name, most likely more so than Colin. My family name is very high up in our caste lineage," Amoli said using a louder voice than usual.

"This may be so, but he is going places with the university and this is probably your way to get around the British imperialists," Rosa instilled making sure she held her lady-like composure. "You will never understand Colin, I am the only woman who really truly knows who he is!"

"Well, if you feel this way about him why did you let him go? You're a liar and he probably left you!"

"How dare you speak to me this way! This is all none of your business," Rosa shouted while growing upset." Does your father know you parade around the streets dressed like this?"

"I'm going to tell Colin how rude you are to me!"

"He won't believe you. You pretend to be such a sweet little thing. I can see right through you, Amoli Sharma you naughty girl!" Rosa stormed off.

Patsy approached Amoli. "Amoli, don't let Rosa Emanuel get the best of you. You should tell her suitor what she's doing. He would probably end his courtship with her immediately."

Amoli sulked in silence. "Patsy, why is she doing this to me? She has Dr. Dimitrikov. She did not want Colin."

Patsy noticed Deep standing in the corner of the room holding his dhal. "Amoli, get Deep to play a very sensual drum beat and you should play the cymbals with your fingers and do a very alluring dance for the Instructor.

You said you were going to demonstrate an Indian dance at this party for the students, so here is your chance. Make Rosa Emanuel crumble."

"I suppose."

"Amoli, where's your confidence? I see the way the Instructor looks at you. He's very attracted to you."

Colin was in the far corner of the large common room speaking with Sasha and Rosa.

***

"What time in geologic history did you two venture off to?" Rosa asked. She snickered at her two gentlemen friends while she watched them indulge in their bad habits. "Let me guess, I bet you two time-travelled to ten thousand years ago?"

Colin and Sasha looked at each other.

"Where did you go this time? Did you meet up with *Megaloceros* again?" She asked.

"I've been encounterin' *Megaloceros* far more so than I'd ever think," Colin responded.

Sasha's cigarette hung off his bottom lip. "We had problem with last time travel, we never closed time vortex opening -- this led to very big problem."

"You had to close the time vortex opening? I didn't know that! Did you know this before, Sasha?

"Live and learn," Sasha said with a shrug.

"Did you close it?" she asked.

"Not easy but great success I think," Sasha answered her.

"Look Rosa, the prehistoric beasts exited the time vortex from our first expedition and we found them roamin' the peatbogs of Wicklow. I discovered this when I brought me students I did. Poor Amoli, the dear lass, almost was attacked by a cave lion she was. I thank the good Lord I was there to protect her. Horrible, it was, Rosa."

"So you ran to Amoli's rescue? Colin, you are such a big hero! Remember, my dear, you are made of mere flesh

313

and bones just like everyone else. You could have been killed just as well."

"Rosa, Amoli is just a wee thing she is, she's not experienced especially with prehistoric animals," Colin said.

Rosa tugged on Colin's arm. "Tell me, Colin find me someone who has experience with prehistoric animals?" Rosa asked.

Sasha looked at Colin, "In order to close time vortex, we had to go through it again. We had very small energy to get us through we ended up in Ice Age."

"The Ice age?" Rosa began to laugh.

"We just happened to arrive at an interglacial period, so it was bloody hot."

"Interglacial? How fantastic." Rosa said.

Colin took another gulp from his bottle. "Instead of freezin', we was boilin'. Uncomfortable it was. Thought I wasn't goin' to live through it," Colin explained.

"And you're both here to tell me about it. Splendid! Sasha, you look so thin!" she said. "And, Colin, you have a prominent shiner on your left eye. Did you get into a fight with something awful?"

"Aye."

"Colin, I know you're addicted to alcohol but you're also addicted to time-travel and Sasha," she pointed to Sasha, "You're Colin's dealer!"

Colin didn't find her comment amusing, "Addicted or not, I've found the most extraordinary way to conduct me research, thanks to Sasha," Colin said guzzling from his bottle of whiskey.

Rosa tried to reach for Colin's face as she started to fondle with his beard, "I like this on you, it's well-groomed, not like when we time-travelled together and you looked crazed and wild."

"Ye weren't a blushin' beauty neither when we got back," Colin commented and continued to drink. Colin looked away, "I'm goin' to try some more food, I'm gettin' hungry," Colin said as he staggered from Sasha and Rosa.

Colin bumped his way through the crowd and heard a South Asian drum beat. Several people in the crowd patted him on the back while greeting him as he meandered through the guests. The guests pulled away leaving a clear way in the center of the room. Deep stood in the middle playing his dhol while the students watched and listened. Patsy ran to Colin pulling his bottle of whiskey from his hand encouraging him to go to the center of the room. Colin had no idea what was happening. Amoli showed up playing her finger cymbals to the drumbeat. She stood still and focused on Colin who stood in the middle of the room feeling awkward. Amoli started to belly dance where she gently demonstrated a story with her body. She seductively glided her way to Colin swaying her hips and extending her arms. She made her way to him and focused on her dance. She rubbed her back against his crotch then turned around and pressed her breasts against him. She bended back and shook her breasts in front of him. She slowly turned around facing him toward the drum then grabbed his arms gesturing for him to kneel onto the floor because of their size difference. She continued to tell a story with her body. She ran her fingers through his hair. Her forward gestures continued where she broke the conservative mold of the young Edwardian crowd. She rubbed her full buttock against his chest and continued to dance extending her arms and then lowering herself on the floor demonstrating her submission to him. Colin felt his impairment where he found himself getting aroused. He tried his hardest not to lose sexual control of himself. The dance lasted for about fifteen minutes. When it was over the crowd let out a roar of applause and screams. Colin's face was red with embarrassment. He pulled Amoli to a single wingback chair in the corner of the room and sat on the chair wedging her between his legs.

"D--do you know anythin' 'bout the male--male

species, lass?" he asked with a slur. He glanced at himself realising his trousers had grown very tight.

"I know my young brother is a fool."

"Yer brother is an arse is he?"

"Do you have brothers?"

"I have one brother I do. His name is E--Ethan."

"Is he a fool?"

"Sometimes."

"So, that's what I do know about the male species."

"Lass, ye embarrassed me in front of everyone. The people here are former class mates, former students, friends from the gym, ye know."

"You don't like my dance?"

He placed his hands on her shoulders. "I did fancy yer dancin' but ye can't draw so much attention to everyone."

"You don't like me?"

He took Amoli in his arms forcing his tongue down her throat. His lips met hers sloppily running his tongue in and around her mouth. He resigned himself to his intoxicated state allowing his over-powering libido to take charge. Patsy tried not to watch them where she tried to interest herself in boring student conversation.

Rosa walked by with Sasha. "Colin can be such an exhibitionist don't you agree, Sasha?"

"What you mean? He having fun, leave him be," Sasha took Rosa's arm pulling her away from them.

Colin pressed the weight of his body against Amoli. "Is it gettin' late for ye, lass?" he asked as he tried to catch his breath.

"I don't care," she replied.

He gasped for air. His hands cupped over her breasts. "Do ye like this, lass?" he bursted his question with a gasp of heavy breathing.

Her body wouldn't relax. "Maybe you could take me home?" She flinched to his touch, which made feel her awkward.

He ran his lips along her neck. "Here? Where's here?

316

Don't really care I don't." He held her waist bringing her to a standing position. "Yer right, lass. I'm makin' a spectacle of us I am. I need to get ye home I do." He stood up, "I'll fetch our coats I will."

Patsy walked to Amoli sitting on the chair. "You got your wish. Colin must be in love with you if he's showing so much passion in public for you. Did you have any idea he felt this way?"

Amoli tried to ignore the gawking students in the room. "Not at all! I thought he just regarded me as a child. He's taking me home now."

"Do you trust him?"

"Trust him? I trust him with all my heart!"

"Do you think he's going to try anything when you're alone with him?"

"I don't know. I never thought of that."

"Are you afraid?"

"I love him, Patsy. I want to be his wife!"

"He is such a nice man. You're right, Amoli."

Colin returned holding their coats and smiled at Patsy. "Yer lookin' like yer chattin' 'bout me, Patsy?"

"No, sir!"

He nudged Patsy. "I need to take Amoli home just now." He slipped on Amoli's coat. "We bes' be goin' now, Patsy. *Sláinte*."

Patsy smiled. "What does that mean?" she asked.

Colin grinned, "Cheers in Irish it is." Amoli held on to his sleeve as they said goodnight to the guests.

***

They walked through the dark damp streets where Amoli tried to keep up with Colin's long strided pace. He noticed she was having difficulty so he scooped her up in his arms. He held her close to him. He brought her to one of the courtyards of the university residence and placed her down in front of him. He looked at her with a serious expression. She could see his breath in the cold night.

"Colin? Why did you bring me here? It's so dark, not a

317

person is around."

He looked at her with a partial smile. "Why you like me so much?"

"Colin, I'm beyond like when it comes to you," she gasped from her emotions.

"I want to tell ye that I wanted ye all night. I want to know before I take ye home -- if ye want me in the same way."

"I wanted you from the day I first set eyes on you."

He stepped closer to her. "I mean I want ye tonight, Amoli."

"I want you too."

He kneeled down to meet her face as he took her hands placing them to his mouth. He could feel the coolness of her hands so he blew on them to give her warmth. "How I want ye tonight, Amoli, I do, how I do."

She stood and stared at his handsome face not really understanding his words. "Colin, I love you. I've loved you for a long time now. Our on-sight camping trip in Wicklow was so very difficult for me. I didn't want you to treat me like just another student. I wanted to be so very special to you."

"I knew it even then, lass."

"Colin?"

"Aye, lass?"

"Do you love me?"

He continued to kneel in the snow and embraced her tightly. "I do."

A large smile formed on her face as her heart started to palpitate.

"Come. Let me take ye inside yer dorm 'n I'll show me love to ye," he picked her up carrying her inside her residence upstairs to her collective dorm. The females that shared that particular dorm unit sat at the common table together sipping tea. They noticed Colin carrying Amoli to her bedroom.

"Is that Amoli being carried over the threshold by the

318

Natural History Instructor?" one of the residents asked as she sipped her tea.

Colin stopped to lower Amoli to the floor as he tipped his hat to the young women, "'Tis I."

"Where are you two going at this late hour?" the one resident asked.

Amoli appeared nervous. "We just came from a party. The instructor was kind enough to take me home."

Colin took Amoli's tiny hand. "Good night ladies," Colin said as he pulled Amoli into her bedroom and shut the door. The other residents started to laugh. "Amoli! Remember the lock on your door still needs fixing!" the young woman shouted.

Amoli ignored the resident.

Colin and Amoli were alone in her tiny bedroom. Amoli stood against her door still wearing her coat. Colin removed his hat placing it on the tiny desk. He then pulled his scarf from around his neck focusing on Amoli. He slowly approached her as she leaned against the door still in her coat. She noticed how unsteady he was on his feet stumbling with each step. He started to unbutton his coat and stepped closer to her. He rested his arm against the wall having her feel cornered.

"I want ye tonight if it's I you'll have?" he asked still slurring his words.

She was so nervous she could hear her own heart beat. "If it's me you want you can have me," she said in a naïve tone.

He pressed his body against hers feeling a little too warm still wearing his long cloth coat. He pulled away from her as he slid his coat off dropping it to the floor. He leered at her while she tried to smile.

"It's a wee bit hot in here," he said. He slid his suspenders off his shoulders.

"W--what are you doing?" She asked with a quiver in her voice.

"Like I said, lass, it's a wee bit hot in here," he smiled

and flopped on her tiny single bed kicking off his big metal boots. He stared at her looking seductive as he licked his full lips like a wolf ready to pounce on its prey. She didn't move, her coat remained buttoned.

"Fancied yer dancin' so I did," he said still feeling the alcohol. "Very sexy it was," he said with a deep raspy whisper.

She looked at him fluttering her eyelashes.

"I'm after teachin' ye me own Irish dancin'," he said in a deep tone.

"Dance? I can't dance to your music, Colin, only to mine," she snickered.

He threw his shirt and trousers on top of her desk. He stood in the middle of her room wearing only his boxers as he began to approach her. She started to slide her body to one side. He placed his arm against the wall to block her from any movement.

"First, ye need to take yer coat off," he said unfastening her buttons. "Second, ye need to kiss me," he brushed against her as he lowered his body to kiss her on the mouth.

"Wait!" she shouted.

"Wait?" he said as he continued to kiss her on the mouth then moving along her neck.

"Colin, this is my very first time ever with a boy!"

"Huh?" he paused but continued to remove her coat.

"I have never been with a boy before, you have to understand. I am not experienced."

"Experienced?"

"Please try to understand me, Colin. You have to be gentle with me."

He tossed her coat onto the bed. "I'll take it easy with ye, don't ye worry 'bout that. Ye can trust me."

She took a deep sigh. "What a relief, I thought you were going to take my clothes off."

He stepped away from her. "Lass, look at me. Tell me what ye see."

"I see you standing there in your underwear," she said partially covering her eyes, "My, this is so very scary for me."

"Scary? Me standin' here in me underwear is scary to ye?"

She slowly removed her hands from her eyes as she scanned his body. "Oh my."

"What is it, lass?"

"I'm just a little nervous that is all. I've never seen a grown man in his underwear before."

"Wearin' me boxers 'is all, lass. There isn't much to see now is there?"

"Um, but, there seems to be more than you care to realise," she said in a jitter as she turned her face away from him.

He stepped toward her. "Lass, please allow me to help ye," he said as he tried to remove her clothes.

"No! Colin, I don't think this is a good idea!" She began to panic.

He gently led her to the bed with her dress unbuttoned. He sat on the bed pulling her onto his lap as he held her tightly around the waist. "I thought ye loved me, lass," he said kissing her along the side of her neck. She crawled off his lap finding a comfortable spot on the bed.

He gently pulled her dress off. He stared at her bare breasts, "Ah, India, how brilliant it is to know Indian damsels don't wear corsets -- they's such a bother to us gents," he sighed as he recklessly pulled off his boxer shorts.

She cupped her ample breasts in her tiny hands. "Colin, don't look at me!"

He tried to push her hands away. "Why, lass? I like lookin' at ye."

"No!" she shouted almost in tears.

He smiled and kneeled on the bed causing the springs of her delicate mattress to buckle while waving his stiffened bold penis in her face. It was at this moment she

321

realized he had done this before.

"Colin, what are you doing?" she asked feeling almost frightened of his experience.

He flaunted himself on the bed. "Well, lass? What ye think?"

She tried to look anywhere in the room. "Oh my."

"Well?" he gasped in an orgasmic whisper as he started to pant like an animal.

"Oh my."

"No comment?" he asked as he flicked his long forelock from his face.

She tried not to look at him as she remained silent.

He moved closer to her. "Am I that awful to look at, lass?" He asked as he brought himself close to her sliding his arms around her waist.

"I've never seen a man's body before. This is such a surprise to me," she commented.

"Surprise?"

She looked into his eyes and smiled. "Yes, I am surprised."

"Not disappointed I hope."

She had a difficult time controlling her nerves. "You look so -- so very nice."

"I do?"

"You - you look spectacular--."

"How so?"

"You are such a lovely man that I cannot believe I'm with you here tonight. Imagine me here with you. I cannot believe this is happening to me. I feel so lucky."

His smile dissipated. "No need to place me so high on a pedestal. I think I'm un-deservin' of yer such kind words."

"Oh no, that is where you are so very wrong, you deserve each and every kind word."

"What ever for?"

Her eyes filled with tears. "Because you are the kindest person I have ever met. I feel I've known you my entire life."

He placed his hands on her breasts where she flinched and pulled away.

"Lass, come to me," he said in a whisper. She moved closer to him. He started to kiss her neck again. "How I want ye, lass," he gasped as he continued to kiss her placing her hands on his penis.

"Don't be afraid to touch me there. A foreign object so it's not. It's still all me."

She looked away from him. "I can't believe this is happening."

"Isn't this brilliant?"

"I don't know."

He secured her hands around his penis. "See, yer touchin' me there, it's not so bad now is it?" He lay on top of her as he fondled her breasts. She wanted to fight him but couldn't. He slide his hands over hers, keeping her tiny delicate hands on his penis.

"Oh my," she expressed.

"So, lass, so what if me package has a wee bit more than other blokes. This shouldn't frighten ye," he whispered to her in a deep romantic tone.

He sprawled his body onto hers. She tried to look at the ceiling but felt the whisking of his long hair drape over her face. His arms supported his body as he hovered over her. His legs were bent like an animal ready to mount its female. He tried to be gentle as he tried to enter her but her screams were uncontrollable. She was very tight for what he was used to. He could barely find her opening. Suddenly the crazed power of his relentless libido took command over him and gentle he was no more. He used the strength of his powerful legs to maneuver his motion. Her cries and screams penetrated past her bedroom door alerting the other female residents. He jolted his pelvis as he entered her almost torn opening. She could barely see his face for she was facing his chest. She managed to catch a glimpse of his face noticing several sweat beads pour off his forehead. He groaned with each sensual pant, which almost frightened her. He was like a wild bull as he devoured her. He thrust with conviction as the room almost shook from the vibration of the bed. Her cries howled throughout the floor as she gritted her teeth. He humped and humped trying to hold back. He was drenched in sweat where she watched his chest expand with power. He continued to plunge as deep inside her as possible. He shot his semen inside her while forcing his well-endowed penis as deep as it could go. He ignored her cries as her narrow walls encased his penis with unruly sensation. He flicked his hair back almost feeling as if he were in a trance while shutting his eyes. Her pain was so excruciating that she felt faint. Streams of tears poured down her cheeks.

Colin wiped her tears. "Why?" he paused, "Why lass? Why ye cryin'? What have I done to ye?"

"It hurts so much!" She wrapped her arms around his neck, "You have to be gentle with me! I've never done this before. I'm a virgin!"

"That I know, lass. That I know." He continued to thrust himself in and out of her. Her screams wailed as she gasped for air. Sweat poured down her face as he continued to thrust. Her eyes filled with tears, he knew he needed to stop but could not pull out for the sensation was beyond his imagination. Amoli could feel his moist skin with every thrust. He hit his climax where he closed his eyes and began to moan with almost a panicked pant of exhaustion. The bed kept banging against the wall making a crashing sound almost ready to collapse. He had never felt anything so satisfying. He wanted to kiss her but he faced only the pillow. He slowly came down from his penetrating ejaculation, which over-flowed onto the bed. His long hair hung partially over his face as sweat dripped off his nose onto the pillow.

Amoli grinned with joy the sexual act was finally over. He slowly pulled out still partially erect. She sighed with relief. He noticed blood on Amoli's genitals as well as his. Stains of blood were left on the bed sheets.

Amoli screamed. "I'm bleeding? Oh my!"

Colin chuckled as he reached for a towel that was sitting on her night table. "I bes be wipin' this mess up. Me lass, don't ye even understand that I broke yer hymen? A virgin ye is no more," he sat up on the bed pulling her toward him as he held her tightly and kissed her softly on the lips.

She looked at him wipe the blood from her inner thighs as she began to cry. "I'm not a virgin?"

"That yer not, lass," Colin said softly as he ran his hand along her face.

"I used to imagine what a night like this with you would be like but I never thought it would be this wonderful. I wish I could hold this moment forever. I wish this would never end," she said with tears and laughter.

He continued kissing her. "This moment doesn't have to end it doesn't. I love ye 'n I'll never stop I promise ye that," he gasped with each hot breath.

As he held her in his arms he could feel her shake with fear. "Lass, look what's around me neck."

"Three chains. It looks like two-silver and one gold with a crucifix hanging off the gold one. One of the silver chains is a huge chain-link and it looks very heavy," she said.

"Which one would ye like, lass?"

"Well, I like the gold but it has a crucifix on it and my family would get very upset with me. The big silver chain link looks too masculine and heavy I think the finer silver one would be best."

He took the fine sliver chain off and placed it around her neck. "Lass, I'm givin' this to ye until I get a diamond for yer finger."

She started to scream with excitement, "Diamond?!"

"Amoli, I am askin' ye if ye would like me to be yer husband. Would ye honour me in bein' me wife?"

"Are you asking me to marry you?"

"So I am."

She threw her arms around his neck as they both sat on the bed. "Yes! Yes! Yes! How I want to marry you so very much! I would love to be your wife and you be my husband! Yes!"

"But, lass, will ye truly have me is me question? I understand ye may seem happy now but will ye in the future?"

"Why wouldn't I, Colin?"

"I suppose we's not the best suited couple, what ye think?"

"Oh no, we are a very suitable couple, Colin. I knew we were meant to be from the first time we met at the Gala Tribute."

He ran his hands through her hair. "I suppose yer right, lass."

"Colin, would you prefer a European girl?"

"Do ye love me, lass?"

"I do, oh, how I do."

"Then it's ye I prefer. But--."

"But what?"

"Ye didn't seem too happy with me makin' love to ye just now."

"It was my first time."

He pressed his body against hers pinning her to the bed as he kissed her on the mouth. The night ripened and they eventually fell asleep.

***

It was approximately 6:00 a.m., the door to Amoli's bedroom slowly opened. Dr. Sharma walked into his daughter's bedroom carrying a stack of clean towels. He paused abruptly when he found Amoli sleeping on top of Colin on her tiny single bed. He was frozen with surprise.

"Amolia?" he said in a curt tone staring at the lovers sound asleep. "Amolia?"

Her eyes flickered. She slowly sat up still on top of

326

Colin. She focused and realized her father standing in the room. She began to cough profusely.

Dr. Sharma threw Amoli's her robe. "Put this on now and get out of that filthy bed!"

Colin sat up. "Shhhhite! Dr. Sharma, how'd ye get in here?" Colin rubbed his face feeling his hang-over pierce his head.

"Better yet, how did you manage to get your filthy way with my youngest daughter?"

Amoli immediately slipped her robe on as she jumped out of bed standing beside her father.

"Dr. Sharma saw Colin's trousers on the desk chair and threw them at him. "Get these on and make it fast! Colin, I thought you were a better man!"

Colin awkwardly tried to get his trousers on while still under the bed covers. "That all depends on yer version of better, sar!"

"Don't be smug with me!"

"Smug, sar?" Colin stood up in front of Dr. Sharma.

"Amolia, you are no longer my daughter! You are nothing but cheap trash!"

"That's enough!" Colin raised his voice.

"Amolia, you have now cursed our family. You have cursed us! Our family name will not continue to thrive!" Dr. Sharma hit her face with his backhand.

Colin watched feeling helpless but managed to pull Dr. Sharma back. "That's enough! Ye made yer bleedin' point!"

"Father! Colin and I are engaged now. We did not commit sin!"

Dr. Sharma threw Amoli against her desk where she fell to the floor. Amoli's shame took control of her and she began to cry. Dr. Sharma turned to Colin with disgust. "You are only supposed to sleep together when you are wed! How much did you pay her, Colin? She belongs on the street corner! She is nothing but used up trash! My wife never gave birth to her!"

Colin's eyes widened with disbelief. He took hold of Dr. Sharma's arm.

Amoli stood up screaming in tears. "No! Do not say this!"

"Dr. Sharma, this is not necessary!" Colin tugged on Dr. Sharma's arm. "Ye need to stop this now!"

Dr. Sharma stepped closer to Amoli as he made a fist to punch her in the face. Colin stood in front of her as Dr. Sharma punched Colin's chest instead.

"Just feckin' stop it already! Ye hurt her again I'll bust yer head over me knee I will. Blame me not her she's innocent in all this. I coaxed her into sleepin' with me last night!"

"Father, I love Colin I wanted to be with him very much last night!"

Dr. Sharma walked up to her. "What's this around your neck?" Dr. Sharma asked pulling on the chain around her neck.

"Colin gave it to me until he places a diamond engagement ring upon my finger," she said holding up the silver chain as her eyes filled with tears.

Dr. Sharma grabbed it yanking it off her neck. "There's your symbol of engagement on the floor and ready to sweep into the trash bin!"

Amoli screamed. "No!" she fell to the floor trying to pick up the pieces of the chain necklace.

"Me parents gave me that piece of jewellery!" Colin blurtedd.

"I am pulling Amolia out of this university. There is a young man in Delhi who needs a wife. I will be sending Amoli to him next week with her dowry. You are now out of the picture, Colin.

"Sar, ye wanted Amoli to marry a western man? Ye can't expect me to embrace yer culture right away! I'm western 'n not all western men wait 'till their weddin' night despite me bein' Catholic. I'm sorry."

"Colin, you are a naturalist, I thought you would

understand culture more than the average man. You and Amoli have committed a sin. I understand I initially was very fond of you and I thought you would be a good man for Amolia; I was wrong. But, what is more important here is Amolia allowed this," Dr. Sharma noticed the bloody towel sitting on the bed. He began to cry. "My youngest daughter, Amolia is dead."

"Dr. Sharma, I love Amoli. I want to marry her! Please try to understand!"   Dr. Sharma stepped closer to Colin. "She has been already spoken for. His name is Prasaad and he awaits her in Delhi. She will be leaving next week. You have no power over any of this, Colin."

Dr. Sharma threw Amoli's coat at her. "Go to the bathroom and get dressed we are going to your aunt's house right now! I will tell the university that you are withdrawing from the programme and this residence will be available for someone else."

Amoli continued to cry and scream and ran to the bathroom in the common area. Colin stood in front of Dr. Sharma wearing only his trousers. "Sar, can we not discuss this?" Colin pleaded.

"Ah, I see you wear a tattoo on your arm. Any reason, Colin?"

"A man of the sea I am, sar," Colin answered trying to cover his tattoo with his other hand.

"Or maybe I misunderstood what kind of a man you really are. I have heard several times around campus that you tend to drink a little too much. I ignored those comments because I thought the Colin Limmerick I knew was a man of respectability."

"Call me as ye wish, sar, but please don't hurt Amoli. She's so young 'n innocent she is. Breaks easily she does."

"Colin, I will continue to work with you in the lab simply because you are a very intelligent and fascinating researcher, our relationship at the university will never change or go beyond that. Amolia has now shunned the family and your relations with her must be terminated."

Amoli stood in the doorway of her room dressed trying to wipe her tears. "I will not go to India and marry Prasaad! I don't love him and I don't want him! I want to be with Colin!" Amoli shouted as tears continued to fall from her eyes.

"Amoli, you have never spoken to me in this manner. You will be leaving as soon as next week. Prasaad is a nice young man. He knows of your dowry very well and he likes it very much," Dr. Sharma said.

"I am marrying Colin! I will not return to India!"

Dr. Sharma walked up to Amoli and smacked her across the face. "You don't tell me what you can or cannot do! You have shamed me!"

Colin took Dr. Sharma and pushed him against the wall. "Don't ye hurt her!"

"What will you do to me, Colin?"

Colin punched Dr. Sharma to the ground. "I'll kill ye! She's goin' to be me wife she is. I love yer daughter very much."

"She will never marry you. You're relations with her are terminated! If you try to see Amolia again I will call the police. Amolia, don't bother trying to see Colin you will need to pack for your trip home," Dr. Sharma grabbed Amoli's arm shaking and tugging at her. He yanked her out of the residence. Colin stood in the common area of the floor. Amoli's dorm mates stood frozen from what they had just heard. Colin sat at the chair in the main kitchen area, the dorm mates stood around Colin and shared his remorse.

330

Chapter Twenty-Seven

One snowy night Colin lay in bed at his London flat staring at the ceiling. He thought about his crew wishing he could be with them but his workload at the university got to be too heavy where he could not leave so easily. He missed Dublin. He tried to hoist himself from his bed as he staggered around his flat trying not to trip on any empty whisky bottles, realising he had run out. "Feck it!" he said out loud to himself. He made his way to the lavatory and looked at himself in the mirror above the sink. "Feck, I'm lookin' like shite I am," he said to himself and scratched his bushy beard. He felt his way along the wall trying not to fall as he almost crawled his way back to bed." He flopped onto the bed feeling almost noxious. He lay down to stare at the ceiling. "I smell like shite," he said with a hearty laugh. "I'm sure to keep the lasses away now." He shut his eyes as he began to recollect a time when he was sixteen. He remembered when his mother caught him having sex with a girl behind the shed at the back of the house. His mother was horrified. What was worse, he remembered, young Ethan was the one who initially found them together. His Catholic guilt weighed heavy on his mind. He eventually fell asleep.

It was approximately three o'clock in the morning. Colin was asleep in his flat when he suddenly heard a crashing sound at his window. A rock had broken through the glass of his second floor window. He immediately awoke sitting up in bed noticing the shattered glass on the floor as blowing snow flowed into the room. He sprung out of bed noticing the rock that had just crashed through had a note attached to it. He picked it up to read what it said.

To Colin, My Dearest, My Love,

A hundred virtues adorn your beauty. In you alone have I found sincerity? I have long esteemed you -- permit me to continue to do so still but forgive me if, beset as I am with troubles, I do not aspire to the honour or our hand. I feel myself unworthy of it and I begin to realise that I'm not destined for such a union.

I will love you until my dying day,
Amoli

Colin put down the note and looked through the broken window. He reached for his glasses and saw Amoli standing below on the road. "Amoli?" he called to her.

"It is I, my love," she called out to him bundled in a heavy coat and boots.

"What ye doin' there on such a cold night?"

"I am here to woo the man I love!" she shouted.

"Oh mother of God! Stay there, lass! I'll come fetch ye I will!"

Colin slipped on his coat and ran downstairs; he walked outside in his bare feet and carried her inside. "Lass, what ye doin' throwin' rocks through windows in the middle of winter with love letters quotin' Molière?

"Don't you like Molière?"

"Lass, why ye doin' this?"

She began to cry. "Don't you miss me?"

He sat her on a chair. "I do very much, lass. I don't want yer father to hurt ye anymore so I didn't persist. I really don't know what to do."

"Are you just going to let me be sent to India to marry another man?"

"I wasn't goin' to let that happen, lass. If anythin' I would have gone to India me-self 'n fetch ye back I would've."

"That wouldn't be so very easy, Colin. India is at war with England. They would kill you at first glance."

332

"I see."

"You are big, white, and English."

"Irish."

"This is too dangerous of a time."

"I have somethin' for ye, lass," Colin opened the drawer to his desk and pulled out a small black velvet box. He brought it to Amoli and opened it in front of her.

"Colin, what is this?"

He opened the box, which sat a delicate diamond ring. He took it from the box placing it upon her finger. He stood her up as he kneeled down on one knee. "Amoli, would ye please consider makin' me yer husband? I wish ye to marry me very much I do. Would ye please marry me 'n be me wife?"

She cried tears of joy. "Yes! I'll marry you!"

He stood up scooping her in his strong arms kissing her lips. He held her up toward the ceiling twirling her around. "Me wife ye will be, lass! Now it's official." He carried her to his bedroom lowering her onto the bed. His room was cold from the shattered window but the two lovers didn't care. He slipped off his long underwear to a naked state as he carefully removed her clothes.

They made love and eventually fell asleep. Some hours had passed where Colin opened his eyes finding himself chilled from the cold breeze. He looked at his clock. "Is it 9:00? Feck! Amoli, ye need to wake up ye do!" Colin tapped Amoli on the cheeks.

While waking, she looked at the diamond on her finger. "Good morning, my love," she said with a smile.

"Yer family will shutter they will when they see yer not in yer room. Do ye share a room with yer sister?'

Amoli sat up rubbing her eyes. "Yes, the two of us share a room. My sister will not say anything to my parents or my aunt."

"She won't?"

"No, she knows how much I love you. I can tell my sister anything. My brother, on the other hand, is a brat."

"I need to get ye home I do!"

"I can go myself, if my father saw me with you he would not be nice about it."

***

It was noon when Dr. Sharma walked into the lab Colin and Sasha were working in. Colin was looking at some of his samples he brought from the interglacial period under a microscope. He wore a white lab coat and glasses. Dr. Sharma stood behind him.

"Colin, we need to chat," Dr. Sharma said.

Colin looked at Sasha sitting at the next microscope. He paused then got up from the lab stool. "Sar?"

"Colin, can I meet you in your office in about fifteen minutes?"

"I will," Colin removed his round-framed glasses from his face.

"Amoli has been very distant from the family lately. She won't leave her room. My wife and I are very concerned."

"Fifteen minutes ye say?"

Sasha overheard the conversation as he watched Dr. Sharma exit the laboratory. "It is none of my business but is this problem, Mr. Limmerick?" Sasha asked.

Colin folded his arms in front of himself, "There's a problem alright. Ye remember the end of term party with the undergraduate 'n graduate students?"

"Da, as soon we arrived back from time travel expedition?"

"Ye remember seein' me with Amoli that evenin'?

"Da, I think she almost had your baby right there," Sasha said with a grin.

"I drank too much whiskey that night. I went overboard I did."

"Mr. Limmerick, many times you are man with no self-control, da?"

"Mate, nobody I know can rub it in like ye," Colin paused as he removed his lab coat. "To make a long story short, Dr. Sharma found me in Amoli's bed the next mornin'."

"So?"

"So? It was a feckin' disaster it was!"

"You screw her before he entered?"

"All night long I did."

Sasha started to pack up his notes. "You have very exciting life, Mr. Limmerick. I sometimes wish I were you."

"Ye don't wish ye was me, Sasha! I witnessed Dr. Sharma hurt Amoli! It wasn't pretty it wasn't! Feck!"

"You no stop him?"

"I smacked'em hard I did."

"As hard as you do to me?"

"Feck off."

"But you screwed her all night?"

"I did. I feckin' told ye this shite already!"

"Did you enjoy?"

"Enjoy? Enjoy what?"

"The screw!"

Colin grew angry as he placed his hands over his face. "Sasha, screwin' Amoli was grand! Do ye need to hear more details now do ye? Sometimes a bleedin' wanker is what ye is."

"I need to get lunch!" Sasha said removing his lab coat. "I also need cigarette!"

"Sasha, he smacked Amoli around the room, her mouth bled. He said he's sendin' her to India to marry some Indian bloke named Prasaad! He forbids her to marry me!"

"So?"

"What is it with ye today?"

"Look, Mr. Limmerick, the world does not center around you. Rosa and I are in great troubles. She wants ring!"

"So feckin' what?" Colin expressed.

"It is obvious she still wants you. I cannot give her

335

ring if she still wants you, besides, I cannot afford big diamond she wants. I am poor Russian scholar."

"Mate, I'm sorry. I've been so thoughtless I have."

"Enough about my problems, Mr. Limmerick, go upstairs to your office don't keep your future father-in-law waiting."

Colin left the lab. He ran upstairs to his office to wait for Dr. Sharma. Amoli walked by his opened door, "Lass?" Colin called out.

Amoli gingerly entered Colin's office. "Hello." She appeared uncertain of herself. "Hello, Colin."

He sat back in his chair at his desk. "Howya, lass?"

She quickly glanced over her shoulder to make sure they were alone.

"Yer father should be here any minute," he said holding his pocket watch.

"Does he want to speak to you about his silly prehistoric plants?"

"Not at all, he wants to chat about ye."

"He does?"

"He does. Lass, why don't ye stay here? I'd much rather look at ye than him."

She made herself comfortable in one of Colin's office chairs. "Alright. Did you notice I am wearing your ring?"

His eyes met hers. "It looks lovely on ye, lass."

Dr. Sharma appeared in the doorway. "Colin? Ah, Amolia is here. I will just make myself comfortable and we can get on with it."

"Colin loosened his tie. "What would ye like to discuss with me, sar?"

"I had a long chat with my wife about your act of sin the other night, Colin."

"I see."

"She cried for hours. We both cried ourselves sick. Even though my wife has never met you. She feels maybe you should be given a second chance."

Colin perked his posture in his chair while he glanced

336

at Amoli. She twirled her hair around her index finger while she pressed her lips tightly.

"Can you meet me at temple tonight?" Dr. Sharma asked.

"Come again, sar?"

"Is tonight suitable for you?"

"Is what suitable, sar?"

"Can you meet me at temple tonight?"

"Temple, sar? I don't understand."

"Yes, of course, Colin, you must now begin your conversion to Hinduism."

"Conversion to Hinduism, sar?"

"Well, I would hardly think you are a serious Catholic if you sleep with young girls half your age long before their wedding night."

"But a practicin' Catholic is what I am, sar."

"I don't think so, Colin. You would be regarded as a sinner and fallen Catholic just like you would in my faith."

Colin took a deep breath while he tried to focus on Dr. Sharma rather than his daughter. "What time do ye want me at the Hindu temple tonight?"

"Half past seven would be very good. I will be waiting for you with Amolia and my wife."

"I suppose I'll be seein' ye there."

"Oh, and one more thing, Colin."

"Aye, sar?"

"Make sure you eat absolutely no meat for the rest of this day."

Colin moved his chair a bit closer to Dr. Sharma, "Sar?"

"Colin, a good Hindu knows they are not to eat animal flesh -- especially if it comes from our sacred cow."

"Huh?"

"Colin, it is still early morning have you eaten any cow meat yet today?"

"I ate breakfast, sar."

337

"What did you eat, Colin?"

"Uh, lets see if I can recall...toast -- I ate toast...fried potatoes, sar, juice, beans..." Colin glanced at Dr. Sharma realising his nerves were starting to react. "Um, I had tea, sar, 'n blood sausage, 'n 'bout four bangers, sar."

Dr. Sharma nodded his head. "Tusk -- tusk, Colin. This is a sin. How can you start your day devouring bovine flesh? How can this be??

"I may've just eaten swine, sar. Do I pass the Hindu test?"

**

It was 7:30 p.m. Colin stood outside the temple watching groups of South Asians gather. Some of the South Asians glanced at Colin for he felt very visible amongst them. Dr. Sharma, his wife, Amoli, and a young boy approached Colin. It started to rain.

"Colin, you are here. I must say I am pleasantly surprised. Let me introduce you to my lovely wife and our son."

Colin tipped his top hat at Mrs. Sharma as he then took her hand. "Pleasure is all mine."

"My, such a handsome man you are. Amoli, you never mentioned Colin was so big and strong. This is a very good trait. You can protect our daughter from so very bad people, " Mrs. Sharma commented.

"I intend to, Mrs. Sharma," Colin replied tipping his hat to her again.

"My son, aren't you going to say hello to the nice man? He intends on marrying your sister," Mrs. Sharma said addressing her young son.

"I do not care," said a fourteen-year old boy.

Colin bent down to the boy as he extended his hand to him. "Hello, and how old are ye?"

"Old enough to know I do not like you."

"That will be enough!" Dr. Sharma shouted as he hit his son on the back of the head. "Say hello to the man!"

"You raped my sister!"

338

Amoli slapped her brother across the face. "I knew he should not have come, mother! He is a terrible brother!"

"Stop your bad behaviour, now!" Mrs. Sharma shouted to her son.

"I think mass is about to start," Colin mentioned to Dr. Sharma.

Dr. Sharma laughed. "We are at temple to pray, this is not mass, Colin."

Amoli held Colin's hand. "Forget about my stupid brat brother let us enter temple."

The Hindu temple had clusters of people walking inside the seating area. Several people dressed in traditional religious robes guided the worshipers to sit in their directed seating.

Colin stepped into the temple. Someone dressed in traditional Hindu attire stopped him. "Please stop, sir!" the person ordered as he pushed Colin against his chest.

"Ye not lettin' me into yer temple?" Colin asked looking concerned.

"You, sir, must remove your shoes!"

"I'm wearin' boots, are ye sayin' boots must be removed as well?"

"Please remove your footwear and then you can precede into the building," the person instructed.

Colin looked at Amoli. "I need to take me boots off?"

"Colin, he is not asking you to remove your clothes, only your boots. It is not so serious of a request," she said.

Colin reluctantly took off his boots. "I'm not comfortable removin' me boots. I practically sleep in'em. They're who I am."

Amoli chuckled. "You can face danger, my love, but it is too much to ask you to remove your boots? You are so silly sometimes."

Amoli and Mrs. Sharma broke away from Dr. Sharma and Colin as they walked to the back of the temple with the rest of the female worshipers.

"Dr. Sharma, what's goin' on?" Colin asked. "Can't

339

Amoli be with me?"

"We must go to the front, see my son is already waiting for us. He saved some space for us."

"I want to be with Amoli, sar."

"No, I'm afraid that cannot be. Amoli and my wife will be at the back of the temple, so they will not be seen by our holy man who will perform the ceremony."

"Why?"

"You are a silly man aren't you? You ask too many questions."

"I do?"

The religious ceremony began as the Guru spoke to the people. Colin didn't understand a world the Guru said, the ceremony was in Hindi. Dr. Sharma informed Colin the Hindu faith has several Gods, which are in charge of certain operations. Several worshipers attending temple stared at Colin as they whispered to one another.

"Dr. Sharma, feelin' like I'm stickin' out in a crowd I am."

"You are."

"Makin' me feel uncomfortable it is."

"Colin, nobody knows if you're from England, Scotland, Ireland, or even Germany for that matter. What everyone is focused on is your whiteness. Your whiteness represents India's enemy."

Colin looked at Dr. Sharma, not really knowing what to say.

"But, you are a lucky man."

"I am?"

"Yes, you are very lucky that we are Hindu...otherwise..."

"Otherwishe, what?"

Dr. Sharma ignored Colin for he was more interested in what the Guru had to say.

The ceremony ended where Colin heard several South Asian languages but no English. They met with Amoli and her mother as they exited the temple.

"Colin," Mrs. Sharma said. "We have several friends who meet with us here at temple. Their comments about you were very pleasant."

"Is that so?"

"Yes, you will be a very good protector over our Amoli."

***

"None of yer friends spoke'bout ye know...that I'm from the Isles?"

"I can't really say much more was discussed, Colin," she said.

"Nothin' else was said 'bout ye know--?"

Mrs. Sharma looked at her husband. "What did you say to Colin? He appears to be upset about something."

"I told him the truth," Dr. Sharma said.

"About?" asked Mrs. Sharma.

"Well, I do not know if our community will accept him."

"Of course they will. Why would they not?"

"Because he's a big bad white man who raped my sister!" blurted Amoli's brother.

Amoli slapped her brother again this time throwing him to the ground. "You are lucky you are just a child, otherwise I would beat you!"

"Amolia! Act like a lady especially in front of your gentleman friend," Mrs. Sharma demanded forcing a smile.

Colin placed his hat back on his head. The London rain drenched the streets. Colin placed his arm around Amoli to shelter her from the rain.

"Well, that is it, Colin. I may see you tomorrow," Dr. Sharma said. "Let me know if you would like to convert to Hinduism and marry Amolia."

Colin stepped closer to Dr. Sharma. "About the conversion, sar. I need to think 'bout this further."

"You haven't made your decision already?" Dr. Sharma asked.

"Sar, I'm kind of havin' a wee problem with yer Hindu faith havin' so many Gods. Me only God is Christ, sar."

"Hmm...this is a decision you must make, Colin. If you love Amolia as much as you say you do, you should be very willing to strip yourself from your faith," Dr. Sharma said.

"Sar, I need to think this over if ye don't mind me doin' so?"

"Fine, you do just that," Dr. Sharma pulled Amoli toward him. "Come, we must go. Until tomorrow, Colin," Dr. Sharma said pulling his daughter, wife, and son away from him.

Colin stood on the street corner in the cold rain, watching Amoli walk away with her family. He watched them walk from him until he couldn't see them anymore. Amoli kept looking back at Colin but Dr. Sharma kept pulling her to turn away. Colin stood still staring at nothing while he continued to get drenched by the rain. He stared into nothing almost in disbelief. He slowly decided to walk the streets where he quickly ducked into the nearest pub.

One of the barmaids approached Colin. "Take your coat and hat off, dear and stay a while. You look quite wet."

"Ah, what's a little rain? However, would ye be so kind in lettin' me have yer finest bottle of Irish whiskey? Oh, 'n please bring me a glass with that?" He asked as he removed his soaking hat and coat.

The barmaid placed a bottle and glass in front of him. He poured himself a glass and gazed at it for a while before gulping it down. He was disinterested in who was at the pub, so he continued to drink until the bottle was finished. The hours passed and it became so late that the pub needed to close down. Colin had just finished his second bottle of whiskey. He held himself up over the bar counter with his head hung down. The manager of the pub escorted Colin out as he could barely stand while staggering into the rainy streets. He walked along the dark narrow roads where he found a pub he was familiar with. He walked in sitting himself at the bar. He drank until the pub closed. The bartenders helped him exit as he staggered across the street. He fell several times until he could no longer help himself up. He remained on the ground as the rain soaked his body. People passed by him as he lay in an alleyway while the rain continued to pour down. He could hear voices as people stepped around him he started to laugh hysterically which slowly transformed to a soft cry. As people walked by they stared at him not able to tell if tears ran down his face or if it was rain. He cried himself into a stupor of unconsciousness where he began to fall into an almost hypothermic state. His thoughts started to run away from him where several images of his past came to mind. It felt like buckets of water from the sky as the temperature dropped and the rain turned to snow. He began to think of a time when he was in his late teens and he was too drunk to go to church with his parents and Ethan one Sunday. He remembered how much he let his family down.

***

It was a new day where the daylight seeped into the alleyway waking Colin who had slept the night on the street. He was covered in snow as he shivered himself into a feverish state. He suddenly felt a subtle tapping on his face. "Mr. Limmerick! What you do sleeping in streets? What you did?" Sasha asked.

Colin slowly opened his eyes. He shivered from the winter dampness looking almost bluish in complexion. "Sasha?"

"Mr. Limmerick, you look terrible. Why you sleep in streets when you have bed?"

"Shite, I'm still drunk from last night I am," he had trouble breathing from his intoxication.

"Mr. Limmerick, I must help you up. Take my arm!"

Sasha suggested.

Colin stood up with difficulty. "I must look bad, eh?"

"You look like hell. What you did last night?"

"I wanted to die."

"Mr. Limmerick, you can't be serious!"

"I'm very serious so I am," Colin started to walk with Sasha where Sasha tried to stop him from falling from time to time.

"Mr. Limmerick, I would carry you but it is not possible."

"Me life's a feckin' mess it is. I finally meet a lass who truly loves me for who I am. She accepts me 'n understands me. Her father, who feckin' teamed us up in the first place now won't let it happen."

"Dr. Sharma, does not like you anymore?"

"What do I have to live for? I might as well die with a bottle in me hand."

"Mr. Limmerick, this is terrible talk. You must stop this immediately! You will find a way to marry Miss Amoli!" Sasha said trying to help Colin from falling.

"I really love'er ye know I do. Her little brother accused me of rapin' er he did. That was pain I'll tell ye. The lass wanted it just as much as I did. I didn't rape'er."

"Mr. Limmerick, you must go home in bathtub and get on decent clothes. You look like vagrant now."

"I do don't I? I have to be in Cushing's office soon."

"Mr. Limmerick, please don't make things worse. Professor Cushing would like to see you in such bad way, don't please him so much. You know what I mean, da?"

"I'll get on home 'n clean up I will. Nobody will know I slept in the rain drunker than a skunk."

"You banged up your face last night. Your black eye has turned to blue."

"I'll be okay, mate, really I will!" Colin staggered away leaving Sasha on the street corner.

Colin staggered to his building, trying to make his way to his front door's main entrance. He stopped as he fumbled for his key, dropping it in the snow. "Feck!" Colin fell to his knees running his hands through the snow in search of the key. He noticed a woman's boots standing in front of him. He slowly looked up.

"Lost something, Colin?"

Colin stared at the woman as his eyes tried to focus. The woman was Rosa. "I've seemed to have dropped me key in the bleedin' snow 'is all," he said as he fumbled around in the snow.

"Colin? Is something wrong?"

"Nothin'."

"You look terrible."

"So, I do."

"You look badly intoxicated again."

He struggled to stand up as he hoisted himself to her, "Again?"

She folded her arms, standing in a long blue cloth coat and wide brimmed hat. "Yes, again. Colin, every time I see you you've had too much to drink. Why do you think you're still not married?"

He could barely stand. "I'm in a hurry. I've got to get me-self to Cushing's office in a few."

"You better not let him see you looking like this."

She found his key taking his arm and led him inside his building. "Colin Limmerick, I don't know what you would do without me," she said while getting the door to his flat opened.

She brought him to his lavatory where he started to urinate in the toilet in front of her. She turned the other way as she drew the bath water for him.

***

A few hours had passed Colin sat in Professor Cushing's office.

"Colin, where the hell have you been lately?" Professor Cushing asked.

"Well, if ye must know, sar, I was time travellin'."

"Time travelling again?" Professor Cushing asked as

he munched on a piece of cake.

"Captured never-seen-before data'n photographs. Grand it really is, so grand in deed."

"Data? On what?"

"Sar," Colin leaned over Professor Cushing's desk to get closer to him, "I'll be provin' me theory, sar, I will. I'll be provin' that *Megaloceros* couldn't survive, not with his antlers he couldn't. Sar, evolution naturally selected him as one of those species that could no longer continue to evolve. I saw evolution in the makin' I did. Fascinatin' it is!"

"I'm not interested in having a time-travelling Ph.D. student. I think you better start facing up to reality!"

Colin pulled off his tie unbuttoning a few buttons around the collar of his shirt, "Reality, sar? Yes, but I know it all sounds all too strange to one's ear it does, but I've got photographs I do. I've got samples I do! Sar, me dissertation will knock ye over it will!"

"Look Colin, let me be brutally honest, the chapters you have already submitted to me are not very good. They are not Ph.D. quality!"

"Why not?"

Dr. Cushing's eyes bounced around the room where he found it difficult to face Colin. "It's a jumble!"

Colin sat up from the cold stool. "A jumble ye say? What the hell is that supposed to mean?"

"Just that! If you continue to base your primary data on your silly time travels I can't see your dissertation carry much weight in this academic institution."

"Sar, if I travel back in time ten thousand years 'n observe *Megaloceros'* struggle with his endowment, wouldn't ye say it would be a damn fantastic comparison to forty thousand years ago?"

"What, during or after the Ice Age?"

"That's what I'm sayin' to ye, sar!"

"The Ice Age?"

"That's exactly it, sar!"

346

"Look Colin, you're going off on one of your tangents again. You need to focus on one thing only. Look at me with the horseshoe crab. It hardly evolved."

"This is Natural History, sar."

"I'm a naturalist, I don't really know what the hell you are!"

Dr. Sharma walked by Dr. Cushing's office where the door was wide opened. "Colin, I thought I would find you in here dazzling your academic advisor with your brilliance!" Dr. Sharma said as he partially stepped into the office.

"Dr. Sharma, have ye met Dr. Cushing?" Colin asked rolling his eyes back.

"I have heard so much about you Dr. Cushing but we have never actually met," Dr. Sharma extended his hand to Dr. Cushing.

"Yes, you're the specialist on prehistoric botany aren't you? Dr. Cushing said as he tried to be cordial.

"Dr. Sharma, would ye be doin' anything special this evenin'?" Colin asked.

"Oh, do you want to meet in the laboratory this evening, Colin?"

"I was thinkin' more me own flat. After dinner would ye 'n Amoli be interested in seein' me at me home?"

"Colin, are you making social plans in my office?" Dr. Cushing asked.

"I am, sar."

"Colin, do it on your own time!" Dr. Cushing shouted.

"Do ye think ye 'n Amoli could come over around half seven? Would that be suitable for yez?"

"This sounds serious," Dr. Sharma said. "Okay, Colin, we will be at your flat then, but now I will leave you two to discuss academic matters, good day," Dr. Sharma left the office.

Colin smiled at Professor Cushing.

347

Chapter Twenty-Eight

It was 7:30 p.m. Colin let Dr. Sharma and Amoli into his flat. "Please make ye-selves comfortable. "What can I get yez?" Colin asked with almost a nervous twitch.

Amoli shied behind her father as she continually smiled at Colin. Colin noticed her gazing at him with a twinkle in her deep dark eyes. He tried to pretend he didn't notice as he tried to focus on Dr. Sharma.

"A cup of tea should be very suitable," Dr. Sharma said.

Colin gestured for them to sit down. "Please, sit make yer-selves at home. Amoli, what can I fetch ye?"

"She sat quietly next to her father but did not speak.

"Colin, Amolia will have tea as well."

"I've got biscuits I do," Colin suggested.

"Colin, please, my daughter and I are not here to eat biscuits or drink tea. Please, let us get on with it. Now, you so kindly invited us here to your home. What is it you would like to discuss?"

Amoli slowly lifted her long gold sari exposing her knee while she crossed her legs. Colin glanced at her gestures as he continued to sit.

Colin placed a few bottles of ale on the coffee table. He started to drink. "Well sar, I need to speak to ye 'bout me havin' yer daughter's hand."

"Proceed, Colin, proceed," Dr. Sharma said looking serious.

Amoli gazed at Colin with baited breath. "What is it you are trying to say, Colin?" she asked.

"Amolia, I will handle this, you must sit in silence!" Dr. Sharma said sternly.

"Sar, I don't think I can convert to yer faith."

Dr. Sharma stood up. "Come, Amolia, we need to settle your arrangements to India!"

"No!" Amoli shouted.

Colin's eyes widened with angst. "Is it possible, sar, for Amoli to convert to me faith instead?"

"Absolutely not! Amolia, come!"

Colin stood up confronting Dr. Sharma. "Sar, what have I done to make ye feel so ill toward me?"

"You engaged in a filthy sexual act with my youngest daughter before her wedding day! Isn't that enough?"

"Ye see, sar, I don't really feel one should be punished for a natural act of love I don't."

"Interesting that you Westerners are so *laissez-faire* about so many things!"

"Well, sar, ye may think me act of love with yer daughter was a promiscuous act 'n such but it really wasn't. Please, could we discuss this more? Please sit down, don't rush off, please."

Dr. Sharma sat down. There was a knock at the door. "Please, if ye could excuse me while I get the door," Colin said making his way to the door.

"Colin! Hello dear!" Rosa blurted barging in holding a large bag of groceries. "Guess what, big-boy? I am going to make dinner for you tonight!"

Colin pulled Rosa's arm. "Rosa, what ye doin' here, eh? With a bag of groceries at that?"

"Study night? Remember? We made a date to study and dine together," Rosa said handing the bag of groceries to Colin.

"I really don't remember the dinin' part, but I thought tomorrow was our study night."

Rosa slapped Colin on the arm. "You are such a big lug. You obviously got your wires crossed!"

"Well, we can't study tonight, Rosa," Colin said in a soft whisper.

"Well, why not?"

"I've got company I do. Guests I have."

Rosa walked to the sitting area of the flat. "Hello Dr. Sharma!"

"Nice to see you again, Rosa," Dr. Sharma replied.

"Oh, and I see your child, Amoli is here with you!"

Amoli pursed her lips while remaining silent.

"Rosa, ye can't stay here, ye need to leave," Colin urged.

"You can continue your little discussion you won't even notice that I'm here. I brought some reading material on Darwin. We really need to do this, Colin. We are scholars!" Rosa said in high volume.

"Fine, I've got to tend to me guests 'is all."

"Go do what you have to do!"

Colin sat down with Dr. Sharma and Amoli. "Sar, I need ye to approve of me takin' yer daughter's hand."

"Well, so far, Colin, you have miserably failed my test," Dr. Sharma said.

Rosa threw a few pieces of wood in the parlor stove. As soon as it started to heat up, she placed a large pot on the stove. "Colin, I hope you like stew!" Rosa shouted.

"Stew? Of course I do."

"I'm cutting up big chunks of potatoes just the way you like it. I'm also making a really thick gravy. And, lots of meat for a big rugged man like you!"

Dr. Sharma looked at Colin. "She cooks for you often, Colin?"

Colin guzzled another ale. "Maybe a few times in the past."

"Was Rosa, by any chance, a special friend of yours?" Dr. Sharma asked.

Colin stared at the floor taking his time to answer. "She was, sar."

"Can you smell the aroma of the stew as it cooks, Colin?" Rosa shouted.

"I can. Rosa, can ye stop yellin' across the room? It's irritatin' me it is!" Colin asked.

"I'll just let it simmer on the stove," Rosa said as she wandered into Colin's bedroom.

"Sar, please don't let religious faith get in the way of

350

the love between yer daughter 'n me," Colin said.

"If I don't hold our faith with high importance, in what style will you both marry and how can the tradition of my family be carried on?" Dr. Sharma asked.

Rosa walked into the sitting room, wearing only a towel around her. "I'm going to take a bath, would you like to scrub my back, dear?"

"She bathes here, often, Colin?" Dr. Sharma asked.

"She doesn't!" Colin sprung from his chair pulling Rosa into the bedroom and shutting the door. "What the hell is gone on with ye? Have ye lost yer bleedin' mind?"

Rosa pulled the towel off her body as she wrapped her arms around Colin's waist. "I just wanted to impress you. You and I both know we must keep feeding your raging desires!"

Colin pushed her away. "Ye never did this when we was a couple! How are ye doin' this now?"

"Doing what?"

"Don't play these games with me! Could ye just help me out? Dr. Sharma found me with Amoli in her bed."

"Did she keep pouring booze down your throat hoping you would succumb to her ways?"

"What ways? She didn't get me drunk, I got me-self drunk. It just happened one night 'is all. I love her, Rosa."

"You love, Amoli?"

"I do," Colin said wrapping the towel around Rosa's body.

"My dear boy, don't you see?"

"See what?"

"You are on the rebound. The one you really want is me. You're so jealous of Sasha you can't stand it."

"Put yer clothes back on, Rosa," Colin walked out of the bedroom.

Colin noticed Dr. Sharma and Amoli standing by the door. "Colin, we really must be leaving, I can see you are very preoccupied," Dr. Sharma said tugging Amoli's arm.

"But nothin' was accomplished here tonight, sar!"

Colin pleaded.

"Amolia is behind in her household chores, we really need to be leaving now."

"Wait, sar, how does this leave us?"

"Amolia will soon be on a ship to India."

"No!" Amoli shouted yanking her arm from her father.

Colin slid his arms around Amoli. "Lass, do ye still love me?"

Amoli began to whimper, "I'll never stop loving you."

Colin bent down to kiss Amoli on the cheek. "And I ye."

"Come, Amolia! Perhaps I will see you in the lab tomorrow, Colin?"

"Perhaps."

The door closed in front of Colin. He slowly walked to his bottle of whiskey and began to drink. Rosa stepped out of his bedroom fully dressed.

"Are they gone?" she asked with a grin.

Colin sat at his kitchen table as he continued to drink. "They left."

"How'd it go?"

Colin stared at the floor. "What ye think?"

"That good?"

"That feckin' good. Yup!"

Rosa sat beside Colin and pulled the whiskey bottle from his hand. "I don't understand why you're so upset."

"I know ye don't get it."

"What's the big attraction to that chubby little Indian brat?"

Colin grabbed his bottle of whiskey from Rosa. "She loves me. She truly loves me. She loves me in a way ye never could."

"I always loved you, Colin. I still love you."

"Ye don't love me!"

Rosa stood next to Colin while he remained sitting. She ran her fingers threw his hair. "I love everything about you. I'd marry you right now. Colin, will you marry me?"

Colin stood up. "Ye don't even know what yer sayin'! Rubbish this is!

"Colin, I'd do anything for you!" Rosa got on her knees.

"Ye need to be tellin' this to Sasha not me."

"Sasha is always so far away. I don't know how to deal with him sometimes."

"A problem of yers this is -- not mine."

"Colin, what has happened to you? You used to be so loving and caring."

"Rosa, ye 'n I was together for a year. It was ye who decided to choose Sasha over me 'n leave me out ye did. Ye didn't care nothin' 'bout me."

"Colin Limmerick, you are no easy man to be paired up with you know!"

"Despite me liabilities, Amoli loves me in a way ye never could." Colin opened his door. "Ye never loved me, 'n ye know it. Ye bes be goin' on yer way, I'm feelin' rather low if ye don't mind."

"You're upset over that plump little girl?"

"Stop pokin' fun at'er! She's beautiful 'n ye know it."

Rosa walked out of his flat into the hallway, "One day you're going to regret this!"

"Regret what?" Colin slammed the door shut.

Chapter Twenty-Nine

The following morning Colin sat in the lab examining his samples from his time travels while Sasha entered the lab.

"Ah, Mr. Limmerick, here you are, working so diligent toward your research, like true scholar!"

Colin hung his head down as he removed his lab coat. "Like a true scholar, mate? More like a true drunk. I'm hung-over every mornin'. Let me take off me specs so ye can see it in me eyes."

"Mr. Limmerick, you look awful. Why you drink so much?"

"Nulls the pain it does."

Sasha slipped on his lab coat. "So shame, Mr. Limmerick."

"Are ye still with Rosa?"

"She wants ring and I cannot give at this time. She is very angry with me now. I do not understand this lady. I think she still wants you."

"I see."

"What happened with Miss Amoli? I hope you have great news to say me."

"Dr. Sharma is sendin' her back to India. I failed her I did."

"Mr. Limmerick, nyet. You not fail her. She will not go to her country. She will remain here for you."

"How, mate?"

"She loves you, Mr. Limmerick, she will find way. I can see she is very determined."

"I don't know, really. I suppose I'm just not understandin' eastern cultures 'is all. It's somethin' that's beyond me."

"Da, Mr. Limmerick, she is girl from India, she not same religion, not same colour, not same culture. You do

354

have problem."

"Thanks Sasha."

***

The following week Colin received a letter, which read that his comprehensive examinations were a success and that he received a high passing grade. He decided it was time to share the news with Professor Cushing.

Colin poked his head in his professor's office.

"Professor Cushing, did ye receive the news?"

"Yes, yes, yes, I did God damn it!"

"Look at me letter, sar!" Colin handed the letter to his professor.

"Colin, I must be brutally honest with you this was a complete surprise to me."

"I'm sure it was, sar."

"Bye the way, Colin!" Dr. Cushing called out as Colin was turning toward the door.

"Aye, sar?"

"You need to include at least a few chapters in your dissertation on a count you'll be doing on the horseshoe crab."

"A count?"

"Yes, Colin, you see it's important for you to include at least two full-sized chapters on the horseshoe crab's legs."

Colin didn't know where to look at this point. "What ye sayin' to me, sar? Yer after me doin' a count of the crab's legs?"

"Yes."

"How many samples ye want?" Colin asked almost wincing with disgust.

"Try for a sample of a couple of hundred."

Colin leaned against the wall as he sighed with frustration. "Ye want me to count two hundred horseshoe crab legs?"

"Yes."

"What ever for?"

"I want you to record the number of legs on each crab and then I would like you to come up with a statistical formula comparing them to their ancestors showing the evolutionary pattern."

Colin shut his eyes. "And, how sar, will I compare their present day legs to the number of legs of their ancestors?"

"Well, I'm sure you and Dr. Dimitrikov will come up with that answer."

Colin moved toward Dr. Cushing's desk as he bent over leaning on it. "Well sar, I just won't do it."

"You'll do it because I'm telling you to. Do you understand, Colin?"

"Me research is on a large mammal, sar, not a crustacean that barely evolved. You got to stop tryin' to turn me focus on somethin' that's more fittin' to ye, sar."

Dr. Cushing sat back in his chair. "Look Colin, I am growing tired of these quarrels. If you need to remove your large mammal then you shall do so. This way if you write a lucid dissertation on a crustacean that barely evolved we can avoid Darwin all together. Do you hear what I'm saying?"

Dr. Sharma suddenly showed up at Dr. Cushing's door. "Excuse me, gentlemen, please forgive me for interrupting your discussion."

Colin stood up. "Dr. Sharma ye've met Dr. Cushing," Colin said.

Dr. Sharma extended his hand to Dr. Cushing, "Yes, so very nice to see you again, Dr. Cushing."

Dr. Cushing remained seated as he nodded his head instead.

"Colin, we must speak," Dr. Sharma said.

"Oh, alright then. Dr. Cushing, I suppose we're finished here 'n I'll be goin'."

"No, Colin, we're not finished here. Whatever must be discussed between you and the botanist of prehistoric times can definitely be discussed in front of me."

Dr. Sharma partially smiled. "Very well. Colin, my wife has been very upset with me. She feels you and Amolia belong together."

"What does this have to do with prehistoric mammals and prehistoric plants?" Dr. Cushing asked.

Colin glanced at Dr. Cushing. "Obviously, absolutely nothin'."

"Colin," Dr. Sharma said, "I am giving you my blessing to marry my daughter."

"Dead feckin' brill this is," Colin commented.

"Excuse me, Colin?" asked Dr. Sharma.

Colin stood up to shake Dr. Sharma's hand, "Thank-ye, sar."

"However, you are never to be alone with her until your wedding night -- both of you must be chaperoned."

"Nay, sar, if she's wearin' me diamond on her finger, she'll be sleepin' in me bed as often as possible.

"Colin, what kind of charade are you pulling in my office?" Dr. Cushing exclaimed.

"This is an outrage!" Dr. Sharma shouted.

"She doesn't belong to ye anymore, sar, she's a part of me for now on."

"Why you selfish brute -- how dare you!" Dr. Sharma shouted.

Chapter Thirty

Rosa was working in the lab on an experiment when Sasha walked in. "My beautiful lady, why I not see you in physics lab these days?" Sasha asked.

"I've been busy."

"Why you so angry with me?"

She removed her lab coat. " Sasha, you are so distant from me sometimes. Colin was never that way with me."

"Oh yes, we must now compare me to Mr. Limmerick."

"Life was so much easier when Colin and I were a couple," she said with tears in her eyes.

"Ah, I see, some regret. I just see Mr. Limmerick and he so happy now."

"Colin is happy? He's never happy about anything."

"Ah, so this is where you incorrect, beautiful lady."

"Will you speak to me in English, please!"

"Mr. Limmerick is engaged to marry Miss Amoli -- you should be happy for him."

Rosa looked at Sasha then burst into a loud scream. "Happy for him?" She grabbed Sasha's tie and yanked it. "What does he see in her?"

Sasha stepped away from Rosa. "He see love. Why you act this way?"

"Sasha, you never once said you loved me. Colin used to always tell me how much he loved me."

Sasha tried not to focus on her. "You act like child, what you expect?"

"No!" she cried out storming off in frantic tears.

Sasha watched her stomp away.

***

Later that afternoon Amoli showed up at the lab. She was feeling excited with happiness as she almost danced into the lab slowly realising Colin wasn't in the room. She could only see Rosa. Rosa glanced at Amoli as she brushed away at a small archeological sample. She slowly turned to Amoli.

Amoli took a few steps back. "Where's Colin?" She asked.

"Professor Cushing wanted to see Colin about something ridicules, so Colin was called away."

"Oh."

"Don't worry yourself, Colin will be right back," Rosa said as she slowly crept closer to Amoli.

"I guess I'll look for Colin in Professor's Cushing's office," Amoli said.

"I wouldn't do that if I were you!" Rosa said, "Professor Cushing has recently made a very illogical request of Colin and things could get bloody."

"Oh?"

"Why don't you make yourself at home, there's plenty of test tubes."

Amoli paused. "What am I going to do with test tubes?"

"Oh yes, I forgot, you have no interest in this kind of work. You're only interest is to wear Colin's ring."

"Miss Emanuel, you have Dr. Dimitrikov."

"Yes, I do. He's my gentleman, but there are some problems."

"That is not really my problem is it?" Amoli commented.

"My my, aren't you a saucy little girl."

"Miss Emanuel, I think I better wait outside," Amoli said lunging for the door.

Rosa grabbed Amoli's arm yanking her toward her. "I'm not finished, so where are you going?"

Amoli pulled away. "Miss Emanuel, stop doing this to me! You better accept that I am promised to Colin."

"Colin doesn't love you. He can't love someone like you!"

"What is that supposed to mean?"

"You're a bratty child, you can't time travel. Only I can time travel with Colin!"

"You don't like time travelling!"

"I'll go anywhere with Colin!"

"Colin is finished with you!"

"Colin must have been drunk when he gave you that ring! No man would get engaged to you in his right frame of mind!"

"I'm not going to take anymore of your insults! I will leave now."

Rosa grabbed Amoli shoving her to the wall. "You will go when I tell you to!"

"By the way, remember I told you in the tea shop a while back that I saw it?"

Rosa stepped back. "All lies, I'm sure."

"You're right, Miss Emanuel, it was a lie. I never saw it at that time."

"I knew you were feeding me lies."

"But now I can say I have seen it -- more than once."

"You're father would never let you sleep with a man!"

"This is true, but Colin convinced him that since we're engaged, we should be together -- so I've seen it alright."

"Impossible. You're father would never agree."

"Go a head and ask him."

"I'm not going to ask your father something like that."

"Better yet, ask Colin."

"Maybe I will."

"You never saw it did you, Miss Emanuel?"

"None of your business!"

"You really missed out on seeing something grand."

"Why are you telling me this?"

"I want to rub it in your face that's why!"

"Colin should know what kind of woman he's marrying. You should never kiss and tell, Amoli."

"I'm only trying to prove a point to you. I'm sure Colin would not mind."

"You obviously don't know Colin."

360

"I know Colin better in ways that you could never imagine."

Rosa pushed Amoli against the wall where she fell over a mobile tray of beakers, "You whore!"

Amoli leered at Rosa as she found herself lying in a menagerie of broken glass noticing her arm was cut and bleeding. Amoli slowly stood up realising she was soar from the fall. She charged at Rosa grabbing her face smashing it on the lab table. While in the process, several test tubes and other forms of experimental apparatus shattered on the floor. Rosa screamed but Amoli would not let go of her head.

The door swung opened where Colin stormed into the room with Sasha following. "What's gone on here?" Colin shouted noticing Rosa's bleeding face and Amoli's bloody arm.

Rosa panted as tears streamed down her bruised face. Amoli tried to cover her arm as she stared at the floor.

"Two women in a physical fight is what I see. Two ladies at that!" Colin shouted sternly.

Amoli stepped closer to Colin as she ailed from the pain of her arm. "Colin, please don't be angry with me," she pleaded and began to cry.

Sasha held an unlit cigarette in his hand and walked to Rosa. *"Ya zdélala vsjo shto v moíh silah."*

Rosa felt she couldn't look at Sasha in the eyes. "In English, please."

"I have tried all I can do," he said shaking his head.

Colin scanned the state the laboratory was in noticing smashed beakers and test tubes on the floor. "Amoli, ye don't love me ye don't. Ye know it that I spend countless hours in this lab, why would ye try to destroy it?"

"No, Colin, please. I love you with all my heart. Miss Emanuel started the whole thing. She's doing everything in her power to end our love."

"So ye felt it was necessary to try 'n destroy the lab? Bullshite this is!" Colin turned away from Amoli. "I need a break from this place I do!"

"What are you saying, Colin?" Amoli cried out.

"I'm gettin' nowhere with Cushing 'n I'm goin' nowhere with yez! I'm tired of yez women born with silver spoons in yer mouths! Ye 'n Rosa have done nothin' but bring me to me knees! I miss me ship 'n I miss me crew! Ah, just feck this Ph.D. programme 'n all of yez as well!" Colin stormed out of the lab leaving Amoli in tears.

"Sasha? Are you angry with me?" Rosa asked.

He looked at her shrugging his shoulders. *"Tako´va dzizn."*

"Pardon?" Rosa exclaimed.

"Ce la vie," Sasha said left the laboratory.

Chapter Thirty-One

It was late evening as the Atlantic Mermaid made her rounds from its 200 nautical miles off its Irish shores. The waters were cool as the crisp winds penetrated through the vessel's walls. Colin cast the net into the water where he drew the bottom line in tightly to net the dense shoal. Colin's scarf was wrapped several times around his broad neck as his auburn hair blew with the breeze almost slapping him in the face.

"Captain, let me give ya a hand! Say, that's a mighty hardy bunch of fish ya caught. Maybe there's just too many of 'em!" Eddy called out to Colin wearing a raincoat and rain hat pulled just over his eyes.

"Feckin' cold it is isn't it?" Colin shouted to Eddy as he worked hard on drawing in the line.

Eddy watched Colin as Séamus and Joey stood a few feet behind. Colin found the reel to be difficult to conquer as he continued to battle it. "Captain? Can't we help ya?" Séamus asked.

"Ye can try," Colin answered where Eddy noticed sweat beads roll down his forehead.

Colin leaped his bulky frame onto the gunnel of the vessel as crouched as low as he could to gain the leverage to draw in the crowded net.

"Captain! Watch yar-self! Whatever ya do -- don't fall in!"

Colin chuckled as he stopped his struggle releasing the bottom line.

"Captain?" Joey said as he walked up to Colin.

Colin looked at Eddy, "It was as if somethin' was tryin' to pull me in or tip the Mermaid. I just had to let go of the line I did," Colin said.

"Captain, this is the first time I ever sawr ya let go of a trawlin' line. It couldn't 'ave been so hard far ya could it?"

"I tell ya, it was as if somethin' was holdin' on to the line. I can't really explain it. I have great strength -- me strength is not the issue here."

Joey looked at Eddy. "Of course, the Captain is stronger 'n bigger than all of us. Then what the feck was it that had ya let go of the line?"

Coln shrugged his shoulders. "The bleedin' feck I know. It was the strangest thing."

"Let's rest in the galley 'n break opened some pints, hmm?" Eddy suggested patting Colin on the shoulder.

Colin unbuttoned his thick cloth jacket as he pulled off his scarf seating himself at the table in the galley. Eddy distributed the warm ale as the nine-crew members gathered at the table while young Timmy remained in the wheelhouse.

"My yar lookin' good, Captain. What is the latest news ya can bring us from London town?" Eddy asked sitting beside Colin.

Colin balanced his chair on its back legs making it squeak as if it was about to collapse. "Latest news ye ask?"

The crew started to howl as they tried to coax their captain into revealing information. They stomped their feet and banged their fists on the table as they hollered at him while in hysterical drunken laughter.

"I don't know what yez wantin' me to tell yez!" Colin laughed with a devilish grin.

"Well?" Murray asked.

"Well, what?" Colin replied.

Eddy pulled Colin's ale from his hand, "Tell us, lad. Tell us -- are ya gettin' married or not?"

"Why yez actin' like it would be such a miracle if I was? What's so grand if I was?"

"Lad, listen to us, it's not as if we's makin' fun of ya. Surely ya got somethin' planned don't ya?"

Colin continued to balance himself on the back legs of

his chair. "Yez all know Amoli don't ye?" Colin asked.

Eddy looked at the crew with chuckles. "We's know this is 'bout the little Indian lass."

"Amoli 'n I had a wee scuffle we's did just before I got to yez here on the Mermaid. But, you'd never guess what she said to me as she expressed her darlin' touch of rage at me?"

"What's that, lad?" Eddy asked.

"She missed a month she has," Colin said with a flushed boyish smile.

The men started to roar with hysterics as they poured beer over Colin's head.

"An ye know what else? We's engaged we is." The men continued to pour more beer over Colin's head. Colin chuckled as he removed his soaked tweed cap from his head.

Eddy placed his arm around Colin, "Lad, I knew it would all happen for ya I did."

"I don't remember ever bein' so happy I don't," Colin said as the crew passed him another ale.

"That explains why ya just gave up the line. The captain of this vessel's never given up a line, eh?" Eddy commented.

"Yeh, so I gave up the line. There'll be more fish to fill the net there will -- there always is," Colin said.

The crew looked at each other while trying to smile at their captain.

Joey started to laugh. "I thought yaz was either too knackered or crazy 'cause knowin' yaz, captain, ya'd never give up the line," Joey said almost with a nervous twitch.

Colin abruptly stood up slamming his beer mug on the table, "Alright, feck! So I gave up the line -- I'll go out there right feckin' now 'n reel in the feckin' next catch I will. I don't want any of yaz to help me!" He stormed out of the galley and rushed to the deck.

Eddy glanced at the crew as he continued to sit and

drink his ale. "Boys, don't bother tryin' to deal with'em when he gets this way -- the lad has a temper as yaz well know," Eddy said looking concerned. "He's in love and things have turned 'round far 'em.

Colin stood on the deck focused on the turbulent waves as a storm started to set in. He tightened his scarf and buttoned his coat while slipping on his gloves. He felt the ale rush to his head as he stood by the net reel. He glanced at the water noticing something strange. He slid his hands along the gunnel trying to feel for the net. The stark blackness of the night made Colin feel like a blind man as he began to panic when he felt nothing at all. He hung over the starboard feeling his way in the darkness not finding what he was looking for. He stopped to catch his breath as he felt the chilled sea run through his icy veins. The moonlight shun over the blackness as he tried to focus his eyes but could not. There was no net and no reel.

Eddy stood behind Colin, "Lad? Somethin' wrong with yaz?" he asked.

"Eddy, can ye fetch a lantern so we can see out here?"

Eddy dashed deep into the hull bringing a lantern to Colin. "Just what ya asked," Eddy said handing the lantern to Colin.

Colin lit the lantern as he stood where the reel used to be. He flashed the lantern on the side of the boat onto the glistening dark waters. "Eddy, where's the reel 'n the net?"

Eddy stepped in front of Colin as he took the lantern. The light of the lantern shun on the water but there was no net. "Lad? What's happened?"

Colin looked at Eddy as he started to walk toward the galley. "I suppose it broke off somehow. Perhaps when I was tryin' to reel the catch in earlier, eh?"

"It's hard to say, Captain, it's hard to say."

Colin slowly went back to the galley where the crew sat and drank. "Men, we's turnin' the vessel back to

Dublin," Colin announced to the crew. The men appeared concerned with confusion begging Colin to explain why there was a sudden change of plans.

Colin sat at the table as he looked for his pint of ale. "The net 'n reel are gone," he said.

Eddy climbed into the wheelhouse looking for Timmy. "Tim, turn the vessel to Dublin!" Eddy called out to him. The ship changed direction heading northbound to Dublin.

Eddy returned to the galley noticing Colin was deep within his thoughts. "Captain?" Eddy sat beside him. "Lad, it'll be alright, it will don't worry."

"No!" Colin stood up. "We'll wait till mornin' 'n look for the net!" Colin called out as he ran to Timmy in the wheelhouse. "Timmy!" Colin shouted to him, "Go back to where we was! We'll wait 'till mornin'!"

***

It was an icy crisp morning the Atlantic Mermaid was anchored in the Celtic Sea off the south coast of Ireland. Colin was sound asleep in the captain's quarters as he rolled over a few times as he subconsciously felt the ship jolt from time to time. Eddy let himself into Colin's chamber. "Captain, are ya awake?" Eddy gently called out.

Colin rolled over toward Eddy with his disheveled hair hanging in front of his face, "Awake? Of course I'm awake now that ye just asked me."

"Captain, me 'n some of the crew 've been up for a while now. We can't seem to find anythin' floatin' in the waters."

"What ye tellin' me?"

"It just isn't there, lad, it just isn't."

"When the mornin' mist burns off, Timmy can climb to the top of the mast with a telescope 'n look for our net's buoys, got that? Go tell him while I get dressed!" Colin ordered.

"Aye-aye, Captain!"

***

367

That afternoon Timmy climbed up the mast. He gazed at the sea with a telescope pressed against his eye.

Colin stood below the mast, "What ye see there?" Colin asked with angst.

Timmy held on to the mast tightly as he scanned the horizon. "I see nothin', Captain -- nothin' at all!"

"How can this be? Ye must see somethin' floatin' in the waters don't ye?" Colin asked as he wrapped himself around the mast. "Do I have to climb up there me-self?" Colin shouted as he started to climb the mast.

Eddy yanked on Colin's arm, "Have ya gone mad? Only Timmy can climb up the mast -- ya're not built for it. Just calm yar-self 'n sit a bit. We have to think what to do!" Eddy suggested.

Colin paced around the deck in a panic while the crew watched. "Do yez have any idea how much quid this trawlin' equipment cost? I'm in no position to be losin' nets 'n reels I'm not!" Colin shouted with anger.

Suddenly a few drastic waves flowed under the ship causing enough disruption to throw some of the crew to the floor of the deck. Timmy hugged the mast for dear life.

Eddy looked at Colin as he helped himself up. Colin gazed at the horizon, "Did we hit somethin'?" Colin asked. "Timmy!" he called to him. "Timmy, don't tell me ye haven't spotted anythin'!"

Timmy kept the telescope close to his eye wishing he could please his captain with an answer. He scanned the horizon shifting the looking glass from side to side. He then saw something in the far distance along the horizon line. "Captain, I think I've spotted somethin'!" Timmy shouted to him.

"What? What ye see?" Colin asked in a hoarse voice caused from panic.

"It looks like a large ship, Captain. Very large I say, Captain. It looks rather strange to be a ship I say!"

Eddy looked at Colin with concern in his eyes. "Lad, a

large ship can't be responsible for the missin' net 'n reel can it now?" Eddy asked.

"I suppose not."

Suddenly Timmy got excited where he spotted two of the net's buoys drifting in the water. "Captain! Look there! The buoys! There!" Timmy pointed.

Colin and the crew ran to gunnel. Colin squinted his eyes to see the buoys. "We can't see them from here, really!" Colin looked at Eddy, "Is Joey in the wheelhouse now?"

"He is, captain," Eddy replied.

"Tell him to steer the ship in that direction. What we can do is go out in the lifeboat for further investigation. Séamus, get prapared to venture in the lifeboat," Colin ordered. "Ya're goin' to find our net ye are."

Séamus backed away from Colin. "Captain that I won't do for ya. Somethin's out there alright."

Colin chuckled. "The Loch Ness monster, perhaps? Looka, I'll go with ye in the boat. I'll protect ye from the monster I will," Colin added with a sinister grin.

Eddy and the crew lowered the lifeboat to the water. Séamus tied his cork-vest life jacket around his body and Colin climbed down the steel ladder along side of the ship and into the lifeboat.

"I'm too young to die, Captain," Séamus commented to Colin as he reluctantly got settled in the boat."

Colin began to row as he ignored Séamus' comment. They encircled the ship fighting every wave with strength and bravery. Colin gritted his teeth with frustration where not a trace of the net could be found.

Séamus sat in the lifeboat with fear as he started to shiver. "Captain, nothin's here, so lets return to the ship now shall we?"

Colin continued to row as he tried to keep the small boat above the waves. As he rowed he noticed something attached to his paddle. Colin stopped rowing as he pulled the paddle inside the boat to examine what was hanging on it. "Seamus, this looks like a piece of the net it does," Colin said. Several buoys suddenly bobbed up from the sea. They were in rough condition as Colin swooped them out of the cold water. He then rowed back to the ship where Eddy threw the cable to the small boat. Colin helped Séamus climb up the ladder along the ship, and then he followed carrying his pieces of evidence. The crew helped Séamus back into the ship and then Colin. Eddy and Murray hoisted the lifeboat up. Colin lifted his leg over the gunnel as the lifeboat was rising up just behind him. Colin stepped into the ship where he was suddenly thrown to the floor of the deck -- the ship severely jolted. The crew yelled in terror as they kept close to the deck. Colin stood on his hands and knees twisting his neck to look behind him. He heard a loud jarring sound that was unfamiliar to him. He turned his body to see large teeth sink into the lifeboat. The lifeboat was gone.

About the Author

D.L. Narrol (Dianne) was born in Toronto, Canada. She grew up reading such classics as Joseph Conrad's *Heart of Darkness* and *Shogun* by James Clavell. As an adult, she admired and loved *The Wars* by Timothy Finley, a renowned Canadian author who put a face to those who fought in World War One. More up to date, she has enjoyed Diana Gabaldon's *Outlander* series.

She has a B.A. and M.A. in Geography, and her writing displays this with vivid descriptions of cityscapes, terrain, and the cultural essence of people. She currently works as a secondary Geography teacher in an inner city Toronto school. Most of her clientele are from India.

She spent four summers in Ireland, hiking the Wicklow Mountains south of Dublin. She researched the life of Irish fishermen of a hundred years ago when there was actually fish in the waters. She learned from the Irish that they are proud of their Great Irish Elk -- *Megaloceros giganteus*. It came to its demise from being sexually selected against where its antlers became a hindrance to its survival.

When communism fell in the former Soviet Union, she spent some time teaching physicists English as a Second Language. Her experiences in Russia taught her a great deal about the life of a scholar under much political change.

Her short story, *Kate's Choice* about the Gangs of Ottawa in the mid nineteenth century will be released in the fall of 2009 with Giant Beaver Publications. Visit her website: www.dlnarrol.wordpress.com, which displays an array of her own artwork for Prehistoric Journey: The First Expeditions.